RELATIONS

RELATIONS

An Anthology of African and Diaspora Voices

Nana Ekua Brew-Hammond

HARPERVIA

An Imprint of HarperCollins*Publishers*

HarperCollins books may be purchased for educational, business, or sales promotional use. For information, please email the Special Markets Department at SPsales@harpercollins.com.

FIRST HARPERVIA EDITION PUBLISHED IN 2023

Designed by SBI Book Arts

Library of Congress Cataloging-in-Publication Data is available upon request.

ISBN 978-0-06-308904-4

23 24 25 26 27 LBC 5 4 3 2 1

CONTENTS

Introduction   1

Nanyuman   12
    by Ayesha Harruna Attah

so long *and* Fuji-san   35
    by Mogolodi Bond

The Body Is More than a Landfill and   39
Less than All That I Am
    by Sarah Uheida

To the woman who accused me of   48
breastfeeding the madam's child *and*
By Any Other Name
    by Phillippa Yaa de Villiers

Ezouga *and* Post mortem   63
    by Bahia Mahmud H. Awah

Daughter of a Bedouin Chief   66
    by Miral al-Tahawy

God's Plan   92
    by Boakyewaa Glover

Her Sweetie, Her Sugarcane   116
    by Natasha Omokhodion-Kalulu Banda

Krifé   142
    by Chiké Frankie Edozien

Contents

Queens *and* Sleeping Beauty (of Borehamwood) *and*   165
Waterstones *and* Ode to a Discarded Face Mask *and*
Denouement
   by Dami Ajayi

Finding Descartes   171
   by Reem Gaafar

Fulbright   199
   by Rémy Ngamije

Dirty Money   210
   by Kim Coleman Foote

The Killmonger Doctrine of Color and Humanity   235
   by Joe Robert Cole

Churai   243
   by Fatima Camara

[Coolitude: ce balisier-mirador]   246
   by Khal Torabully

This Tangible Thing   249
   by Yejide Kilanko

In a Yellow Dress with Red Flowers   271
   by Lillian Akampurira Aujo

A Honey-Headed Child   287
   by Nana Nyarko Boateng

Napoleão   303
   by Conceição Lima

Atat   306
   by Arao Ameny

Sontem and *Në na'a mpúrí haalo* and   317
En la puerta primavera
   by Recaredo Silebo Boturu

Contents

Lagos Wives Club   321
by Vanessa Walters

I Am Lost!   337
by Richard Ali A Mutu K

Poor Men Have Too Much Ego   346
by Edwige-Renée Dro

Sundays in Nairobi   361
by Jacquelynn Kerubo

Mbuya Baines   370
by Makanaka Mavengere

The Swagger Stick Man of June Fifteen   384
by Chuma Nwokolo

The Heart of the Father   390
by Enuma Okoro

Trophy   415
by Nana Ekua Brew-Hammond

Célebrons la culture   417
by Salma Khalil

Word maker.   419
by Ayi Renaud Dossavi-Alipoeh

Contributors   427
Thank You   447
A Note on the Cover   449
About the Editor   451

RELATIONS

INTRODUCTION

Years ago, I was at a party in New York. I was single, and I presume the man I stood on an invisible island with was unattached, too. Separate from the clusters of aspiring photographers and models, and friends like me who had tagged along to this photographer's studio, the two of us huddled together, gripping cups of clever bravado, our heads tilted toward one another at an angle of intrigue and lust. He was witty and worldly, and as we spoke, we discovered we were both from other places: he had moved to the United States from Morocco, and I was the daughter of Ghanaian immigrants who had sent me to live and school in Ghana when I was twelve years old.

"Oh, how cool," he said, "I've never been to Africa."

I blinked at my cup and then at him, sure I hadn't heard right. "But, aren't you Moroccan?"

"Yes," he said, the blank stare in his eyes not following my point.

"But, Morocco is in Africa."

He appeared genuinely unconvinced.

There was a whiteboard in the middle of the studio. I left our island to draw a map of Africa on it, and traced out two jagged rectangles.

"Morocco," I said, pointing to the rectangle in the top left corner. "Ghana," I said of the other one. "Africa," I concluded.

After a slight pause, he nodded with the sincere acquiescence of a knowledge transfer. The spell of flirtation broken, we floated away from each other, absorbed by new conversations, our atoll permanently abandoned.

1

Unsure how—or why—a man born and raised on the African continent truly seemed to believe he had never been to Africa, I wish I had probed him further, but I was still forming my own sense of who I was, and I had not come to the party to interrogate the vastness of African identity. I never forgot the exchange, though, and years later when a Frenchman I was dating noted casually that I was from "Black Africa," I felt the same befuddlement and irritation at the implication in his racialized delineation of the forty-eight countries known as "sub-Saharan Africa" that cover the northern, southern, eastern, and western regions of the continent. I told him to never describe them in that way again, especially not in public.

As far as I was, and am, concerned, the distinction between "Black Africa" or "sub-Saharan Africa" and Africa's northernmost nations reflects the continuation of a centuries-old distancing of lighter-skinned peoples from darker-skinned peoples largely due to the stigma projected onto the enslaved African. Chouki el Hamel's *Black Morocco: A History of Slavery, Race, and Islam* notes how the legacy of the enslavement of Blacks has complicated contemporary racial relations and Black identity in the country. I would add that it has complicated racial relations in every country where people of African descent live.

In October 2021, while I was on a weeklong stay in Cape Verde, the stunning necklace of ten islands off the northwest coast of Africa, a man on the island of São Vicente explained to me that Cape Verdeans, "whether rightly or wrongly," don't really consider themselves African. He pointed to the Portuguese heritage evident in the local complexion as his exhibit, but to me therein lies the rub. The relations between the Portuguese colonizers who controlled the archipelago and the people they kidnapped from their homes and families in "Black Africa," and the others who came by force or by fare to settle there, have complicated the assignation to a single identity so that what one claims, or doesn't, is a deliberate statement—a choice of who and what they want to be associated with. "Of course we're African," another Cape Verdean man from the island of Santo Antão told me with the Pan-African conviction of Bob Marley. "Look where we are."

Relations obfuscate the convenient and comfortable narratives we tell ourselves about who we are. They expose our hypocrisies and truths, and they attest to our inextricability from one another. They trounce boundaries erected by religion, class, race, and rhetoric. They force us to admit we're deeply interested in each other, and because there is so much at stake in this admission, relations are rife with the pain of disappointment, compromise, rejection, and exploitation. They are equally heavy with expectation, hope, and obligation. They are pregnant with possibility.

The relationships in my life were on my mind when I pitched this anthology in August 2020—the fifth month of the global coronavirus pandemic that had abruptly sent the world into quarantine. Businesses and schools were shuttered, public transportation was restricted to essential workers, travel was initially banned, then highly discouraged, and a flurry of edicts from national and global health organizations advised people to maintain a distance of six feet/one meter from each other and wear protective face masks.

When the pandemic was officially announced in March, I was based in Queens, New York; my siblings were two different bridges away in Brooklyn; and the man I love was resident on the West Coast. For the first time in my adult life, I felt acutely alone.

Usually, I flew to visit my parents in Ghana at least once a year—would that still be possible? I had relished attending the Pa Gya! and Aké literary festivals in Accra and Lagos, respectively, the past two years—would I ever again be able to engage with the community of writers and friends whom I had come to look forward to seeing in person?

I thought, too, about the network of family and friendships I had spread across Africa, North America, and Europe that I wasn't sure when I'd get to see again. And I thought of my relationship with myself, how much I admired that I wasn't "needy" and had a "full life" of exciting travel and work, and how much my independence was predicated on the assumption that the people and systems that made my nomadic life possible would always be available to me. I was palpably weakened by the shaking of that presumption and the realization that like everyone else, I needed people.

Intuiting my cries for help, my big sister and her husband risked their health in those early days of the pandemic when the official guidance encouraged minimal contact. They dropped by my apartment with groceries and stayed for dinner. A few weeks in, we moved the dinners to our brother's place, as his roommates had left New York, planning to ride out the COVID-19 lockdown in their respective hometowns. Before "pods" of trusted friends and family became a way people who weren't immunocompromised could safely connect with each other, my siblings and I were each other's safe spaces. On the recommendation of a friend, I also joined a virtual women's prayer group that met twice daily. I didn't know any of the women, except my friend, but they quickly became my extended community, a consistent network of support thirty minutes every morning, thirty minutes every night.

Two months into this fog of isolation, on May 25, 2020, in the American midwestern city of Minneapolis, Minnesota, a Black man named George Floyd was murdered by a white police officer who knelt on his neck for nine minutes and twenty-nine seconds. The asphyxiation, filmed by a brave teenager, Darnella Frazier, looped online and lassoed the global conscience, underscoring the heartbreaking point the #BlackLivesMatter movement had been trying to make since its 2013 founding in America by Alicia Garza, Patrisse Cullors, and Opal Tometti. Protests erupted in response to the killing in the United States and around the globe, from Australia to Antarctica—the whole world in agreement not only that the kill-first-ask-questions-later murders of

Black men and women at the hands of police officers would no longer be accepted, but that the explicit and tacit assignment of inferior and nefarious status to blackness had reached its expiration date.

Corporations vowed to hire and elevate more Black people—and many actually did! Brands built on avatars of antebellum slavery changed their names and logos. White people were pressured to "check on your Black friends." Two weeks after Floyd was killed, members of the US Congress donned Ghanaian kente cloth, given to them by members of the Congressional Black Caucus, and knelt for a moment of silence to honor Floyd. Karen Bass, the chairwoman of the caucus, told reporters that the kente cloth represented "our African heritage" and those who wore it were "acting in solidarity" with the same. She added, "That is the significance of the kente cloth—our origins and respecting our past."

As whiplash-inducing as this change felt, it reflected a culmination of decades of committed and consistent labor of activists in every sphere who had built or rebuilt systems to support a new generation of Black voices.

I have seen this steady build in the African literary space up close.

When my first book, *Powder Necklace*, a young adult novel inspired by my boarding school experience in Ghana, was published on April 6, 2010, few outlets were dedicated to covering, engaging, or supporting contemporary African literature and writers, and the modern era of social media was in its infancy. Today, there is an infrastructure specifically set up to bolster African voices.

There are African literature news platforms like *James Murua's African Literature Blog* and Ainehi Edoro's *Brittle Paper*. There are literary festivals like Aké in Nigeria, founded by Lola Shoneyin; Writivism in Uganda, cofounded by the writer and lawyer Bwesigye bwa Mwesigire; Africa Writes in the United Kingdom, launched by the Royal African Society; and Pa Gya!, produced by the Writers Project of

Ghana, which was founded by the Ghanaian writer Martin Egblewogbe and the US writer Laban Carrick Hill. There are literary magazines like *Kwani?* in Kenya, which was founded by the late, great writer and champion of African voices Binyavanga Wainaina; *Kwee* in Liberia, led by Managing Editor D. Othniel Forte; and *Doek!* in Namibia by Rémy Ngamije, a contributor to the anthology you're reading now; as well as an army of bloggers, bookstagrammers, and podcasters who review books by African authors and catalyze conversation.

There are publishers like Bibi Bakare-Yusuf's Cassava Republic Press, Valerie Brandes's Jacaranda Books, and Dzèkáshu MacViban's Bakwa Books. There are literary advocates like veteran publisher Ako Mutota; the author, publisher, and editor Zukiswa Wanner; and the founder of the Library of Africa and the African Diaspora, Sylvia Arthur. There are awards like the Miles Morland Foundation Writing Scholarship and the Etisalat Prize for Literature, which have joined the AKO Caine Prize for African Writing in earmarking funds for winning African writers. There are allies like the Goethe-Institut, the Alliance Française, and the British Council, which partner with many of the abovementioned to sponsor readings and events. And there are critically acclaimed and commercially successful writers who have created opportunities for new, emerging, and overlooked talent. The author Chimamanda Ngozi Adichie, one of this generation's most powerful and laureled voices, established the Purple Hibiscus Trust Creative Workshop to spur unpublished and published wordsmiths in their craft. Bernardine Evaristo, whose works have been translated into close to forty languages, founded the Evaristo African Poetry Prize (formerly the Brunel International African Poetry Prize) to honor and encourage African poets.

Contributors to this anthology are also investing time and resources to foster African literary creativity and community. Edwige-Renée Dro founded 1949, a library of women's writing from Africa and the

Black world, in Yopougon, Abidjan. Ayesha Harruna Attah started the Pomegranate Book Club in Popenguine, Senegal. Richard Ali A Mutu K, as head of the Wallonia-Brussels Library at Kinshasa in the Democratic Republic of the Congo, organizes activities that bring the Congolese literary scene together.

All of these join publishing pioneers like Margaret Busby, Jessica and Eric Huntley, and Verna Wilkins, as well as resources like the African Books Collective, which began in the late 1980s, and the African American Literature Book Club, founded in 1997 by Troy Johnson, and many others. This list is by no means exhaustive—the company of individuals and organizations who have built this sprawling contemporary African literary complex is long enough to merit its own book.

Literary anointers outside this community have been increasingly recognizing the art of African writers, too. Celebrity-powered book clubs by the actresses Reese Witherspoon, Sarah Jessica Parker, and Emma Roberts, respectively, have selected books by African authors for their millions of followers to read, just as their groundbreaking forerunner Oprah Winfrey was doing ten and twenty years prior. The Booker Prize has laureled three Black writers since 2010, including the aforementioned Nigerian-British author Bernardine Evaristo, who shared the prize with Margaret Atwood in 2019. In October 2021, the Tanzanian writer Abdulrazak Gurnah earned the Nobel Prize in Literature.

Just like in the 1960s through the 1980s, when the Heinemann and Longman African Writers Series respectively published the works of African and Caribbean writers like Chinua Achebe, Ama Ata Aidoo, Buchi Emecheta, Tayeb Salih, Wole Soyinka, and Ngũgĩ wa Thiong'o to the wider English-reading world—and in the 1980s and 1990s, when publishers and imprints like Amistad Press, Dafina Books, and One World published African American and Caribbean authors like E. Lynn

Harris, Terry McMillan, Bebe Moore Campbell, Eric Jerome Dickey, and Jamaica Kincaid—this most recent incarnation of interest in and infrastructure surrounding Black stories has begun to offer readers a deeper diversity of thought, experiences, and forms to connect with.

Authors like Chinelo Okparanta, Diriye Osman, Akwaeke Emezi, and Chiké Frankie Edozien, a contributor to this anthology, center queer stories. Writers like Nana-Ama Danquah, Tope Folarin, K. Sello Duiker, Songeziwe Mahlangu, and Yejide Kilanko (also a contributor to this anthology) engage mental health issues. Some like Kiru Taye and Empi Baryeh write romance, while others like Nnedi Okorafor, Tomi Adeyemi, Namwali Serpell, A. Igoni Barrett, and Nana Nkweti offer a new wave of science fiction and speculative fiction. Some write for young readers, and many of the writers here named and unnamed do all of the above—and more—showing just how membranous the borders we erect around topic and genre can be and should be.

Add all of this to the fact that we are living in a post–*Black Panther* world. The 2018 global blockbuster film based on the Marvel comic book hero brought Afrofuturism—the future-focused exploration of African Diaspora culture that fuses history, science, and technology—into the zeitgeist and ignited a multitude of conversations around "authentic" African identity in the process.

Free(r) from the burden of explaining our existence to "mainstream" audiences, and from the expectation that we document or comment on the African continent's every historic landmark, cultural contribution, or contention, a new generation of Black writers is introducing ourselves to each other, like our forebears Maryse Condé and Maya Angelou did. We are crossing the lines of land and language erected by colonialism and the slave trades, and trying to get to know ourselves. We are engaging in the awkward and painful conversations about the stereotypes and prejudices we hold about each other. We are defying notions of extra- and intra-cultural respectability and confronting what has long been considered taboo.

It isn't pretty literature—it's beautiful.

With this anthology, my goal was to create a meeting place for those of us connected by shared color or continent, but often separated by country, language, history, experience, or outlook. I wanted this collection of works to reflect the intimacy of honest exchange, with all of its irony, humor, vulnerability, and relief. In it you will find the work of writers hailing from, based in, or moving between Botswana, Canada, Chad, Côte D'Ivoire, Democratic Republic of the Congo, Egypt, Equatorial Guinea, Gambia, Ghana, Jamaica, Kenya, Libya, Mauritius, Namibia, Nigeria, São Tomé and Principe, Rwanda, Senegal, South Africa, Sudan, Togo, Uganda, the UK, the US, Western Sahara, Zambia, and Zimbabwe. Here, you will encounter a fictional Congolese journalist, noted for his rigorous commitment to exposing corruption, who considers compromising his country and his morals to please an out-of-his-league girlfriend. In an essay, you will meet an African American woman who compares being cheated out of money in Ghana to the sale of her ancestors into slavery. The co-writer of *Black Panther* also addresses the complicated relationship between Africans and African Americans, a topic that is explored in the film.

One woman in South Africa invites us into her body, heart, and mind as she moves through every step of her decision to terminate her unwanted pregnancy, while another woman in Ghana navigates the surprising religious objection of her family when she explores IVF.

One narrator rebukes the hypocrisy of legislators in Ghana who publicly promote anti-LGBTQ legislation and privately attend sex toy parties while the poor in their country ascend through sex work. Another story set in Khartoum, Sudan, makes a stinging comment on laws that give men—specifically, able-bodied married men, and fathers, in particular—outsize power over women and children. And another writer from Egypt dismantles Orientalist depictions of "desert life."

Woven into many of the works are reflections on place and home. Many of the women protagonists, for example, decide the marital bliss portrayed in books, films, and church is false "advertising." Some of the authors grapple with exile—"cursing the distance to my Sahara, as it grows," writes a Sahrawi poet—and seek to strengthen cords stretched by migration and generation. One examines her African identity through the lens of her European name, while another introduces us to a Caribbean-British protagonist negotiating the fact that she will "never be of" the Nigeria her husband and sons belong to. Others weigh the cost of leaving Africa to pursue opportunity abroad. On this topic, one character muses on the "Americanisms" that await him as he flies from Windhoek, Namibia, to New York to begin a Fulbright fellowship. Will it matter to a racist police officer, he wonders, that he is "Africa African" versus African American? Another, from Equatorial Guinea, ponders:

> If all of us leave,
> Who will tidy up our village's house?
> Who will write down our nòkonoko monster stories?

Many works contemplate Christianity and Islam, and the role both have specifically played in shaping thought on marriage, family, femininity, and masculinity. Others place traditional African cosmology at the center.

In terms of form, there are short stories that read like songs and essays that read like poems. Some engage legends, others document headlines and reference Facebook.

This gathering of stories, essays, and poems from new and established writers living in Africa and the diaspora is not the definitive authority on the African or Black experience; nor does it assume the pretention of offering answers to centuries-old struggles. What it does offer are deeply personal meditations on a diversity of human experiences, and a safe space for the kind of contemplation, confrontation, celebration, and revelation that characterize the most profound relations. It is also an invitation to continue the conversation about who we are and who we want to be, in a mélange of languages and expressions that reflect our ancestral tongues, the foreign nations many of us have settled in, and the interplay between the two. A school of pidgins.

One conversation I hope to continue is one that Bahia Mahmud H. Awah, a contributor to this anthology, rekindled in me—one that started that day years ago in the photography studio. In an early correspondence about his contribution, Mr. Awah mentioned that the name "Nana" derives from the African name "Aichanana" and that it originates in the African language Senhaya—a Northern Berber language spoken by the peoples who inhabit the southern part of the Moroccan Riff.

Nana Ekua Brew-Hammond
Queens, New York
October 2021

Ayesha Harruna Attah

Nanyuman

STORY

The waves of the sea crested and frothed, lapping Nanyuman's toes as Maimouna crouched next to her, selecting mussels from the recycled yogurt tub the vendor had ambushed them with. Nanyuman's phone rang and her heart leapt from its sea-induced calm. They didn't call each other. It couldn't be *him*, could it? Her screen was too cracked to see who was calling. Still, like an infatuated teenager, she could dream, couldn't she?

"Hi, Mama," Danny said on the other end of the line. Her dreams, stupid bubbly things, popped and fell to the sand.

"Oh, hi, Danny," said Nanyuman.

"When are you back home?"

"Soon," she said, trying to shove her irritation into her belly. It was *his* evening with Aissa, hers to breathe. And she'd told him countless times, she didn't like him calling her Mama.

"Aissa wanted to say goodnight to you," said Danny.

"Tell her I promise I'll give her a kiss when I get home."

Nanyuman pressed the red button.

"It was who?" asked Maimouna.

"Danny." She was sure his name came out flat. She could have tried to inject a little more enthusiasm, but she just couldn't summon it from her body.

"Bluebeard *cannot* live without you," Maimouna said, satisfied with her mussel pickings. She put the glistening black shells into a plastic bag and stood up. Her gray hair, woven in stunning braids, settled just above her shoulders. Maimouna had always worn her hair out, not wrapped in scarves like most women of a certain age in the village.

"Does the excitement ever come back?" Nanyuman asked.

"I've been married to Bouba for decades, my sister. If *you* don't make it exciting, it'll get even worse. If you're so bored, why don't you spend the evening with us? I need to get some white wine, some butter, garlic. Bouba is cooking, and it's going to be—" Maimouna smacked her fingers.

Nanyuman shook her head. It was too beautiful an evening to be stuck making small talk. Or any kind of talk. She kissed Maimouna bye. She just wanted to feel the sun's last rays on her skin. Nothing on under her dress, as she walked along the ocher and red cliff that hugged the seashore, she relished the feel of her thighs rubbing against each other. She wanted to replay images of her afternoon with Natan and how just thinking of him diffused electrical pulses from the crown of her head, through her slice in the middle, down to the tips of her toes. She wanted to soak it all in, because soon, sameness was going to seep back into her life.

The sun burned its power into Nanyuman's pores, melting all her guilt away. She was glad for destiny, for the story that was inscribed in the glyphs of her name.

• • •

RELATIONS

When Nanyuman had first arrived in the Sahelian village by the sea, it was to work with Maimouna on a translation project. Their contract ended and Nanyuman stayed and worked on new, local projects. It seemed an improbable place for a woman in her early thirties to want to settle—a village with one restaurant, no nightlife, no shops—but there was the sea, solitude, and something that made her feel as if this could, finally, be home. Her grandmother was Sahelian, her name was Sahelian. It made sense for her to finally settle in the Sahel, after years of traveling and decrypting other people's languages.

When she met Danny, camera around his neck, on the same stretch of beach on which she meditated, bought fish, and discussed local politics with the women selling cloth and beads, the whole thing seemed like destiny. He had bought a house in the village, he was English-speaking, and he gave her a break from her job of thinking in other languages. There was something alluring about his being much older than her, especially after her many failed romances with indecisive young men. He took her picture and it was the most beautiful capturing she'd ever seen of herself: she looked free. In those early days, Danny seemed as energetic as she was. She mistook hours and hours of lovemaking and talking about what their future could look like for passion.

• • •

"I'm going to start calling your boyfriend Bluebeard," said Maimouna.

"Bluebeard?" said Nanyuman, brow raised.

"You know the legend of Bluebeard?"

Nanyuman shook her head. Was it about pirates? She couldn't care less about pirates and didn't understand why little boys were so obsessed with them.

"It's a French classic. Danny's beard is blue, haven't you noticed?"

"Is it?" Nanyuman considered.

Bouba, Maimouna's husband, was hacking a piece of mutton to bits, while Danny stood watch close by, wincing every time the blade struck bone. Nanyuman and Maimouna sat outside, with a view of the sunset, glasses of wine in hand. Nanyuman and Danny had been seeing each other for just about a month.

"You think it's gray, but look at it in the light," said Maimouna, sipping from her glass. She was right, there was a hint of cerulean in Danny's beard. "Don't look so alarmed. Okay, shall I tell you the story of Bluebeard? Great. Bluebeard is a man whose beard is blue, which repulses all the marriageable girls in the village around his castle. Eventually, a young girl from the village decides to give him a chance, and they get married. He goes away on business and gives her keys to all his rooms and tells her she can go into them all except for one. Does she listen?"

"If she's anything like the two of us, my guess is no."

"Exactly. So she goes into the forbidden room, and turns out Bluebeard has murdered all of his former wives exactly because each disobeyed him."

"And this is the person you're comparing my boyfriend to?" Nanyuman said, laughing. "Are you suggesting I'm about to get murdered?"

Maimouna grinned.

"No, look at him. He can't stand watching Bouba cutting through meat. You have nothing to worry about."

• • •

And yet, stories have a way of weaving their words and taking over minds. Nanyuman started to wonder if maybe Danny was hiding something. When she first visited Danny's house, she chirped to her friends back home in Ghana that it was like a castle. It had many rooms, a large garden, a pool with a bridge over it that reminded her of a moat.

"You don't have a secret chamber, do you?" she asked, when they lay together on the bed in the largest room in the house.

"My garage," said Danny, light from the moon shining off the dome of his head, even in the dark. Nanyuman's heart raced. Maybe Danny *was* Bluebeard. "It's my form of a bachelor pad. My dad was crazy about his garage, and his dad was crazy about his carriage house. I suppose, it's hereditary. Tinkering with things in there."

It was a boring answer, but it was an answer that seduced Nanyuman because it was safe. She had met many people on her travels and no one had wanted to settle, except for Danny.

"How come you bought this house and didn't move back?" she asked him, because it was also improbable for a fifty-year-old white man from Minnesota to settle in their village by the sea.

"There's something about this village, isn't there, that lures you to stay?" said Danny, propping himself on his elbow; the moon had now lit up his whole face and his beard glowed blue. "It's a good place to start a family. I'm ready."

Nanyuman would learn that for Danny, whose parents died young, family was everything. Until he discovered their little village by the sea, he had simply struggled to find a place that rooted him.

• • •

About a year after they had started dating, Nanyuman's belly swollen with new life, she asked Danny what his deepest fear was.

"That I'll lose you and the family we're starting." Nanyuman was relieved that it wasn't something to the tune of, *If you cheat on me, I'll never forgive you.* "What's yours?" Danny asked, rubbing Nanyuman's belly with his soft hands.

"That I'll live up to my name," she said.

"Tell me the story."

"You know it already. I told you on our first date."

"Tell me again." His voice was tinged with a low rumbling.

"Fine. I'm named Nanyuman, after a woman who lived with her gentle husband. She and her husband hosted a kola trader who was passing through their town. When Nanyuman's husband was at the farm, the kola trader seduced Nanyuman with kola nuts and gold, and she eloped with him. Soon the kola trader tired of Nanyuman and whined that she'd spent all his money. He left her and moved on to the next town. Disgraced, Nanyuman returned to her father's house. When Nanyuman learned of her only son's circumcision, she organized the best musicians in town to throw a celebration. Then, she took the oldest shoe she could find, went to her husband, and asked him to spank her bottom. Her husband took her back."

Danny said nothing.

"So what happens if I do this to you?"

"It's just a story," said Danny. "I'd like to think we have more control over our lives than that." He switched to talk of what they would name their baby. She found herself yearning for less talk and more skin. And yet, he barely touched her anymore, because he was scared of hurting their baby.

• • •

Nanyuman and Danny had lived together for about three years when they first met Natan at a celebration of Bob Marley's birthday at Bouba's restaurant. Nanyuman and Maimouna spent most of the evening dancing, all the while trying to avoid the self-styled Bob Marleys with their spliffs and accompanying sugar mamas. Danny sat at the bar, talking with Bouba, barely drinking his beer. He didn't look at Nanyuman once.

She wondered at what point desire had packed her bags and left their marriage. Had she even existed in their marriage?

Natan, whose wife was nowhere to be seen, chain-smoked, drank beer after beer, talked with everybody, was back on the dance floor. He zipped here, there, and everywhere. He stopped in front of Nanyuman, shook his shoulders at her and twirled her around. His skin was damp with sweat and flushed from all the dancing. He reminded her of the boys she'd pined after in secondary school. No, he was more than that. Virile. Like the kola trader must have been. She didn't want to give any more weight to that thought.

Then Danny told her Natan had invited them to a barbecue at the house he and his wife were renting not far from theirs.

· · ·

Danny had no friends. Bouba was too avuncular for him and Maimouna was always hovering, watching him. Natan, he enjoyed, Danny admitted after the barbecue. Natan was a live-and-let-live kind of person. Nanyuman was glad that Natan and Danny could become close. Angela, however, she didn't see the need to befriend.

"How do you like living in our village?" Nanyuman had asked her over a plate of charred fish at the barbecue.

"It's quiet."

"Do you get to go to the city much?"

"For work, and my family's there."

"When I first moved in with him, Danny was always off watching soccer games and whatnot. It can feel lonely in the village. I make sure that I'm always busy."

Angela smiled. Nanyuman thought herself a quiet woman, but Angela was painful. Nanyuman wondered what Angela and Natan could have had in common. Being Catholic Senegalese?

Over the next year and a half, Danny and Natan grew closer. Angela was often not around, because sometimes her work spilled into weekends or she preferred to stay with her family.

• • •

Natan was a year younger than Nanyuman. He turned thirty-five and wanted to celebrate in grand style. Angela was not in the mood, especially since she was with child. She stayed in the city to rest. It tickled Nanyuman, that one would go to the city for quiet, to escape a party in the village.

Danny and Nanyuman toted over two bottles of red wine to Natan's, whose garden was spilling over onto the street outside. They found the host surrounded by an entourage of limbs and miniskirts, and Nanyuman wondered if it was Angela who decided not to be present or if Natan had insisted she leave.

"Hey!" Natan shouted and bounded over, his curls bopping up and down. He pecked Nanyuman and Danny on the cheeks, his fragrance eau de cigarette.

"Great party," said Danny.

Nanyuman downed a glass of wine, then nursed another. She'd come to have a good time. Parties like this one were rare in their village. She sidled over to Maimouna. They clinked glasses and danced when the DJ proved able to play tracks that were not rock headbangers. For someone who had spent most of his life in Senegal, Natan's musical taste was shockingly European.

Nanyuman went to the bathroom and on her way out was swooped off the floor. She looked down and saw Natan, his arms wrapping her legs. Caramel over coffee. Their skin together, a delicious drink.

"Where do you think you're taking me?"

"To the trampoline."

Tucked in the corner of the garden, the trampoline was filled with adults jumping up and down like five-year-olds. She'd worn a short red dress. No way she was going on that contraption to flash the whole village with her undies—even if they were a particularly good pair.

"Put me down or I'll scratch your eyeballs out," she warned, digging the pads of her fingers into his arms.

"Feisty and strong," said Natan, conceding and lowering her down. "I like."

She wondered who had seen as she went back to Maimouna. Maimouna? Bouba? Danny? No one seemed to have noticed.

"Natan knows how to throw a party," said Maimouna, who handed her another glass of wine.

The wine raced through her system, and on her way back to the bathroom, she crossed paths again with Natan. She twiddled her fingers at him and he marched to her.

"You're dangerous," he whispered, lips grazing her ears, as they looked in Danny's direction, and her heart sprinted. Around him, everything seemed to speed up.

"Me? Why on earth would I be that?"

"My friends are saying I'm hitting on Danny's wife."

"Are you?"

"Maybe."

And then he was off, cigarette smoke trailing behind him. Nanyuman's belly warmed. What was wrong with her? He had a baby on the way, he was married, she was married. Why was she getting lured into whatever it was Natan was trying to weave?

Later that evening, Danny huffed and puffed on top of her. The last time they had tried this, months before, Danny was out of her in seconds. This time, she allowed Natan to eclipse her thoughts, and only then did she reach a toe-curling finale.

. . .

I forgot to give you Aissa's birthday card at the party, Nanyuman texted Natan. Hope the rest of your birthday went well.

Her daughter had designed a card Nanyuman had forgotten at home. Aissa was not pleased one bit and insisted that her mother get it to Tonton Natan "*now!*"

Who could resist a four-year-old dictatorial fairy godmother sprinkling magic dust over two lusty adults?

We'll get drinks and you'll give it to me, Natan texted back. ;)

Heart racing, she deleted their messages.

. . .

Natan's hands were as soft as Danny's. This, she learned weeks later when Natan dropped off a very tipsy Danny after they'd watched a soccer game together. Nanyuman groggily opened the door because Danny had left his keys goodness knows where, as usual. He was about to shut the door, but Nanyuman squeezed her way out to say hello to Natan. She didn't care that her nipples poked through her sheer nightgown or that the filmy garment traced the moons of her butt. She tossed out her good training, passed down from grandmother to mother to her, admonishments that she be decently dressed when in company, that a lady left people guessing. But Natan had suggested that they have drinks and had done nothing more. Now she wanted to remind him of the thing that had been building up between them since his birthday party, and show him.

He smiled brightly when he saw her, and his mop of curls bounced as he poked his head out of the car window. She couldn't kiss his cheeks, not when his lips were puffing out clouds of smoke, and certainly not with Danny near. Her husband knew just how much she abhorred cigarettes. So she reached out to high-five him and he clasped her close. The surprising tenderness of his hand pressed into her eager palm. She wanted all those fingers squeezing her flesh, pinning her against a wall. Could such soft hands go rough? Danny had never quite been able to go there. He always had to be a gentleman.

"I suppose I have *you* to thank for his current state," she joked, pouting, arching her back, and retrieving her hand.

"Any time," Natan said and laughed, driving off with the crazed speed only he seemed to possess.

Back in bed, as her husband snored next to her, whiffs of beer and cigarettes also her bedfellows, she thought of what it could take to get Natan in her. The divide between her legs moistened.

• • •

Mangrove Hotel. 3 pm. And burn after reading.

• • •

"Do you still think I'm dangerous?" Nanyuman asked, as they stood in the shower of the hotel room. She'd insisted on the shower, because their respective drives from their village to this town had drenched them in sweat.

"Isn't it a compliment to be called dangerous?" said Natan.

"In the story of my name, you're the dangerous one."

It must have been her see-through nightgown that made Natan text her. She was glad she hadn't had to work too hard.

Drinks had not happened, even though the Mangrove Hotel bar was semifamous for its bissap cocktails.

He'd sent her a room number and she'd gone over with Aissa's card, each step on the seashell-bordered trail trying to convince herself to turn around and go back home. And yet, her attraction to him was like water boiling in a lidded pot. *Bubble bubble, puff, spurt*, the lid *tack-tack-tack*ing and threatening to blow off. She needed the release. The full-throttle release. It was coming out in whiffs of irritation toward poor Danny. She convinced herself that this entanglement would be good for everyone involved as she violently shoved the image of Natan's unborn child from her mind.

Now they lay side by side, drained. What had she done? It was too late to go back to when this was all a fantasy. What had Danny ever done to her but be kind? No, she would not let disgusting, oily guilt slog through her. She was doing this because it was written in her cards.

• • •

"You have the same faults I detest in my husband," Nanyuman said to Natan, as smoke wisped over their naked bodies, his bare chest supporting her beaded braids. "I'd never let him smoke inside. And certainly not in bed."

"Only difference is I'm young," said Natan. "Which is why you're fucking me."

"Maybe," Nanyuman considered, turning over to kiss Natan. The beads in her hair clacked. "And the melanin. But don't be crude." She smacked her lips. "Somehow cigarettes taste different on you. They don't disgust me as much."

"Forbidden fruit."

"It's strange, how your names even rhyme."

"Natan and Danny do not rhyme, Nanyuman."

"Natan is derived from Nathaniel. Danny, Daniel."

"This is why you work with words," said Natan, taking a drag from his cigarette. "And I'm just a poor merchant."

"Poor merchant," scoffed Nanyuman. "Two words that don't go together. You're who my husband was some years ago. You're going to turn into him in ten years. Into mush. And your wife will find a younger version of you."

"You're cruel."

"Just the facts of life. Unless she truly is an angel."

"No one is an angel."

• • •

Aissa was Daddy's girl. She spent more time with Danny in his garage than she did anywhere else in the house. Nanyuman had tried playing dolls and teatime with the girl, but fixing her bicycle in the garage or hammering away at some invention was more Aissa's preference. The only time a hint of girly oozed out was when Natan came to visit or to borrow a tool from Danny's garage. He would lift Aissa off the ground and throw her into the air and she would shriek in delight. In that moment, they looked like father and daughter, their copper-toned skin glistening in the harsh noonday sun.

"I will marry Tonton Natan," Aissa professed one such day, after Nanyuman had had to wrestle her out of her father's arms to get her into bed.

It was as if the girl knew that something was going on. Aissa's words turned Nanyuman's lust into guilt. Oily thing, it slid right over what Nanyuman had thought were high defenses, walls she built up the first time she got into bed with Natan.

• • •

They were in the kitchen. Nanyuman doing the dishes. Danny had cooked, as he always did. She and Maimouna joked often that they were lucky to find men who cooked in super-patriarchal Senegal. He had made a delicious prawn sauce with rice. He went to tuck in Aissa for the night.

"I want to throw a party," said Danny, when he returned.

"You?" said Nanyuman, and she laughed. Who would come? "Why?"

"The music at Natan's party was terrible, and I want to throw a party where we play good music. To throw a grown-up party with no trampolines or silly games like that."

"You know I'll end up doing all the running around and I don't have the energy for that."

He said nothing. Then he grabbed Nanyuman's phone and flung it against the wall. The crack preceded a long quiet. Did *he* know something was going on?

"I'm sorry," he said. "I'll get you a new one."

She picked up the phone. The screen was cracked into a thousand shards.

• • •

"I don't believe in hell, but I might be careening into some version of it."

"Don't tell me you're feeling guilty about this," said Natan, shifting on the creaky bed, and now lying on his back. Nanyuman sat up and watched him, his feet splayed on the furry blanket with some striped wild animal motif.

"It's easy for you to say. You have no conscience. Your wife is expecting her first baby, and yet, here you are."

"Angela and I will come to an arrangement."

"You will, as I will, as will Danny, just so we feel better about ourselves. Actually, this will be easy for you. I'm the one who risks losing everything. If this affair ever got out, people would say, 'Ah, you see, we told you, Ghanaians in Senegal, prostitutes and bandits. Real sai-sais.'"

"My people have all sorts of rigid ideas about things they don't understand. They're allergic to anything slightly foreign. Like me, because I'm mixed, people always regard me with suspicion. And yet, Senegal is home."

"But, you and me, we *are* evil, Natan." She smiled. It started out as a joke when she'd said it, but inside, her words deepened and turned into truth. This would hurt people.

"Are we? I think it would be wrong to ignore our attraction. What if I died or you died? We'd be forever left with 'What if'? What a horrible thing to live with—regret."

"You're incorrigible," said Nanyuman. Her grandmother might have agreed with Natan, that she shouldn't feel guilty about an act that seemed fated from the very minute the griot had whispered the name into her ear, four times. "Tell me about this scar." She pulsed her finger on the rubbery keloid on his chin. "You have many scars. I want to know about all of them and when we reach that point, we'll stop this thing. Let's start with this one."

"I got it when I was four, just after my mother and I moved back from France. I had just learned to pedal and I thought I ruled the world. Went crashing downhill. Hit a rock and was thrown up in the air, landed on glass. Next day, I was back on my bike again. Haven't stopped since."

"I would never have ridden again," said Nanyuman.

"Yes, you would have. You're here, in bed with me. You're not as cautious as you think."

• • •

"Sing me the Nanyuman song," said Natan.

"Not you, too," said Nanyuman, spent, as Natan's head lay in the gap between her breasts, a space in which she often imagined miniature horses passing through with loads on their backs, a mountain pass. If she narrowed her eyes, chopped off Natan's hair, paled his skin, and aged him a smidge, he looked like Danny. Danny, who was still insisting on his party.

"I've never heard it," said Natan.

"I don't know the words—they're in Bambara. Only the tune."

"You say I'm the kola trader?"

"Yes, and you're going to tire of me one of these days."

"Never. Me and little Natan could never get tired of you."

"Don't be vulgar," she said. "But why are men so obsessed with your penises? In any case, your baby will force you home."

"Sing it."

Nanyuman summoned the song her grandmother had hummed when she'd told her about the adulterous Nanyuman at the age of sixteen.

"Why name me after someone so bad?" Nanyuman had asked then.

"Was she bad?" her grandmother responded.

"She left a good man to chase after riches."

"But she did something good for her soul. She was disheveled and not thriving before the kola trader came along. She would have died if she hadn't left him. She came back a whole woman."

· · ·

"Natan De Jong, you're a Viking," joked Nanyuman, pushing a limp onion into her mouth, as they sat in a different room in the Mangrove Hotel. She had left home before lunchtime, feigning a meeting with a client. "This is what you do: raid. After me, there'll be a lot more. And who knows who has gone ahead of me? But if your wife did this to you, you'd clobber her."

"Says the person living with Bluebeard," said Natan. "In any case, I like to think of myself as warmer than that."

She paused over her room service plate of yassa au poulet. "Sorry, what did you just say?"

"That I'm warmer."

"About Bluebeard." Nanyuman couldn't believe that Maimouna had shared the secret nickname.

"We live in a village," Natan said. "People talk and sometimes spill things they didn't mean to share. It was a slip, when she called him that. I thought it was hilarious, because Danny is the furthest thing from Bluebeard out there. He's so gentle."

Nanyuman didn't want to be upset. Natan was supposed to be a blissful time. She would force herself to forget about Maimouna's treachery. The woman was getting old anyway; Nanyuman couldn't fault her. And she didn't want to think about Danny.

"Your father's blood has to be stronger than your mother's. Nathaniel the Young. There's no hint of Senegal in you."

"You don't think it's my warm Senegalese blood that's running this whole show?" He pointed to his groin.

"Oh no, that's the Natan that likes to cuddle and spoon. The conquering of me is totally your Nordic blood."

"Well, and you, who left herself so open to conquest?" He reached for a piece of chicken on Nanyuman's plate.

"I'm a hundred percent African. Too trusting. Of everyone."

"What will Danny do when he finds out?"

"He already knows the story of my name. And I think he knows about us."

"Me and you, like, me Natan?" He sat up.

"Uh huh."

"How? And he's okay with it?"

Nanyuman shrugged.

"I like your confidence. Danny is all Nordic, too, isn't he? From Minnesota somewhere? Should we be worried about getting clobbered?"

"His blood is diluted," said Nanyuman. She didn't like the way she was feeling—itchy inside. "He even insists he has African blood. But, can we please stop talking about him. Are you having a boy or a girl?" She took a forkful of rice covered in translucent onions, then chewed slowly.

"Way to change the subject." His voice went up a register. "*Enough about me, Natan. Your turn. Let's talk about your wife.*"

"God, I don't talk like that."

"Your voice *is* sexy," said Natan.

"Boy or girl?"

"Angela wants us to wait. She's buying lots of yellow and green."

"You seem distant from your baby. Is it your Viking blood making you so macho? Babies are for mothers alone to worry about because they can die in one swoop when the neighboring raiders come?"

"You're too obsessed with lineage. It's because I'm in love with you."

Nanyuman paused. Was he being genuine? She looked at him and he was regarding her, expecting a response. She suddenly felt transformed back to that teenager who wrote poems in her notebooks, waiting for someone to say those words. When Danny said, "I love you," it felt like he said it out of duty. He had the family he had always dreamed of, the house he had always wanted, a beautiful wife on his arm. All the boxes were checked, and would remain checked if he just kept saying those words. When Danny said those words, nothing stirred in her. Now something pulpy shifted in her chest with Natan's declaration.

"No, Natan," she said, finally. "I'm wiser than my namesake. I know this is not love. I'm not going to leave my home behind and elope with you. I can see this for what it is. A good fuck."

He squinted and pursed his lips. "Ooh, I see I'm rubbing off on you. What happens at the end of the song?"

The plate of yassa was now clean. Nanyuman placed it on the floor, then sat by Natan.

"Nanyuman goes back to her husband with her tail between her legs, but he doesn't scorn or shame her. Her husband is praised for being a good man."

"Angela wants to move back to the big city," Natan said, suddenly.

"Good," Nanyuman said, ignoring the painful beat that tripped in her heart.

"Why are you so happy about this?" Natan asked. "I'm gutted."

"After Nanyuman has spent all the kola trader's gold, he says, 'I have nothing more to give you.' It's exactly what's supposed to happen."

"Up to me, I would be staying here."

"When are you moving?"

"Next month or so. I have to go search for an apartment."

"Did you mean what you said about loving me?"

"I did. I do." They were quiet. "Why did you give in to this?"

"This question is so unlike you, Nathaniel. Because it's my destiny."

"Bullshit. You've been using destiny as your cover for everything and I've let it slide. Why did you seduce me?"

"*I* seduced you?"

He nibbled Nanyuman's cheeks.

"You did. That nightgown . . . I still want a straight answer."

"Marriage is boring. And everything the movies and books have taught us is advertising. The real thing is so humdrum and ordinary. This feels like a chance to live. You?"

"You're irresistible."

She palmed his head, suddenly feeling protective of him. She remembered a dream she'd had a few nights before. In it, her grandmother lay in her hospital bed and whispered last words into Nanyuman's ears: "Don't forget, your name also means good mother."

• • •

"Natan and Angela are moving back to the big city," Nanyuman said as she lay with her back to Danny. She with a finger hooked in *Rebecca*, he crouched over his iPad.

"His wife's doing, no doubt," said Danny, swiping his finger on the glass screen.

"You'll miss Natan?"

"I like the guy, but he's always been on another wavelength. Too high-speed for me. Imagine what it's like being married to him. I don't envy Angela. You could never be married to a man like him."

The last sentence said as fact. Nanyuman toyed with telling him.

"Danny?"

"Yes, Mama?" He raised his brows but his eyes remained fixed on the glow of his screen.

"Never mind."

• • •

She was still seething at Maimouna's flippant sharing of Danny's Bluebeard nickname, so she had done everything in her power to avoid the woman. She canceled their walks in the reserve, and once, when she'd seen Maimouna at the market, she turned right around and walked home with an empty basket. But now, Maimouna was standing at the door to their home.

"I miss our walks," said Maimouna.

Nanyuman was dressed in yoga pants, a tank top, and sneakers. She couldn't come up with an excuse. "Let me tell Danny I'm going out," she said.

She and Maimouna went down the hill from their house, turned onto the main laterite road and walked toward the entrance to the natural reserve. They usually didn't talk much on these walks, so Maimouna wouldn't have known that there was something out of the ordinary. They entered the reserve by its rubbish-filled path, where the pond was filled with storks, gray herons, and millions of mosquito larvae. Squirrels with striped tails scurried ahead of them, and the sea—which hugged the reserve—slapped the shore right next to it.

At the top of the Cape de Naze, the sea glittering below, Nanyuman felt emboldened.

"How and why did you tell Natan about Danny's nickname?"

"He told you?" Maimouna said. Her skin was dark and striking next to the gray of her hair. "It slipped. I'd drunk one glass of wine too many. And you know how he loves to make sure your cup is never empty. I said it in Wolof, so I'm even surprised it stuck in his head. And I didn't think it was a big deal."

"We have to stop calling him that."

"Fair enough," said Maimouna. "Natan says you two are working on a project?"

"I was helping him edit some work," said Nanyuman. She should have been like her namesake and had an affair with someone from out of town. This village by the sea was too small. "But it's over."

• • •

"One more time," Natan urged, over the phone. "Please. Just one more time."

"Our project ends after this," Nanyuman said.

So they went back to the hotel of their trysts.

"I found your song," he said, thumbing through his phone. She knew it well, the Orchestre Régional de Kayès rendition. It started with a slow guitar strum, followed with a doleful saxophone. "Dance with me."

She slid off the bed and went to him, closing her eyes to fight the tears that were about to roll out. The vocalist began and she was transported to her grandmother's bosom. "Naaa-nyu-man," the old woman had hummed.

"When Nanyuman left her husband, he said he didn't have a quarrel with her and that God would go searching and would bring her back," Nanyuman told Natan, wiping the tears that had broken the dam and pooled in the dent of her neck. She didn't like that it hurt. This wasn't supposed to hurt. The song didn't mention a thing about Nanyuman's pain. Or how she'd just wanted to come alive. "I'll miss you, kola trader."

• • •

Nanyuman picked up her cruddiest of slippers. Shoes that had trodden on laterite, cow dung, grass, and just recently, mud, as the rainy season was in full force. She went to Danny, who was in his garage tinkering with an old rusty lamp. She set the mud-caked slipper by the lamp, turned around, and lifted her boubou up. She closed her eyes and waited.

"You did it." Danny sighed.

"You knew I would. It's why you asked me to tell you the story over and over. So you would know as soon as it happened."

"I convinced myself it was just your African superstitious side."

"I'm sorry," Nanyuman said.

"Nanyuman's husband doesn't spank her, does he?"

"I'll feel better if you do it."

She clenched her backside, waiting for the sharp sting of plastic against skin. Instead, she felt Danny's soft hand cup her butt. He pushed her against his workstation, cluttered with wrenches and screwdrivers of all sizes, and took her.

"You owe Aissa and me a party," he said, as he limped out of her. Then just as suddenly, she was filled with an urge to laugh. All along, she'd been trying to chop up Danny and stuff him into the stanzas of the gothic tale to feel better about her own story. *She*, Nanyuman, was Bluebeard.

Mogolodi Bond

POEMS

so long

she loved me
for
who I was
for so long
but
who I was
was not
who I was
for so long
she could not love
me anymore

Fuji-san

All my life
I've been dreaming
dreaming of becoming
dreaming of being
someone
some thing
somebody

It nearly killed me

I went to bed
in a mood
there was Tokyo
and a spooky moon

I woke up
before sunrise
then the sun rose
and there was
Mount Fuji

Fuji-san

That dormant volcano
formed this island

I'm on an island
again

All my life
I've been *obsessed*
with rising
rising and climbing

I can't rise
like the sun
I can't set

I never believed
in windmills
ghosts
god
or failure

All my life
I've been fighting

Gotta fight
life is hard
fight harder
fight for my life
my rights

For seven straight years
I stood
in front of a mirror
every day
at war
fighting
like Travis Bickle

fighting with
him
her
me
in the third person
HE
fighting for he
with he

HE is a fiction
his dreams
and his fight

Mount Fuji isn't dreaming
rising
or fighting

Señor Quixote
befriend your sheath
I have a new dream:
to fight no more

Sarah Uheida

The Body Is More than a Landfill and Less than All That I Am

ESSAY

I have knelt and howled over smaller things. I have been shown more tenderness over smaller things. I have looked my suffering in the eyes before and *this* is not it.

April begins and ends the way a poem does. There is first the expectant disquietude of a white page, and then, the severe scorch of a confession: *mifepristone & misoprostol.*

Inaccurate.

April begins with me in the man's bed, dark blue sheets, light blue eyes, a stinging blue bruise on my left breast. My teeth on his artery, soft as scalpels; the sound of my body splitting against his—think peaches smashed against a window, syrup soaking sleeves, spellbound and almost certain of the semantics of sex.

Irrelevant.

RELATIONS

April begins with an orgasm and does not end.

Incriminating.

April is turning into June and I am still suspended somewhere, say Monday the twelfth of that month, say against the bathroom wall at Pulp Cinema, waiting for the second blue line to appear, knowing long before I knew. The blood was only a day late; the blood was an entire day late. The body—which used to be mine and which I had to give up on the thirteenth of April, in a green room, alone, on a metal table, legs spread wide open—has its own ways of declaring war. How for two weeks I watched my breasts (blue bruise and all) become someone else's, some far foreign woman of abundance whose flesh obeyed her and whose nipples were perpetually hard. I turned myself on. I looked in the mirror and thought *this* is what I'm meant to look like. For those few weeks after conception and before we found out, the man spent long minutes touching them; called them "decadent." But the man is also just a boy who did not notice that I was going to the toilet every twenty minutes, or that I was ordering the same food every single day. The man is a boy who stood still for only a single second before aging ten years right then and there, pulling my frozen body to the barstool, fetching water and coffee, buying a second test so that we could rule out a false positive. Let me shatter my world twice. We drove to Jonkershoek and were stopped by a police officer who asked for his driver's license, watched us scramble and stutter as we dug around the car for the wallet we well knew was on his desk like an untouched box of condoms. The police officer, who could have taken us to the station, let us go with a "Now you can't say the police aren't nice." She is the first policewoman I've ever spoken to. I like to think that my uterus—which became a womb on the twelfth of April and then was again reduced to a uterus on the thirteenth—whimpered some embryonic plea that touched hers. We sat silent on a bench in some abandoned field and stared straight ahead at the lawless lavish forest that we'd fucked in two months earlier. Sun-strung sky spilled onto a still river and whatever metaphors lust sleeps with. Pants off and panting. Something so pleasurable it borders on disgrace. Some guttural forehead kiss afterward that sees me through the days before I can have him again. Now here we were those long-gone groans grabbing at our ankles as we sit stupefied and splendid. There was something unbearably beautiful about the way I closed my eyes and saw a hundred different ways in which Father would find and flay me. Bare breasted and belly curved. Aglow and even in body-slashing ache. I was Crucified Jesus *and* Mary. I laughed and looked at the man and for a selfish solipsistic second I thought *I must keep it—no, her.* A small soft thing tore open inside me and I saw the woman in the mirror tying tiny shoelaces. He said: "Say the words and we are out of here." He said: "Your body is yours, but I will keep it alive as though it is my own." I just kept lighting cigarettes. He said: "Tell me what you want me to do, I will do it for you." Then there was a shift in the air and all of a sudden I felt unsafe in that exposed field and asked him to drive me home. We parked somewhere behind the Language Centre building where we'd fucked a month before—in broad daylight, both half wishing someone would catch us and witness what a feminist's sophisticated mouth is capable of doing to the causes that she believes in. Now here we were, the man calmly scrolling through his phone looking for a place that seems legitimate enough. *Marie Stopes.* I take the phone from him and dial them, force the guilt right out of my mouth as I tell the recep-tionist what we did and what I need. She asks the last time I bled and what color it was—I am dissociating, thinking only of the times I've looked the man in the eyes and said "Come inside me": bed, floor, desk, wall, dark cinema, empty building, full bathroom, wine farm; quiet and then so goddamn loud and in my mother tongue that he loves but does not speak. Now the woman on the phone is telling me to come in tomorrow and bring sanitary pads and a change of underwear. When she hangs up, the man and I split the abortion bill into two as if it were a little hotel stay or the countless times we'd each insist on paying at the restaurant.

He drops me off a street down from where I live and that walk costs me an entire year's worth of willpower. Mother unlocks the door and I look straight ahead and right through her. Father's "Hi" cuts through the soft skin just below my stomach and I think I black out with shame. I spend the rest of that evening sitting by the window in the dark, the cigarette's ember hissing and hissing as my thoughts short-circuit. My first fixation: when was the particular day of conception? What underwear was I wearing that day, and what mood were we in, and was it my hands or his that led the chase? I think about the vodka Red Bulls that I have been drinking all month, and the triple espresso shots, and the bipolar I medication I am on causing heart defects in infants, and the skin-tearing sex we had last weekend after splitting a bottle of white wine at Jan Marais Nature Reserve. I collapse into an uneasy sleep at seven p.m., just like most nights of late, but not before coming to a uselessly gut-wrenching maternal resolution: *tomorrow I will quit smoking for the sake of the daughter that I am going to flush down the toilet.*

Motherhood begins with the two blue lines on the thirty-rand test kit. It is the man emptying the last little bit of his bank account on a spinach wrap and orange juice for me so as to counteract the blood loss. It is the drive to Cape Town in utter silence save for the friend I mistakenly asked to accompany us. Motherhood is harsh like that: when the friend says that I am not killing anything, that it is just a bunch of cells right now, I tell her to shut the fuck up about my child. And then the forty-minute wordless drive while a playlist that the man and I made love to plays on repeat. When we get to the clinic I ask them to give me a moment in the car. I think: what if I ruin my uterus with complications? What if I cannot bring myself to do it and then am hunted down by Father? I think: *what if it breaks the man to the point where my love is no longer enough? What if we can never bring ourselves to undress again?* I am just beginning to savor this sovereign feeling of fullness but must now rip it away from my body. I get out of the car.

They do not let the man or the friend come through the main door with me. I wait for a long time in the yellowed room, old posters peeling, pale and pained women in the row of chairs in front of me. When at last the receptionist calls my name, she asks whether I am fasting, too. It is the first Tuesday of Ramadan and with a surname like mine I can never leave a religion that I left a long time ago. I say no. I say, "I am an atheist." Her eyes roll: *look where that got you.* She spends ten minutes digging through her pile of papers looking for my proof of payment and then calls the nurse to take me to Room C. Inside the room, I am a ghost who takes off her shoes and hops onto the scale. I am a watercolor painting on my dead grandfather's wall and when the nurse pricks my finger, I leak the wrong thing. She makes me retake the test just to make sure: still bad news. "Rh negative. Your body will create antibodies that attack your baby in future pregnancies. You will need a RhoGAM shot within seventy-two hours of the abortion. We are out of stock." She leaves the room to fetch something and I take a shaky photo of the blood sheet with the labels so that I can remember to tell the man because right now I am neither able to process her words nor care about their implications. Just get me through this; *tomorrow* is a word no longer meaningful or even utterable. Just scrape this thing out of me. She comes back and asks me to follow her outside, past the man and the friend, and into the toilet, where she hands me a reusable metal cup, washed after every use, and tells me to urinate in it while she waits by the sink. I obey. I am giggling against the coolness of the metal toilet seat and have lost all sense of self. She sticks a pregnancy test into the cup and tells me something I already know. I follow her out and back into the room, once again whishing past the man and this time winking at him. Inside, she says: "Do I have your permission to give you an ultrasound?" She takes my numb sneer for a yes. I remove all my clothes, hiding my panties at the bottom of the pile, and get into some blue and white backless cloth. She smears gel on my stomach and presses her device way too hard against it. She looks disappointed in me. She says: "I cannot see the pregnancy which means it might be ectopic." I manage to utter an eloquent "What?"

"It is when the fertilized egg implants outside of the uterus, usually in the fallopian tube. This can cause the tube to rupture, leading to internal bleeding. It can be fatal if not treated." She says one in fifty women will have an ectopic pregnancy at some point during her lifetime. I am leaning against the pillow looking at the empty gray grainy screen, aware of the man's absence, the space right next to the bed where he should be standing, smiling, but no, I am alone and my loneliness is made more disgusting by the fact that it is being witnessed by this woman who keeps asking me the same questions. She apologizes, says she's done the same procedure six times today already.

She says: "Do I have your permission to conduct a transvaginal ultrasound on you?"

At this point I am a neglected child left at the door of a mosque. She puts a condom onto a rodlike device and asks me to relax, tell her when I am ready. My answer is immediate: "Now." She shoves it into me and the sensation of my body tensing up is masochistically good. And there it is. A small round object to the right of the grainy screen, something pounding. The nurse isn't giving me any more instructions, isn't saying anything at all, and for a piercingly long minute I just alternate between looking at the bundle of a baby on the screen and the silver cross around her neck. Later, when I tell the friend that the nurse at the abortion clinic was wearing a silver crucifix pendant, she hides hers under her collar and says she's sure I got it wrong. Right now the woman is asking me to change back into my clothes as she scurries around the room collecting things. She gestures for me to sit down on the bed and asks me to sign a form that says I cannot hold Marie Stopes responsible should something go awry with the pregnancy termination. I am a twenty-two-year-old woman sitting on the same bed that hundreds of other women have used as a Noah's ark of sorts, and what do I know? I'd sign a thousand of those. If a woman's body is not hers to begin with, she finds it is much, much better, even cathartic, to give it up formally. *I, the undersigned, have no one but myself to blame: the ovaries for working, the heart for wanting, the body for forgetting its perishability.*

She puts a pile of pills on the table, pushes two toward me: "These will stop the embryo from growing. You have to take them here and in front of me so that we are sure you do not go home and change your mind." She says this and walks out of the room before I have put them in my mouth. So it's just me and whatever is inside my body and the oval white pills. Again, some useless maternal gut-wrenching need to save it—no, her. But all the feminist fights I've fought, all the protests for Arab women's right to choose, all my plans for activism, the resistance poetry, all of it is gone. And even here, in one of only three countries in the entire continent where medically induced miscarriages are legal and safe, what choice do I have? I am weak and defeated when I put the two pills on my tongue and that is that.

Twenty-four hours later, at 15:30 p.m., alone in my bed the next day, I place the second dosage under my tongue and leave it to melt for half an hour. At exactly 16:03 I have my first cramp. I walk to the bathroom and sit on the toilet seat, stare at the water until I see that first bead of red. I breathe for the first time in seventy-two hours but am being strangled by a kind of loss, too. I stay seated and the uterine contractions start rippling through my body in heaves, higher each two minutes, oceanic and turning the water into an opaque bright red. I think: *what a waste of labor pain.* I have to support my body against the wall as I make my way past Mother and Father and into the room, popping painkiller after painkiller until the ceiling starts looking like a pathetic sky. I have never known pain like this before, as if my femaleness is speaking for the first time, as if my body is punishing itself for things that are beyond me. I am feverish and my spine is splintering and my bed is white except for the expanding bloom of red where I am sitting, and in the dim light I am an angelic presence whose embryo is worth more than seven Always Maxi sanitary pads worn and buried in the bin that night.

When the morning arrives, it finds me bloated and barren or desolate or whichever adjective one uses to describe that which is uninhabitable; a colosseum of *what else could I have done?* And how for weeks following the termination I would cry every night and blame the man for not having a uterus until he collapses, too, sobs, swears, says watching me go through this is deathly. How, for weeks following the termination, I could fall asleep only to the sound of some woman describing the process of pregnancy week by week. How, for weeks following the termination, I stopped eating for fear that the abortion was not successful. I thought: *I will have to starve it*—no, her—*to death.* How, for weeks following the termination, I had to learn how to live with the fact that things cannot be reversed, was forced to sever and sever and sever an invisible umbilical cord knotted around every time I began a sentence with the words "I want."

And then three weeks later, when it was time to take another pregnancy test to see whether the abortion was successful, how I did my hair and nails and put on black lace underwear and went to the man's room, told him to fuck me one more time before we face the facts again, the yellowish green room, the surgery that would have to happen. We did not hold back, bodies pressed against each other and heat and heave and *how do you want it?* I came as hard as I could and then got off him and put my clothes on and walked to the bathroom with two tests hidden under my sleeve. It struck me then, as I was waiting for the second blue line, that the abortion clinic did not give me a counselor as they said they would on the phone. No one gave me options or told me that relief tastes a lot like grief sometimes. I waited and waited for the second lines on both tests, but they did not appear. I ran back to the man and, when I told him, he held me hard and long as if my empty body still meant something equivalent to "enough."

April is turning into June and I now know the exact number of days that sperm lives inside you and that the egg has a lifespan of twelve to twenty-four hours. I also learnt how to pour my shame right down the drain as if it were the blood in my menstrual cup: I deserve to have and be had as often and as loud as I crave to. Loss is loss is loss. I wanted but could not have and so needed to want something else. The body is more than a landfill and less than all that I am. The man and I still flinch at the mention of the twelfth of April, but last week we walked past the toddler clothing rack and we let our mouths merge into half smiles in the name of *one day.*

Phillippa Yaa de Villiers

POEM AND ESSAY

To the woman who accused me of breastfeeding the madam's child

You cannot know the conspiracy of blood:
Europeans are not god, although you seem

to believe that you alone can see into my savage
soul. Haughtily you stopped at the roadside

where I sat feeding my son to accuse me, of what,
exactly, theft? Is it kidnapping to nourish

someone else's child? Could you tell me which
commandment I have betrayed? All mantled

by the golden morning I must have shocked you
back to church, a brown Madonna with a tiny white

infant drinking from my contented breast, the ultimate
subversion of mankind's perversion of life's perfect

establishment: the embodiment of love. There is so much
that evades you, madam, this here, now: the mystery of touch.

What has been lost can never be reclaimed. While
I dwell in salt; you reframe a dead monument, unnamed

you cannot stem the flow of time nor break the link:
the child is mine, we all together at the river's brink.

By Any Other Name

haste to repay / the debt of birth.
—Wole Soyinka, "Dedication"

Identity is a drama in minor key, except if you live in a country that persecutes people of a certain identity, like South Africa used to be, like India is, Myanmar, and Israel. All the places where sexuality makes people into targets.

The minor dramas of identity fall into two types.

Same-name dramas: imagine that you lose your driver's license. One day your phone rings and a stranger asks if you are [your name]. When you agree, they tell you that they have found your driver's license at such and such a place. When, after following directions to a place known or unknown to you, you arrive to collect your document, and find that it bears your name, but not your face.

Same-face dramas: when I lived in Los Angeles, I had a living nightmare that I would get lost in the maze of identical stucco housing. After some time searching, when I found my unit, I would let myself in with my own key only to meet my identical twin, who calls the police on the intruder she doesn't recognize.

I want to write a story about a character called Antionette Gouws, but I know a real human being with an almost-identical name. When I joined Wits University in 2015, Antonette Gouws was the creative writing department's administrator. Likable, cheerful, and helpful, she moved to a different division after a couple of years, taking up a well-deserved promotion.

I wanted to write about Gouws because her name, like mine, at times denies, or should I say *disavows* us, and at others enlarges or enables us. In a defunct value system, it could also be said to *ennoble* us.

By this I mean that the surname "Gouws," like the surname "de Villiers," promotes a certain ease of movement in our society. If you call a store, for example, to complain about a faulty appliance, or poor service, wielding the name de Villiers or Gouws has a certain impact. People move around, reprimand others, try to make you happy.

This is because de Villiers, Gouws, and hundreds of other names arrived in Africa on ships bearing refugees from King Louis XIV's papist regime. The Huguenots were Protestant religious objectors who left France and joined the Dutch, who had elbowed themselves into the southern tip of Africa in 1685. We quaff Huguenot wine, and their rumbling "r" adorns certain dialects in the Western and Northern Capes of our country.

Antonette Gouws is a real character, with a wacky sense of humor and a unique sartorial style. She is nothing like Antionette Gouws, the character whose story this is. Possibly they have some things in common, as I do with both of them. We're not sure what. We are still getting used to each other, to know each other.

The character Antionette Gouws appears at the tide line on Strandfontein Beach, just before dawn on a Wednesday. Long before the sun breaks free of the horizon, the sky is full of its radiance and the air is full and soft with promise. For several years, weather permitting, she has worked her way along the wave line, sifting through the flotsam for pieces of plastic, which she then places in the largish bag that she wears diagonally over her shoulder. As she proceeds, a sense of peace rises in her. Perhaps overcautiously, she sports a wide-brimmed straw hat. As the sun skates across the sky, the bag gets fuller and heavier.

There are no starfish on the beach today, or beached whales, or turtles, but she has handed their lives back to the ocean at various times over the years. As her hands, now practiced and swift, scuttle over the bits and pieces left by the tide, she imagines her forebears walking naked on this beach. With an essential pride that can't be restored once it is taken. Before the advent of plastic, before the great waste that seeks to wipe her people from the face of the earth.

She's not a poet, but she remembers lines like those declaimed by Khoisan !Xaribusai: "relegate my people to walking trash / talking brash / statements in a futile wish / to reconnect with the land / to which we / are now refused entry."

Something that lies beyond the waves has called her to the beach, compelled her to this labor that makes more sense than any other work she has ever done. The lines hum through her memory as she pauses to measure her fatigue. Now Antionette knows that the land does not refuse her feet, nor the ocean her long and loving regard.

We are all trying to make sense of the fragments of which our lives are made. I, like Antonette, our administrator, constantly have to deal with cases of mistaken identity. We have to often help people process the shock of the Black body. "Oh, *you're* Antonette Gouws!" After growing up in Australia, my sister told me that seeing Black people en masse for the first time in Ghana gave her a strong feeling she can't quite name.

The word I would use is awe. Like when I saw my biological father, Black and born in Ghana, with my own eyes, for the first time. But this is Antionette's story.

Antionette's beach forays began when she discovered something she had somehow always known, but had learnt to deny. She knew, for example, from the age of six, that neither she, nor the neighborhood

51

children, looked anything like the people in the books she loved to read. Because she enjoyed the stories, she forgot what she looked like, and it took someone outside her to remind her. This was often shocking, because sometimes the means of telling her were aggressive, and she'd go home and tell her father, and he would threaten to go "knock his or her block off."

Antionette found the whole business distasteful, and far too dramatic. She worked out that one can entertain other people's impressions of you, and react righteously, challenge their authority, go head to head. Or one can nobly turn the other cheek, offer one's energy to teach them their error. Or one can watch, take note, and step lightly and purposefully on.

Like that post office clerk whose disgusted look follows her, ten years later.

She had gone to collect a registered letter from the university. "Gouws," Antionette had said, handing over the parcel slip with a smile. The woman had looked dubiously from her peppercorn hair to the slip, and repeated the name, with a questioning tone that seemed to say "Your name may be Gouws, but we are NOT related. If we are related, it's because *my* people owned *yours*."

"Yes, Antionette Gouws," she said, her smile getting slightly glassy.

"It's spelled wrong," pronounced the clerk, and stumped to a pile of letters and parcels. *I know how Antoinette is spelled*, thought Antionette for the two thousand, seven hundred and forty-ninth time.

The woman had begun rifling through the mail with one eye on the reference number on Antionette's slip. Antionette had watched the two folds of fat on either side of her spine, creasing the woman's blue shirt as she sifted through the mail items, and remembered how her own mother had suffered from diabetes. The clerk returned with a white envelope and pointed to where Antionette should sign. As she handed back the pen and parcel slip, and pocketed the envelope, she noticed the woman's faux brass name tag. Marie Gouws. Antionette paused as the name sank in. She stepped out of the cool, dim room, into the tree-dappled sunshine.

Are you with me? Are we, as they say in the townships, together? My former husband used to get irritated with the rambling threads of my stories. How I had to make things up to get to the truth. Can you please get to the point? he would bark, as the story riffed in and out of reality.

How does one map a feeling? Imagining it as a substance, the vague sense of shame that Antionette should have felt followed her like a cloud, a swarm of bees, righteous resentment that she could order a painful revenge. But Antionette had not felt the shame that the woman's certain hostility had intended. She felt slightly annoyed, and then relieved that she was not a post office clerk, and did not have to work in this woman's environs.

Of course, she was now in her midtwenties, and it was not the first time she had had this kind of response. Like an iceberg in a warm ocean, these encounters remind us that circumstances beyond our control are melting us. We are not who we think we are. We learn to see by traveling, the seTswana proverb states. *Ho tsamaea ke ho bona*, a school friend had once told her.

Back home in her community she was a child like all the others. It was only when her small ship hit this kind of iceberg that she was hurled into the water and she became somehow other than herself; a process that unmakes and, she observes, somehow remakes her.

"Antoinette," like "Phillippa," is a queenly name. I found out recently that Philippa of Hainault was the first Black queen of England. Antionette was, of course, named after the French queen who famously said "Let them eat cake." From the beginning of her life, she had thought of herself as somewhat above the ordinary people around her, especially her family. The family legend told to her was that her father, who was in charge of registering the birth, had forgotten his glasses at home in his excitement and misspelled her name. Later, piecing the story together, she realized that he had probably been drunk at the time.

Everyone who has misspelled a name on an official document knows that correcting the mistake costs the time it takes to download and fill in a BI-85 form, as well as the amendment fee of seventy or one hundred forty rand, depending. At sixteen, Antionette, on the threshold of majority, had considered correcting the error. She was tired of the misspelling being pointed out to her by those who claimed ownership of the name, the stiff patronizing breeze.

But then she had decided that she liked the "Anti," because it seemed to put her against the family, the squalid childhood street, the grubby school to which she was heir, the preordained career of teacher or nurse, which were the only professions to which her type was welcomed. Against all this, her surname shone out proudly, because was not the famous Zimbabwean cyclist Pierre Gouws possibly a relative? Even if he wasn't, he just showed the world what a Gouws could do with their life.

After finishing school top of her class, Antionette, unpregnant and ambitious, had been sponsored to study at university. She had kept herself aloof from all the revolutionary rumblings, which earned her the name "Sturvy" or "Play-White." Truth was that the demands of her course made for little free time—coming from a poor school, she had to basically reteach herself mathematics and science in order to compete with the rest of the class. It was a lonely course, but she stuck to it, although she often felt like a crab moving sideways.

Antionette, queen of an unseen kingdom, celebrant of a buried catechism, studied marine biology and quietly built herself a career.

The registered letter, which she had opened when she had settled down with a cup of tea on the front porch of her small house, congratulated her on her appointment as a coresearcher on a prestigious international project, investigating the role of plankton in regulating the ocean's ecosystems. Somehow she did not feel triumph or pride, perhaps because the letter pointed out that the post she had been awarded was specially designated "affirmative action," therefore to fulfill the quota of "formerly disadvantaged" staff, not entirely due to the merit of her contribution to the field.

She had gazed at the sun as it gradually sank closer to the horizon. She thought about the post office clerk then, and the tiny, silent centuries-old war that had taken place that afternoon. Suddenly she had stood up and gone to the laptop. Feeling almost possessed, she had done a Google search of the Gouws surname, and felt curiously affirmed by the congested enthusiasm:

"Billions of records. Millions of fellow family-history seekers.

"You could find an infamous relative. Or perhaps a photo of your great-grandma as a little girl. But whatever you find, it's sure to change the whole way you look at your family history, and yourself. After all, the story of your family is the story of you."

A story of me. As I shadowed my character, performing the Google search on Antionette's behalf, the webpage's hyperbolic assertions triggered a thump in my chest.

I remembered telling Onkel Albrecht that I wanted to find my biological family, and him replying, as he always had, "It doesn't matter who they are. What matters is who is here with you now." Years later, when the laws changed and it was more than a dream but a potential reality, my mother-in-law, worried that I might find out something awful about my family, cautioned me not to. But her husband said it was my right.

My name seemed like the bits of plastic Antionette collects, so important at the time of purchase, now, after years in the ocean, warped and hardened, barely recognizable. The name de Villiers tells very little about me. My achievements do not enlarge a dynasty, or contribute to the clan's mythos. I write about Gouws; like my own surname, it is not mine.

When the name de Villiers was conferred on me, it created a kind of bridge over an ocean of doubt. If my mother's teenage pregnancy was a result of a historical or societal problem like rape or slavery, perhaps I'd be able to claim a place in a more noble, if tragic, history. Instead, her relief for the embarrassment and social censure was giving the baby up for adoption. An almost-new family, a mom and dad whose racial difference made their role, as parents, at my most vulnerable and angry, parenthetical.

Bridging the ocean leads to wet feet. Saltwater permeates everything I try to create. Separate from myself, my story, a hidden tide, rises again.

I called the real Antonette Gouws this morning because it seemed ethical to ask her permission before bringing her doppelganger into print. She laughed, and said, "I could tell you stories about this name. Of course you can use it."

These days, ethics matter, unlike in the 1990s, when an unknown scriptwriter used my name as a character in a television series. Look, it may have been a coincidence, but it's a small industry, and I knew people who worked on the show. It was quite a strange feeling. It was around 1997, when I was still working as an actress, and I went into my agent's office to collect my tax receipt. Next to the photocopy machine, in the cramped cubicle occupied by the accounts lady, I saw a casting brief with my name on it. "Phillippa de Villiers," it said. Incredulous, I read again. Truly, there it was: my name on a briefing document from a reputable casting agent.

I leapt into the open plan office, with agents' desks arranged in three corners of the room. The fourth corner was a ceiling-high glass sliding door, open this spring morning on our agent's lush yet manicured garden.

FINALLY somebody wants ME: not a type, but ME. Chortling triumphantly, I wagged the page in front of Linda's (not her real name) face. She was on the phone, and put her finger to her lips. Still listening to the squawking voice I could faintly hear in the background, she squinted at the casting brief.

She was at that age when the use of a good pair of spectacles makes reading so much easier but she'd never thought of herself as shortsighted, so she kept forgetting to deal with the problem, until she needed to read something. Without putting down the phone, she said some comforting generic words to the squawker and shook her head at me, pointing at the description under the name.

"slim, white, 35-year-old woman"

I was a character, a made-up person, not my body. My genealogy cut me out of the family photograph. It was at this time that I was confronted by one of my inner contradictions: I was the lead singer of the Race Doesn't Matter band. We all know that there were a lot of extramural activities between the former masters and "their" slaves. Paper will tell you that you can own a human being, but it will take an army of cruelty, jail, whips, and chains to make it real.

What can a human really own?

Our slave DNA is no longer a source of shame, nor of legal consequence. With the first democratic elections in South Africa in 1994, it seemed that the whole world shifted, and all those monuments assigning ultimate power to that particular group came crashing down. Black friends called themselves their African names. In tiny incremental ways, these actions brought me back to myself, or to a potential I'd never considered. Adopted by white people, I had denied myself, or refused, the dramatic space to fight for the right to exist, just as I am, without disclaimers.

Technology allows humans these days to, instead of going for a drink and a chat with a friend who's hurt you, "cancel" them, which amounts to a social assassination. I have pretty much weaned myself off social media, so I'm not sure what people are saying about me. Like Antionette, I have to work really hard to keep my place at the university, so I try to minimize things that cause anxiety. I have a small group of friends, whom I see in person, except those who don't live in my city. If there's a breakdown of some kind, we deal with it.

Like A and A, I was phlegmatic: I had not allowed myself to be moved by these misunderstandings, even though they happen at least five times a month. Unlike A and A, however, the "passing" game I had been playing was a performance that my family and I created to make them feel safe and comfortable. They thought it was the same for me, that the pretense made me feel secure. If nobody mentioned it, I would be a white person. If I brought it up, I had a chip on my shoulder, or was manipulative. If somebody else brought it up they were a bigot.

When I grew up, and South Africa was no longer an apartheid state, I made friends with many Black people. At first I felt like I was fronting, passing and pretending. In conversation I often couldn't relate to the memories and feelings because I'd grown up elsewhere, otherwise. After some years I began to feel accepted, and accepted myself as a Black person. But it still felt uncomfortable, relating with people because we're Black. I realized that even though it was a relief to come out of the closet as it were, I had internalized a truth: if race didn't matter, neither did I.

One of my best friends, the African American poet, Myesha Jenkins, who taught me so much about love, also told me that at times I would step over her boundaries because I'd been raised by white people and I didn't understand. She was patient and, most important, honest with me, and asked the same of me.

As we lived our lives, with poetry sessions, holidays, picnics, and discussing the men we had, lost, and lusted after, we became like sisters although she was eighteen years older than me. I realized that I had tried to pretend that pain didn't matter. Not belonging had turned me into a very sad monster.

When we became friends, I started to feel as if all my friendships with white people had been dishonest. All the things I'd grown up doing: swimming, hiking, loving dogs, were not African.

Language itself broke in my mouth, in my mind. For two years I spoke haltingly.

Dogs were simpler, they didn't see race. Myesha helped me to identify the love in all my friendships, pointing out the truth in our lives, the way we weave in and out of each other's dreams.

Names: how language calls us, how we are called by others, how we call ourselves.

Calling: a greeting, a vocation; strangely, a cancellation, rescission. Destiny. All of the above.

Language is a haunted monument.

I'm not sure if I'm the ghost, or the Doric columns at the top of a hundred identical steps, or if I am the steps themselves.

Or if I am Antionette, whose story this actually is.

It's getting hotter now, and sweat is rising on her skin and soaking her cotton blouse. The tide recedes. Like the waves, she retreats from the thick blond sand. Her feet wind homeward. Each foot falling tells her that five hundred years ago, this place did not know the name Gouws. How was her great-great-great-great-great-grandmother called?

After adding today's plastic to the dumpster in the driveway, she lets herself in the kitchen door. The house is filled with sunlight. She boils a kettle and makes herself a cup of tea.

Gouws, the website had told her, is a Dutch reinterpretation of the French word *gauche*, which means "left." She had grinned to herself, as, for the first time in her life, she was considering joining the local Socialist Party.

On the website, after the introductory paragraph, someone had inserted: "**Weird things about the name Gouws:** the name spelled backwards is *Swuog*. A random rearrangement of the letters in the name *(anagram)* will give *Owsgu*. How do you pronounce that?"

Was that supposed to be a joke? She was not a laughingstock. She had imagined the person who compiles heritage websites in America, possibly in the Midwest, hee-hawing like a donkey at the weirdness of the Gouws name. She imagined this person being a right-winger, someone with a Confederate flag hanging on their wall, or maybe not, just an ordinary American called Chuck or Britney, who thinks someone whose name is anything more complex than Trump or De Niro is abnormal. She knew her conclusion may be seen as bigoted, but she wasn't putting it out there on social media. It was her private thought, so it could do no harm.

She had balked at the paywall halfway down the page.

"You've only scratched the surface of **Gouws** family history." The price, in dollars, was way out of her reach.

Then she had stopped. She had looked closely at the coat of arms. The name Gouws emblazoned on a beige pennant below a simple white crest, surrounded by a lush background of leaves. Were they lily leaves? There was something in the shape that reminded her of the fleur de lys, which her mother embroidered on one of her school blazers, with thick yellow thread. Also her childish imaginings of pageantry, knights and ladies, somewhere between the excitement of an aunt's wedding and sports day at school.

Then the small badge at the center of the crest, with a red star at the top, and one on each side of the … how curious: a person, as opposed to a lion or a dragon.

A person who looks like her.

The Black woman's face in profile, neither smiling nor frowning, just staring into her future, as Antionette was staring into hers. A future with a coat of arms. Antionette, now wondering what lay outside of the frame of that stylized, captured moment. Antionette, suddenly aware of the warmth of the sun in the room, the sound of her own breath and two quick tears which fall, surprised, into her lap.

Perhaps she did have some work to do for the Gouws name, although the quota committee would never recognize it. Her namesake at the post office would also never know to whom she would dedicate her everyday work.

She observed the woman's profile. Her full, silent lips. Her steady gaze. The cap of her neat, kroes hair. Suddenly a distant clash of weapons rose in one sharp sound and the smell of dust and blood filled the room; a loud mourning cry from thousands of throats. Antionette felt filaments of connection spreading between the families of the Cape peninsula, and over the oceans to people on other continents, netting them in a web of black threads, like a shock of gasping fish.

Then she had laughed, long and loud. Of course, it could never be that simple.

The website was selling merchandise with emblems that they had designed. There was no information about the woman, or the meaning of her profile on the Gouws crest.

This was a research project. Perhaps she should see a heritage consultant. There might be slender evidence, but she wanted to collect and serve it.

She had looked out then, at the long blue sky, and briefly admired how the sun outlined the grasses growing wild in her garden in bright gold. Those who claimed that their ancestors had owned hers, were now owned by her, even if only in name.

Bahia Mahmud H. Awah

ازوك
Ezouga
Exile

متوحشتك يا باهي   و انت يا غرت عيني

بيك لرافع عن قديتي   كيف انطالب بالحرىى

نطلب مولانا يجمعنا   فوق الراضينا مبني

و اجابرنا و امتعنا   و يجمع شمل الفرق ازكي

بيه الطير اللا من فركو ا   و انا ذي طيري باهي

Even in exile

as they say,

"the bird belongs to its flock"

I fly in formation

free like that bird

cursing the distance to my Sahara, as it grows

I yearn for my nomadic dwelling

and for all the birds

that still remember it

I yearn for my exiled bird

in the homeland we have built

for he is the light of my eyes

imploring God for a reunion

my struggle is my guarantee

soon the scattered will reunite

because "the bird belongs to its flock"

as they say,

and my bird belongs to me

Translated from the Spanish by Vivian Solana Moreno

Post mortem

In tribute to my mother and teacher "Detu" ذكرى رحيلك عنا في

When the long night of exile struck,
my mother started walking
days and nights,
And left footprints in the warm
and dusty sands of the Hamada,
and beneath her firm footsteps
loose horizons yielded.
There she became a teacher.
There she became a mother.
There she became a scholar.
There she became a partisan.
And in the books, it became a gleaming lamp.
Tore the belly of heaven
in search of stelae toward the homeland,
Grandfather's abode.
And seeing that the time of the exile was long,
indifferent and without horizons,
mom in her immaculate bowl of esparto
offered everything,
life, children, the nonagenarian grandfather,
the cattle and the friends of social gatherings.
For freedom and the return home
She dialogued with the beads of her astral rosary.
Mama then heard under the altar of her parents
resounding voices,
crowds of firm fists,

and fiery eyes that cried out:

"Here we are in union of fists and loud voices,

in defiance of the dark days of exile,

and here we are,

on the roads back to the steppes and abodes of the grandfather."

And about the mother, everything has already been said by the Prophet,

"If you seek paradise, find it in the firm tread of her foot."

Translated from the Spanish by Bidi Salec

Miral al-Tahawy

Daughter of a Bedouin Chief

ESSAY

The stars that mapped the journey of the tribes, the routes they traveled, and the stops they made, said nothing about the term *Bint 'Arab*—daughter of an Arab—the succinct phrase that my grandmother uttered with a certain grandeur, and which the fellahin of our sand-blown estate repeated warily, with a tinge of resentment or even hatred. I have always found the phrase perplexing. On the way to school, along the winding paths between my father's house and the houses of my uncles, across the yellow, sand-strewn ground and grassy drainage channels, past mulberry trees and irrigation ditches, I'd throw pebbles into the canal that meandered through the sand, the circles of perplexity growing ever wider. I was puzzled by the expanse of silt-rich soil my ancestors had inherited among the dunes dotted with roads reserved for the tribal encampments across the vast estate.

Long, long ago, one of the great-great-great-grandmothers had landed here by way of an old-fashioned caravan. Her belly swelling with one child after another, over time the vast estates of sand were parceled out among the progeny of the Arab Bedouin who settled those territories. Known as *'urban*, or Arabs, these people never forgot the history of eastward and westward migration that brought their tribes to inherit this land, regardless of their wishes. Little remains of their lengthy migration across North Africa but the dust that whittles aging features, the nearly buried desert stations of the ancient caravan routes, and the glories of a vanished tribe whose sole bequest is a genealogical tree that forever maps Bedouin expatriation on either side of the river.

In Egypt, *'urban* settlements were not a scattering of tents but rather borderland desert towns: ringed by mud walls, they looked like fortresses in a desert expanse dotted with tiny tribal hamlets on their periphery. The desert demarcated them from the city as the site of civilization.

From my father's house, which stands side by side with the houses of both paternal and maternal uncles, I'd walk along the myriad irrigation channels abutting the cultivated land. The dwellings around me were a collection of watching eyes—those of my cousins, whose white garments and headcovers I recognized, as they lounged around the open sandy spaces or sat between the entryways of scattered houses with dilapidated mud-brick walls and bolted doors. I'd go past the hamlets toward the hills over which flew a large banner signaling the town center where my school was located; I'd press my books against my chest, hiding my fear and looking down at my shoes; I'd walk in the rhythmic and poised steps expected of a young woman trying to cast herself as the image of a well-brought-up *Bint 'Arab*—someone who'd been graced with favors not bestowed on her mother or grandmother.

In the early mornings, *Bint 'Arab* would unlock the front door, gather up her schoolbooks, and run through the mist and the dust rising from the irrigation canals and the sand dunes of the Bedouin estate. She was always on the alert for the ethereal apparition of tribesmen watching her every step, their eyes as tight as a bridle around her neck like the heroine of Bedouin lore, Aljazia Alsharifah. And she was dogged by her grandmother's songs, which added to the circles of her perplexity. Polite and demure, *Bint 'Arab* dared not raise her eyes to meet her interlocutor's gaze, for it was deemed shameless and improper—her dutifully hunched back so bent from bowing to tradition that she resembled the she-camel trudging through the hills.

She-Camel

Bint 'Arab must be compliant as a she-camel on her herder's bridle, accepting of harshness, and untiring of the travelers she carries on her back; because she is a beast of burden, seeking neither pleasure nor pasture, she is stoic in the face of hardship and tolerant of the constant migration, from one hill to the next and from one expanse of sand to another. Making her way through hills as undulated as her back, the she-camel knows the route; she is resigned, long suffering, and subdued, as is expected of her.

Bint 'Arab kisses the hand of her grandmothers, uncles, and older brothers.

She is betrothed to the cousin after whom she is named. Since she is named after him, and as his own flesh and blood, she is his due. My grandmother would shake her long falcon's nose and her earrings would shiver with anger as she repeated within my earshot, "The crocodile devours her and the peasant will not take her"—a warning so constantly reiterated that it clung to my skin and seeped into my flesh. Then she would tell her favorite story, the tale of a girl with a she-camel's long neck and wandering eyes, hazel, the color of mountain honey. With her fierce good looks and her stubborn pride, the girl scared her cousins off; since they were afraid to ask for her hand in marriage, she remained husbandless, a spinster of fearsome beauty who disarmed anyone bold enough to propose to her—for who would dare try to tame such haughtiness?

She waited and waited for her fate until finally a rich Egyptian merchant came through the lands of her tribe and fell victim to her charm. He proposed, they married, and as she was about to set off with her groom on the wedding howdah, her cousin came up to them on his horse. He grabbed the white dress she wore, wrenched her off the howdah, set her before him on the saddle, and rode her to the Nile, where he threw her into the water to be devoured by crocodiles thirsting for blood. Her body was the tribe's honor, and the tribe will not have its blood tainted by the lineage of strangers.

Caravan

My grandfather was, they said, the owner of a soap caravan plying the route between Gaza and Quft, the land of the Copts (Upper Egypt); *his* grandfather guarded pilgrimage caravans from the Maghrib to the Levant; and his great-grandfather, who traded in slaves, ran his caravans from the Sudan to the lands of the Turks and Berbers. Their forbears, conquerors from Najd, left the drought-stricken and parched territory and went, as enjoined by the Almighty, to "inhabit Egypt and find that for which you have asked" (the Cow, verse 61). The Bedouin who settled in Egypt chose to inhabit the virgin terrain of the desert-bound periphery, suffering for centuries the anguish of estrangement in the land of black silt populated by emaciated fellahin.

Living on the desert's periphery in those long-gone days, the Bedouin maintained their right to raid the immiserated fellahin settlements that bordered their lands. As a result of this history filled with injustice, a deep and centuries-long enmity was born that was further entrenched by cultural and ethnic differences. Each branch of the tribe lived within small mud-walled enclaves barricaded by locked gates, which they called hamlets. In time, the movement of caravans came to a halt: covered with sticky tarmac, the ancient trading routes were now criss-crossed by memory-less cars. The desert no longer had need of guides, caravans, or horsemen to protect its hills; the tribe surrendered to the adversities of time and to the decline of its political clout but remained faithful to the traditions and customs of its gloried past.

Although modern vehicles sped along the asphalt roads, my grandfather continued to light a blazing fire in front of his house, sitting every evening, waiting for passing caravans to stop before his tent. In earlier times, the glow of the fire and the scent of his Arabic coffee could be detected from afar, his tribal tattoo telling of his noble and ancient lineage as he hosted guests and welcomed passersby. It took him a long while to understand that times had changed, that there was no further need for his services as a caravan guide or as a patrol force to protect the borderlands from bandits. He eventually announced his retirement, since no further good was to be found in the world after the city had encroached on the desert.

In his will, my grandfather instructed that all his camels and she-camels be slaughtered over his grave, and that their bones be combined with his own in a single burial ground. In the darkness of night, the inhabitants of nearby villages still see the ghost of an old Arab sheikh striding among the hills, proudly singing of his past: *Life of honor and plenty / Among his camels and she-camels / A commander of men / His sons neither soft nor effete.* Hearing the sheikh's laments and songs, they see the ghosts of camels and she-camels processing after him like distant shadows dancing on a dream.

The Tent

My grandfather's tent is spacious, it is like a lost desert city. It stands inside the courtyard of the mud-brick compound because only there does he feel at ease. It is divided into portions, each of which is like a separate room; at one end is the *khiba'*, the women's space, whose perimeter men do not venture to approach. My grandmother, who abhors barriers and walls, sits beside my grandfather. She looks out from the chink in her *khiba'* and softly intones a traditional Bedouin song:

> *About your dearness, have no concern*
> *It is planted between my eye and its lid*

> *There I have placed you as their sentry*
> *Where, O stone, is the abode of the dear ones*

Aunts, both maternal and paternal, clad in black—gowns, tattoos, and inky kohl—gather around her for the evening conclave in traditional Bedouin shifts, brightly embroidered with the figures of lions and brides. Braided gold bangles aglitter on their wrists, they quietly chant *ghinnawa* (literally "little song" or short folk lyric) verses in a ritual they call *darb al-'alm*—the performance of the *'alm*—the art of sorrow and loss, of pain and yearning. I don't understand how such dense and succinct verses, replete with symbolism, love, and passion can tumble out of their hearts extemporaneously. Have they even experienced the thrall of love, longing, and separation, these women who never left the houses of their husbands other than to go to their graves? I squat at the end of the rug, writing the verses down in an attempt to record the impassioned feelings they invoke. My grandmother reaches over to me, her rough hand strong and angry as it takes hold of mine. "What is concealed may not be revealed," she says. Clutching the ends of my loose-flowing shift, my grandmother's hand was the first to teach that revealing emotion is a disgrace, that expressing love is shameless, and that to record the plaintive laments of women is a transgression of tribal norms. Although the prohibition is categorical—*ghinnawa* are women's secret songs that may not travel outside these intimate evening gatherings—her warning only exacerbates my desire: I collect the fleeting and anonymous ghazals and copy them into my notebooks; I dream of breaking every taboo, of uncovering the splendors the verses describe fearlessly and far from scrutiny, and of ripping to shreds that preconceived image of me: the *Bint 'Arab* who lives and dies like a mute she-camel, without complaint, evincing no emotion, and certainly never daring to write down or otherwise express her feelings or longings.

Geography of Illusion

In primary school, we were four little girls who spoke and listened to each other eagerly during recess and in between classes. When it is my turn to speak, I tell the girls I am *Bint 'Arab* and let them make of it what they will. I repeat my grandmother's stories about (faraway) lands, about people and camels wading through the deserts, as the girls, utterly puzzled, shake their heads. It is then that I realize how strange my worlds must seem, how they may even be cause for mirth, how there is a true chasm between what I narrate and how I live. As I recount the tales bequeathed by the tribe, I realize that next time I must tell them in a different way. Those stories were my only escape from my father's house, the one surrounded by uncles' dwellings and sand dunes on every side, with the camphor trees separating us from the adjoining fields.

Ours was just like any other tribal home with a grandmother sitting in her *khiba'* singing (one of) her favorite verses: *"Neither shall you slay bandits / Nor shall you be the shepherd's prey."* Looking around me, however, I see neither prey nor shepherds, or any sign of loot or banditry . . . Just our compounds, in which the tribe settled after its incessant wandering, with their mud-brick houses and wide-open court-yards, and the high walls that keep us separate from the tiny hamlets dotting the land the Bedouin elected as their final destination. Was this tribal architecture with its fortresslike enclaves a response to the desert expanse? Was it a way to prevent the dissolution of our Bedouin lineage and our assimilation into Egyptian society?

The massive gates that enclose my childhood and surround the compounds that keep us separated from the outside world give rise to existential questions: Who are we? Who created this isolation? And, how did this fractured identity evolve, I ask myself. Vestiges of vacuous splendor, the abandoned horse stables still standing were our childhood playgrounds, the homes of the female jinn, and the stuff of tales no one believed. "Your grandfather's horse was called Mawzoun, 'the bal-anced one.' It was the purest of thoroughbreds. Your grandfather's herd counted a hundred head of camel, their resting place so wide that a mare could gallop around it," my grandmother would tell me. But today, the sole remaining witness to the rise and fall of the 'urban kingdom in the land of Egypt is a frail filly painfully pacing back and forth under the camphor tree by the fence. A few scattered horseshoes and metal hitching posts testify to these ruins' past glory.

My uncles' houses flaunt photos and mementos from those bygone days. The proud displays of their tribal heritage—the brass coffee utensils, the rifles, the swords—are evidence, they claim, of the splen-dors that recorded history has elided. Trying to unravel the complex relationship between the 'urban and local landowners, between the tribe and fertile land, and between sedentary life and its nomadic counterpart, becomes my sole preoccupation. I really want to understand the struggle between two proximate cultures that for centuries have shared Egypt's history, land, and riches, in a troubled and antagonistic relationship that is punctuated in alternation by esteem and contempt. I comb through a plethora of books—on history, migration, and tribal heritage—in search of an explanation, looking for an opening that might shed light on our existential place as an ethnic minority. But formal history is sparse, down to its footnotes: I discover that the 'urban of Egypt are not the only ones whose existence merits little more than an odd note in the margin; official histories make no mention of the frequent conflicts between Egypt's other racial and ethnic minorities, on the assumption no doubt that obfuscation yields a prettier picture of the country.

My grandmother, sitting on her mattress chanting verses about camels and caravans, gave me a gift: her poetic recitations opened up a space of imagination that led me to understand the "desert" as a particular culture with views about life, love, loss, and migration that differed from the norm; a culture rooted not so much in history or geography as in the orally transmitted legacy of spoken lore, whose truth is imagined and founded in a collective belief that we, as 'urban, were driven to a land which imposed its terms on us and forced us to settle down against our will—waiting for the seasons, waiting for the tithe assessments, waiting for the river waters rather than wandering and moving in search of rain-fed pastures. It was with her imagination that my grandmother—who knew only that slaves came from Java, soap from Gaza, and woven cotton from the land of the Copts—created verses that sang of destiny and despair, of homelands and drought, of loss and separation, and of the tears shed over the vestiges of times past, even though she herself had no acquaintance with or experience of that particular desert life.

Grandmother drew her own maps—the Land of Haysh was here, below the hills of Manazi', and the red plateau there, bordering the Gulf of Mahjoub—in which all the cartographical names derived from an extensive lineage: Mahjoub, Manazi', and others are all names connected to the bloodline, the very foundation of tribal formation. For my grandmother, that genealogy represented actual history, a history worthy of being preserved, transmitted, and sung from generation to generation. She gifted me narrated imaginaries of the *'urban*: a "world" geography that does not look to "real" history or geography for its validation, but was born entirely of her imagination . . . the imagination of a woman who left her father's house only to enter her husband's (which in turn became her son's), the houses all lined up one next to the other, folded in on their secrets . . . a woman trapped inside her own understanding of the past and of life itself. That is how my grandmother created her own history of mankind, one based on relations of lineage and pedigree, where a man was the son of so-and-so, who was the son of such and such; she established her own class hierarchies, characterizing her relationships with people on the basis of their descent as, for example, being from Upper Egypt, or *gharabwa* (gypsies) or fellahin. What they all meant to her was summed up in the short phrase "beloveds, and our lifelong servants." What then was the tribe if not the feeling of being caught in the stranglehold of faded glory?

The "desert" to which I refer is simply the tribal culture that delimits our place in the world; it is a culture we, the *'urban*, brought with us after drought laid waste to Najd and we were led into sedentariness in search of pasture and grassy riverbanks. And although we were nomads without a desert—pitching the goat-hair dwellings we carried with us in the courtyards of mud-brick houses—and feudalists who disdained agrarian life and scorned the local fellahin, with the passage of time, here "we" are still using those ancient turns of phrase—Bedouin being intrinsic to a normative legacy that is difficult to undo or question. Could I write something that approximated our place in the world as "Arabs" and as Bedouins who experienced such isolation in a sedentary agrarian culture? Could I trace the roots of the struggle, the reasons for the hatred between those who for centuries shared bread and salt?

My quest to extrapolate from a narrow sample and formulate a more comprehensive proposition about this minority's existential crisis drove me to research: I was determined to understand what the specificity of the Bedouin implied about other minorities living in Egypt.

Deep down I knew that I belonged to a human community that I could not properly describe: certainly not peasants, whether in the accepted sense of landed gentry or "simpletons," but rather a group whose bond with the fellah was characterized by vindictiveness and hatred; nor were they Bedouins in the semantic sense of the word, since they were no longer nomads; they also weren't a local aristocracy with links to Europeans or a European way of life. Their vainglorious tribal pedigree may have harkened back to earliest history, but it was one that meant nothing at school—neither the Beshara elementary school (named after my grandfather), which was little more than a heap of sand, silt, and broken benches, nor the high school from which I graduated that was located in the hilly woods of a small village. Walking several kilometers there and back, I'd wend my way between the open sarcophagi of pharaonic tombs, an area some people still call "Pharaohs' Hills" in the belief that it was the site of a temple dedicated to the ancient Egyptian god Bes, the god of laughter and forgetfulness in Egyptian mythology.

The tribe's houses were scattered across the vastness of this large province east of the Nile, known as the Eastern Fringe during the Islamic conquest. It was the first abode of the Arab tribes that landed and settled in Egypt before they acquired (vast) tracts of land on which they built stables for their horses and hostels for their guests on the ruins of ancient cities dedicated to ancient Egyptian gods. As the number of kinsmen grew, the tribe was eventually composed of many "tributary" branches, and as they settled the province, the 'urban established tribal villages and enclaves named after one descendant or another. The hamlets and settlements were thus named on a patrilineal basis designated by the grandfather's name—such as "Naje' Manazi', Naje' Beshara"—the "hamlet of your grandfather Manazi'," or "your grandfather Beshara's hamlet." Every tribe of the Eastern Fringe tilled its share of the desert, whose fertile pastures bore the names of the tribal "tributaries."

The tribes were not a monolith. On the one hand were the generally more humble and less haughty southern Arabs who had been "ruralized" and eventually surrendered to their environment's nurturing embrace: of lower standing in the tribal hierarchy, they allowed themselves to assimilate into Egyptian life, abandoned mythical notions of pure bloodlines, and sullied their tribal "purity" through intermarriage with the native population; because they allowed the hallowed tribal past to fade, they were disdained by the *'urban*, who refused to intermarry with them and snubbed them as fellahin. On the other hand were the northern Arabs, the warrior Adnani tribes, who arrived on the scene later and considered themselves notables, or pedigreed families with political aspirations: proud of their Arab bloodline to this day, they insist on their distinctiveness from both the indigenous population and the humbler tribes whose origins had dissipated in the valley after they had "Egyptianized" and mastered agriculture.

The relationship between those that went native and those that didn't bore no trace of friendliness: the chasm between them, fueled by hatred and contempt founded in class and tribal differences, led to wars as well as compacts. Neither joint destiny on the banks of the Nile nor Islam, with its emphasis on fostering a spirit of justice, could eradicate the racism and arrogance embedded in tribal culture. In order to resist dissolution into the greater whole, the latter tribes, the ones that did not go native, hung on to their traditions and customs, and the heritage bequeathed to them, and in order to preserve what they considered their distinct identity, they resorted to isolationism within their own milieu.

Bedouin culture wasn't an exotic space I chose to write about in order to gain attention as a writer. Nor was it a knowledge base that I acquired firsthand. It was something that survived inside me like a living organism. It evolved, nurtured by a vernacular oral tradition, including the tribal *diwan*, myths and legends, and verses and songs that bore little resemblance to the sensibility of the society in which the tribe lived. In all its expressions, this cultural heritage forged a sense of distinct identity whose impact was far greater than mere geography, history, or the inexorable forces of assimilation. We, the younger generation, may have wearied of its moral code, and even mocked its value system, but the ever-present sense of longing also meant we understood it, and were able to engage with both its positive and negative manifestations. As a writer, I found myself preoccupied first and foremost with the condition of women in that culture.

That is how my sense of identity fractured between a world whose value system was founded, on the one hand, in tribalism and nomadism, and on the other, in the sedentary life of the settled, with the hegemonic pull of the latter thwarted by the former's feelings of superiority and isolationist attitudes. Living in the midst of their antithesis—the subtext of the history of Egypt's Arab tribes—was not the only imperative for the *'urban*; they also had to lose themselves in an immense cultural vessel, as the tribal hamlets were established alongside the villages of the Egyptian Delta. Thus, assimilation, which naturally appeared inevitable, not only drove the tribes to surrender to their fate but also to preserve their own history and legacy, which they bequeathed orally, first and foremost. The songs that trill on my grandmother's lips reverberate with an anguished longing for the empty expanse and beauty of the lost paradise, the imprint of that inextinguishable history.

The Translator

When a publishing house overseas decided to issue a translation of my first novel, *Al-khiba'*, they gave a copy of the Arabic original to the translator, providing him with some information as to my real name and whereabouts (I had published my first novel under a pseudonym). Curious to discover this "desert" of which I wrote, and to experience the world I narrated to better evoke it in translation, the translator got into a crowded Peugeot, this being the preferred mode of transportation in the Egyptian countryside, and went from village to village, poring over his map for what they called Naje' al-'Urban. He traveled along the delta's narrow agricultural roads, from one gorgeous desert oasis to another until the small rural settlements scattered over the agrarian plain yielded to the desert's great expanse, or its periphery. Having reached the town's large public parking lot only kilometers from my tribe's homes, the translator stood there, uncertain about which direction to follow. There were no street signs or a discernible grid pattern to help him situate himself on the map, only a taxi stand on either side of the paved street, and a few passersby.

Much to the embarrassment of several young boys hanging around the area, the translator asked after me using my personal rather than my kinship name. None of the boys responded. One of them, lying on top of a pile of dirt, laughed at the translator's accent and pointed toward the dunes in the distance and the winding desert tracks that led there, behind which our old houses rose up like ships afloat on the sea of sand. The translator roamed between mud-brick walls scattered across the sandy expanse until he reached the old wooden gates of our compound. He stood there waiting for someone to come out to greet him for quite a while, as he knocked on the gate that is the only opening in the wall of the compound that encloses the homes of my extended family. It is, in fact, that gate which separates my father's compound from a large area of sand and fallow land, that carried the echo of a voice calling my name. My name was all I could discern of the translator's words, and fearing scandal, I locked myself inside my room. Women's heads poked out of various relatives' houses in the compound, inquisitively following the voice of my mother. Standing on the balcony, "Who comes here?" she asked disapprovingly of the trespasser. "The translator," came back the faint echo of a deferential voice.

At that moment, it felt as if all my problems would start and end with him. My mother gestured at the translator to take a seat in the *madyafa*, an enclosed space bordering the compound wall especially reserved for hosting guests. She then went in search of the male in the house who could go out and greet the stranger; not yet ten, my younger brother came back from the encounter saying matter-of-factly, "It's a foreign translator and he wants to meet her and ask some questions about her book." My mother came to find me. "What's all this about a book? And a translator?" she asked. "What's going on? Oh, my, the scandal!" Then she added disapprovingly, directing her words straight at me, "And what exactly does the translator need to ask you? Let him translate to his heart's content, far from here."

The whole time my mother was thinking about how she was going to account for the aberration of this foreigner standing at the tribe's door repeating my name shamelessly, without the respectful qualifiers that tradition and propriety required as "daughter of so-and-so, sister of so-and-so," or "the kin of this family or that." But it was the word "translation" that proved insurmountable. During the family's evening gathering later that day, she summed up the situation in a few words: "The man is a guest," she said. After a moment's silence, she added, "He's come to study the history of the tribe," making no mention of me whatsoever.

Following much questioning and deliberation, the translator found himself surrounded by a huge entourage of volunteers, my male cousins, hosting him on my behalf. They took upon themselves the task of explaining everything in my novel about which he had questions—and being men, they naturally knew more about the life of the desert than I did, or ever would! The translator would frequently come to find his way to the *madyafa* as the tribe's houseguest, and he soon learned not to blurt out my name shamelessly, enquiring instead after my father's household. He learned to knock at the door and to ask to sit in the company of my brothers or cousins. Having understood that he should never mention me by name, if, for some unavoidable reason, he needed to consult me about something to do with the book, he would forward his question in writing . . . and, naturally, the go-betweens would take it upon themselves to answer him with eloquence far surpassing my own!

It took a while for the translator to understand that I was a *Bint 'Arab*, and that the appellation permeated every aspect of my being, as indeed was the case for all "proper" Arab girls: I was the daughter of so-and-so and the sister of this or that man, having no existence of my own since there was always someone to represent me or speak on my behalf. It had been drummed into her that "*Bint 'Arab* was like an obedient she-camel, "neither raising her head nor straying from the herd"—faithful to their preconceived notion of her as delicate, polite, and demure, bowing her back because only men may stand erect as swords.

After a number of his visits, I can say that the translator learned that the desert was no joyride, or something from one of those nineteenth-century travelers' watercolor paintings of sand dunes and women's smiling faces. The desert was also not geography: having sedentarized, the Bedouin were no longer perfect specimens of their kind; nor was being a Bedouin a matter of herding a bunch of sheep. The translator grew to understand that being a Bedouin was a cultural identity that had been fought for and preserved in an attempt to resist assimilation, and that the life of the delta's Arab "nomads" was in fact a form of cultural isolationism cemented by the ancient bequests of tradition, custom, and right conduct.

Those born, raised, and steeped in the desert's transformation did not view things in the way that the translator imagined, especially after the city began encroaching on the desert. The dwellers of this barren expanse chose to create this isolation by living on the desert's periphery, in tribal communities or hamlets, where extended families could live in close proximity, still surrounded by the desert, but fenced in from its boundaries by walls. The homes of the Bedouin I belong to and of the Arabs who settled other areas of the Egyptian desert were not scattered tents, but dwellings that look like ruined old fortresses: they keep the Bedouin separate from the city to which they do not feel they belong and with whose population they prefer not to interact.

Explorers

Orientalists and foreign explorers have left us extensive descriptions of the desert, in general, and of Egypt's Bedouin, in particular. In their writings, they commented on Bedouin traditions and customs, on the variety to be found in desert architecture, and on the jewelry worn by women during their evening gatherings. Their accounts speak of caravan routes and of she-camels flowing majestically across the sand dunes, of hunting and shooting, of falcons and thoroughbred horses, of guides and highwaymen, of tribal sheikhs and honor. But their "Arabian" desert—an eroticized Orientalist space, aglitter with fantastical tales and stereotypes—isn't so much a romantic expanse of sand as it is a legacy of traditions, norms, and taboos that imprisons people within its confines. Nor is it as wide or free as imagined. Fear, isolation, and harshness are embedded in its history, as is the burying alive of both female bodies and voices.

The desert isn't the Romantics' paintings of barren expanses of sand and crystal-clear blue skies. Rather, it is full of hills strewn with metaphorical tents full of stories, poems, oral traditions, on a land inscribed with a long history of conflict, raiding, banditry, looting, tribal strife, abductions, surprise attacks, and bloodshed. In this landscape, Egypt's Bedouin are human communities steeped in layers of tradition and custom as well as a hidden heritage, little of which remains but an oral reliquary that has been largely ignored.

The explorers of this desert world were motivated by a wide range of incentives, from political espionage to cultural anthropology, or simply the pursuit of adventure. Their portrayals of the Bedouin from Najd and Hijaz, of the tribes of Iraq and Jordan, and of Oman's Jabal al-Akhdar—such as the Anza, Al-Rawala, and Awlad 'Ali—also vary a great deal: some accounts speak positively of the desert and its people, with admiration for Bedouin values, especially the qualities of courage, generosity, and loyalty to the tribe. Others are more neutral and descriptive, portraying the desert as a natural enchantment but a harsh passage, and offering romantic depictions of desert life as the most extreme forms of unrestraint and freedom. Yet other accounts are shallow and one-dimensional, full of trite generalizations that stereotype the Bedouin and their ways.

Egypt's Bedouin in the Traveler's Mirror

Nineteenth-century travelers classified Egypt's 'urban as either "peasantized" or "genuine" Arabs according to their tribal hierarchy, ethnic origin, class status, as well as their ability to adapt and assimilate. Edme-François Jomard, of the Napoleonic Egyptian expedition, speaks of the 'urban as belonging to two categories, distinguished by tribal origin and cultural heritage: the first, who had been settled in Egypt a long time, he describes as being of Asian origin, cultivating their own land, and living in mostly riparian towns along the Nile; the second, descendants of the warrior Qaysi tribes, entered Egypt in successive waves following the Islamic conquest and settled on the western bank of the Nile, where they eventually turned to farming and allowed themselves to assimilate.[*]

The former group, the tribes that came to Egypt early on, were of Qahtani Yemeni origin, while the latter included the Hilali al-Sulaimy alliance that left Najd for North Africa. As noted by Edward Lane, those who have been longest established in Egypt have retained less of Bedawee manners, and have more infringed the purity of their race by intermarriages with Copt proselytes to the Muslim faith, or with the descendants of such persons; hence, they are often despised by the tribes more lately settled in this country, who frequently, in contempt, term the former "fellaheen," while they arrogate to themselves the appellation of "Arabs" or "Bedawees."[**]

Similarly, scholars attached to Bonaparte's Egyptian expedition distinguished between the eastern and western Bedouin. Pierre-Simon Girard, for example, classified as eastern 'urban those Qahtanians who, for the most part, had reached Egypt during the Islamic conquest

---

[*] See Edme-François Jomard, "Observations sur les Arabes de l'Egypte moyenne" in *Description de l'Egypte, ou Recueil des observations et des recherches qui ont été faites en Egypte pendant l'expédition de l'armée française* (Paris: Imprimerie Royale, 1822), 1:545.

[**] Edward William Lane, *An Account of The Manners and Customs of The Modern Egyptians, Written in Egypt during the Years 1833–1835*, p. 178 (London, New York, Melbourne: Ward, Lock and Co., 1890); electronic edition available at https://scholarship.rice.edu/jsp/xml/1911/9176/71/lanma1890.tei-timea.html.

and had easily acculturated to Egyptian life. He noted that the tribes arriving directly from Yemen had settled on the eastern banks of the Nile while other Arab tribes had spread throughout North Africa over successive epochs and settled on the river's western banks. The Bedouins maintained their nomadic life, living with their herds at the outer edge of the desert.*

The travelers noted the *'urban*'s self-imposed isolation in their effort to prevent any kind of mixing with the indigenous population, and that endogamous marriage was deemed a requirement for the preservation of their identity and the purity of their bloodlines. Although the men could marry Egyptian peasant women whenever they pleased, Bedouin daughters were prohibited from marrying outside the family; a girl was married to her cousin regardless of her preferences. The *'urban* thus resisted assimilation by all means possible, and those who migrated westward to North Africa lived there for centuries with little change in their customs or way of life. Only the manner of their dress became distinct: the Levantine Bedouin maintained the traditional head garb, the *agal* and *ghutra* (headcloth), while those farther west adopted the fez and the North African *burnous* or, as in Upper Egypt, the turban and the abaya.

The *'urban* continued to regard their assimilation into the indigenous population as a betrayal of their already-threatened identity, and thus lived for centuries in semi-isolated inward-looking communities united by a common history and genealogy. In addition to emphasizing their distinctive way of life, some of them so feared the dissolution of their bloodlines that they forbade their daughters from marrying into tribes

* See M. P. S. Girard, "Mémoire sur l'agriculture, l'industrie et le commerce de l'Égypte," part I, sec. IV, "De l'état des cultivateurs en Égypte; quelques notions sur l'administration des villages," in *Description de l'Égypte, ou Recueil des observations et des recherches qui ont été faites en Égypte pendant l'expédition de l'armée française* (Paris: Imprimerie Royale, 1822).

that had embraced sedentariness and agriculture, viewing these as having spurned parts of their identity.

Clot-Bey tells the story of a rich Bedouin sheikh who "overcame" his innate preference for desert life after embracing urban living and becoming a high-ranking provincial official; when he sought a marital alliance with one of the Arab tribal elders, he was denied the privilege on the grounds that his adoption of sedentary life clearly indicated his predilection for furnished houses over goat-hair tents, and for a life of comfort and ease over fertile land; he had lost his taste for the harsh nobility of Bedouin life, his courage and sense of 'asabiyya had been watered down, and he was therefore not fit for the intermingling of their bloodlines.*

"Mrs. Noon"

Mrs. Noon was an upper-class Egyptian lady who'd lived in France for many years. After a long and failed marriage in which she felt lonely and worthless, she decided to buy a professional video camera to capture on film storied Egyptian destinations such as the Pyramids, Sakkara, camel markets, and others. She wandered around, camera in hand, perpetually in search of a purpose to life, or so it seemed. She had apparently decided to make a documentary about emerging Egyptian women writers. I don't know how she came across me: at the time, I was a young author with two novels to my name that had been consigned to the genre of desert or Bedouin literature. It was apparently sufficient to bring me to her attention and include me in the documentary, which featured interviews with a number of young Egyptian female authors.

* Antoine-Barthélemy Clot-Bey, *Aperçu général sur l'Egypte*, vol. 2 (Brussels: Hauman et Compagnie, 1840), chapter 7.

When Mrs. Noon shared some of her footage with me, I was at a loss as to what to say about my so-called Bedouin worlds. The women writers Mrs. Noon had interviewed were quite different from me: their literary worlds were born of knowledge and readings that were diametrically opposed to my own experiences; their registers echoed those of an intellectual class, their tone imbued with a certain haughtiness toward intellectuals from other worlds than theirs. I did not belong to any intellectual circle, and the only thing that spurred me to writing was the oral tradition sung by all the women around me. I did not belong to an urban upper-class or even middle-class milieu. Using the phrase that I most often heard summing up my existence, I described myself as *Bint 'Arab*. But my belonging to the world of the *'urban* was also imprecise and tenuous, conditioned as it was on stereotypical representations of the Bedouin that ignored the history of the Arabian Peninsula tribes and the stages of their journey to North Africa, as well as the evolution and decline of the remaining ethnic enclaves, postmigration.

Mrs. Noon was not happy when she arrived at the family home. What she found didn't conform to her mental image of the Bedouin. My father's house and those of my uncles were the homes of notables, considered to be upper-class and quasi-aristocratic, and whose occupations involved neither cultivation nor herding—and, thus, who could not be described either as Bedouins or as fellahin. "Where are the Bedouins then? Where are the tents and the herds?" Mrs. Noon asked, her tone sharp. My mother stiffened. She took offense at the question, which, in her view, betrayed a lack of understanding and needed correction. "We are Arabs," my mother said, "not nomads." Socially, the word Bedouin is a put-down, implying ignorance, lowliness, vagabondage, something akin to *ghagar* (that is, gypsies), and the term is of course also applied literally to nomadic tribes. In Mrs. Noon's ill-formed mental image, the Bedouin were a combination of gypsies, herders, and primitive groups of seminomadic and nomadic people. The connotations of the term in no way conveyed the historical stature of the *'urban* or their standing in Egyptian society.

As the camera rolled, my mother rested her back haughtily against the armchair and crossed her legs—something I seldom saw her do because it was considered shameless and contrary to proper etiquette. Attesting to her well-bred ways, she recalled what she could of French expressions she had learned at the Mère Didier school from which she'd graduated, noting that her father, Sheikh al-'Arab, had acquired the title of bey, and that her uncles were related to the famed Lamloum Pasha—as far removed as one could possibly be from desert life and the state of being "Bedouins."

Mrs. Noon was impervious to the offense she had caused by insisting on the label "Bedouin." The word was one with painful connotations in tribal memory. She didn't apologize in spite of the rest of the family's persistent correction with the (equally problematic) statement, "We are Arabs, not Bedouins." Mrs. Noon was adamant about my wearing an embroidered shift and some flamboyant Bedouin jewelry for the interview. She then chose where I would sit, a remote spot by the garden fence where the dilapidated walls overlooked an orange grove full of withered thornbushes. Her preconceived notions had her providing a backdrop to the interview that invoked seminomadic sheep-herding tribes—people living in encampments bordering the valley who wandered among pastures wearing their gaudy gypsy garb. The setting was satisfactory only at the approach of evening when a few shepherds were crossing the sand-blown track by my uncles' houses. Finally, Mrs. Noon alighted on what she was looking for. As the poor shepherds went in search of some fodder in the courtyard, Mrs. Noon's camera swung into action, capturing the sheep roaming freely among the thornbushes and the young shepherdesses' brightly colored garments, and then panning across toward the herd of sheep before my mother delivered what she thought would be a decisive blow to the lady's cinematic curiosity.

"These are not Arabs," my mother said. "They're shepherds—*ghagar*, vagabonds, and herders." Although trenchant in tone, her words had no impact on Mrs. Noon.

The term "Bedouin" has been used indiscriminately to stereotype many kinds of herding and migrating communities that could not be more different from the Arab tribes—which is why confusion has persisted in depicting the *'urban*, whose political weight and social role in North African history has been illustrious, and confusing them with other nomadic communities like shepherds, gypsies, and seminomadic Bedouin. One of the reasons for this confusion arises from the similarity in certain aspects of Bedouin culture—the imperative to travel and migration; tribal and clan structure; and customary law, to name a few—and other pastoral communities. In addition, some of the Arab tribes that went on to acquire quasi-aristocratic status and influence in North Africa did have connections with other herding communities, and over time, gypsies and herding groups turned into quasi-tribal communities that pledged fealty to the Arab tribes of Egypt: gypsies and panegyrists, for example, who specialized in the memorization and sung recitation of the life stories of popular figures from Bedouin lore. They also extolled the Bedouin Arabs as an ethnic group, composing odes that glorified legendary heroes like Abu Zeid, Yunis, Al-Jaziya, Al-Sayid al-Badawi, Fatima al-Aqliyya, Al-Khadra al-Sharifa, and others.

Walls

My grandmother would soothe me if I cried of oppression. Patting my broken back, she would say, "You are neither a prey for hunters nor are you a war bounty for strangers. You are the descendent of a freeman, who is a descendent of courageous men."

I collect songs of the grandmothers in silence; I repeat them to make myself believe that I am that girl who cannot be caught by a hunter, cannot be a war bounty or be enslaved at the hands of strangers. I am the Bedouin girl who falls on a long lineage of fathers and grandfathers revered by other tribes.

Bending to rules teaches me loyalty to writing as my only area for freedom. I wrote my first novel *Al-khiba'* (*The Tent*) to tell the story of Fatma, a young girl, who lived in her father's high-walled house. Fatma was not an obedient she-camel; she had the soul of a gypsy that dreamed to dash out into the open space. Like myself, Fatma attempts to escape traditions, to escape fear of everything. She climbed trees, walls, and gates, but never succeeded in getting away. She was caught by her old grandmother, who chased her with her cane and then incited her father to marry her off at an early age, admonishing him, "Grave her before she graves your reputation and your honor. Tie her with a happy bond and throw her away in a happy home." Fatma fell one time after another, and eventually lost one of her legs. In that story, Fatma became an invalid who crawls like a puppy forever looking for an exit, her exhausted body that looks like a tent pole, or a swastika, stands to confront the heart of the cruelty of traditions.

In my novel *Nakarat El-Zeba'a* (*Gazelle Tracks*), I wanted to illuminate the myriad facets the desert world offers. I wrote my second novel about a girl called Muhra, whose grandfather was a caravan guide who talked to her about his travails from east to west; he told her about his eagles and camels, about his Arabian breed of horse that went extinct. He used to sit on the asphalt road that divided the desert into two halves and would put up his tent. During the day, he would wonder among the hills and light up a fire at night to guide the passersby. But no one sees that fire, as the desert needed no more guides, nor knights, nor caravans that reaped the sands. Ultimately, the grandfather died of grief, believing this world has no good left in it, and that it would never have any again so long as iron vehicles run over the black asphalt roads.

The desert I know, and about which I write, is not merely a landscape or a vast space of sand. It is rather a heritage of traditions, customs, and taboos that imprison people within their invisible walls. The desert is not as spacious as some would believe, and not a free space as they depict it. It is a long history: of killing daughters at birth, of fear, of isolation, and of being strange. The Arabian desert, especially, is not a clear open sky as romantic painters draw it. It is hills full of secrets, tales, and poetry, as well as a long history of disputes, raiding, and robbery. It is a fertile land for ethnic and class struggles, kidnapping and raiding, as well as a long line of women captives.

Boakyewaa Glover

God's Plan

ESSAY

[Names have been changed to protect individuals' privacy]

I am a tomboy. People don't use that term a lot these days, but that was my label growing up in the 1980s, an identity given to me by others but also acknowledged and accepted by myself. I grew up with two brothers and several male cousins, and I knew nothing else but the lifestyle of boys. I was one of them—climbing trees, kicking around footballs, throwing stones and sticks, and playing hard-core video games like *Mortal Kombat, Street Fighter, After Burner*, and *Out Run*.

I never engaged in any of the typical Ghanaian games for girls, for instance, ampe, jump rope, and the numerous singing and clapping games that I cannot even name now. My mother, hoping to curtail my boyish phase, bought me a slew of Ken and Barbie dolls, and her prized gift to me, a Fisher-Price kitchen set. She spoke endlessly about the Fisher-Price brand, and the exorbitant cost of the set. I don't know if the constant mention of the brand and cost was meant to guilt me into playing with it, but the thought of cooking, whether in a real or make-believe kitchen, sent dread through my soul. I hated cooking and everything associated with it! I was constantly evading our housekeepers, who wanted me to wash, chop, or grind vegetables, do the dishes, or do anything in that space they called a kitchen. Why in the world would I willingly play with a toy kitchen set?

I remained a tomboy right into my teen and young adult years. When pressed by people curious about my affinity for loose-fitting, nondescript clothes; my aversion to makeup, heels, and bags; and my preference for video games and sports, I would casually explain that I grew up with boys. That wasn't quite true, though. In my heart, I truly believe I was born this way.

I went to an all-girls school, and even though I was surrounded by girls, day and night, I still didn't unearth any buried interest in what is typically regarded as "female" or "feminine": a focus on appearance (makeup, clothes, heels, etc.); an interest in marriage, children, or taking care of a home and family; excitement about pretty and sweet things like flowers, chocolates, and colors. Nature or nurture, who knows? I have just accepted that I am not feminine in any Ghanaian or global sense. To this day, at age forty-two, I hardly wear dresses, skirts, heels, makeup, or fancy accessories. I am not interested in bags, shoes, and clothes, unless they provide comfort, ease, and practicality. And my favorite color is black—it helps me remain obscure.

I am a heterosexual female, but growing up as a bona fide tomboy, clothed constantly in dark, baggy clothes, I was concerned that others would interpret my boyish looks and interests to mean I was gay. The specific label I was familiar with and concerned about back then was "dyke." Another label that concerned me was "goth." *Merriam-Webster's Collegiate Dictionary* describes goth as "a person who wears mostly black clothing, uses dark dramatic makeup, and often has dyed black hair." This definition eerily describes me—99 percent of the time I am in dark or completely black clothes. If I ever paint my nails (which is rare), it is always black nail polish, and if I ever wear makeup (also rare),

I lean toward dark lip colors and black eyeliners. I also went through a phase where I constantly dyed my brownish-black hair "1B"—jet black—every couple of weeks.

Now that I am older and more open-minded, I am not concerned about others' assumptions regarding my beliefs and sexuality due to my looks, but as a youngster, I suspect that my fear of those ignorant and hurtful labels pushed me to develop an unhealthy adoration of men.

I dated indiscriminately, bounding from one complicated relationship to another. It was all temporary satisfaction of emotional and physical needs. I fell in love, multiple times, but I never contemplated or envisioned marriage. I was open to the idea of a partner, not necessarily a husband. I liked the thought of companionship more than the idea of the full gamut, husband and kids. I wanted a man to watch movies with, discuss politics, be my plus-one to events, especially family events, and help cover expenses and vacations. I wanted to be in a committed relationship for purely practical and added-value reasons. I wasn't sure what a child had to offer, so I didn't crave children.

And now I must admit that something profound has changed.

Due to complicated circumstances, I became a foster parent overnight, to a five-year-old boy, Kweku, a wonderful, incredible ball of energy. His previous guardian, a relative of mine, had passed away tragically. The situation with Kweku was complicated and fraught with family strife from the start. A few months later, when I turned thirty-nine, I gave my life to Jesus. I had always believed in God, but I wasn't a committed, practicing follower of Christ. That same month in church, the pastor preached about saying yes to God when he calls on us to do something difficult. The pastor encouraged the congregation to raise their hands and say yes, no matter how challenging the ask was.

It all seemed to line up—suddenly I am a parent, then a Christian, and then the first message in church is about saying yes to God when he calls us to do more than we imagined for ourselves. What were the odds of all that happening within months? And so, like Jesus's disciples, I left my job to heed God's call to be a parent and to focus on this vulnerable and precious child. My work environment had become extremely difficult anyways, a situation I was certain that God had orchestrated to get me out of there, to set me on the right path.

Initially, I approached my full-time parenting duties as a God-given task, an obligation. That is all it was at first.

Then someone put my little boy's welfare at risk and it was a heart-wrenching experience. In that moment, I was fully prepared to trade my life for his. I had never, ever felt like that before. There was just something about being responsible for a vulnerable, dependent human being that completely and thoroughly changed me. I wanted to love him and protect him forever. Parenting was no longer an obligation. It was the most important aspect of my life.

By my next birthday, my fortieth, I became so completely smitten with my foster son, enamored with parenting itself, and I wanted more. I wanted a baby.

The thought was exhilarating and scary. I was forty years old. I had an inkling the journey to giving birth would be a little challenging, but I had achieved a lot in my life through sheer tenacity. I had built my own dream home with no debt. I had self-published three books that were reasonably successful, and I had a good bank balance. I had done all this without financial or emotional support from a man.

I also regarded myself as a fixer. There was absolutely no problem I couldn't solve. I felt confident that I could approach having a baby by myself as a project and be successful. There was nothing to worry about.

I was wrong—so very wrong.

Shortly after my birthday, I planned a trip to the United Kingdom and the United States to visit family but also to kick-start my baby-making journey!

A few weeks before I was due to fly out, I fell sick—excruciating headaches, fever, fatigue, weakness, nausea, the whole nine yards. It felt like my body was shutting down. One of the specialists I saw conducted erythrocyte sedimentation rate (ESR) and C-reactive protein (CRP) tests. An ESR test measures the level of inflammation in your body. ESR is not conclusive on its own, but it is typically indicative of autoimmune conditions, cancers, or severe infections. CRP is also a measure for inflammation in the body. My results for both tests were through the roof. The normal range reference for ESR is 0–20 mm/Hr, and mine was 100! And the normal range reference for CRP is 0–5 mg/L; mine was 24 mg/L! Both tests are not diagnostic tests on their own, but strongly indicative that something is wrong in the body. I told the specialist that I was going away on vacation, I didn't have time for follow-up tests to investigate. He strongly suggested that I see a doctor as soon as I arrived at my destination.

And I did. I spent close to one thousand pounds consulting with a rheumatologist in the United Kingdom and conducting a slew of tests. The rheumatologist concluded that my ESR, CRP, and other protein markers were most likely indicative of an autoimmune condition. Unfortunately, despite all the tests and money, he couldn't make a specific diagnosis. I was devastated. It felt like my baby journey was over before it even started. I was sick, but I didn't have a diagnosis to even begin treatment.

My relationship with my health, doctors, and the entire medical community has been basically nonexistent over the course of my life.

I have been fairly consistent with annual health checkups, but breast exams were occasional. I wasn't seeing an ob-gyn, and I also didn't have a consistent physician. I had been to countless doctors over the years, but these doctors were all general practitioners assigned to me when I visited the hospital with complaints. The doctors differed from visit to visit. Even when I lived in the United States for years, my attitude toward health care was no different.

My lack of proper, consistent, and reliable women-oriented health care led to a life-threatening situation when I was about twenty-three years old. I had been suffering from immense back and abdominal pains for over five years, but my pediatrician (yes, I was still being treated by a pediatrician at that age), just couldn't figure out what was wrong. Eventually he did some blood work that alarmed him. My infection level was sky high. My pediatrician referred me to a specialist, who immediately ran some scans and discovered that I had ovarian torsion caused by a cyst that had twisted on itself and my fallopian tubes, impeding the blood flow to the ovary and also other parts of my body. This specialist, a surgeon, told me that the torsion was so severe that I had to have surgery within twenty-four hours or I wouldn't survive. It was all very dramatic. The surgery was immediately performed and the entire ovary was removed. I was treated by the surgeon and another gynecologist for a couple of months, and then that was it. I moved on.

That surgery was one of the scariest experiences of my life, a situation that came about because I remained with my pediatrician for far too long. And yet, I didn't learn my lesson from my near-death experience. I didn't find one doctor to take care of me consistently, monitor my health, and provide advice as I aged, particularly regarding women's health. Ignorance knows no bounds.

I left the United Kingdom feeling anxious. Within days of my arrival in the United States, I was in a fertility doctor's office in Virginia. I was forty years old, with two degrees in psychology, top of my class at each level of my education and rated as a high performer at each organization

I had ever worked. I was a complete overachiever, and yet I had absolutely no inkling what it took to have a baby.

Unlike the rheumatologist, the fertility specialist, Dr. Mishra, had a diagnosis, and it was grim.

First off, Dr. Mishra informed me that there were three main aspects of female reproduction: the ovaries, the fallopian tubes, and the uterus. I began to wonder why we studied the eye and the ear so intensively in primary and secondary school, and even university, when we should have been studying the female reproductive organs! Why did the Ghana education system have such an obsession with the eye and ear?

Starting with the ovaries, Dr. Mishra indicated that the blood work she asked me to submit was for a series of hormonal tests to determine the status of my eggs; specifically, if I had enough eggs to yield a pregnancy and the quality of those eggs. She added that these were two very important factors for women my age—the quantity and quality of eggs.

Dr. Mishra said that I had a low ovarian reserve. Apparently, women are born with a finite number of eggs, a number that diminishes over time. Women cannot produce new eggs; we actually shed eggs.

I felt like I was sitting in a biology class that was being taught in an alien language. Worst of all, my mother, who was in the consultation with me, was equally clueless.

My maternal grandmother had seven children. Only five of her children were alive when I was born—the others suffered and died from sickle cell complications. My mother had three children. From the stories I've heard, my mother was gunning for more, but my younger brother was born premature, and my mother coded during delivery. Apparently, my grandfather physically threatened the doctor, who managed to resuscitate my mother. My paternal grandmother also had about six children. To be honest, I keep discovering new uncles and aunts on that side, so my grandmother could have churned out more than ten.

Perhaps she stopped counting at a point. Getting pregnant and having children was not a problem that ran in the family. It was expected that the women would marry, have sex, get pregnant, and have children. The actual mechanics of it? That was "something God deals with."

My mother also said that she was not taught about the intricacies and details of fertility in school when she was growing up, and my mother went to some pretty good schools, in Ghana and the United Kingdom.

My mother was keenly listening and learning, intrigued by what Dr. Mishra was sharing. On the other hand, I felt that as a modern, independent, smart woman, I should have known all this, so my naivete completely floored and embarrassed me. I wanted to sink into the floor and disappear. How had I missed this? How did I not know all of this? I knew that age was somewhat of a factor in pregnancy, but I didn't know it was *this* much of a factor. My mother felt the same. She knew bits about the challenges of getting pregnant, but she had never been briefed on the details. We could both probably reflect and cite examples of friends or relatives who had struggled with getting pregnant, but we just didn't realize that fertility was this complex and nuanced.

Dr. Mishra recognized that I was overwhelmed and disappointed, but she couldn't stop now. My late-stage education had to continue.

She said that my eggs weren't completely depleted, but with the levels indicated in the blood work, the chance of success of live birth using my own eggs was 10 percent. Ten percent!

Secondly, since I didn't have a sexual partner whom I was planning to have kids with, she told me in vitro fertilization (IVF) was my best option. Even if I had a partner, trying to get pregnant naturally with my shrinking ovarian reserve would be incredibly difficult. And guess what? The cost of IVF was between twenty and thirty thousand dollars inclusive of drugs! Twenty thousand dollars for a 10 percent chance of success of live birth! I was livid at myself.

To improve my chances of success, though, Dr. Mishra suggested that I consider an egg donor or embryo adoption. I had never heard of either of these terms before. Women got eggs from other women? With an egg donor, multiple viable eggs are retrieved from a younger woman and merged with sperm from a partner or donor, and then implanted into the recipient. With embryo adoption, already existing viable embryos that have been freshly produced or frozen from others' previous IVF cycles are implanted into the recipient woman. Both options gave me about a 50 percent chance of success for live birth.

I couldn't react. I wanted my own baby, flesh of my flesh, blood of my blood. It was one thing for me to use an anonymous sperm donor, but to have both contributions be completely anonymous? Nothing at all from me? I would just be a carrier? It didn't make any sense to me, to go through the pain, stress, and expense of IVF and pregnancy, just to carry someone else's genes.

Third, Dr. Mishra said I had to prepare myself physically, which included taking vitamins, eating healthy, and losing weight. Turned out, weight was another factor that affected pregnancy and the success of live birth. Dr. Mishra shared some weight- and pregnancy-related studies, including research that she had directly contributed to. The research, available on the fertility center's website, compared overweight and obese women with women of average weight using assisted reproductive technology (ART) treatments. The results showed that excess weight had negative effects such as lower pregnancy rates, increased miscarriage rates, and a lower rate of live birth. Further, excess weight could complicate pregnancy, with a higher likelihood of gestational diabetes, high blood pressure, preeclampsia, and birth defects. Oh, but that wasn't all. For the IVF process itself, excess weight could lead to "higher and longer doses of ovarian stimulation medication, fewer or more immature eggs to retrieve or more canceled cycles due to an inadequate response, higher risk of bleeding, damage to surrounding organs, and anesthesia-related complication during surgery or egg retrieval."

Whoa!

I had been trying to lose weight on and off for twenty years of my life without much success, but also without much intentionality. If I had known all this, I would be in model shape by now!

After all the talk, Dr. Mishra dragged me into a room and conducted a vaginal ultrasound. At that point, I didn't expect good news from the scan, and Dr. Mishra did not disappoint. She confirmed that I only had one ovary, which I knew, but also discovered that I had fibroids. Fibroids! I was stunned. How could I have fibroids and not know? She explained that some fibroids, depending on their placement, didn't cause any pain or discomfort. She didn't think it would be necessary to remove my fibroids, due to their placement and the potential for scarring if removed.

As I got dressed after the exam, thoughts were swirling in my head—I should have frozen some eggs, I should have had a regular gynecologist, and I should have lived a healthy lifestyle and lost weight.

Overall, I should just have been proactive, purposeful, and deliberate about my future. Instead, I had my head buried in books and somehow had forgotten to get my health in order.

It was an overwhelming consultation. My lack of knowledge regarding fertility and women's health was just astounding, irresponsible, and unacceptable.

For a few days after the discussion with Dr. Mishra, I wallowed in guilt, blaming myself for not learning or being proactive. Then I started to think about the educational system I grew up in. Information is everything. Knowledge is power. Where was my exposure to fertility information supposed to come from?

In 2021, the Ghana Coalition of NGOs in Health and the Human

Rights Advocacy Centre (HRAC) presented a report* titled "Sexual and Reproductive Health Rights in Ghana (Comprehensive Sexuality Education & Adolescent Reproductive Health Rights)." The report stated:

> Comprehensive sexual education (CSE) is absent from the curriculum in Ghanaian schools . . . [even though] the National Population Policy has a policy objective specifically on educating the youth on sexual relationships. Nevertheless, the absence of legal provisions for comprehensive sex education in the Ghanaian school systems limits young people from receiving the correct information and the resources in order for them to make *informed choices concerning their sexual health.* (Emphasis my own.)

Tell me about it! Without information and resources, how can anyone make an informed decision regarding when and how to have a child?

The report adds that "since it is *culturally unacceptable to discuss sex and sexual issues with adolescents,* parents do not discuss reproductive health issues and sexuality with their children." (Again, the emphasis is my own.) Yup, same experience for me and many others.

In 2019, Ghana introduced a "comprehensive sexual education" (CSE) policy.** The introduction of this policy generated a lot of unnecessary and unfounded fears and controversy, with parents and religious groups pushing back against the teaching of sensitive topics, like sex, to students. I've scoured the policy and looked at the suggested topics and

---

* The Human Rights Advocacy Centre and the Ghana Coalition of NGOs in Health, "Sexual and Reproductive Health Rights in Ghana" (2019), https://uprdoc.ohchr.org/uprweb/downloadfile.aspx?filename=4490&file=EnglishTranslation.

** Ghana Education Service, "Guidelines on Reproductive Health Education in Schools," January 25, 2020, https://ges.gov.gh/2020/01/25/guidelines-on-reproductive-health-education-in-schools/.

curriculum for each grade, and it is the most basic and safe information that can possibly be provided. The CSE topics are centered on leadership, family life, morality, religious and social values, hygiene, self-esteem, interpersonal relationships, and fertility/reproductive health (introduced in junior high school). I haven't been able to get access to the actual teaching materials for the fertility and reproductive element of the curriculum, but I skeptically wonder if it'll touch on any critical details.

The CSE is definitely a start in the right direction and I hope the government is able to push through and implement the program broadly. I can't find any details on the curriculum from my time in school (the 1980s to 1990s), but I have a pretty vivid memory, and I do not remember being taught anything about reproductive health besides a basic introduction of the male and female reproductive organs.

To be fair, I do not believe that formal education is where details like ovarian reserve, and the relationship among age, weight, and fertility can adequately and effectively be covered. And a parent most likely wouldn't know most of those details either. That's why I don't really blame my mother for being uninformed about most of this. In my opinion, the detailed mechanics of reproduction can (and should) be handled by a physician like a gynecologist, not a teacher or a parent. In the end, I pivot back to health care, and in that regard, I bear most of the blame. I should have been proactive and smart about seeking appropriate health information and resources (a gynecologist, at least) through my adult years.

· · ·

By August 2019, just a few months into my fertility journey, I had been hit with a possible autoimmune condition, low ovarian reserve, fibroids, and weight issues. I was not off to a good start.

When I got back to Ghana, I did what many Christian Ghanaian women trying to have a baby would do—visited my pastor. Even before I had the urge to have a baby, it had always appeared to me that most prayers and prophetic interventions were focused on four main things—wealth and success, healing, marriage, and having children. It was my turn to tap into this menu. I just needed spiritual intervention on two items on the list—my health and having babies. A few members of the pastoral team at church were already praying with me regarding my foster son and the complicated custody situation I was embroiled in on that front. I felt comfortable enough to approach them about my desire to have a baby of my own, through IVF.

I was met with two very different reactions to my plans.

The head pastor was completely supportive. He said God's ways are not our ways, and we cannot begin to understand his plans for our lives. He encouraged me to pray and trust in God for healing and direction. He assured me that the baby would come.

The second pastor I spoke to had a radically different reaction. When we spoke, she didn't say much. Instead, she sent me a text hours later, a text I have saved and read over a hundred times since:

> Thanks also for sharing about your plans for IVF. I want to share a few thoughts with you to consider before you go ahead with this decision. I have two concerns with IVF. One is the moral/ethical question that arises from creating multiple embryos, all of which may or may not be used. As each embryo is essentially a person, this raises a lot of ethical concerns. I say this to draw your attention to the matter if you were not aware of it before. I am aware there are different options for the embryo process, but it is worth praying and considering how God would view this.

My greater concern, however, is that I do not believe God intended for a child to be created outside of a sexual relationship occurring inside a marriage covenant. The Bible clearly states God's instructions regarding fornication and adultery. One reason that He forbids them is because they have the potential to conceive a child outside of a family unit which is not God's plan. The only time in the Bible that we see a pregnancy without the act of covenant sex is the birth of Jesus. Even then, it wasn't outside a marriage because Mary and Joseph did marry.

You raised the point that God brought Kweku into your life even though you are not married. I do believe that is a different situation from you becoming pregnant through IVF. As Christians, God commands us to help orphans and take care of the poor. When the parents are no longer present to take care of a child, God can raise up other men and women, whether married or single, to stand in the gap. An example of this in the Bible would be Esther and Mordecai.

I would be happy to talk more in person about this if you would like. As you pray and search the Scriptures, may God speak to you and guide you.

My reply to her was respectful, but the text exchange affected me greatly. I really wanted this particular pastor's support. She had been good to me and to my foster son. I regarded her as a friend. I knew she meant no ill will, she was simply voicing her spiritual opinions. All the same, I was pained and confused.

This pastor was not the only one who had strong opinions about my IVF intentions.

I have a tendency to involve my close family in my life plans. Unfortunately, the reception to my IVF journey wasn't welcoming. At least two close relatives told me that I needed to trust and wait on God to provide me with a husband and kids in that order, and by pursuing IVF I was skipping ahead of God's plan, showing a lack of faith and trust in God.

At the time, as a young Christian, only one year into my journey with Christ, I regarded these family members as pioneers in the faith, the same regard I had for the pastor who raised moral and ethical objections to the IVF. These were people who were deeply steeped in scripture, so I assumed they had to be right. Perhaps I was stepping ahead of God's plans. And yet, I was also triggered that they purported to have insights into God's plans for my life.

I did what I often do in most conflicts, when I feel verbal discussions would lead to interruptions of my thoughts: I sent an email—my thoughts, feelings, and beliefs just flow better in written form. The email I sent to my close family was the longest note I had ever written in my life. It was a lot. It was intense. I dug deep within and poured it all out. I have provided an abridged version.

Some of you have said to me—do not go through with this IVF and just wait on the Lord. I'm curious—wait on the Lord for? For the traditional, normal sequence of things? Husband, marriage, and natural birth? Because somehow you feel God works in a very linear, sequential way?

What about little Kweku? Should I return him to Social Welfare or maybe to an orphanage because I'm waiting on God for my husband first and then natural pregnancy and birth? And anything that is not in that sequence means I'm jumping ahead of God's plan? Should I therefore return the child I am taking care of because I am skipping steps?

I am reminded of the story of the man who was stuck in a tree during a flood and was at risk of drowning. Several people came by and offered him help, but he said he was waiting for God. Eventually he died, and wailed that God didn't rescue him, and then God listed all the people he sent to him that the man didn't recognize as God's hand in his life. This man didn't accept the help offered to him because he had a particular way he expected the rescue to happen, and so he was waiting for that particular way. It's a powerful story because that's how a majority of people treat God, prayer, and blessings. There's an expectation of how the blessing should manifest.

God is not moving in my life in some carefully planned, sequential, and traditional way. He brought Kweku into my life, and no matter how difficult that situation is, I know it is God who brought my son into my life. Why would God do that? Why would God interrupt the accepted natural sequence of marriage/husband and then kids, and bring this child into my life when I don't have a husband? It comes down to one basic thing—God's ways are just not our ways.

My email was extremely cathartic for me. It helped me come to terms with my motives and my faith. After I sent it, I read it over and over again, and decided to take my own words to heart and take a leap of faith.

Over the next six months, I worked out regularly, took the vitamins that Dr. Mishra prescribed, and started seeing a fertility specialist in Ghana, Dr. Adi, to help manage my care and tests in Ghana. I also decided that my first attempt with IVF would be with my own eggs. I believed in miracles. God could turn 10 percent into 100 percent!

Dr. Mishra and I set a date for the IVF—April 2020. A month before my flight to Virginia, the COVID-19 virus hit the globe, and Ghana went into lockdown. I was devastated. The lockdowns in Ghana were lifted three weeks later, but the United States was in a mess with rising case numbers and lockdowns across multiple states. The fertility clinic paused treatments until further notice. I spiraled into despair. My chance of success using my own eggs was dwindling. When I first met with Dr. Mishra in July 2019, I'd had a 10 percent chance of success with my eggs—what were my likely odds a year on? I wasn't creating new eggs! My reserve was depleting with every month that rolled on by.

Disappointed with my odds, I stopped taking my vitamins and I stopped working out. What was the use? I was certain I had missed the window for using my own eggs. As the pandemic relentlessly wore on, I decided to research and explore getting a donor embryo, but I really struggled with the concept. I wasn't sure I could take on the risk of a geriatric pregnancy for a baby that wouldn't have my genes. It was too painful to comprehend. And I couldn't figure out what I actually wanted—to just be pregnant and have a baby, or to have a mini me? I had my son, whom I loved dearly even though he was not biologically mine. I loved him unconditionally, so I had no issues being a mother to a child who was not genetically mine. My struggle was with taking on the risk of *pregnancy* for a nongenetic baby. I also wasn't very keen on initiating another adoption, because the situation with my foster son had soured my experience of adoption in Ghana.

I had a lot of questions, so I joined a virtual support group organized by the Virginia fertility clinic for women considering donor eggs or embryos. These single women and couples were all struggling as I was, coming to terms with carrying babies that would have no genetic connection to their parents. The support sessions were really good for me. We had guest speakers who had gone through IVF with donor eggs and embryos. These women, who had done what the rest of us in the group were hesitant to do, expressed how completely they loved their babies, babies whom they considered theirs in every sense. I gained incredible insights from the sessions, and the process prompted me to be open-minded and take some time to work on my psychological and emotional reaction to the concept of a donor baby.

The support group also made me realize that the lack of information and education on fertility is global. Most of the women in these groups were in their forties, and prior to seeking fertility treatment, almost all of these women were clueless about the intricate details regarding fertility.

Living in the West, these women were also bombarded by images of fortysomething celebrities popping out babies. In 2019, *Harper's Bazaar* posted an article on celebrity moms who had children "after 40," and the article, by Megan Decker, stated, "The challenges that can go along with trying to conceive and have children at an older age are often obscured by the number of celebrities who give birth after 40—which can, in turn, perpetuate a belief that it's easy to get pregnant later in life." Many of these celebrities are silent on how they actually "acquired" their babies. I get that it's a personal process, but the silence also feeds a harmful culture of ignorance regarding fertility.

Selfishly, it was comforting to know that my naivete was shared by many women who grew up in Western cultures, women who, like myself, were educated at prestigious institutions of higher learning, women who were smart and independent but had somehow missed educating themselves on fertility.

I had other friends who had either emigrated to the United States or United Kingdom, or who had moved there after high school, and they were in the same boat as I was—ignorant and clueless about fertility and now experiencing the pain and disappointment of their ignorance. We were coming out of the woodwork now. Or maybe we were always there, but only recently vocalizing our experiences. One of my closest friends, who has lived in the United States for over twenty-five years, is so irate about the whole experience that she plans to launch a platform focused entirely on fertility and women's health. I hope her platform goes viral and reaches the millions of women out there who are living in blissful ignorance, thinking that when they're good and ready to have a child, it will just happen. My friend and I recently spoke for over an hour about menses. Menses! There was so much we didn't know even about our menstrual cycles!

Just over a year after my visit with Dr. Mishra, I started to feel excruciating pain in my lower belly, unlike anything I had ever felt before in my life, except for when I had the ovarian torsion. I was in denial for two months, fearful of what was happening with my body. Eventually, unable to bear the pain any longer, I dragged myself to see Dr. Adi. He was also concerned about my pain, so he performed a series of tests, and the results completely tore me apart. I was done for.

The debrief was somber. Once again, my mother was next to me. Dr. Adi explained his findings, one by one.

First, I had adenomyosis, a mass in the inner lining of my uterus. With each menstrual cycle, the mass or tissue in the lining thickens, causing excruciating pain. The only treatment for adenomyosis is a full hysterectomy. The onset of menopause was also known to stop the growth and impact of adenomyosis, but I was a few years away from that. With the positioning of the adenomyosis, if a baby were implanted in my womb, the baby and the mass would compete for space as each would be growing.

Second, I had hydrosalpinx, a collection of fluid in one of my fallopian tubes. Typically there are no symptoms, but sometimes, a hydrosalpinx can also cause pain. If I were to proceed with pregnancy, the fluid could also backwash into my uterus, infecting the baby and killing it before it even had a chance.

Third, I had an occlusion in my other fallopian tube. There was a polyp buried at the back end of the tube. So one tube was blocked by fluid and the other was blocked by a polyp.

Fourth, my fibroids had shifted, pressing against my uterine wall. Surgical removal could lead to scarring, affecting implantation and pregnancy success.

Fifth, my uterine wall was thin. Ideally, for the successful implantation of an embryo, uterine wall thickness should be at least seven to eight millimeters. I was at five millimeters—implantation at that thickness would not be possible. The catch was that I could take hormones to improve my lining, but the hormones would also stimulate the growth of the adenomyosis.

I just couldn't win. I was numb after that download. My mother was asking Dr. Adi some questions but I couldn't speak. I wanted the appointment to end. I wanted everything to end. Later that day, I sat alone on my bedroom floor and cried. I had been wrong all along, I thought. God didn't want me to do this. He had spoken very loudly to me that day. I was stubborn, so perhaps God needed to bombard me with multiple issues for me to truly realize that having my own baby wasn't God's plan for me. I had been so stupid to even think that having a baby was in the cards for me. I had lived a very reckless and wanton life before I gave my life to Jesus. I knew the Bible spoke of grace, that no sin was too great to be forgiven, that salvation is not by works. I knew all that, but what I was going through just didn't make any sense.

From the very moment I had the urge to have a baby, I had been plagued—lingering autoimmune symptoms; depleted ovarian reserve; lack of support from my favorite pastor, close family, and friends; and now adenomyosis, hydrosalpinx, fallopian occlusion, fibroids, and thin uterine lining. All in one person! One body! It all felt too severe not to be some sort of biblical punishment. I refused to believe it was all a coincidence. This had to be God, sending me a clear, unambiguous message.

For a couple of months after the consult with Dr. Adi, I refused to address or acknowledge what I had been told. I didn't have the courage to think about the implications of my multiple diagnoses. I was depressed.

That December, I scheduled a consult with Dr. Mishra and we went through Dr. Adi's findings. Dr. Mishra was very direct with her plan of action.

First step, I had to remove the hydrosalpinx and possibly the other blocked tube through a surgical process called laparoscopic salpingectomy. A keyhole incision would be made along my belly and the whole tube with the fluid would be removed. Dr. Mishra suggested that once the surgeon was already in my uterus, the surgeon would need to examine my other tube and make a determination about the removal of that tube as well if it was diseased or would create pregnancy issues due to the polyp placement. Once both tubes were removed, natural pregnancy would be off the table permanently. Although, with hydrosalpinx in one tube and a polyp in another, both tubes were essentially blocked, with no pathways for an egg or sperm to naturally meet, so the natural pregnancy ship had long sailed. This surgery would also require general anesthesia.

Second step, I had to improve my uterine lining. There would be no IVF without getting the thickness to at least seven millimeters. Improving my lining would cause growth with the adenomyosis, but Dr. Mishra felt the pain could be managed.

Third, I had to recognize that using my own eggs as part of an IVF process was completely out of the picture. In addition, my chances of success had now been dramatically reduced, even with a donor. Without any health complications, a donor egg or embryo would provide 50 percent chance of success for live birth. With adenomyosis, my chance of success of live birth with a donor had dramatically reduced, to 15 percent.

Fourth, I had to continue to manage my weight and health. With all these complications, weight could not be an additional factor. I had to take control of that.

I proceeded with Dr. Mishra's plan on autopilot. In January 2021, I found a US-trained doctor, Dr. Lucca, who could perform the laparoscopic surgery in Ghana. Dr. Lucca, Dr. Adi, and Dr. Mishra had a joint consult on my case. They came back to me, aligned with the plan Dr. Mishra had shared with me back in December. It was now up to me to decide. Dr. Mishra's plan started with surgery, but I wasn't ready for that, especially surgery that required general anesthesia. I informed all three doctors that I was going to start with step four—manage my weight and health. We established some timelines—March to August to lose weight, and then a consult with Dr. Lucca in September to proceed with surgery if I felt physically and emotionally ready.

It is now more than two years since I had my first fertility appointment, and I am not ready, psychologically and emotionally. Physically, I have made incredible progress, losing twenty-two pounds over the six months. Psychologically, I am conflicted. What lies before me just doesn't make sense.

First, a surgery to remove one, maybe two, blocked tubes. Then weeks of hormone therapy to improve my uterine lining, which would feed the adenomyosis, causing excruciating pain. If my lining improves for implantation, it would have to be via donor embryo, with no genetic connection to me or any member of my family. Obviously, I could select from a donor menu and pick an ethnicity or mixture of an ethnicity that closely matches mine, but the fetus still wouldn't have my DNA. And then I would carry this baby in a hostile womb, surrounded by adenomyosis and fibroids, which would likely compete with the baby and threaten its survival. Pregnancy isn't a walk in the park. Pregnancy can be dangerous. Maternal mortality is a real thing. Do I really want to take all that risk, just to carry and birth a baby?

My analytical mind simply can't come to terms with my options. Spiritually, I am devastated that I am even going through this. I can't figure it out. I don't know if God wants me to stop, or if he wants me to persevere. I am lost. I have been to prayer camps at dawn. I have joined prophetic hours at midnight. I have given generously to the church and church causes. All to what end?

There are days when I am overcome with emotion, wondering if the journey is truly over, thinking about the likely possibility that I will never carry or birth a child. The thought pierces my soul. Then there are other days, when I look at my foster son and think, *He is enough*—until I am reminded that he is not yet mine.

I have no control over anything—pregnancy or adoption—I have no control. So, I have surrendered. I have decided to just focus on my health and well-being, and continue to work out, eat well, get enough sleep, and relax. Losing weight is no longer about fertility or the surgery; I want to be around for my foster son. I won't stop fighting for him, and I would rather fight for him, a child whom I know and love, than to risk my life for a fetus I do not yet know.

I also want to get back to writing, to refocus on the passion that I shelved in pursuit of the baby dream that is likely not my path. I tried really hard to make the baby thing happen. I gave it my best shot, but it is no longer part of my story right now. I am still blessed because I am still here, standing, breathing, writing, living, and loving. All I can do is take it one day at a time. I have no other moves to make.

Natasha Omokhodion-Kalulu Banda

Her Sweetie, Her Sugarcane

STORY

Lusaka, 1972

Elizabeth Moyo's wedding day forecast had promised that the weather would shine; that the sun would be sweet. Instead, raindrops braided down silk frangipani at the entrance of the Cathedral of the Holy Cross. In the distance, faceless picketers huddled under trees, their upended signs reading OPPOSE ONE-PARTY STATE, and she wished they would do it somewhere else. Her hips ached from the contortionist dance lessons of that week, which were dispensed to her like bitter medicine from the old ladies who now encircled her. She sweltered, her joy shrouded in a puff of lace that pressed upon her head and crawled down to her ankles. Her dress was so heavy, she felt she might be flattened into the concrete steps. Just a few minutes before, her older sister and chief bridesmaid—Chipo—had kissed her on the cheek ever so softly. "Goodbye," she'd whispered. "No matter what happens, I'll always love you."

Her eager reflection had drowned in Chipo's glistening eyes.

Trying to rationalize the heartbreak in her sister's kiss, she twisted her bougainvillea bouquet, letting the ribbon that bound it blot her palms dry. *Dennis chose me. Dennis chose me.* Her mouth fluttered open to ask Chipo one more time if she still felt anything for him, even remotely, but Father linked his arm in hers. She felt a slight tug as Chipo lifted her train, and took her cue to move.

Organ pipes released an ecclesiastic horn. The audience twisted their heads before they sprang up. In front of her, preening children whom she barely knew took their first steps; tiny fists grasping rose petals from their baskets to parachute along the endless red carpet. Because Father squeezed her arm reassuringly, Elizabeth marched on, her head bowed, the red carpet beckoning her white satin shoes.

She'd read somewhere that siblings compete for attention from the moment they are born and that's what it felt like right now; it was how she had always felt. It pained her that Chipo's presence pulled the hall—her beauty turned heads even though she was not the one getting married—and Elizabeth wished she could turn around and ask her to stop it.

The burden of being born two years later than the first child was a heavy one. To be less shiny, less beautiful, less novel, was a worn path Elizabeth had walked. It was the small things, like how the house had countless studio photos of Chipo, but very few with her. "By the time you came, I was too busy with my nurse training, and A Tate was climbing up the civil service ladder at the Ministry of Housing. We just didn't have the time to go out and spend the day taking photographs," Mother would say. Many times, among both guests and strangers, Mother attributed Chipo's beauty to the happiness she felt early in her marriage to Father—the days he called her pet names like chisankonde, *sweet sugarcane.* Elizabeth would never know the state their marriage had been in when they had her, because no one had ever cared to carry the discussion further. They looked at Elizabeth, and patted Mother's shoulder with a flash of sympathy in their eyes.

The scales, however, began to tip when Chipo began kissing boys after sunset at the end of their cul-de-sac, beyond the pink hibiscus hedge; or smoking Rothmans cigarettes outside the gym at school. She got away with it most times, impressing the thick band of friends she walked to class with, but she also spent many afternoons slashing grass on the terraces at school in punishment. Yet it was expected always, that she, Elizabeth, would be on her best behavior. So far, she had never disappointed, and she wasn't about to today. No, today was her day.

Her parents were ecstatic, and so were Dennis's. To have their joy so openly expressed—the smart suits, the fuss over preparations, the distinguished guests—made her beam with pride. To be in this moment, floating down the aisle toward Dennis, meant the world to her. *See, I too am worthy to be his bride.*

* * *

The first time Elizabeth and Chipo met Dennis and his family, all she could smell was money. It clung to the plastic-covered chairs, the Supersonic gramophone in the corner, the too-large carpet that curled against the floor skirting, and the soundless chrome fan that gleamed, spreading cool air against their faces. All she could hear was the counting of notes, like fresh newspapers spitting off a press, and the subdued chink of coins. Women sat at a desk counting and recording, bundling and packing. "His daddy owns almost all the butcheries in the African township," Father had told her along the way. " 'Big Tee's' is also the red brand you see when you want to buy some sweeties," Mother had said.

Father worked as a clerk in the Town Planning Department, and Mr. Tembo wanted him to plan the strategy for his new shops. Mr. Tembo spoke, resting his folded arms on his potbelly, his loosened cross-bands swinging at his knees. "I want all the key corners, and all road frontage—nothing less." Independence was well on its way, and so their fathers' voices muffled outside as they pored over drawings and plans for the future. She imagined her father squinting through his thick-rimmed glasses tracing translucent paper with his forefinger.

A five-pound note sat framed above the piano. "That was our first profit, September of 1957," said the smiling lady to Mother. "I can't believe it's only been two years since then."

Elizabeth and Chipo perched on either side of Mother. Mr. Tembo's wife sat opposite them. Chipo was as beautiful as Mother. She wore her hair long, in two braided ponytails with checkered ribbons that clenched tightly at the ends. Elizabeth's was shorn to her skin because she was prone to ringworm. The girls' legs were too short to reach the mottled carpet, so Chipo's swung, while Elizabeth's kicked. Elizabeth hadn't started school yet, so she wore no socks, and her legs had caught all the dust from the road along the way. She wished that her mother had not insisted on coating her with so much Vaseline.

Elizabeth's eye averted to the frosted cupcakes that sat in a pyramid on the table draped in lace, even though, on the way, her mother's wagging finger had warned not to accept any offer of food. Chipo must have noticed, because her face split into a toothless grin, and she stood up to take one. Mother's sharp sideways glance cut enough to make Elizabeth shrink back, but by the time Mrs. Tembo sprang up to serve them, Chipo was wolfing hers down anyway. "Please, let her have as many as she wants. Come on, dear, that's why I made them, so you can have plenty."

Elizabeth hadn't sunk her teeth into anything as sweet or fluffy for as long as she could remember. The cupcakes caressed her little mouth and made her wobbly teeth ache, and even under the stern eye of Mother, she let her jaw loosen to move in slow sticky circles.

"Thank you, Mrs. Tembo."

"Please, call me Aunty Vivian." She smiled, and Elizabeth's eyes absorbed the copper glow of her long thick shoulders, admired the palm print of her sleeveless dress, the way everything seemed so breezy to her. Elizabeth felt in that moment that she wanted to be rich someday, to have her own colorful home whose entrance smelled like freshly baked cakes. "Why don't you run out and play while we wait for your fathers to finish their discussion? My son Dennis is about your age, he should be playing somewhere outside."

Outside was cluttered with statues of frogs and mushrooms that peeped among jostling creepers and discarded toys. Dennis came from around the corner and they stood in awkward silence before he asked, "Would you like a Penny Sucker?"

He had on a pair of red shoes that looked like they'd been dipped in baby oil. His hair was soft and curly, so clean that it glistened in the afternoon sun. The girls nodded, and his hands rummaged in his pockets before he presented one in each palm. When the three of them rolled the sweets against their tongues, their eyes met to set off a fission of giggles.

A lone guava tree bent over a small hedge, and they clambered up its branches. They sat in awkward silence in the crook of the tree, while the township shifted in a hum beneath them, their eyes focused on anything but each other's. Returnees from work rang bicycle bells, while in the distance, at the corner of the T-junction, children lined up for a bucket bath from a plump lady perched on a wooden crate.

"Come and try my seesaw. A Tate made it for me." They climbed onto a welded seesaw painted bright blue. Chipo pushed up with her feet, and as she rose into the warm impression of the sun behind her, Elizabeth felt that what she'd always suspected might be true. That Chipo was an angel, and the way Dennis looked up at her sister, she knew he felt the same way, too. Chipo's shadow flung itself over Elizabeth, making her shiver from the coolness of the breeze. When Elizabeth pressed her feet to go up, Chipo squealed, swooping down in an exhilarating descent. They did it again and again, Dennis running to help on each side of his seesaw, until Big Tee called out for them.

"Let's take a photograph! I've been waiting for a chance to use this thing." The fathers had finished their discussion, and Mr. Tembo called the mothers out. The girls posed, Chipo grinned, draping her arms around Dennis's neck like he was a new pet. Elizabeth found the courage—from where she was not sure—to throw her arms in the air. And Dennis was cool in the middle, wearing a half smile. Big Tee's English inflected like a song, like the way Mother spoke Chichewa. Only the words were different, but the rhythm was the same: "Look at the children, how well they get along. It's good to introduce them early? I'm very sure one day they will marry and we shall be referring to each other as Ba Sebele." Elizabeth noticed how everyone looked at Chipo while they said this, and something in her wished they would look her way, too.

When the Moyo family left that day, Mother's mouth twitched at the corners, and the mustache above Father's lip spread wide. They marched into magenta skies, each one of them lost in thought, reflecting on the different ways that this new family friendship could grow. Elizabeth's heart thumped, her body bloated with sugar, and her sister squeezed her small hand. The adrenaline from the seesaw game rushed through their veins, and made them jump to clap their hands in the air.

Although they'd both known Dennis since they were children, it was in secondary school that Elizabeth first noticed him. She watched him through the obstruction of wooden scaffolding as he practiced his lines for *A Midsummer Night's Dream*. Backstage, her throat parched. She was transfixed by the ripples in his arms. He stood bathing in the glow of white floodlights. His back was tall and stiff, his green shirt rustled from the fan; he looked like the smell of sugarcane fields before harvest. She felt her heart race a little, her imagination escape for a short while, and she saw, for the first time, an image of her and him holding hands.

At home that night, a State Lottery announcement on the television poured through the gap in the kitchen door: "In every draw, there's a winner!" Elizabeth washed the dishes, so full of this new feeling for Dennis that it threatened to burst her chest. Meanwhile, Chipo pretended to towel-dry, stacking cups and saucers into baby blue cupboards, gasping when they overheard the lady on the television screaming because she had won twenty thousand Kwacha.

"She's rich forever. What would you do if you won all that money?"

"I think I have feelings for Dennis," Elizabeth blurted, washing a cooking stick smeared with gravy.

Chipo's silence punctured the balloon that had been swelling in her chest, and the stick in Elizabeth's hands slipped, clinking in the sink. In front of Chipo, drops of water blotted the *Times of Zambia* lining the cupboard shelves.

"You have nothing to say?"

"No. I don't."

"Please say something."

Chipo sucked the air as she always did.

But what did Elizabeth expect? No one despised Dennis as much as Chipo. She'd thwarted all his efforts to take her out. She said nothing nice about the slow but confident way he moved, or the cheer that rested in the corners of his smile, or the dazzling white cubes he had for teeth. She said nothing complimentary about his parents. In the silence, she heard something that surprised her: envy. Elizabeth gathered the courage to ask her sister, "Do you like him?"

"Can't you see his eyes are spaced too far apart? You can even see the back of his mouth whenever he laughs. No, I could never like him."

"Why do you always have to be such a female dog about everything?"

"You can't even say the word, can you?" Chipo laughed. "You're worried what I might think if you say it? Go ahead, call me a bitch. I know you all think it."

"I prefer not to use bad language."

"Listen. I know what's best for you. Just stay away from him."

• • •

Chipo had a new boyfriend who went to Evelyn Hone College. He looked like a Jehovah's Witness. It was the way he dressed exactly the same every day: white shirt, black trousers, white sports socks tucked into black dress shoes. By then, Chipo's hatred for Dennis had grown tenfold, even as Dennis began visiting their house frequently, talking politics with Father and complimenting Mother's delele. While he did this, he eyed Elizabeth over his plate, and Chipo rolled her eyes. Sometimes the phone would ring, and Mother would answer, both of them waiting to see who it was for, and she'd say, "Lizzie, it's for you."

When Mother was out of range, Elizabeth lay on her back, twirling the coil around her finger. While he asked her what her favorite color was, or what upset her most, she could hear Chipo on the other end in Mother and Father's room, pretending she was not there, but she was— her jealousy reaching across the line in even breaths until it clicked just before they said goodbye. "Who was that?" he asked.

"No one." Embarrassed, she touched her warming cheek with her free hand. "I'm sure it was just a crossline."

"Good, because I have a question to ask. Can I take you out?"

He picked her up on a Friday afternoon in his Datsun and they zoomed past Chipo and the man-boy from college. He clasped her hand as they walked up and down Cairo Road, dipping into restaurants to meet his friends. Later, when they sat in the cinema, he squeezed her hand and kissed it, and it felt just as she'd imagined: decadent. It was so sweet it made tingles run up and down her spine, her skin, between her toes. At recess, in the toilets, the girls circled her. "Aren't you Chipo's younger sister?"

"Of course I am."

"So why are you here with Dennis? Hasn't he been chasing her all of secondary school?"

She assumed they were saying this because they couldn't believe Dennis would want her instead of Chipo. But he did. Right? She let their laughter roll off her back as she twisted the tap open, cool water running over her hands, her bangles jangling as she negotiated a leftover slice of Rexona soap. Then she looked in the mirror and wondered what she was doing. Of course he didn't like her. Chipo was the pretty one.

Dennis waited outside near the popcorn stand, one foot resting on the wall, his black shirt buttons opened down to his navel, a silver chain glinting in the lights. His sideburns were shaped like the split stem of a wineglass, swooping into the deep hollows of his face. He wore a thick mustache, and his lye-cooked Afro stood about four inches tall; a sheen of dripping curls. He was a beautiful man.

"Ladies, enough gossip," Dennis answered the questioning girls, "leave me to my sweetheart." He pulled her into an embrace, so that they all kept quiet. Her heart soared. She knew she could never fill out her jeans like a Coca-Cola bottle, or carry a chest as round as Chipo's, but Dennis saw her as worthy to hold his hand. She was his and he was hers. She was going to treat him with dignity and respect, the way a good woman should, because she saw in him what Chipo had failed to.

At home, her sister's eyes were dark after he hugged her goodbye at the doorstep. "What's going on with you and Dennis?"

She smiled and twirled, hugging the sweater he'd given her that still smelled of his Palmolive tonic.

"You're wasting your time. His family has other plans for him. I hope you know this."

"What plans?"

"The same plans every one of these new families with a little bit of money have—a virginal bride to give their son in holy philandering matrimony. But you never know, maybe even someone like you." Chipo laughed aloud, inflating Elizabeth with anger.

"You are jealous, aren't you? You wish it was you in his car and in that cinema today, don't you? Do you have feelings for him or not?"

"Even if I do, little sister, I'll always be too much for them."

• • •

At the altar, Elizabeth didn't look above the suede burgundy blazer Dennis wore over a ruffled white dinner shirt; her view was limited to his black bow tie. She wanted to look into his eyes, but the old ladies had told her not to raise her gaze from the ground whenever her husband was nearby. She obeyed, even though Big Tee and Aunty Vivian used to stare into each other's eyes in front of them. "The Tembos may be modern, but we are traditionalists," Mother said. "Bow your head outside, but in your home you can meet him eye to eye." All Elizabeth wanted to do was to make them proud. She also wanted the congregation to know she deserved to be his bride, even though she suspected they were whispering that it should be Chipo in her place. "Isn't that the one he's always pined for?"

At the priest's dictation, they parroted their vows. The tips of Dennis's moon-shaped nails burned red. He retrieved the ring from the page boy, but squeezed so tight that the gold band escaped his grip. It bounced onto the marble floor three times before it rolled to a stop.

Gasps rose.

Fans pumped.

Handkerchiefs swiped.

Columns of sunlight inched away from the pews, and Chipo bent over to collect the ring. "Face this way please, Mr. Tembo." A small ripple of laughter. Chipo's heels clicked toward them. The priest made Dennis repeat the vows as he slid the cold metal onto her finger.

"You may now kiss the bride."

At last her veil was lifted. Elizabeth took a deep breath and tilted her face upward in anticipation, but his expression was empty. It told her nothing. She wished he would smile, even just a little. Summoning the confidence of her new last name, she turned her cheek toward him, but his lips barely scraped her forehead.

Incense unfurled into a smoke screen, and the bells of the clergy chimed.

· · ·

Mother and Father turned on only a few lights, but the old hinges on the doors squeaked, and their hurried footsteps gave them away. The girls sat up in their beds, their James Brown posters glowing in the moonlight. It was past midnight, and Big Tee had come to their house; his Buick rolling silently into the yard, lights off. He had only ever come home twice, both times to pick up Father. But now, Big Tee's Chichewa-English voice was trying to fold itself into whispers that rose and fell in steady waves. From behind the closed door, they listened.

"If you can testify for me, and absolve me of the accusations, I will ensure you never have anything to worry about financially."

"What do you mean?"

"UNIP is out for my blood. The party and its government have arrested everyone I was supporting in the opposition. If the National Council passes one-party democracy, they . . . we will all become outlaws."

Mother made something between a cry and a yelp.

"Are you sure?" asked Father.

"They sent hooligans to beat us up in the market. Looting my shops. Just this afternoon, they sent a pack of tax auditors to inspect our books. I told them to look, because there's nothing there."

"So what are you proposing?"

Silence.

"If we are bound through family, we are assured of legitimacy, you are assured of wealth. If we have a marriage, the government will not doubt my loyalty. In the long run, it might give me even more business, which will mean *our* profits. If you remain in the system to keep us protected, then I think we can set a solid foundation for the children and the children's children. The more I think about it, the more it makes perfect sense."

Elizabeth wondered what he meant.

Mother asked Aunty Vivian if she'd like some tea. "The children have been friends since they were young. There is no other way to repay you without the flag being raised. There's so much talk of corruption and wastage, people are afraid to use ink and paper at the government offices. No one's safety is guaranteed. Look at them." Big Tee's laugh sounded a little shaky.

Chipo pressed her ear closer to the door so Elizabeth did the same.

"Elizabeth and Dennis should get married. It will be good for both families."

"Doesn't he like Chipo?" It was Mother's voice.

Aunty Vivian cleared her throat after an uncomfortable laugh. "But he's always moving around with Lizzie."

The girls looked at each other. Elizabeth's heart was dropping fast. Her sister's eyes were large, seemingly terrified. For once she did not pass a snide remark.

"Like has nothing to do with suitability when it comes to marriage." Big Tee was talking now. "Chipo is beautiful, no one can deny that, but a man wants a wife he can trust. No offense intended at all. I think we can be candid among old friends, who we have always considered family."

Father agreed audibly.

Chipo closed her eyes and slowly turned around. She leaned against the wall, bringing her knees to her chin, and tucked her head into the crook of her arms. Elizabeth wanted to hug her, but she wanted to listen on, too.

"I told you so, didn't I?" her sister mumbled. "They want a virginal bride."

• • •

Outside the cathedral, the rain had stopped, replaced by a blinding shower of confetti. Elizabeth stood planted to the concrete steps while everyone arranged themselves around her. Flashes snapped from a small cameraman, and she watched Dennis brush confetti from Chipo's bare shoulders. She saw the upward smile, the way her sister's dark gums shone in his direction, and felt Chipo's high-pitched giggle work its way through her marrow. Again, Elizabeth chose to turn instead to the glory of her parents' approval. "Everyone move away now, only Mr. and Mrs. Tembo please." Her sister sashayed away: her chin high, her waist twisting from side to side, making Elizabeth blink back her tears.

• • •

There was a time when Chipo leaned over the lip of the toilet bowl every morning before school. A time when her face blackened at the sight of sunny-side ups wobbling on toast and she spoke to no one. Mother and Chipo hurled tumblers past each other, screaming, while Elizabeth squatted in a corner of the living room, scooping the broken shards into a dustpan. "You will tell me who he is today! Who is responsible for this . . . thi . . . ?"

Father's voice agitated, Mother's sobs seeped through the walls and into the girls' room, spilling into muted shades of gray at dawn. "It's going to be okay, I promise," Elizabeth said, her arms wrapped around her sister, "just do as they say."

"I hate them both. I wish they would both just die."

Mother took her out of town to terminate the pregnancy. When they returned, Mother forbade her from seeing anyone. Elizabeth tried to stay close to her, her back pressed to the other side of the bedroom door, when she locked it, Chipo's sobs breaking her as they rose and fell. Elizabeth slid notes through the gap at the bottom of the door until the night sucked the daylight and she slept in the living room.

When they returned to school, Chipo murmured, "Sorry," into Elizabeth's hair as they hugged. "I'm sorry, too."

She pulled back, and Elizabeth looked into what used to be the brown glimmer of her sister's eyes, only to find blank tunnels, hollow and dark. She watched her walking along the long corridors, hugging her books, speaking to no one. She knew something inside her had died, and this new thing would never leave, not until it was placated.

• • •

After the speeches, it was time to dance, but Dennis was nowhere to be found, and neither was Chipo, so she danced with Big Tee, Father, and a drunk cousin. The wedding ended with forks scraping plates, wires winding, chairs piling, linen flapping, and guest exits—Dennis and Chipo were still gone.

"Ah, ah! Where is the groom?"

"No, calm down," she told herself. "They'll be back soon."

When they left the reception, the old ladies led Elizabeth to an empty marital flat, singing and beating on drums that echoed against the walls. Her heart whirled. Anger and humiliation twisting, fighting hope from the advice of her parents and the old ladies: that marrying Dennis had been the right thing to do, not just for herself, but for the clan.

"Wait at least a week for his return. That's what a faithful wife should do. Shipikisha," they said.

"But where have they gone?"

"We don't know yet. But don't worry, we will deal with Chipo when they return."

"Something must be wrong. What if there's been an accident? A Tate should call the police!"

"Breathe, Lizzie. Breathe," Mother said.

"And what if they—if he doesn't come back?" she asked through clumps of wet mascara.

"They always do," they hummed.

But he didn't. She sat in the tub, emptying and filling, emptying and filling—wondering when the pain would ever go away. Elizabeth waited for the front door to unlock, to hear his voice announce his return. She waited for him to hug her and say how sorry he was. But her world was shrinking into a dark hole that squeezed smaller and smaller with each passing day. She'd sleep into the afternoon, hoping it would prevent her from feeling the numbness, from living the reality of a jilted bride. She mourned a life that could have been, a future that should have been theirs. She pictured him living unscathed, eating his food each day, laughing at something he found funny on the television—his tranquility intact.

Even though she stared into Dennis's gaping wardrobe, walking around in his too-large shoes, crying herself to sleep on the mustard couch he'd chosen, Lusaka city carried on, as life tended to do. From the safety of the straw chair on her balcony, she watched the season's sullen tufts begin to give way to cloudless blue skies.

A key fumbled in the front door. She breathed in deeply facing the traffic, hoping and dreading at once.

It opened.

Paper bags rustling, tin cans landing on the kitchen table. The smell of her daily bribe in the form of chicken stew wafted through the grill door. Mother came to sit next to her. "They're at his father's house, but not for long though, because Big Tee is as angry as we all are." She didn't have to confirm that "they" were Chipo and Dennis. "You can remain here. His parents have agreed it's your due."

"My due? That's all they have to say?"

Mother kept quiet.

"All is not lost. You can get married again. Everyone knows that it wasn't consummated. There are many eligible men who will marry you."

Elizabeth refused to look at Mother.

"Since the wedding I have banned your father from going to the golf club with Big Tee. Aunty Vivian has quit the knitting club, stopped baking cakes on Sundays, and when did you last see her?"

Aunty Vivian had visited a few times, making small talk at the door, her fingers hovering over a nervous cake. Her apologies were cool and correct, but not sufficient to plug the bottomless sorrow that Elizabeth felt.

"She has retreated into herself and her home." She spoke softly. "It's not only you, Lizzie. We're all hurting. You need to get up and give yourself a new start."

Elizabeth understood, but she couldn't bear to imagine Dennis and Chipo together, or to answer questioning eyes at the shops or the theater, so she no longer opened her door confidently. Instead, she peeked first through voile curtains whenever guests arrived. She walked around the house mumbling to herself in mirrors, replaying the vows she made at the altar. Sometimes, she practiced clever lines of what she'd say to Chipo when she saw her again. What she'd say to Dennis. But it left her exhausted, and all she wanted to do was climb back into bed.

Dennis finally sent for his clothes, and her in-laws sent a sheepish emissary who gripped a white chicken at the base of its wings. The bird clucked until its throat was split. It splashed crimson at the edge of her sandals. Over several visits his people begged her forgiveness, because now it was clear that he'd chosen her sister, Chipo, and there was nothing anyone could do about it.

• • •

She got their new home address from Mother, but she was not ready to see them yet. In the meantime, she decided to try to live a little: try going on a date with a new man. He wore an all-white tailored suit, his cologne cloying her small living room. She let him woo her, maybe because his teeth were as perfect as Dennis's, and maybe because she needed to be wanted. She didn't have much else to lose.

After a dinner of chicken-in-the-basket at Ridgeway Hotel, served with a glowing narrative of all of this man's achievements, she chose to smile and let his ego inflate some more. She reduced herself to his request—yes, he was right—they were old enough to book a night at a hotel. Yes, she technically was single. She let the stranger take her hand, his smell foreign, his eagerness cheapening. She drew her coat closed when they climbed up the stairs.

In the sterile room, with crisp folds and severe corners, she continued to oblige him. She lay on her back, spreading her legs slowly. If she could only see this as gaining an experience, rather than losing her dignity, then she would have won something. Right?

As he kissed her, she kissed Dennis. Her eyes shut tight: willing him to touch her deeply. But it was nothing like she'd imagined making love to Dennis would be: passionate nights with warm rain pelting against their window, her straddling him while he fed her his love.

It was quick, unsavory, surface; it left her emptier than she was before. She'd won nothing. When he dropped her home that night, she knew she'd never see him again, and all she wanted was to see her sister.

• • •

Her hand shielded her eyes from the sun as she looked up from the flat number scrawled on the paper. Dripping laundry hung from balconies. Creepers grew out of their corners. Big Tee had punished them at least. This was not somewhere she'd expected Dennis to live.

"Tenth floor," Mother had said.

She clambered up a dark winding corridor.

Offals. Hooves. Dried fish. The smells crowded each other, charging through her nostrils. Voices of DJs on the radio floated through the frames of the numbered doors. She gripped the banister and continued upward. She dabbed her forehead with a rectangle of tissue from her purse and closed it between her arm and her breast. She raised her fist to the door, but silence met her knocking.

A neighbor craned his neck out of a blaring E43. "Madam, there is no one there. They moved."

"Where to?"

The man shrugged. "I have no idea, I'm also new."

Downstairs, her Peugeot shouted a message printed into its coat of dust.

WASH ME PLEASE

She followed some children, a photograph of Dennis and one of Chipo, shaking in her hands. *Do you know them?* But the bell of an ice cream bicycle rang, and they zoomed in its direction.

She opened the car door, and threw herself inside, banging it closed before she began to weep from the relief and the frustration of not seeing them. In the rearview mirror, she picked her afro puffs. She'd hoped that somehow the new hairstyle might give her a new edge, show that she was bolder now and impress Chipo and Dennis. Her new high heels pinched her feet. She'd been determined to arrive looking her best. She dabbed her tears with a powder puff.

She locked the gear into reverse, and her foot pressed the accelerator. She began to curve her way out of the yard, when they all screamed for her to "STOP!" The man from upstairs appeared in the side mirror, slapping the body of her car, his words punctuated by the claps of the woman behind him. "This lady says the woman and the man live here. They moved a few floors farther down."

Elizabeth stepped out of the car and slammed the door, its hot metal heating her back, the small crowd staring at her before she asked them to excuse her. The walk was endless, her heels shaky, the stairs steeper than the first climb.

She rummaged through her leather handbag and cursed under her breath when the door opened.

There she was, perfect as always, her right hand in the air, massaging a morsel of nshima. Elizabeth rushed past her sister before she could protest. It was only a few paces to the living room. Chipo's quiet footfall was steady behind the severe click of her heels.

"Why are you here?"

Smoke rose from Elizabeth's ears, plumed through her nose.

"Where is Dennis? Where is my husband?"

"Ha," Chipo answered.

"How could you do this to me? To us?"

"I love you, you know I do. You just forgot that he loved me first."

• • •

It was humid: hot-hot. A jug full of iced Mazoe clinked on the dressing table. James Brown was in town. They sat on her bed. Chipo carved Elizabeth's eyebrows with a razor blade. She was getting her ready, although Chipo was not allowed to go to the show. "Ow!" Chipo pushed earrings into tiny holes, still raw from the home piercing a week before.

"I'm nervous," Elizabeth said, jerking her legs like she always had since they were children. Chipo hugged her tight, her large bosom pressed against her flat chest. She kissed her cheek. Their eyes locked for a long while. Chipo's expression was sad even though she smiled through her pink lips.

She swiveled Elizabeth toward the mirror, to their combined reflection. Sisters opposite in complexion, in bone density, in disposition.

"What was it like? When Mother made you take out the baby?"

She clutched her belly. "She didn't go in with me. She just paid the strange woman and left me there."

"Did it hurt?"

"You see this razor?" She nodded. "It was like someone was scraping my insides with it."

"Will you tell me whose it was?"

135

She took a comb and began to line her tresses with Dax. "It's all in the past now. It doesn't matter."

Her sister's hands soothed her hot scalp and Chipo hummed while she styled her hair. Elizabeth wished she could take Chipo's hurt away. "Being with you like this, makes me happy. I miss this."

"Enough about me. Tonight is your big night."

She was anxious about seeing him later. She hoped he'd like her new jeans.

"Do you think Dennis will like me?"

Chipo clutched a fistful of hair. "Ow!"

She pantomimed the question, "Do you think Dennis will like me?" She let go, and began to pace the bedroom. "Why does everything have to be about him?"

"It's not."

"Don't you love *me*? Don't you care what's happened to *me*? Don't you ever think about those monsters? What kind of parents would do this to their child?" She clutched her belly again.

"I'm sorry, I didn't mean to upset you."

"When I walk down the road, I know what they all say behind my back. I'm the loose one. The damaged goods, and you're so delicate and good, you shine without even trying."

"I do try, all the time, but you never let me in."

"Then take me with you. Tell Mother and Father that we'll go together and I'll be on my best behavior."

"They won't let you. And where would you get a ticket? It's much too late for that."

"Not if you tell them Dennis will chaperone us. Big Tee certainly has tickets to give away. I saw the promotion at his shop just yesterday."

• • •

They went together, a threesome joining the throng at Mulungushi Hall. Crazed women clad in hot pants and over-the-knee boots crashed against railings, climbed over each other yelling their devotion to the King of Soul. He slid onto the stage like it was coated in sunflower oil, and the girls grew even wilder. Elizabeth jumped and screamed, it was magic, watching the man from their bedroom posters come to life, twisting his waist, flicking his wet perm while he sang "Sex Machine."

But behind her back, she felt Dennis's long fingers swipe Chipo's, as though they'd been searching for something and then found it. They locked fingers while she screamed and sang, sang and screamed. She knew because she tried to push it to the back of her thoughts, but she stopped, and they were so wrapped up in each other's stares, neither of them noticed. She inched away, and they didn't even search for her. By the time they found her at home, Chipo mumbled a "Sorry," and Dennis came by with roses from his mother's garden the next morning.

· · ·

A plane flew low over the flats, rattling the windows. Elizabeth stared at her sister, and the sight of her made her tremble some more. She perched on the edge of the farthest seat determined to stay until she saw him, too. She wanted each of them to roll on the floor with an apology. Chipo sank into the couch sucking her delele, spitting fish bones.

"I know that you want to punish me, so I'll take it." She stopped eating suddenly. "Hit me."

Elizabeth shifted, feeling the corner of the cushion press against her thighs. When she wouldn't look at the cheek her sister offered, Chipo asked casually, "Have you had lunch?" She shook her head to decline the offer, but Chipo stood up to get a plate. After waiting in silence for a few long minutes, while she wondered what else to say, a key turned at the door, and Dennis walked in. "I'm hom—" He froze in the entrance, and Chipo smiled up at him.

"Lizzie has come to pay us a visit."

She needed to breathe. She stood up to part the curtains at the window. She watched the afternoon traffic move slowly, not quite sure what she wanted to achieve. Dennis clearly loved her sister, and he had proved it to the whole world, so why was she standing here?

"Why did you let me go through all of that? You stood there in church, and watched me humiliate myself when you both knew exactly what you wanted to do. Why didn't you just say something before?"

"You will never understand," Chipo said. Dennis was still quiet. "We didn't mean to hurt you, it's just—"

"Are you happy?"

He walked over to Chipo and sat down next to her. "Yes, we are."

"I gave him a million reasons to not love me, but he still did. He still does."

Watching them together was painful. It seared when he sat with his arm wrapped around Chipo's shoulders. Elizabeth wanted to be angry, but she saw Chipo, for the first time since the abortion, appear at peace. "They would never have agreed to us being together, even if we had said anything. Neither of us wanted to hurt you with the truth."

"And me? Was our relationship a lie?"

"I like you Lizzie, I really do. But I've always had an attraction to Chipo and everyone knows it, even you."

Had she? For as long as Chipo was her sister, the question of Chipo's feelings for Dennis had been like sugarcane nectar: difficult to extract. Chipo had had to be snapped at the joints, shred open and pressed, and she, Elizabeth, was the skin tossed out of a moving car, burned to ash along the side of the road.

Watching him hold her sister's hand and plead gently with his eyes,

Elizabeth hated what they'd done, and loved them still: her sweetie, her sugarcane.

Her parents did what had always been done: through their children, they planned their future in the hope for a better tomorrow. After the romance of Independence, politics had become personal, and the personal had become politics. Perhaps there was another place for her where anonymity could grant her a new beginning.

· · ·

Chilenje Township bustled around her. Buses honked. The warmth of frying chips and sausages wafted from red-and-white mobile restaurants marked "Big Tee's." Between the colorful awnings, bouquets of maize cobs sprung from tire rims. Gaggles of pedestrians drifted under the shade of arched jacaranda trees. Only when the sun lowered behind Lusaka's buildings, and dust no longer rose from the sidewalks, did she gather the courage to face him.

Big Tee leaned back in his armchair, surrounded by a team submitting their takings for the day. When he saw her, panic climbed to his face.

"Ba Pongozi."

She hoped it was hard for him to say those words.

"How can I help you?"

"I'm here to collect my due."

He laughed a little, and coughed into a lavender handkerchief.

"But what do you mean? I thought the issue was settled when we sent our people?"

"I want money. A lot of it."

He stood up and gestured for the workers to leave the room. "You must be mad if you think I'm some sort of Father Christmas."

"Give me twenty thousand kwacha or I tell my story to the *Times of Zambia*. How you actually believe in a multiparty state, how you funded the opposition, but want to hide behind my father to save your own skin."

At first, he looked ready to dismiss her, shuffling his papers and closing his books. Then he seemed to ponder the consequences. She jingled her car keys impatiently.

"Let's go outside, we cannot be seen here talking like this."

And so, they negotiated quietly in the dark garden.

"Little girl, fifteen thousand kwacha is the best I can do." She turned to walk away, but he called her back. "Twenty-five thousand kwacha if you promise we'll leave this matter behind once and for all." She stopped, and her heart leapt.

"How do I know you won't come back for more?"

"You don't."

. . .

The airport was busy. Capped captains and air hostesses flowed in bird formation; smart and smiling. A xylophone tinkled and a woman announcer called for a flight to Harare. Elizabeth sat on the edge of the emerald fountain with a copper antelope at its center, and remembered a story Father once told her. He'd said if she dropped a ngwee coin in the water, she'd be able to close her eyes and wish for anything she liked.

She remembered the State Lottery announcement the night she told Chipo how she felt about Dennis: "In every draw, there's always a winner." She listened to the bubbling from its jets and ran her hands through the lukewarm water, smiling at the enormity of what she was about to do. The exhilaration of a fresh start and a new life she could live on her own terms invigorated her. She tossed her gold wedding band into the air and watched it sink to the mosaic floor.

A suitcase bursting with brand-new clothes from Margot's bumped against her thigh; her heart against her cotton blouse. At the Booking Hall, she pulled out a stiff wad of kwachas from a manila envelope before she slid a Croxley pad to the lady at the desk. The lady removed a pen from the slit at her breast pocket. It had four colors to choose from—and after Elizabeth watched her deliberate on which to use, she pressed the red lever down. Elizabeth studied her as she scratched some words. She peered at a couple ahead of her, Zambia Airways tags waving goodbye from the handle on their cases.

"Return ticket?"

"One way."

"Destination?"

"Kingston, Nairobi, Accra—anywhere the weather shines, and the sun stays sweet."

Chiké Frankie Edozien

Krifé

STORY

As Akosua blew out the flickering flames of the thirty candles on the large lemon merengue cake her friends had organized, it seemed the entire dining room at Bistro 22 was applauding. All the waiters had trooped behind the one who brought the cake, singing their version of the "Happy Birthday" song.

> *Happy Birthday, to you, to you.*
> *Happy Birthday, to you, to you.*
> *Happy Birthday, Happy Birthday, Happy Birthday to you.*

They must have done this often. Without the need to learn the person's name, they just drummed and clapped and caused a happy stir. This was a warm night on a holiday weekend and the restaurant was filled with well-heeled and nattily dressed diners. It was the cream of the crop of Accra society here tonight, the folks who are often chronicled in the society blogs. At one corner sat the socialite daughter of the president of Ghana with the oil magnate she was rumored to be secretly married to. An ice bucket holding a chilled bottle of Taittinger was by their side.

Across the room was the handsome former Chelsea Football Club midfielder. Now retired, he still traveled with an entourage of excited women and fawning men. He held court at a round table for twelve. And not far from them was the superstar architect of the National Cathedral complex, who had once been given a knighthood by the British monarch. Sir and his Lady were dining together, giggling at each other and oblivious to the world around them. The *Vogue* editor who popped into town from London every so often was in another corner with a lover and some hip bespectacled and tattooed photographer types. All were chatting quietly but animatedly, and seemed like they were celebrating something. Maybe they had just completed a successful photo shoot in Accra.

But at the drumming and singing of "Happy Birthday" all the diners paused their chewing and sipping, and joined in. And as they were clapping, Akosua stood up and demurely clasped her hands above her breasts, smiling shyly, keeping her head down. Akosua turned to look at her best friend, Lizzie, and her smile got bigger. It was she who had really organized the dinner and it was sophisticated Lizzie who was now ordering crème brûlée for the gaggle of four ladies at their table.

Akosua had never celebrated birthdays before she met Lizzie. For the last four years, Lizzie had made a fuss about celebrating and this year was no exception. But this time it wasn't drinks at some pub somewhere. It was a high-heeled, slinky short dress, and expensive perfume kind of night. So much so that Akosua wondered if Lizzie had something else up her sleeve. Perhaps one of the diners here was a man she was soon to reel in? Akosua looked around the room. The men eating and drinking this Saturday night out were definitely all in Lizzie's target demographic. Rich and married. And at the moment, they were all being super attentive to the wives or women they were out with. Which one of them would end up at Lizzie's East Legon flat later? Which one of them,

Akosua wondered, would after dinner go home and say to his wife that he had some business emergency that had to be handled that Saturday night, only to end up frolicking at Lizzie's for hours on end?

Lizzie was beautiful in a classic way that a certain kind of Ghanaian man loved. And she knew it. Lizzie was tall, lithe, fair skinned with long hair. Hair imported from India that she had paid a good sum for. Tonight, Lizzie was ravishing in her form-fitting sundress bursting with yellow flowers. Her gold necklace shone bright, and the bold pendant that rested just between her full breasts dazzled. The way this woman squealed and radiated joy, one would think it was her own birthday. She oozed of jasmine. A fragrance that she had recently picked up from her new boss.

Many of these men here found her irresistible. And they never seemed to understand how calculating and cold Lizzie could be. How she could easily discard them once she'd had her fill. Lizzie could have any man she wanted at Bistro 22 tonight and their women would not be able to do anything about it. The only question was, which one?

Some of the wives smiled at her in a brief greeting. Giving her the kind of smile that ends at the lips, and is devoid of warmth. Some hissed and gave her a side-eye. Many didn't acknowledge her, even though their husbands looked, as Lizzie came in, and some of said husbands gave a quick hello. Many of these married women here tonight wanted to be like Lizzie, statuesque and sexy. And many more hated her for reasons they couldn't articulate. That she lived a life they wanted perhaps? Maybe it was that she took risks and was in control of her sexuality and her body. Maybe it was the idea that she could take their husbands and discard them so easily that irked the so-called Christian girls who hissed at her antics.

It wasn't that long ago after all, when the king of spare parts himself, Nana Dankwa, moved out of his marital home, leaving his wife and four children in pursuit of Lizzie. Nana Dankwa is also a pastor at the Synagogue church and lives the life of a beneficiary of the prosperity gospel. Well, the rumor was that after he moved into a house in Cantonments, Lizzie declined to move in. Lizzie supposedly told some of her pals something about how happy she was to be a guest star in Pastor Nana's world, but not a series regular. And just like that, she broke it off with him. Pastor Nana has since moved back in with his wife and kids. And everyone at the Synagogue pretends like nothing extraordinary happened.

It was these same wives who routinely tried, unsuccessfully, to shame Lizzie. They deemed her skirts were too short and her face too painted.

Ghana has been this way forever. Men like adventurous, sexy women to frolic with, but want to marry only religious, pious-presenting women. Some of these women had played the game in their dating days and had gotten the husband, but were now trapped in forced piousness as "married women." It seemed grating that their hard-fought-for husbands were smitten by the likes of the sexually adventurous Lizzie, who didn't seem to care about getting married. Lizzie wasn't even a husband snatcher. When she wanted someone, she got him. She often said, "A wife is not a mountain." Lizzie then discarded the men once she'd had enough. She was free and they resented her for it.

• • •

Once upon a time, Akosua herself had been one of those women. A judgmental hater. When she and Lizzie first roomed together at the Kwame Nkrumah University of Science and Technology in Kumasi, she was a different person. Today, Akosua barely recognized that version of herself.

Back then, she had been one of those Bible-thumping virgins who was saving it all for marriage. Marriage to a man whom her church elders had introduced her to and approved of. A good man. A kind man. A God-fearing man she would make a family with. Akosua never really had a family of her own. Sure, there were the aunts who came to take her from the Motherless Babies' Home when she aged out, but they dumped her on some church elders and rarely checked in on her. She was born of sin, as far as they were concerned, and then abandoned. No one adopted her.

Akosua never knew her parents, and she went from one church elder's house to another, going to school and performing domestic work in each home. She remembers a clutch of women, aunts or maybe a grandmother, who visited her once and looked at her with pity. If only her parents had not been sinners who brought shame on them. That's all she remembered. Fragments of a conversation about her mother, a child herself but "grown enough to bring shame" and who then disappeared.

For most of her teens, she was essentially a house girl who was paid primarily in clothes and meals and shelter. She still doesn't even know when her real birthday falls and so her age is a guestimate. She could be thirty, the age of her schoolmates, or she could be twenty-seven. It was anyone's guess. But she remembered a primary school teacher registering her for junior high school on a very hot Monday and writing the nation's birthday as hers, since he had no records. "When we celebrate Mother Ghana, we will sing 'Happy Birthday' for you, too," Mr. Frimpong said. He said, like her classmates, she would be twelve years old. That was how March 6, Ghana's Independence Day, became her answer whenever she had to write down a date of birth on a form.

As a teenager, all she did was study the Bible and focus on her class-work. Her only ambitions were to go to school and find a good Christian husband. The kind of man that came to church with his wife and sat up front. The kind of man that made his wife look to sit under the ceiling fans in church so her husband stayed cool. The kind of man who boldly stood up to give his offerings and tithes each week without fail. Careers were dreams for others, those kids who had parents. All she ever wanted was to be in a home where she wasn't the house girl. She couldn't wait to be a madam. She wanted the husband who went out and worked to provide for her and their children. The church guardians would have found someone sooner, but she got admitted to university and so they let her attend. It wasn't like there were suitors lining up for her, as there were for the other young women in church.

But it wasn't too long after when Nana Osei, a member she had not really noticed at services, began talking to her after worship. He was nice, into computers, and had big dreams. He came from a family of fisherfolk and had grown up on the shores of Lake Bosomtwe. He was short with a big head of hair. The church elders approved of the match as he was a good man, a working man who was ready to settle down.

Fellow congregants told Akosua she had hit the jackpot to have a man like that interested in courting her. Yet it seemed to her that no one who said that was actually envious. He wasn't the type to make any of them swoon. But the elders said he had prospects.

When they started spending time together, Nana Osei and Akosua just talked and read the Good Book together. On weekends, she cooked for him. Meals that lasted him all week. She packed the food in plastic containers and put them in his fridge, which had very little in it. Her time as a house girl had honed her cooking skills. The first time she spent alone time with him in his home, she brought ingredients with her and made palm nut soup with cassava and plantain fufu for him. Nana Osei kept licking his fingers and praising God. She laughed and he smiled more. He told her then and there that they were meant to be, that she was his gift from God. One Sunday in church, after praying for a wife, he looked up and she was the first person he saw. It was a sign, he said, as was her delicious fufu.

She liked that he listened to her, but mostly Akosua imagined what her life with him would be. She could see his vision for the future and bought into it wholeheartedly. Akosua believed she would be a good wife for him. Nana Osei liked that she was plump. He loved that she wore her hair short or plaited, and that she adorned her dark round face only with shea butter. Nana Osei called her a "natural beauty." No one had ever associated her with beauty. She believed that he meant it, and also that he was going to be quite prosperous one day. After all, his name was also Prosper.

Maybe he would even propose before she finished school, and she wondered if she would even need to complete her degree once he did. What would be the point of finishing school, if she was to be married?

After her first year at KNUST, she had to move into off-campus housing. There was no guaranteed housing for second-year students, as there was for first-years. Akosua opted for the cheapest place she could find in Ayeduase, just outside the university grounds and where all the hostels were. It was still too expensive, and she couldn't ask the church elders for any more funds at this stage. The old men had made it clear they owed her nothing and, if she was married, she would not be their problem anymore. So, while they gave her allowance for school, it was tough for her to ask for more than they gave. Which was the barest minimum. She would need roommates with a similar budget. As the semester was coming to an end, and quite out of the blue, Lizzie announced that they would continue living together as she didn't want to get a new roommate or live alone. Lizzie liked her company and didn't want the hassle of new people.

Akosua had mainly been quiet about her roomie's short skirts and painted lips, but she disapproved, like all the other Christian "year one" girls. She once invited Lizzie to Bible study but after Lizzie laughed so hard, she didn't bother anymore. "People are judgy, and you are, too," Lizzie told her one evening after accepting Akosua's invitation to eat some rice and stew she had prepared. "But you don't say much and are very quiet. Plus, you can cook!"

Akosua laughed. She did judge her roommate, but she still found her warm and neat. When they moved in together off-campus, she found that Lizzie had so much more money that she handled the rent and took only what Akosua could afford. Akosua had been so busy with her studies that she never paid much attention to Lizzie's spending before. But now, Lizzie often didn't even bother to take Akosua's share of the rent. They ended up living together without other roommates, which was a rarity. Lizzie laughed at the idea of the fiancé Akosua was so proud of. One who didn't touch her, and hadn't yet bought a ring, but who needed Akosua's cooking every week. When Nana Osei got a scholarship to go to London for graduate school, Lizzie just smiled and declared: "You're free now."

Akosua thought of "freedom" and asked herself, *What does it even mean anyway?* Lizzie had had options in her life, parents, friends. And now Lizzie had Ashanti men who gave her things just because she pouted.

Their lives couldn't have been more different growing up. Akosua had grown up tolerated. She knew that ultimately a good marriage would be the key to her success in life. And after all the suffering of her youth, God had smiled on her and sent her Nana Osei. The man who promised that from afar he would look after her and that, in three years, they would be man and wife.

As soon as he was settled in London, he did. Each month, they FaceTimed and then he sent her funds to her mobile money account for her upkeep. Nana Osei was a very frugal person, and that didn't change, but the money he sent came regularly.

Akosua studied hard but, to indulge Lizzie, and also quell her boredom, she began accompanying her friend to places in Kumasi she'd never been before or even knew existed. Lizzie always seemed to be happy, carefree, and unbothered. "Come and hang out for once," she would say. "All this praying, you'll probably still go to heaven if you came out with me."

So, she did go out with her. Akosua enjoyed watching as men sent them cocktails and fell over themselves for her roomie. She knew nothing about alcohol but, to fit in, she would ask for a virgin piña colada.

Soon, she began to emulate Lizzie in all things. It started with Lizzie lending her a small clutch with matching low heels the first time they went out. The next time, it was a dress that seemed demure but clung to her body as she moved.

Then she went on a run, and later to the gym with her. And slowly the evening sprints and gym sessions replaced Akosua's Bible study groups. And some of her Nana Osei allowance went to things that Lizzie helped her pick out, like new not-so-sensible shoes, ones with small heels. Then she began to buy more dresses and skirts. Akosua started to use imported apricot face scrubs and she got to experience her first manicures and pedicures. A truly luxurious indulgence that her friends in Revelation Mountain Church would disapprove of. It would never even cross their minds. Lizzie encouraged her to wear makeup on their nights out.

"Just let me put a little eye shadow on you and let's go. Don't be too Krifé tonight," she would say, mocking what she called Akosua's severe Christian faith practices. Practices that began to wane as their undergrad years went on.

It started slowly, and as Lizzie took Akosua everywhere she went, Akosua's skirts got shorter, and her dresses got tighter. She started routinely working out, the pounds dropped, and a svelte figure emerged. One that was accentuated by a pair of skinny jeans Lizzie gave her when she returned from Dubai.

As these small changes happened, Akosua was moving from side-kick to equally desirable babe for a certain kind of generous man. With Akosua's hair braided long, and her body skinnier, and her heels higher, and her firm breasts out, the sophisticates who fawned over Lizzie and showered her with gifts began to notice her, too.

Her plump self. The one with the short hair and downcast eyes that oozed modesty. The self that was marriage material in her church and village circle had disappeared.

Akosua knew Nana Osei loved the old version of her, so during their video calls she always wore head ties and no makeup. He often railed against how the African women he attended school with in the United Kingdom were all painted ladies and didn't go to church. How he would have befriended them if they were not so in the ways of the flesh. How he missed her and her fear of God.

Akosua studied and passed her exams in tourism and culture, but her dream to end up as Nana Osei's wife was evolving. What if she got an opportunity to manage hotels? What if she could travel all over the world like Lizzie had?

She realized that Lizzie used her as a security blanket when they were out with her high-end friends, but Akosua couldn't figure out why. Lizzie was worldly. She'd been to London and Cape Town, not just the Arab Emirates. She capitalized on her looks and wasn't shy about taking whatever was offered to her. She barely looked at folks on campus. Her "dating" life was on a whole other level. She was an okay student, but she didn't spend more time on things than she needed to. She never went to French class, but always got As. It turned out she had picked enough of it up on her forays to Geneva.

Akosua realized her life was changed forever when Lizzie asked her to go away with her and some friends for some beach time. "You'll be able to show off your nice body in a bikini." Akosua had never even been on a plane at this point in her young life, so an all-expense paid weekend trip was tough to resist.

On the plane she could barely control her excitement and kept taking selfies as the plane rose up into the clouds. When they landed, two men, both American, picked them up. The men said they worked in "oil and gas," and all four were to join some more friends for a weekend of laughter and frivolity at the Blue Moon private island, a luxury resort almost two hours' drive from the Takoradi Airport and very near to Axim. They stayed in an elegant villa with stunning views of the private bay and sea and with a gigantic heart-shaped pool. Akosua had never seen or experienced anything so luxurious and was wide-eyed the whole time. Even the fresh air felt opulent. All this was here in the Ghana she had lived in her whole life, and she never knew of it.

Lizzie was at home in this crowd and in this environment. Akosua met the two other ladies and two other guys on the trip with them once they got to the resort. The man in charge was Lizzie's "date" and benefactor, it appeared. He had organized the break. It was a weekend filled with decadent meals, boat trips on the ocean, pool parties at the villa, and massages in between. The women danced in their bikinis and the men admired them, chomped on cigars and talked business. One of the American men, Ben, took an immediate liking to Akosua and, with trepidation but serious encouragement from Lizzie, she agreed to go to his room after dinner that first night.

"He could be your ticket to this life. Don't be difficult and get all 'krifé' on him," Lizzie warned her as they downed even more champagne.

Ben, the muscular engineer, was soft-spoken and had showered her with compliments since they arrived. He was even more charming when they were alone. Ben shared more bubbly with Akosua, and she kept sipping from the tall glass that everyone called a flute. She kept trying to be as classy as Lizzie and act like she belonged. Before long, she and Ben had clambered onto the king-size bed.

She didn't always understand him—his accent and the champagne kept her wondering if she was hearing him right—but she looked up at him wide-eyed and pretended she did. She pretended he was fascinating while her mind thought about how wonderful the room was. She lost herself in the fluffy pillows and soft sheets and thought it was probably the nicest bed she had ever been in. Akosua wondered what it would be like to have a bed this large and this comfortable to sleep in all day. She wondered what she would do with all the pillows if she did indeed have a bed like this. This is what Lizzie meant by the "suite life."

The moonlight softly lit the entire place, and she could see clearly even though the room's lights were off. Akosua could hear the waves crashing down on the beach below. Once Ben began to caress her, all she felt were sensations shooting up all over her. She seemed to feel his hands and fingers everywhere and found herself moaning when his tongue found her nipple.

"Ssssh, just relax," Ben whispered as he pulled her closer, his muscular arms enveloping her, his whole body now on top of hers. There was something about his scent that was intoxicating, that coupled with his accent and the way he slowly gave her instructions made her just submit to him.

She did as he told her to, raising her arms, spreading her legs, opening her mouth. All she felt were electric sensations when he touched her. She had never felt that good from a touch.

It was only when Ben rolled over after emptying himself into her that they noticed the line of a crimson stain on the sheets, and he realized just how new she was to womanhood. He had broken her hymen. Ben, who had been in Ghana for just a few months, then took a tender approach to her all weekend and allowed her to cling to him like Gorilla Glue. The days went by quickly, and before the end of the long weekend he nonchalantly mentioned his kids and his woman back in Louisiana.

Akosua returned to Kumasi a woman, walking on air. She'd left a naive college girl on an adventure. She felt no unease about Ben's marital status, just a huge desire to see him again and again. To feel him on that large fluffy bed again and again. To have his tongue make her go crazy, and his sizable manhood inside her again. To be taken care of by him. Her "thank you for coming" envelope from Ben was more money than she'd ever had before. He promised to stay in touch but warned that life on the oil rigs gave him limited opportunity to have weekend breaks.

Lizzie laughed at the prospect of Akosua falling for him. "There are many more engineers in the sea," she said. "Keep his number. He will call again and maybe next time we will all go to Dubai, but don't wait for him to call. He might not." Akosua's heart sank. And so it began. With Lizzie's tutelage, Akosua said the right things and provided excellent company to a certain kind of businessman who passed through Kumasi. The men provided fun weekends out and generously thanked her for the pleasure of her company. And her body. Akosua learned from her friend about birth control and safer sex practices, and she realized how little of the world she actually knew.

Slowly, Akosua disengaged from her former life while creating a well of savings for her future. After graduation, with the connection of one of the men in her rotation, she secured a spot at the reservations desk of the Golden Tulip Hotel Kumasi and she did her mandatory National Service there. Lizzie relocated to Accra to do her service year. Akosua had wanted to break up with Nana Osei, but had learned from Lizzie to keep her options open—and the allowance coming—so each week she took his calls, updated him like all was well, even prayed with him. Like clockwork, he sent her monthly allowance. Of course, when he returned, she went over to his place and broke up with him citing the need for a career and not wanting to rush things.

Nana Osei looked good from his years in the United Kingdom, but he was still the same devout churchgoing fisherman who'd left Kumasi. He came back with an advanced degree and a nicer haircut. But he was still the same. A traditional Ashanti man in all senses. His patriarchy was on display. What would she need a career for if he was ready to marry her, he wondered. He was also confused and broken by the Akosua he found. In the years he'd been abroad, he had fallen even harder for her, or at least for the version of her that he knew. Nana Osei fumed about what had happened to her: her transformation from a girl who loved Bible study, cooking, worshipping, and hoping to start a godly family with him to a wannabe slay queen. Just like those African girls in London who lived for makeup and passing men around.

Akosua knew it wouldn't work with Nana Osei, who wondered incredulously how on earth she had become a painted lady with little modesty. When did she start wearing heels? Why did she have two mobile phones? And why did he have only one of the numbers? He hurled so many questions her way, but she kept her cool and never got agitated.

Even though she was a changed woman, Nana Osei was willing to make things work. He still wanted Akosua to move in with him and for them to get married while he set up his technology business. He still saw her as a good woman. One who had just gone wayward because he had been gone so long. But once Akosua wrapped up her National Service, she relocated to Accra and cut off ties with Nana Osei and everyone else in her church. Finally, she was in control of her life.

Lizzie was happy to have her in town and they picked up where they left off. Akosua got work as a front desk associate at one of those boutique hotels that expatriate businessmen love in Osu, Accra's pricey and noshing district. The rest of the time she ran with Lizzie's slay queen posse. She was popular with Lizzie's businessman circle because she never had a business plan or project to push. She was just "Akosua" and there for the fun. So far, she was loving Accra. There were weekend trips to other places she'd otherwise never have gone to.

One weekend, she could be dancing up a storm with Lizzie and others during one of the nighttime jam sessions at the exclusive Sandbox Beach Club. The next, they would be sailing on the Volta Lake and chilling out in a bungalow at the Royal Senchi resort in Akosombo. On another she could be found paragliding over the Odweanoma Mountains and then relaxing poolside at the Rock City resort in Kwahu.

Her bikini collection was growing, as was her collection of lingerie from Victoria's Secret. Soon enough, just as Lizzie predicted, they were invited on weekend jaunts to Dubai, where they shopped. They were invited to London, where they shopped more. They were invited to Lisbon, to Marbella, and to Luanda. On each trip they provided their good company to benefactors busy inking oil deals during the day. Ben, the engineer whom Akosua had pined for after losing her virginity to him, was a distant memory. Nana Osei, whom she once hoped to marry, never even crossed her mind anymore.

For Lizzie, providing a girlfriend experience was something she had made work for her, and Akosua was not only reveling in it but taking notes. She realized that Lizzie's "it" factor wasn't something that came as naturally to her as it did to Lizzie. Akosua had to work at looking great and being super easygoing. But what she no longer wanted right now was to be someone's wife and someone's mother.

Soon, she thought. Just not yet. After she had set up her own concierge traveling service, she could get married. Lizzie agreed that Akosua could have organized some of the trips they had taken, just as well as any other travel agent. So they set about to come up with a small travel concierge consultancy in Ghana.

Lizzie, who had all the wealthy admirers, would casually mention that "Akosua's company can organize a long weekend for us in Lagos or Abidjan," and it would manifest. Lizzie began to think of cultivating a small select stable of girls who could come along and provide company if there were a few more men than she and Akosua could handle. When the money came, they split it all down the middle.

• • •

After Akosua's birthday dinner at Bistro 22, Lizzie disappeared, leaving the gaggle of girls to continue celebrating while she reeled in a big fish. It turned out just as Akosua suspected. An expatriate beer manufacturer ditched his date—his wife, really—for the evening and ended up with Lizzie for the rest of the night and into the early morning. "We were talking Bitcoin" was all Lizzie would say the next day. The relative success of their little travel business had given both Lizzie and Akosua ideas about their future. Akosua knew she was not as desirable as Lizzie, so her own shelf life giving the girlfriend experience to wealthy men would be shorter than Lizzie's. Akosua had always felt she was just not as pretty. Her skin didn't glimmer like Lizzie's always did, and she didn't have half of Lizzie's femininity, which made every man swoon. And she was okay with that.

She wanted to grow the business, yes—being a concierge travel expert who owned her own business was far more desirable than going up the ranks in the hotel she worked in now—but she began to think seriously about reeling in a wealthy man as a husband. Once, she had dreamed of being a reservations manager. Now she had seen a bit of the world and would gladly stay where she was with the right husband.

Lizzie had other ideas. She wanted to be a mogul. She was seriously fangirling her new boss. In all these years, Lizzie had a blasé attitude about everyone and everything. Until now.

She had, for some time now, been working with a Nigerian business-woman peddling high-end sex toys to Ghana's fetish obsessed. Everyone seemed to be a prayer warrior in Accra, but behind closed doors, people were freaky. Her boss satisfied those cravings at a steep price. Akosua had seen the price tags of some of those CynthiaJele boxes that came wrapped like jewels. They were big boy toys.

"I've been talking to Amina about you. I think you can be a new brand ambassador for the CynthiaJele line."

Lizzie explained that her boss, Amina, was very private, and that very few knew of the line because it was so expensive and for men with discretion. And big wallets. "You could make so much more money just by being a rep here. She's conquered the Nigerian elite and the wealthy Ghanaians are salivating over the fact that she is spending more time here."

Lizzie told her of a luxury cruise Amina was planning on the Ankobra River in a couple of months. Amina and her brand ambassadors would unveil new products that her high-end customers could sample and play with. The trip would be on Amina with food and beverage covered, but the customers would buy and buy. This would be a chance for Akosua, Lizzie said, to lock in a profitable cruise, and maybe snag that husband she'd been going on about of late. Akosua nodded as Lizzie told her that Amina had been spotted several times at dinner at the Gonja Kitchen, the most expensive and exclusive restaurant in Ghana. Tables there were booked months in advance and the place never seemed to have a lull. Even getting a reservation for lunch was tough.

Lizzie had already secured an invitation to Amina's Airport Hills home for an interview. Apparently, Amina had already looked her up and the interview would not be conventional. Amina would be hosting an exclusive soiree by her pool. Cocktails, dinner, and drinks would be followed by a screening of a new Netflix film produced and directed by the Nigerian wunderkind Makuochi.

The movie's director would be on hand to mingle with the select few who could finance the next Makuochi production and raise the profile of the film in Ghana. Makuochi had already given hints that he would love to shoot a film in Ghana, so this would be a good opportunity for him to meet some financiers. But in the end, it would be a party, and Amina would be able to watch and see how Akosua conversed and dressed and mingled with the crème de la crème of Accra society: the potbellied moneymen and the dainty madams dripping in diamonds who formed the base of her clientele. And then they would take it from there. It was Thursday, and Lizzie was just dropping this on her now. "She just finally asked to see you," Lizzie explained. "This is your chance. Win Amina over, and you could be an ambassador. Besides the money, she opens doors, so let's make this happen."

Akosua was ready. She would get a mani-pedi and a facial, bring out one of the minidresses she bought in Dubai, and throw on her special occasion Manolo Blahnik heels for Saturday. She knew she needed to glam it up, but not so much that she upstaged anyone. Lizzie would do her makeup, and they would go together like they belonged. She needed to land the gig. And to meet Makuochi.

The man used just one name. The blogs always showed pictures of him with a neatly trimmed beard and wide smile, and depicted him as fit as a fiddle. He was young, sexy, and photogenic. A filmmaker with an upward-trending profile and movie star looks. Maybe she could show him Accra. She could even take him to some hidden beaches past Kokrobite where the monied went surfing. She knew from his Instagram posts that he had a thing for the beach and open-water swimming. Maybe she could show him other places, too. They could take an afternoon to see the baboon families in the Shai Hills. She could show him an even better time than he expected in Ghana. From her experience, Nigerians were not that hard to please.

Fortunately, Makuochi wasn't married so Lizzie probably wouldn't have her eye on him, except maybe to party and take pictures for her Instagram followers. And if Makuochi was involved with someone— well, that was just an obstacle she would have to climb over. Akosua smiled and thought, *What if I aced Amina's test and left that party with not just a job, but a cute Nigerian boyfriend?* Yes, that would be her goal for the weekend.

• • •

From the outside there was nothing remarkable about the Airport Hills home they were going into. But once Akosua and Lizzie got past the gun-toting guards, it was breathtaking. The huge brown gate opened up to a wide driveway shaded by large trees on each side. As the guards directed Lizzie to where she could park, Akosua gasped.

Akosua knew houses in this estate were nice, but this was something special. There were flowers and towering hedges everywhere, and a large villa-style main house in the distance. Meandering stone paths in the middle of well-tended lawns led to even more artfully crafted hedges that shielded a gigantic oval swimming pool from view. They were led around the corner and followed the music coming from one end of the large pool with deep blue tiles to find a full bar at the end. At one corner, a group of about ten musicians, the Chorkor Symphony Orchestra, was playing Ghanaian highlife music with classical instruments.

Hunky muscled waiters and reed-thin waitresses were passing out avocado and salmon hors d'oeuvres. There was already a large pavilion screen set up at one end of the garden to show the film once the time was right. They had been told to arrive early, and they had, but others were already on hand. Lizzie pointed out several starry-eyed, very conservative members of Parliament. She winked at two in particular who were always in the news for opposing Ghana's LGBTQ population and women they considered immoral. Lizzie told Akosua they were good clients of Amina's. They were the morality police in public, but privately they engaged in all manner of sex play. They all seemed to be equally gobsmacked at the opulence of the topiary. Lizzie spotted a tall guy in a white kaftan, took Akosua straight to the hunk and excitedly air-kissed with the man, whom she introduced as "Abba."

"This is the chef and mastermind behind the Gonja Kitchen," Lizzie said. Abba gave Akosua the once-over and winked at her. "Nice Blahniks," he said with a big smile.

Soon, more people were coming in. Ambassadors, tech industry folk, and the like. Akosua and Lizzie mingled, smiling and relaxed. The bubbly was flowing.

Then Akosua spotted Makuochi and made a beeline for him. She introduced herself and they got to talking. He was a bit shy but genuinely interesting and receptive to her flirtations. He asked her why she wasn't an actress, and said he'd be happy if she could show him around Ghana. Lizzie found them, and he asked her where she'd been hiding Akosua. They exchanged cards, and Makuochi confessed he wasn't good at public speaking but that their hosts had told him it would be an easy crowd. "That reminds me, I promised I would make a proper Nigerian Chapman for them. Come with me, please."

They made their way to the pool bar, where he moved past the bartender on duty, grabbed two jugs, and mixed the drinks. He measured the Angostura bitters, the grenadine, and the lemon juices as intently as he did the Fanta and Sprite. Then he finished them off with large slices of cucumber. "I'm a bartender in my spare time," he said to Akosua as she flashed him a genuine smile.

Makuochi was more beautiful in person than in any image on social media. No photo out there did him justice. Makuochi also had no airs about him for someone who was a major deal in film and the guest of honor at this shindig. Akosua liked this guy and no matter how long it took she would end up with him, she thought.

Makuochi grabbed a tray in one hand and took the finished drinks and Akosua to a corner hedge where a small cluster of folks were chatting.

Akosua felt great. She could already envision herself as Makuochi's lady and one day his wife. She was comfortable with him, which was hard for her to fathom since she had just met him, but he could definitely be *the* one.

"Prosper. Your Chapman is here," Makuochi bellowed when they reached the group of men. Prosper turned around and grabbed it. As he said thanks, his eyes locked with Akosua's.

They both stared at each other. Speechless. Akosua couldn't believe she was seeing Nana Osei. It had been a few years. He looked the same and yet he looked so different, and utterly amazing. His skin shone bright. His hair was neatly trimmed, as was his mustache. He was trim in his designer clothes. He'd even had a manicure. He seemed so at ease. This Nana Osei who looked back at her was sophisticated and sporting a gold Cartier watch. And this was his home? What had happened? What was he doing here in Accra? In this mansion?

"You two know each other?" Makuochi asked.

"Yes," Akosua mumbled. "We dated when I was in the university."

Prosper found his tongue and added, "It seems like a million years ago, but we were actually engaged." He looked at her intently for a bit and then back at Makuochi, before settling his eyes on her again. "You look well."

Just then, Lizzie appeared with a very stunning lady sporting matching diamond earrings and a choker. She wore a flowery sleeveless sundress and a big smile. Her Louboutins clacked on the stone pathway, and her jasmine scent punctured the awkwardness. Makuochi handed her a Chapman and give her a kiss on both cheeks. Amina smiled at Akosua and said, "Lizzie has told me so much about you. I'm happy to meet you. And I see you've met my husband."

Makuochi, with a twinkle in his eye, jumped in with, "They used to be engaged!"

Prosper slid his hands into his wife's and whispered something into Amina's ears. She smiled warmly.

"Thanks so much for having me," Akosua mumbled, feeling even more ill at ease. She was totally intimidated and yet captivated by Amina. "Your home is exquisite," she said.

"Oh, it's all Prosper's doing," Amina responded. "We were happy living in Nigeria, but he had to come home to Ghana so here we are." Amina then asked—well, really, told—Akosua: "Go mingle." She wanted her to meet some of the other guests before the dinner was served and the film screened.

Akosua wanted the ground to open up and swallow her. She had just been sweetly dismissed by the woman she meant to impress. She knew mingling was to be part of the interview, yet she didn't really want to move. It seemed Prosper, Amina, Makuochi, and even Lizzie were just staring at her as she turned and slowly walked away trying to look and feel confident. Any confidence she had was now shattered. Makuochi told her he'd catch up with her, but he remained with his hosts. As she turned and went to go mingle, she looked around at all the elegant, high-powered, and wealthy guests who had come to pay homage to Amina . . . and Nana Osei.

She looked at the immaculate surroundings and admired the care taken with the simple things, like the place settings on the poolside dinner table. Akosua wondered what might have been if she had never let Nana Osei go. She could be sitting on tech millions with him.

Akosua grabbed a champagne-filled flute from a hunky waiter in a muscle T-shirt and downed it all at once.

She wondered to herself, *What if I could get him back? What if I could have this life with him? After all, Lizzie always said, "A wife is not a mountain."*

Dami Ajayi

Queens

(after Patrice)

To the Queens of my nickel days,
days blurred by memory's stain.

To the Queens of my jackal days,
days landscaped by sepia dreams.

To the Queens of my Lagos nights,
days pierced by shrilly brass & fast cars.

To the Queens of my liminal nights,
Nairobi nights, Cologne nights, Delhi nights.

Nights restive in their nocturnal shifting,
nights that spill into crayon dawns.

To the Queens of my London days,
days edged like a bet,

RELATIONS

days of intense feelings & scarred healings,
days interrupted by squeaky train announcements,

days trembling from denouement,
days hoisted like a painter's easel,

days notched by uncertainties,
days weighted with misery's dram,

days seasoned with searing pain,
days salted with sodium & absinthe,

days beaten by monkey wedding drizzle,
days welded with grief & duty,

days watered with wine & whining,
days stretched thin with longing,

days of microwaved lunches,
days of absent queens & promises,

let love songs pour out of radios &
let lonesome poets sing the karaoke of memories past,

audit love songs for love,
audit love songs for soothing words.

Sleeping Beauty (of Borehamwood)

Be grateful
when your lover's afternoon snores
segues with Ali & Toumani's guitar strings.

This morning we fought
a small war over toilet rolls
at a Tesco till, our affection
smoldering out of what we have
chosen not to call ourselves.

When the sun sets
you will take your beauty
& a supply of essentials,
out of my grasp
away into the waiting hands
of uncertainty, COVID-19 & a fast train.

Waterstones

& when the minstrel's wails filter
into the alcove of your dreams,
listen for the words beneath the wail:

it says, don't close your ears
to the gentle strum of tides,
aiding and abetting destiny.

When chance wheels itself in,

do not reach for scales,

statistics, fantasies or traumatic pasts,

reach inward,

      for dove gentleness

& sit out the gale outside Waterstones.

Ode to a Discarded Face Mask

Dark, like my skin

not black, call it beige or brown,

but for its rumpled form

it could have been beautiful.

How lonely it must be,

velvet brown,

to journey from a cotton farm,

spin through textile machines,

be woven into fabric,

manhandled by a tailor

for this fate of abandonment.

Your fate reminds me of breath

& George Floyd lying on asphalt,

an American knee weighing

against his neck.

Perhaps this was the notion

that spurred your principal

to tug at your fine velvet
in a survival haste for air hunger.

Nothing is promised,
your immaculate cut,
exquisite stitching,
delicate embroidery
did not promise the warmth
of exhaled air.

The future is grim & tragic
lying on the concrete's skin
to be trampled upon by the
insouciant wayfarer.

Nothing is promised,
not even the grip of the
litter picker.

Denouement

(after Derek Walcott)

A time will come
when, with a sigh,
you shall exhale.

That evening,
the gloomy weather may persist

RELATIONS

the world brimming with COVID disease,
but your heart will rid itself of grief,
fluttering pigeons & embrace ease.

Then you shall raise a glass of wine
to your portrait in the gilded mirror,
your favorite songs streaming,
supper stewing on an electric stove

& suddenly your solitude
will be tolerable,
enjoyable, even

Reem Gaafar

Finding Descartes

STORY

Ustaz Awad marched briskly down the road toward the school gates, kicking up dust and pebbles as he walked under the bright morning sunshine. Boys of various ages and stages of shabbiness scurried hurriedly behind, around, and in front of him to reach the building before the morning bell rang. They scuffled at the gate to get in, their backpacks torn and sewn together several times, some of them clutching their lunches in plastic bags, and not a few dragging along a chair. Some boys wore sweaters, others had layered shirts, but most wore only their discolored school shirts with little to protect them from the biting winter air. It was probably a blessing that the sun shone just as fiercely throughout the year, warming the thin bodies hurrying along under its rays.

Ustaz Awad looked at his watch as he stepped into the schoolyard that morning: eight more minutes to the bell. Gadir—the retired *saul* employed by the school to man the gates and whip the children—was perched on a three-legged plastic chair by the gate, dressed in his faded dark green army fatigues, whip resting on his lap, his long legs crossed in front of him just in the way to trip the children up. He was also looking down at his watch, getting ready to shut the gates when the bell rang.

171

Often, he slammed the gates closed a minute early just to hoard as many children outside as possible for whipping.

Ustaz Awad started to loiter by the gate to keep an eye on the old *saul* and make sure he kept the gates open right up until the bell rang, but the cluster of teachers next to the principal's office huddled in deep conversation yanked his attention. Ustaz Awad knew exactly what they were talking about, and after a moment's hesitation decided that today the children would have to fend for themselves at the gate. He strode across the yard toward the teachers.

". . . can't ignore us forever, can he?"

"And what if he agrees to talk to us? What else does he have to say that we don't already know?"

"He can at least give us the dignity of an answer instead of hiding away from us in this pathetic manner. He's the principal!"

"You know what he's like. He's nothing but a coward." Sit Amna, the Arabic teacher, noticed Ustaz. "Hey, Awad, how's your leg?"

Ustaz Awad had tripped and fallen a few days ago and twisted his ankle but had insisted on coming to school after staying at home for two days, ignoring the doctor's advice to rest. He lived alone, with nothing but pictures of his dead family to keep him company, having firmly resisted the best efforts of his mostly distant relatives to marry him off to an underage cousin he had never even met before. The only thing his life revolved around was teaching his students. But even that was now at the threat of being lost.

"Much better, thank you. Has there been any news at all?" he asked Sit Amna.

"Nothing," she replied, her look of disgust amplified by her jet-black, unequally drawn eyebrows. "That man won't even open his office door anymore. I say we raise a complaint to the ministry."

"The ministry *is* the problem," snorted Ustaz Kamal, a teacher of religion and science. The other teachers murmured their agreement. The ministry had been steadily downsizing expenditure, and now even the teachers' pathetic salaries had stopped. They hadn't been paid in three months, and things were getting desperate.

"My wife had to sell another gold bracelet yesterday just so we could pay for that damned electricity and get to our jobs." This bitter statement was from Ustaz Jad Alradi, a short, gray-whiskered man balancing his books and whip under his arm. His subject was geography. Sit Amna frowned and clicked her tongue at this news.

"There must be something we can do," Ustaz Awad ventured meekly. "Maybe we should write a letter? To the ministry?"

"You mean write *another* letter?" growled Ustaz Elsheikh, the English teacher. "We've already written three letters, and no one has replied. What are they going to say anyway that we don't know? 'Sorry, but at this time our defense budget is so swollen it's eaten up all the other budgets and so no money for your salaries'? We were desperate for a raise to start with, now we just want our stupid eight hundred pounds again. We're going to starve!"

More murmurs of assent from the teachers.

"Maybe they'll respond differently this time after those protestors burnt down the NCP building in Atbara. And there are protests picking up all over the place," Ustaz Kamal said hopefully.

"I say we should go back to charging the students."

Ustaz Awad looked in alarm at Ustaz Jad Alradi, who had voiced an opinion that had been on the teachers' minds for a while now.

"Either that," he said, "or we go on strike."

"How can we charge them anything more? They already pay for the utilities and exam paper printing and registration. Their families are even worse off than we are!"

"Strike sounds good to me. But it would be useless if it was just us.

We need to organize a mass protest or something. All the teachers in the locality!"

"There's that new Sudanese Professionals Association movement, they're marching to the Republican Palace on December twenty-fifth to demand minimum wage. We could join them."

"That's what they were protesting initially," Sit Amna corrected Ustaz Kamal, "but now they're marching to bring down the government. An even better reason to join them in my opinion!"

"It won't cost the students much more than what they already pay. About two or three pounds per child. You're the math expert, you add it up," Ustaz Jad Alradi continued, ignoring the interruption.

Ustaz Awad was flabbergasted. A couple of small boys ran past them to their classes, laughing. Both had torn trousers and were carrying a few tattered exercise books tied up with bits of string. One of them tripped and fell, got up almost immediately and tottered off after his friend. The teachers all saw the familiar fungal bald patches on the back of his receding bony head.

"They don't have two or three pounds to pay. It's bad enough they threw twenty-one children out this year for not paying the original fees. I don't agree with—"

Whatever Ustaz Awad didn't agree with was lost in the noise of the morning assembly bell and the shouts of the boys pouring into the yard to get in line. The teachers disbanded to organize their classes. Ustaz Awad looked toward the gate and noted that, again, Gadir seemed to have shut it early, with dozens of terrified boys trapped outside. He sighed, wishing he could gather up the courage to march over and demand the gates be opened and the boys let in, *or else*. But of course, he wouldn't march anywhere or demand anything. There just wasn't enough in him to do it.

As the students pushed and squirmed into their crooked lines, the teachers roaming between them waving their whips in the air, the words "strike" and "protest" rang faintly in his ear. Go on strike or march to the government's head office? Them? *Him?* They must be crazy, or desperate, or both, to consider such a thing. They couldn't go on strike; who would take care of the students? (The thought that the students would be the happiest of all about this decision didn't occur to him.) More pressing was the question of what these forms of protest would accomplish. Would anyone even bother with them? The authorities would probably just go on ignoring them and their problems. Or worse, they might punish them like they punished those doctors who went on strike a few years ago demanding higher pay and better working conditions. They would bring in the riot police to beat the demonstrators into submission, and then either fire them or fine them or throw them in jail. Or worse: they would shoot them dead.

With a heavy heart, Ustaz Awad turned with the students toward the flag as they blasted out the national anthem in a tone-deaf sing-shout. Looking up at the faded strip of material, he thought how much they and this flag were alike: diverse in color yet segmented and separated, battered, and almost unrecognizable. And just as much as the tattered flag waving on its rusted post, they were at the mercy of the wind that decided whether they would flap up with dignity or droop in surrendered despair.

• • •

All through the morning assembly, the teachers whispered and hissed. The principal remained holed up in his office, sending his deputy Sit Afaf instead. Sit Afaf stood on the opposite side of the yard keeping a safe distance between herself and the rest of the teachers, gaze averted. Ustaz Awad watched her standing alone at the edge of the crowd. He knew how difficult this was for her. Not just because she was being used as a scapegoat, but because she was unable to join the group and share her enormous and constantly updated wealth of gossip.

Under normal circumstances she would be right in the middle of them, chattering away in low tones on ongoing stories, or imparting new bits of news about other people's personal lives, while the children drawled their poems and plays and exercises. Ustaz Awad wondered if the subjects of these gossip were aware of just how many people knew such intimate details of their lives. Did the distant niece twice removed of Sit Afaf's in-laws' neighbors know just how many people disapproved of her marriage to a Black American and were waiting for the marriage to fall apart just to prove that Sudanese women simply *cannot* be happy with anyone other than a Sudanese man? Did that high-ranking government official whose uncle happened to live near Sit Afaf's maid's family in the village have any idea that the fact that his birth had been the result of an illegitimate relationship between his father and the woman who came twice a week to make kisra for the family, was well-known among everyone within four degrees of separation from the deputy principal of a thirty-five-year-old boys' elementary school he had never even heard of? Ustaz Awad could almost see Sit Afaf bursting with all the untold news as she fidgeted and adjusted her *tob* for the eighteenth time, and for once he actually felt sorry for her.

• • •

When the bell rang for lunch break, Ustaz Awad almost cheered with the students. No matter how old one gets, few things rival the happiness those two sounds bring: the lunch break bell and the end-of-lessons bell. He gathered up his ruler, bits of chalk, and battered notebook, and headed out the classroom door, almost getting knocked over by the stampede of children running for the grounds, shouting at the top of their lungs. Some of them were already opening their plastic bags and stuffing their sandwiches in their mouths. Others clutched some pennies and crumpled banknotes and raced to the school canteen for a fried falafel sandwich, joining the screaming and shoving mob in the fenced-in square of dirt covered by a zinc roof, battling for the servers' attention. Outside the school walls, a few ladies sat in the shade selling fava beans, falafel, aubergine, *tahniya* and jam sandwiches, little bags of powdered *dom* and spicy baobab, and peanut sugar sweets.

However, quite a large number of children either stayed behind in their classrooms looking down into their empty hands or gathered around the water pipes to get a drink. Every year, Ustaz Awad saw the number of these unfortunate boys grow, until now they would easily be more than half of those in school.

Ustaz Awad stepped into the teachers' room amid roaring laughter about a joke someone had cracked. He had his own sad little aubergine salad sandwich in his bag and took it out as he sat down on a creaking, dusty chair with ripped upholstery, but didn't open the wrapper. Eating lunch was a struggle every day. He kept thinking about whom he could give his sandwich to. But how would that help anyone? There were around twelve hundred boys in this school, half of whom hadn't had a proper meal in God knew when. Even if there were just two boys, this sandwich would barely be enough for them. Sighing, he put it into his pocket and got up.

"Hey, Awad, where to? You should try this *fatat adas* Samira made, don't make me say how good it is in front of her, her head will get all big!"

Smiling weakly, he motioned the need for some water and walked out of the room, across the yard, through the gate, along the outside wall, and around the corner. The vast *meidan* behind the school was dotted with white shirts and green trousers, as children roamed around enjoying their break, not a few of them up to no good. Ustaz Awad leaned against the crumbling and chafed wall and put his hands in his pockets, his fingers brushing against the sandwich. He had no appetite but was trying to convince himself to eat the sandwich anyway since lately his blood sugar had taken to dropping before the fifth period. He should go and get checked, he kept telling himself, but couldn't seem to find the time. But it wasn't really about finding time. He didn't want to know what was wrong, just like he didn't particularly care about eating, or about his hurt leg, or about his empty house. Perhaps he was depressed?

As he uninterestedly contemplated his mental health, his eyes wandered aimlessly across the grounds until he realized that he had been staring at the same object for the past several minutes. About fifteen meters away from him and the school, a boy was curled up in a wheelbarrow, apparently asleep. From this distance, the boy looked more like a pile of rags, but the sandals perched on the skinny legs sticking out gave away the occupant inside. The scene wasn't particularly striking. The school was located in close proximity to the Central Souq of South Khartoum, where dozens of young boys worked during the day pushing wheelbarrows for customers. The concept of shopping trolleys did not exist outside the fancy uptown hypermarkets.

But now Ustaz Awad knew whom he was going to give his aubergine salad sandwich to.

Looking at his watch he noted that only a few minutes remained until the end-of-break bell rang. He would have to hurry. He pushed away from the wall and took off in long strides across the *meidan*. The afternoon sun beat down mercilessly on his balding head, reflecting off the ground and heating the soles of his tired shoes. He was trying not to limp, as his hurt leg smarted with each step. He had hurt it while getting off a bus a few days earlier in front of this very same Central Souq on the way back from a family funeral, shoved unceremoniously off by the passengers behind him, who were unwilling to wait until the bus came to a complete stop.

Ustaz Awad stood over the wheelbarrow, looking down at the sleeping boy inside. He was on the smaller side, with a closely shaved head and large ears that stuck out. But the clothes he was wearing were not rags at all, nor were his sandals the shabby, mismatched affair you would expect. They were just dusty and a little worn down on the insides of the soles; the boy had flat feet. He looked around twelve years old, so that would put him in the eighth grade if he was in school. But he wasn't in school. He was asleep in a beat-up wheelbarrow in the shade of a tree, a few meters from his apparent place of work.

Ustaz Awad's blood was boiling in harmony with the sun scalding them both. Ever since this damned government had hijacked the country three decades earlier, everything had fallen to ruin, starting with education. Children were pushed out of the system because they couldn't afford the fees, the uniforms, or the food, or were simply sick of being beaten mercilessly day in and day out by people twice their size.

The school bell rang in the distance, and both Ustaz Awad and the boy jumped awake. The boy looked up in alarm, instinctively raising his hands to protect himself, as all signs of sleep disappeared from his face. He was clutching a small piece of carboard in his hand. Ustaz Awad stepped back and raised his own hands.

"Hey, relax," he stuttered, trying to smile reassuringly, although the boy's reaction revealed what he was used to receiving from grown men, and that made his blood boil even more.

"I didn't do anything! It wasn't me!" the boy shouted, his arms still raised to protect himself as he struggled to get out of the wheelbarrow.

"I know! I know! It's fine. I just want to give you a sandwich!"

The boy managed to dislodge himself from the wheelbarrow and, backing away a few steps, he kicked his sandals off and picked them up, keeping his eyes on Ustaz Awad. Typical flight preparation, as Ustaz Awad knew from a lifetime of close contact with boys. He was still clasping the piece of cardboard close to his chest, as if afraid to lose it.

"I thought you might be hungry and wanted to give you my sandwich," he repeated. He reached into his pocket and pulled it out. The boy didn't move.

"It's aubergine salad," Ustaz Awad said, a little embarrassed at the pathetic contents and the three-day-old bread that he was offering. "Do you like it?"

The boy stared mistrustfully at the sandwich. He didn't reach out, but he didn't back farther away either, so that couldn't be bad. Ustaz Awad kept the sandwich in full view as he studied the boy closer, trying to place the face in one of his classes. He had a faint bruise under his right eye and a dried scab on his lower lip. A few buttons were missing from his shirt. All that coupled with his terror and mistrust screamed out the obvious, and Ustaz Awad wondered who it was who was beating him. A father? An uncle? A teacher?

It was getting late. The kids had disappeared from the grounds behind the school and people would be wondering what had happened to him. His class would be in full party mode until his appearance.

"Here," he said as he tossed the sandwich into the wheelbarrow and stepped away. "It's just aubergine salad, I'm sorry."

He took a few steps back, then turned on his heel and walked away. Halfway to the school walls he turned around to see if his gift had been accepted. It had. He saw the boy throw the piece of cardboard from his hand, clutching the sandwich with both hands, wolfing it down. He even licked the wrapper. Then he climbed back into the wheelbarrow and curled right back up.

. . .

It was the end of the school day and the children streamed out of the gates like a swarm of locusts, scattering in all different directions at varying speeds of light. The teachers plodded out among them, avoiding getting trampled by the small feet. They shouted their goodbyes to each other, a few of them getting into a couple of beaten-up old Toyota Coronas, pooling with each other, and the rest heading in the direction of the main road to wait for public transport. Ustaz Awad lived within reasonable walking distance and usually headed home in the northwest direction, but today he had something else to do. He turned in the opposite direction, around the back of the school and across the empty space toward the trees where he had met the boy earlier. Of course, neither child nor wheelbarrow were anywhere to be seen.

Ustaz Awad stood under the trees, feeling deflated. He wasn't really sure why he wanted to find the boy, or what he would have done or said if he had. Did he want to hear a thank-you? Of course not. More likely, he wanted to know why the boy wasn't in school. Although that wasn't much of a mystery either. There was an abundance of reasons why children were outside the educational system in Sudan. Ustaz Awad remembered reading the statistics recently: almost 60 percent of school-aged children were outside the system. It was the kind of fact that was stated dramatically in conferences and NGO budget meetings and academic papers, which raised eyebrows and drew gasps of horror—but then was quickly forgotten and pushed to the back of everyone's minds.

Ustaz Awad scanned the ground, looking for nothing particular until he saw it: the piece of cardboard that the boy had been holding. Maybe it had a name or phone number. The wind would have blown it farther down the road, and there was no shortage of trash in Khartoum, especially around the area of the souq. But he was sure it was the same piece.

He reached down, picked it up, and flattened it out, turning it this way and that to make sense of the crooked scribbling and lines crossed out with what looked like a piece of coal.

At first, they looked like random scratches but in a series of straight lines. A seasoned mathematician, however, Ustaz Awad could spot an equation in the blink of an eye, even if he couldn't read the numbers properly. And this was very obviously an equation of some sort. Indeed, it was a Cartesian equation, an eighth-grade problem. It was almost complete but missing a step. No, missing two steps; one in the middle and one in the end. The one in the end wouldn't help solve anything because of the missing step in the middle.

Ustaz Awad stared curiously at the problem for several minutes, wondering. Had that boy been trying to solve it? He was sort of the right age, a little on the smaller side. He had obviously been a student himself once upon a time. Maybe even in Ustaz Awad's same school. Without thinking too hard, he could remember at least a dozen children who had stopped showing up to his eighth-grade class, mostly because their families could not afford to keep them in school anymore.

He raised his head, looking around himself. Where had the boy gone? Where had he come from? Where did he live?

Looking back down at the problem in his hand, he reached into his shirt pocket for his Bic pen, inserted the missing steps, and solved the problem. It was a difficult problem, quite advanced for an eighth grader. And the steps written down were, for the most part, accurate. This was a smart kid. And he was beaten up and hungry, pushing a wheelbarrow around for an income, carrying the maddening burden of this unsolved math problem around with him in his head.

The hot, dusty afternoon breeze brushed against his face, rustling the trees over his head and the piece of cardboard in his hand, carrying with it the noises of the souq in front of him. Ustaz Awad wondered why there was so much misery in the world, and why the vast majority of it fell on the small heads of children, especially in this country.

The *meidan*, momentarily deserted, was now being populated again with the same schoolchildren from that morning, now out of their school clothes and in shorts and T-shirts and *aragis*, kicking their footballs and setting up their goal posts, playing tag, shouting and laughing. People were scurrying across in all directions, hurrying to get out of the direct, unshaded sun and poorly aimed footballs, heading to their different destinations, mostly toward the souq to pick up their evening groceries.

Ustaz Awad looked down at the problem, thinking it over in his head. It didn't take long for him to decide. He would find the boy and show him how to solve the problem properly. Then he would find out why he was pushing a wheelbarrow for a living instead of staying in school, especially at such a crucial school year. He wasn't exactly sure what he would do next, but he would cross that bridge when he got to it.

• • •

The Central Souq of South Khartoum, or Almarkazi as it was known, was the typical Sudanese marketplace, which also doubled as a busy bus stop. Previously a small collection of vegetable and fruit stalls, it now spanned more than several hundred acres with ill-defined borders, bleeding into the surrounding neighborhoods and streets, its noise further amplified by the roars of the aging diesel buses that stopped and started within it. A few years ago, the dual-carriage road alongside it leading south toward Al Azhari, Al Salama, and eventually the Soba agricultural scheme, was transformed into a three-lane highway flanked by service roads and concrete pavements. The road crossed over the intersection via a flyover bridge, under the shade of which scores of passengers entered or alighted from lines of buses defying all traffic rules and policemen. Pedestrians crossed in all directions. It was also where a small population of homeless people lived and lounged.

A bus revved noisily behind Ustaz Awad making him jump, and as he moved out of the way, he heard the young *kumsari* grumbling behind:

"Itfakfak ya ammak."

Ignoring him, albeit with slightly bruised dignity, Ustaz Awad crossed the street and headed under the flyover bridge. The noises, the smell of burnt gasoline and fried fish, the shouts of *kumsaris* and vendors and speaker phones, the laughter and the squabbling, felt like an assault on the senses. He paused and waited for the passengers of a bus that had stopped directly in front of him to disembark so that he could move forward, and saw a young, overweight woman step off and almost topple over, just as he had those few days ago. She caught her balance at the last minute, wincing and moving embarrassedly along. It looked as if her sandal had broken.

Around the line of buses, a large concrete mastaba arose under the flyover. It covered the entire width of the bridge with wings on either side leading back up the road. Here, dozens of people were sitting and lying around, there was graffiti and layers of posters on the walls, and dirt everywhere. Several homeless men and boys in various stages of filth and lucidity, at least one of which had a lower limb missing, were spread across the ground. There may have been some women as well, but it was always difficult to tell with the state of their clothing and hair. There were also "regular people" collected around the scattering of tea ladies, sipping tea and coffee and hibiscus, some in formal clothing on the way back from a civil service job, and others in casual clothing, also probably on the way back from a civil service job.

But most important to Ustaz Awad, there were several boys with wheelbarrows. They looked like they were on break, with their vehicles leaning against the walls or flipped upside down and used as a table on which they played ludo.

Ustaz Awad stood on the raised ledge opposite the mastaba with the road between them, looking over the vehicles passing through. A couple of beggars pulled at his trousers, demanding an offering, and each time he reached into his pocket and brought out a coin. The beggars looked at his modest offering in disgust, and one actually gave his coin back to him.

Ustaz Awad screwed his eyes to try to focus on the faces of the people sitting around the mastaba across the road. At least three of them were the right size; elementary school–aged boys, all somewhat undernourished. None, though, were the boy he was looking for. The rest were too big or too old. He looked around him for a while, examining the different faces in the crowd, then walked along the ledge around the mastaba, stepped down, and crossed to the other side of the road. There, crowds of people were standing waiting for a bus to take them back downtown, the opposite direction from which he had come. He didn't think he would find the boy there, but he looked, just in case.

Back across the road, through the turbulent flood of vehicles and people and animals, Ustaz Awad headed toward the souq trying to formulate a plan in his head. The place was huge and the boy could be anywhere. He could go around in circles for days and they wouldn't bump into each other. If he had known his name, at least, it would have been easier; he could have asked any one of the other boys pushing their own wheelbarrows.

The more he thought about his feat, the more ridiculous it felt. He didn't even know if it was the boy who had written down that math problem in the first place. He put his hand in his pocket to finger the folded bit of cardboard sitting alongside a few bank notes. He needed some aubergines and peanut paste anyway. And some new bread.

And so, into the souq he went.

• • •

Where the souq actually began was a tricky question to answer. The stalls and sellers started from all the way down the intersection, on both sides of the asphalt, with merchandise spread out on sugar sacks and canvas mats and on the backs of donkey carts and pickup trucks. Further in, there were stalls with shades and signs and more canvas mats.

For the untrained eye, the place looked like complete chaos, but there was a method to the madness. The souq was divided into sections for fresh produce, grains and legumes, spices fresh and dry, plastic and glass goods, meat and chicken, canned goods, and even clothing.

If he were to find the boy, he would have to somehow cover all those sections in some organized way.

Ustaz Awad couldn't remember if there were always this many boys with wheelbarrows or if he was only noticing them because he was looking for one of their own, but they were everywhere. They roamed the narrow aisles between the stalls and vegetable mats in a hurry, steering their vehicles professionally and a little recklessly, looking around for a customer who looked like they would be buying large quantities. They were particularly focused on women, a task made easier by the abundance of women doing their shopping. Although, it didn't seem as if many people were buying things in large quantities. The prices were just too high.

"Have you seen a boy in a green shirt with a wheelbarrow? About this tall?"

The boy Ustaz Awad had stopped to ask this question looked up at him impatiently.

"What?"

Ustaz Awad searched around for something that was more specific, trying to keep the boy's wavering attention as he strained his neck, looking around in all directions for a potential customer.

"His buttons were torn and he had a black eye, and he was trying to solve this math problem."

Ustaz Awad brandished the crumpled piece of cardboard in the boy's face, making him flinch. Carefully, he looked Ustaz Awad up and down, then leaned a little forward. Ustaz Awad bent toward him to hear what he was about to whisper. But rather than say anything, the boy sniffed his breath. He thought he was drunk.

Flabbergasted, Ustaz Awad whipped his head back and was about to deliver a stern admonishment of some kind, but the boy simply rolled his eyes at him and pushed his wheelbarrow on and away.

Well then, so much for asking around, he thought vexedly. There wouldn't be any help from anyone, he would have to use his own eyes to find the boy. Again, he tried to make a plan so as to cover as much area as possible without missing too much. It made sense to comb the aisles in one direction and come back down in the next, but also, covering each produce section would allow him to scan several aisles at the same time, minimizing the risk of missing him. He would do that. Starting with the area nearest at hand: the vegetable section.

This was the section he was the most familiar with, mainly because it was as far as he had actually ventured into the souq before. Usually he bought whatever he wanted from whomever was closest to the road. Everything else he needed, he bought from the local corner shop and attached butchery. The souq made him uncomfortable with its crowds and loud noises, and the nonexistence of personal space.

Passing the mats on the ground and the open stalls, he soon entered what was actually the real souq: huge metal hangars housing lines of high, tiled platforms. Perched on top of the platforms were the vegetable sellers, with narrow dirt aisles running between them, up and down which customers strolled, observing the produce. The men called out to the women, not at all shy to use what they thought of as flattery but which was in fact sexual harassment.

"Hey, beautiful, don't you want to see these tomatoes? A kilo for eighty-five, best price around. And for those big lovely eyes of yours, I'll give them to you for just eighty."

The women either ignored these catcalls, responded with laughs, or hurled a couple of insults and threats at the caller. The callers didn't care either way; it was how they made a living, after all.

Ustaz Awad moved up and down the aisles, occasionally standing on tiptoe to see over the neighboring platforms into the adjacent aisle. He couldn't move very quickly; people kept blocking the way and he was trying to avoid putting too much pressure on his injured leg. The wheel-barrow boys—and other boys carrying plastic bags for the customers, or balancing trays of plastic sieves and sets of glasses and cookie cutters, or lugging crates of cold water and drinks—weaved in and out of the crowd, almost bumping into buyers as they offered their own merchandise for sale or to carry things for them. The ground was covered in small puddles of muddy water caused by the sellers' constant spraying of their vegetables to make their produce look shiny and attractive.

Ustaz Awad passed lines of cucumbers, tomatoes, pumpkin slices, carrots in bunches, onions, marrows, green peppers, and sweet potatoes. There were large bushels of *molokhiya*, piles of okra and spinach, and bunches of those green herbs that he could never tell apart. An abundance of produce, and an even bigger abundance of empty stomachs, because the prices being called out were simply ridiculous.

And the boy was nowhere to be seen.

He was near the end of the vegetable hangar now and was trying to make his way out, but the way was blocked by a woman who was haggling with a young boy over the price of sweet potatoes.

"Are you crazy? You're trying to sell me half a kilo of *bambay* for forty-five pounds? How stupid do you think I am?"

"That's how much it costs today, *ya okhot*, take it or leave it." The boy waved the plastic bag in her face, one foot on the step, ready to get back up on his platform.

"I'm taking it, and I'm taking it for thirty only. Take your money and give me that bag."

He laughed at her and pulled the plastic bag out of reach. "It's forty-five, lady, and won't go down a single pound."

Ustaz Awad was not particularly interested in this discussion, nor did he have the time. But the problem was the woman was blocking the aisle with her enormous backside, at which a group of young boys were standing and openly staring on either side, further closing off any other way of passage. He turned around to go back down and try another way, but that way was blocked by a group of women who had come over to see what the commotion was and egg the woman on. They shouted that the sellers on the other side of the hangar had sweet potatoes twice that size and for twenty-eight pounds only.

Behind him, Ustaz Awad heard one of the boys whisper "If you don't give it to her for thirty, that woman will sit on you and break you in half," at which the rest of the boys burst out laughing.

"Stop wasting my time or else I'll call your aunt Safiya and tell her you're cheating everyone! Give me that bag!"

The boy flinched at the name of his aunt and the smirk on his face instantly disappeared. Whoever she was, Aunt Safiya was terrifying enough to knock the price of half a kilo of sweet potatoes down from forty-five to thirty without being present. The boy practically threw the plastic bag at the woman. She slapped the thirty pounds against his chest in disgust, picked up the rest of her bags and, turning around to leave, knocked Ustaz Awad clear off his feet with her expansive backside. He let out a small shout of surprise as he toppled backward, saved from falling into the mud by landing in a wheelbarrow parked just behind his knees.

• • •

Ustaz Awad emerged from the vegetables hangar with both his back and his ego sorely bruised, and without his aubergines. In all the commotion he had forgotten he had even wanted to buy them. It didn't matter, really; he would just buy a couple of those dried-up things sold at the local corner shop that looked more like shriveled figs.

In front of him was the section housing wholesale spices and dried grains and goods, including dates, which Ustaz Awad had a particular weakness for. It came from his being raised in the Northern State, where dates were a nutritional staple, a source of income, a measure of wealth, and a means of inheritance. They were the first thing a newborn tasted, and were served at only happy ceremonies. Other people usually remembered them only in the month of Ramadan to break their fast with, but where he came from, they were relished all year round.

He had memories of the huge piles of dates lying in their expansive front yard, fussed over by his elderly aunts during the date-harvest season, brought in from the fields on camelback, set down and threshed, divided by type and inheritor, and left to dry before being packed into sacks. The harvest season brought in an influx of people from all around the region, seeking work or begging for their share. They climbed the palm trees, collected the fallen branches, offered their carts and camels for transport, helped the women shake off the vines and cleaned everything up.

Ustaz Awad stood at the edge of the hangar, momentarily forgetting about the boy and observing the different piles of dates around and in front of him. They looked out of place here in the humid markets of Khartoum, laid out so unceremoniously on the ground. He could name at least fifteen different types, each with a different shape, size, taste, and shade of brown. His personal favorite was the Tamod, a thin, wrinkly, very dark brown date with a nutty flavor. He liked it not just because it was the sweetest, but because it was one of the few things that he knew his mother had liked.

He couldn't remember what she looked like and there were no pictures of her. This wasn't because cameras didn't exist at the time. It was because, in that strange old Sudanese tradition, she had been forcefully disappeared from his life once his father had divorced her. Knowing his father to be the tyrant that he was, Ustaz Awad knew he had taken him from his mother at the age of three purely out of spite rather than from any actual affection on his side, maliciously incited by the women in his family as was usually the case. Children—especially boys—belonged with their fathers.

It wasn't just tradition that let this happen; the Sudanese Family Law of 1991 gave fathers the right to take their children from their mothers at a certain age, while other laws such as the Immigration and Passports Law gave them the freedom to travel with their children without the permission or even the knowledge of their mothers, regardless of guardianship. Not a few of Sit Afaf's morning stories involved custody-battle updates of couples they had been hearing about since their weddings, and how messy everything got after divorce—especially when the mother decided to remarry.

Ustaz Awad bitterly remembered his own father's almost daily beatings, the constant insults, and always being compared with who was smarter, faster, and stronger than him. How he wasn't allowed to wear glasses for several years because, to the older man, eyeglasses were a sign of weakness, until one day he fell into a shallow ditch behind their house and broke his ankle. How, once, in a fit of rage over his failure to fight back against a school bully who had ripped his shirt, his father had picked up a bare palm frond discarded from that afternoon's harvest cleaning and beaten him within an inch of his life, leaving him curled up and sobbing on the scattered dates in the front yard with a broken rib. How, the only reason he knew that his mother loved the Tamod was because when she died, a few days before his fifteenth birthday, his grandmother had bitten into one, found it full of insects, and spat it out in disgust.

"Of course, she has to keep reminding us of her miserable existence, even after she's dead."

Perhaps that was why he wanted to find the boy so badly. Not just to help him solve that math problem. But because, in a way, the boy reminded him of himself.

Head down, Ustaz Awad walked straight through the dates hangar and out the other side without looking around.

$$\bullet \ \bullet \ \bullet$$

"My son is taking me to Nairobi to get my back checked. He works with the UN."

Ustaz Awad was sitting on a plastic chair, his hurt leg stretched out in front of him, resting in the shade of a juice stall on the far side of the souq. He had a glass of orange juice in his hand. It looked and tasted more like lemon juice, was half filled with sugar and the rest with ice, and cost about as much as a dozen oranges itself. But Ustaz Awad was tired, deflated, and dehydrated. And he had given up his search.

He had been circling the souq for almost three hours, and had seen roughly one hundred and fifty boys pushing wheelbarrows. Some boys he had seen more than once. There was no sign of the boy he was looking for. The boy could have simply gone home. Or maybe he was never there in the first place. Maybe he had just fallen asleep in some random wheelbarrow he'd found lying around. Ustaz Awad felt a scratchy, heavy knot forming in the bottom of his stomach at this thought.

Sitting in the plastic chairs next to him were two women in black abayas and large scarves; a new fashion brought in by the Islamist government's copying everything Saudi. He hated the sight of those things. They didn't suit the weather or the usual colorful, cheery nature of the Sudanese. And they were everywhere now.

One of the women talked about how her son was going to let her find a wife for him.

"Of course, he knows that only *I* can find someone suitable for him," she boasted importantly. "He works for the UN, like I told you, so he can't marry just *anyone*. But I'm taking my time. Don't want to rush these kinds of things. Maybe someone from the Nifeidi family, or perhaps Al Mahdi."

In the meantime, the son would take care of all her problems in the most expensive manner possible. He was fixing the bathrooms in their family home, buying spare parts for her younger son's car, and covering the costs of her other son's extravagant upcoming wedding. And he was taking her for a full checkup with the best doctor in Kenya. No, not Kenya: *Nairobi*. Ustaz Awad and the woman's companion watched her curiously as the name rolled around her mouth and off her tongue, making her sound more sophisticated as she mentioned a country by its capital—which she knew—instead of its name, which any commoner used.

Ustaz Awad looked down at his drink. The whitish froth and small bits of orange peel swirled lazily around the ice cubes, just like he had been swirling around this damned souq, and to no avail. He had searched through towers of sugar sacks and behind the butcheries with their huge piles of stinking animal skins, intestines, and severed cow heads. Between aisles lined with plastic tubs of cheese and metal cans of tomato paste. He had been stepped on and bumped into and pushed over, called out to and laughed at, and even followed around for several minutes by a curious group of boys.

A few meters away from him was a section of the souq he hadn't bothered looking in. It was the tobacco section, where crowds of men lined around the different stalls with their little plastic bags to be re-filled. The big names in the tobacco industry also came from up north, but that was something Ustaz Awad had no appetite for. Yet another thing that had attracted the disgust of his father. A man who didn't chew tobacco? Even the old women in his family chewed it, keeping their stash in small orange Creme 21 containers under their pillows.

He sighed, took a sip of juice, and leaned back in his chair, thinking about the man Descartes, who had developed the Cartesian math for-mula that was at the center of the day's saga. The man who had been not only a mathematician, but a philosopher and metaphysicist, most famous for his quote "I think, therefore I am." The same man who had painstakingly reasoned and examined, and eventually proved—to him-self before others—the existence of God in a time when challenging this conviction was the norm. Ustaz Awad wondered not for the first time about the effort this feat had taken from the man, and if his insistence to prove the existence of God had been purely a scholarly endeavor or for his own peace of mind. He further wondered—also not for the first time—how people not born into surroundings where the existence of God is an unquestionable fact ended up searching for him and finding, say, Islam. He wondered if he himself had not been born Muslim, would he have searched for God? Would he have reasoned and examined until he could have proved his existence? Would that proof, if found, have led him to Islam with the horrific way Muslims now behaved in the name of their religion? He couldn't say for sure, and that troubled him.

Anyone observing the current ruling Islamist regime and mistaking it to be representative of the religion it alleged to follow would have a hard time believing that this religion was about anything other than bloodshed, racism, and thievery. Ustaz Awad was sixty-two years old:

he was born the same year Sudan gained its independence from the British Empire. He had witnessed all the short-lived democracies the country had experienced, all the military coups, the rise of Sudan as a beacon of education, women's rights, and agricultural excellence in the region, and its descent into poverty, corruption, and conflict following the Muslim Brotherhood's coup in 1989.

He had also witnessed the countless protests over the years, brutally crushed by the riot police and the terrifying National Intelligence and Security Service. So, when protests had started in Damazin on December 13, 2018, Ustaz Awad—like others all over and outside the country—barely took notice. Then protesters took to the streets on the other side of the country in Atbara, and burned down the ruling party's headquarters on December 19. And that was a whole different level. Suddenly fires were lighting up all over the country and calls to join a united front were made by a previously unknown group called the Sudanese Professionals Association: doctors, teachers, engineers, and tradesmen. Ordinary people, like him. *Like Sit Afaf.*

And then, there was hope.

"When it is not in our power to follow what is true, we ought to follow what is most probable," was another one of Descartes's sayings. Ustaz Awad had no idea what the truth was in order to follow it, but what was most probable now was that he would never find the boy, and would never help him solve the problem.

Morosely, Ustaz Awad took another sip of his juice, trying to block out the woman's annoying voice as she described the type of wife she would be finding for her son. Light skinned, not too old, university educated—but not a doctor, of course. No one wanted their son to marry a doctor; she would leave him alone at home for her night shifts at the hospital and throw her kids to be raised by a maid. Nope, no doctor for her son.

The sound of the *azan* reached his ears, making him jump. It was time for *maghrib* prayers already, and in his panicked search he had forgotten to pray *asr*. Suddenly the air was filled with the calls to the sunset prayer. Typical of Sudan, where a mosque minaret rose above the buildings every few kilometers, the calls to the five prayers sounded from dozens of different directions. Different voices and tones, calling the same words to the same people, to come and pray to the same God. It was jarring and beautiful at the same time.

He gulped down the rest of his juice, set the glass down on the low plastic table in front of him, and got up, looking around for the nearest prayer mat and wincing as he stood on his aching leg. A short distance from where he was, a couple of young boys were laying out the traditional green and black plastic mats in front of the shops lining a yard, with a couple of metal holders on either side from which hung the *abareeg* filled with water. Men were already taking off their shoes and sandals, rolling up their sleeves and trousers, and taking turns to do their ablutions for prayer.

Ustaz Awad walked over and stood to the side to wait his turn, but was quickly ushered to the front of the line as the younger men stepped aside for him to go first. He feebly protested, but as usual no one was having it, and he was actually a little grateful. He sat down on the tiny *bambar* and pulled off his dusty shoes and colorless socks, rolling up his sleeves, and started washing his hands and mouth.

As he proceeded with his ablutions, his mind drifted back to the events of the day. They were already becoming blurry. He felt he couldn't remember exactly where he had gone and what he had seen; couldn't even remember the boy's face that clearly anymore.

He washed his feet and put the *ibreeg* down, pausing a little before pushing himself up, shoving his shoes into the growing pile, and stepped onto the mat to get in line. There was no time to pray *asr*, he would have to pray *maghrib* with everyone else. Again, he was pushed to the front out of respect for his age, and was almost made to lead the group in prayer, but he managed to escape and blend back into the crowd. He had never led a large crowd in prayer before. The thought terrified him.

"Allahu akbar," the appointed imam called, and the crowd repeated after him, as did the many worshippers on the other mats all over the market and the street, and those inside the mosques around them. Ustaz Awad called out to Allah along with the thousands of other beings around him, then listened to the lovely recitation of the graying man standing in front of him, his voice mingling with and almost inaudible over the voices coming from the mosque microphones. Again, it was both jarring and beautiful. Ustaz Awad forgot his aching leg and mind and just listened, letting the words flow through him, feeling that heavy knot in the pit of his stomach disintegrate little by little. The worshippers bowed and touched their brows to the ground, and when he sat back up, the knot was gone.

After prayers, Ustaz Awad sat on the side of the mat, putting his shoes on but stuffing the socks in his pocket with the boy's piece of cardboard. Lights were coming on inside the hangars and kiosks and over the wheelbarrows piled with lemons and *tasali*. On the road outside the souq, lights were coming on inside the buses carrying their exhausted occupants to their destinations. It had been a long day, and he wanted to go home and lie down. Tomorrow, he would wake up, make himself an aubergine salad sandwich, and go to school, where the same discussions on salaries and protests would be held. And where he would wonder—and worry—about the Cartesian boy.

Again, something Descartes had said came to Ustaz Awad's mind: "Except our own thoughts, there is nothing absolutely in our power." But it seemed to Ustaz Awad that at this moment, he had lost control even over his own thoughts. Perhaps it was the image of the boy's black eye and busted lip that had taken over his mind, and the fact that he wasn't in school anymore even though he very obviously wanted to be. Or maybe it was the memories of his own miserable childhood, bullied and insulted by his father, and now oppressed and humiliated by his government.

Whatever it was, now his thoughts were telling him that he couldn't keep taking all these punches silently without fighting back. How long would he lie curled up on top of the scattered dates, crying from the injustice of it all? How long would he keep bleating politely, writing letters to ask for what was rightfully theirs?

Tomorrow, when the other teachers asked him for his opinion again, he would say it.

The teachers—all of them—would march with the Sudanese Professionals Association to the Republican Palace.

This time, he was going to fight back.

Rémy Ngamije

Fulbright

STORY

"Columbia University, in New York City."

That's where I'm heading. When I tell my seatmate, Caroline—
"Caroline Weaver but, please, call me Carol!"—a chatty British lady
on her way to the United States to visit her family, she's startled. She
sits up straight and fussily adjusts the seat belt's pinch. Our destination:
Trump's America. I'd have preferred going to the United States in the
Obama years, when the promise of Black excellence in that country was
high, when that proverbial four-hundred-year corner had been turned.
Still, it has to be admitted, even by me, that Agent Orange steers the
ship that is the United States. If there's a country with a reputation that
can survive a despot, it's the one that gave us Muhammad Ali, Michael
Jackson, and Michael Jordan—the three Ms whose reputations and
achievements remain unimpeachable by scandal wherever Black people
are found.

Caroline is headed to some tumbleweed town in the Midwest with a
biblical name. Her daughter teaches at a university there. That's how we
started talking. "I'm going to see my Katie. She's an art history lecturer."
I wanted her to leave me alone so I could return to my podcast. With a

199

robotic smile, the icy stewardesses glided through the plane checking seat belts. When we taxied onto the runway, Caroline took a break from telling me about Camden, where she worked at the British Library, her interest in tap dancing—"Keeps the old legs going, you know"—and her Katie's move to the United States, which "was just bad business, really, what with this Trump fellow in charge now. And where are you headed, dear?"

I dropped Columbia University between us, like the armrest, letting her know which side was mine and which was hers. The plane sprinted down the runway, vibrating with its effort. Caroline's eyebrows lifted as the wheels left the ground. "You don't say."

I do say.

I'm going to New York City. *Nueva York.* The Big Apple. *If you can make it there, you can make it anywhere.* Frank Sinatra's "New York, New York." Home of the Yankees, the Knicks, and the Notorious—RIP—BIG. I don't have to send my family pictures of the Statue of Liberty or the Empire State Building, because they've all seen them—I'm the only one who hasn't been to the United States before.

I'm going to find out what a New York minute is. I'm going to Madison Square Garden. I've booked tickets for a jazz concert at Lincoln Center. I'm going to read my way through the Harlem Renaissance. I'll have a hot dog on a corner. Bagels, burgers, soda, milkshakes—I might even watch an ice hockey game. I'm going to play Dean Martin's "Let It Snow!" as I watch the snowflakes descend from the sky.

"That's quite impressive." Caroline pulls at her earlobe. The airplane strains for the sky, searching for the necessary altitude. Wherever her Katie is, it certainly isn't Columbia. "And what is it you'll be doing there?"

"I'm a Fulbright scholar, ma'am. I'll be in law school."

"Oh my—and please, 'Carol,' not 'ma'am,' 'miss,' or 'missus.'"

I say I'll try my best to drop the titles even though I won't. Familiarity between traveling strangers might be good, but cultural upbringing supersedes everything.

"You're one of those, are you?"

I laugh and say, yes, I'm *one of those*—a Fulbright scholar at Columbia University in the city of New York.

. . .

My father has a doctorate from MIT. My mother has one from Stanford. My sister did her first master's degree at NYU; she's busy with her second at UCL. My family was anxious I wouldn't pursue a higher postgraduate qualification, shamed, as they were, by my longstanding status as an honors degree holder—"Yes, yes, from the best university in Africa," my mother would say, "but still . . ." They hinted and nudged at family dinners about there always being more to know and learn. They never quite said "abroad" but I knew what they wanted: a degree from an international university—in this way, the family could finally be whole. It is wonderful to have studied *here*, they said, but if you really want to make it you need to go *there*. Conversations steered toward some conference paper my father was working on; my mother's latest citation; or which university would pursue my sister for her PhD after she finished up in England.

Being less than a minor academic—"At best," my mother said, "more like an advanced undergraduate"—I never joined in their lofty talk about research methodologies, thesis defenses, or journal publications. I think what irked my parents the most was how much I didn't mind being left out. They reluctantly admitted I wasn't pursuing higher qualifications whenever they met family friends at weddings or funerals. "He has too many interests and talents," my father lied, "so, naturally it's taking time for him to choose a focus and institution." The scandal of it all made my mother sigh like a sea breeze. She tried to corner me into a Yale application by saying she'd told a colleague I'd already applied. "It would be really embarrassing if you didn't go on to do it," she said. I let her explain that situation on her own a year later when her colleague saw us in town as the academic years in the United Kingdom and United States commenced. After that, when my parents learned to live with my grossly underqualified shame, I told them about Columbia.

"And I got the Fulbright."

"*Ehen*, another one in the family!" my father said. He'd been one, too. My mother clapped and danced. She'd been waiting for this day since high school. My sister, via FaceTime, said, "Well done, bro. Now you're officially part of the family. You had us worried for a bit."

We still have cases of beer and bottles of wine from the celebration party they threw.

• • •

I told my girlfriend.

All she said was, "Oh."

She knew I'd been applying. When I had told her I was considering getting my master's degree in New York, she'd said it would be the perfect opportunity for her to practice slow-bandwidth stripteases for me. But she must've thought I wouldn't be accepted. She cheered up and said, "I'm so proud of you." She hugged and kissed me.

Three days later she broke up with me. New York, she said, would test my resolve and commitment to a pixelated girlfriend.

"Long distance," she said, "is the wrong distance." She would've been willing to try if I was "going to a place that didn't have girls from the music videos." Kampala. Accra. Ibadan. But she wouldn't compete with girls from any of New York's boroughs. "The Bronx," she said, "that's where all the Jamaicans, Haitians, Puerto Ricans, and Dominicans live." She paled talking about the biracial girls New York churned out at a whim. "I haven't even started with the white ones." The wisdom of Kanye West lives on in strange ways.

I said she was being silly. There was no need to pause or end us. She wouldn't wait—couldn't wait. "I've seen how these things go. You'll come back changed. Don't deny it. You changed the moment you told me you got the scholarship—and you haven't even left yet. Imagine when you've been gone six months, or a year. You'll be a Fulbright, and I'll just be—"

"What?"

"Me."

She's a makeup artist. Early on, when we were dating, I told her I liked her eyes and she'd asked me about which part and in what style. I said, "Err, the whole eye . . . ?" She'd pointed out that, on Monday she had smoky eyes, cat eyes on Tuesday, and double wings on Wednesday— I was schooled on their differences and attributes. From then on, I took care to be particular with my compliments; after I noticed the slit in her eyebrows she said I was learning—that maybe there was hope for me and us yet.

We were enough for each other until I, apparently, became too good for her. I wonder if this occurrence should be listed as a possible consequence of being accepted into whatever the world considers to be prestigious academic programs. *Our alumni pool consists of world leaders, global thinkers, problem solvers, and practical doers— corporate careers can be fast-tracked, breakups might occur.*

She texted me when I was at the airport: You're on a different track. I've always known that, even if you didn't. I'm happy for you. Have fun in NYC. And if you ever think of me, don't be too angry.

I contemplated replying. I aimed for something amicable but the hurt of her kindness soured me. Instead, I deleted her message, shouldered my bag, and made my way to the immigration counter at Hosea Kutako International Airport.

From Namibia to the world. I am told that this is the way of things: when you want to make a positive change, you have to leave the place where that change needs to be made and learn how to solve it elsewhere. Africans know: local problem, so-called global solution.

Fulbright. Columbia University. As far as prestige could carry me. I am positive change personified.

Maybe, after I arrive, I shall find comfort in my classes and distance from her in my dissertation. But, secretly, I know I carry too much knowledge about gel and cream eyeliners. My newly minted skin-care routine is hers.

. . .

My friends threw a farewell party for me last night. The guys clapped my back and spoke about "all the fine-as-hell honeys in Noo Yaawk." Never mind that my girlfriend had recently broken up with me. The scholarship, Columbia, New York, the Atlantic Ocean between us— "You'll be good, bro. You'll forget about her in no time at all." They petitioned me to look out for Supreme hoodie sales, iPhone discounts, and Bose headphones. I'd be an outpost for free shipping; already I am thinking of the excess luggage tariffs I will have to pay when I come home for a visit.

"Dude, I can't believe you're leaving," another friend said, eyes glazed with drink.

"I'm only *going*," I said. "I'm coming back."

"For what? And to what?" He sipped his beer. "This?" He waved his hand at the party, with everyone drinking beer, wine, or whiskey, with the genreless music coming through a hidden speaker, the laughing, the rude jokes, the collected camaraderie that my departure fostered, and at the rest of the small city, the slow region, the wide country, and the challenging continent. "No, trust me," he continued, sagely, "this is the first of many tickets away from this place. Just accept it. You're a Fulbright now."

. . .

My boss was disappointed by my resignation. "No point in keeping your post for you then, eh? I mean, when you come back, I don't think you'll be challenged by this place." I told him I rather enjoyed my job. "Yeah. But *this* will change you."

My colleagues offered a mixture of praise and sadness. Kieran, the program coordinator, said I should connect with some of his friends living in New Jersey. "They're good people, even if they're from New Jersey." Laura, the other junior researcher, said I'd managed the impossible and successfully clawed my way out of NGO work. "All I want to hear about you from now on is world domination." Sydelle, our HR manager, said, quite ruefully, that we'd never even had *that* date. I told her I had a girlfriend at the time and she, you know, was in charge of HR. She said, "Yes. But still."

. . .

One of the local newspapers did a profile on me for the youth section. To inspire young Namibians to follow in my footsteps, I said the best thing was to focus purely on one's studies: "Don't be distracted by boyfriends or girlfriends. Your studies will take you further, to bigger and better things."

My ex sent me a message: Cool interview.
I didn't reply.

. . .

Some university friends emailed me their congratulations. One
other friend, Mathabatha, from Johannesburg, also got a Fulbright—
Berkeley in the fall. We joked about how he'd called it *fall* and not
autumn: "We're practically American, dude. I'm ready to be a
Democrat-voting, tortoiseshell-spectacle-wearing political consultant
from Portland. I have my bow tie ready."

We traded Americanisms: trunk instead of boot; a truck, not a *bakkie*;
football is soccer and TV is cable; pizza is sold by the slice; everything's
bigger in Texas except the voting rights; inches, feet, and yards; miles
instead of kilometers, pounds instead of kilograms. Back and forth, we
wrote to each other about the -isms we'd pick up.

"If there's a vice, America probably has a drive-through for it,"
Mathabatha said.

I'd read about the presidents out of curiosity. Washington. Adams.
Jefferson. Madison. There's a hazy period between Andrew Jackson and
Abraham Lincoln filled with anonymous heads of state. Polk, Taylor,
Fillmore—such strange and unfamiliar names. Naturally, I wound up
rereading about slavery and the Civil War. I didn't really have to be-
cause we covered it in detail in high school at the expense of our own
local history. We knew all about the injustices of the world outside, but
not of the violence in our own heritages. We had to learn about the
world, but not our place in it. World history was, basically, the study of
empire and the trafficking of Black bodies. There was one bit about the
Aztecs that was interesting, but by the next page-turn, we were reading
about Hernán Cortés and the Spanish arrival in the Americas. Clicking

through the histories of pirated and peddled flesh brought back questions I had in high school.

How could they?

How could they for so long?

How do they live with themselves?

We asked our history teacher and she shook her bottle-blond head and said it was the most shameful period of history the world has ever known. When we reached the Holocaust, a grade later, she shook her head—now sporting silver highlights—and said that *that* was the most shameful period of history. When we read about the settling of the Cape and Apartheid in our final high school year, and asked her the same questions she said, "You know, the Afrikaners weren't bad people. They did what they thought was right at the time."

Fidel—yes, after Castro—raised his hand and asked her, "Now, ma'am, with better information, how does it feel knowing you're descended from the devil?"

Fidel was suspended for a week.

The plane levels out. Caroline makes herself comfortable with the provided blanket.

I wonder if I'll ask white people in the United States the questions that were never answered in high school.

• • •

I worry I'll be another Amadou Diallo, target practice for racism, or fall victim to the pavement special, the headlock American policemen love using on African Americans. I don't want to be another Black man waiting to become a white chalk outline on a curb somewhere. I'm the real deal: *flesh of the sun and flesh of the sky*—I'm from Africa-Africa, not Zamunda or Wakanda. I'm not one of those brothers who, in a few years, will say he never knew he was Black until he moved to the United States. I'm Black on this flight. I'll be Black when I land.

I'm scared some gun-toting white man will see me coming home from the library and be threatened by the books I'm carrying—"Your Honor, I've heard these people can throw Thurgood Marshall's biography at killer speeds!"—and confuse me for a Cairo Jenkins, Kenya Townsend, Zaire Jones, or Azania Martin—and just shoot. I don't want to be another closed casket, fodder for open letters and thought pieces.

I want a sweater that warns people I'm valuable to someone back home: TIA—THIS IS AFRICAN. PLEASE RETURN UNDAMAGED.

Do they have Fulbright jerseys? Or a special ID I can show the police when I get pulled over?

• ′ • •

Another friend called me. He hadn't made it.

"Again," he said, sighing with despondency. "Commonwealth Scholarship and Chevening—five; Fulbright—four; YALI—three; Mandela Rhodes—two."

I didn't know what to say to him. "You just have to keep trying, man. Maybe it'll be next year. You never know."

I do not tell him that I got it the first time around. There are some things even friends are not allowed to share. It is not worth it to provide the minor gods with a target for petty jealousies.

He says he is happy for me. I tell him I am hopeful for him. I really am.

"Yeah, well, enjoy it. Don't waste it."

I won't.

• • •

I adjust my seat. Caroline says she'll stop prattling. I lie and tell her I don't mind her conversation. "Oh, never mind me," she says. "I'm certain I don't have much to say to the likes of you."

I tell her it isn't like that at all and settle into my seat, looking out the window.

The likes of you.

A Fulbright scholar at Columbia University in the city of New York.

Kim Coleman Foote

Dirty Money

ESSAY

It feels like a scene from a gangster movie. Mr. Sumina rolls up to the Standard Chartered bank in Cape Coast and cuts the engine. The reflection of his car sparkles in the blue-tinted glass windows. As we get out, Mr. Sumina brings along his empty black duffel bag. The uniformed guard by the ATMs nods at us tersely. Mr. Sumina cuts me a smile and holds open the door, bringing a welcome whoosh of air-conditioning.

"Well, Yaa," he says breathlessly, using my local name, "shall we?"

The lobby is empty, as if we've planned it that way. I feel like I should be watching out for the security cameras. The teller, who responds to my greeting with a British-tinged Ghanaian accent, wears the Standard Chartered uniform, a white blouse printed with blue and green triangles. I slide her a withdrawal slip, and she punches the long string of numbers into her computer.

"One moment, please," she says, raising a manicured finger. She turns and reaches into the safe behind her and pulls out several brick-size bundles of cedi notes. She continues to swivel in her chair from the safe to the counter until the bills form a pyramid. More than eleven million cedis.

It's the last week of 2002, and the American equivalent is far less impressive, around $1,300. Yet, it's the most money I've ever seen in person. And for a twenty-four-year-old whose two years after college consisted of low-paying internships and part-time work, it feels exorbitant, even if it's less than what I paid for two months of rent over the past year in Washington, DC.

I remind myself again that I'm getting a sweet deal for it: four months of stability and security—housing *and* research assistance. All through a handshake agreement with Mr. Sumina. It's a relief, considering the first few months of my Fulbright fellowship, which I'm using to conduct research for a novel about the slave trade. Since arriving in Accra in September, I'd been unable to locate informants for my proposed oral history interviews in Elmina. Ghanaian friends as well as professors and scholars I'd contacted for advice warned me my project would be difficult; slavery is a taboo topic, they said, so people wouldn't talk openly.

With no one from Elmina to interview, I spent my time in Accra conducting background research, reading historical texts at the University of Ghana library and the national archives. Additionally, I'd lived in three different households. I preferred to stay with a local family, based on my study-abroad experience in Ghana three years earlier, when living with families allowed me to practice Fante and Twi, eat local food, and get to know the community. I befriended families in Cape Coast, Komenda, Takoradi, and Accra through my study-abroad program and personal connections and would have loved to stay with them during my Fulbright term, but their homes were inconveniently located or cramped. I lived with two of them on an emergency basis during my first weeks in Accra, but eventually relocated to private housing closer to the university.

Two former Fulbrighters had endorsed Mr. Sumina as a reliable one-stop resource in the Elmina area: he had experience as an informant and translator; he could chauffeur me to interviews; and he rented spacious bedrooms in his family's house in Cape Coast, located near public transportation. In early December, I visited for a weekend to sample his services. He arranged three interviews in Elmina, along with private tours of the town and its historic slave castle, the focus of my novel. It being the furthest I'd gotten with my fieldwork thus far, I decided to hire him. I also gladly agreed to rent a room in his house, where meals and laundry would be included. There is also a TV, a radio, and a phone I can use for local calls, unlike in Accra, and Mr. Sumina said he can arrange language and even drumming and dancing lessons for a reasonable fee. The rent is the same as in Accra.

Only $1,300, I tell myself, as he places the duffel bag onto the counter and grins. He unzips and starts packing, grabbing the bundles two at a time. When the bag is full, he chuckles, joking how heavy it is. Outside, I expect to see a limo waiting. It would pull into a dank alley for the money handover, with hopes that the recipient would make good on his verbal promise. But Mr. Sumina's green sedan is the sole vehicle in the parking lot.

. . .

It's the first morning of Edina Bronya, and I'm emerging from a dream about furry things. Something bumps against my bedroom ceiling and it sounds huge. I've had an unexplained fever since moving to Cape Coast, and despite feeling hot, I pull the sheet over my head. I can't decide which is worse, the chance of this giant bug landing on me or the chance of having malaria. Yet I don't feel motivated to get out of bed. I have no family to observe Edina Bronya with. Mr. Sumina guaranteed me we would find one easily. Wishfully hoping to see some of them and learn more about Elminans' historic involvement in the trade, I had stressed to Mr. Sumina the importance of getting to know families in advance of Bronya to gain their confidence. But that has not happened.

Thump! Thump!

I groan and chicken out of thoughts of killing whatever that thing is. Keeping the sheet over my head, I make a mad dash for the hallway. Once there, all is silent inside my room. I peer in, and there's no giant moth hanging out on the ceiling, no water bug sputtering around. Was it a hallucination from the fever? The tail end of that morning's dream? A bit of it flashes into my head: several kittens were lined on their backs as though in a nursery. I kept thinking they were baby bats, and soon they morphed into them.

I'm tempted to call myself a fool and go back to sleep but decide to check the floor, just in case. All around the bed and armoire is bare. I tiptoe to the bed and glance under it. I let out a bloodcurdling scream and bolt. Prosper and Esi, Mr. Sumina's six-year-old son and eight-year-old niece, run out of their bedroom next door.

"Auntie Yaa," Esi says, "what is troubling you?"

Plastered to the wall, I point into my room. Esi goes to check it out, then squeals and scurries to me. Prosper—all three feet of him—swaggers inside, stretches a bare foot beneath the bed, and kicks. Esi buries her face against my stomach as the gray lump slides to the doorway.

It's not a moth or even a mouse. There's the scrunched head, the teeny skeletal fingers clutching wings, the same as in my dream. My stomach flips, and I reach the bathroom at the end of the hall just in time. Esi comes to the doorway, watching as I vomit into the toilet.

"Auntie Yaa, you are feeling ill-o."

But my fever is breaking. I sweat so much that the boubou I slept in sticks to me. I'm still shaken, though, wondering how the bat got into my room. I lock the door overnight, and the screen on the outdoor window is intact. There's a hole in the window screen facing the hallway, but three fingers can barely fit through.

Some say bats are messengers. If so, what has this one come to tell me?

When I leave the bathroom, I find Prosper using the bat for soccer practice in the hall. It's on its last legs, scrambling after Prosper kicks it. Esi clutches me as we pass him.

"Prosper," I say, "*mepa wo kyew!* Don't play with it."

He ignores me and I feel too light-headed from the fever to argue. I continue downstairs, Esi following closer than my shadow. I'm relieved to find Priscilla, Mr. Sumina's wife, standing outside their bedroom. "Prissla," as it's pronounced in Ghana. One hand is on her hip and the other is balled into a fist over her mouth. She jumps when she sees Esi and me approaching.

Her skittishness sends my thoughts back to New Year's Eve. I would have slept feverishly, missing the swelling voices at midnight from a nearby church choir, if not for her yelling downstairs. From the sound of it, she was throwing things, too, and I could hear Mr. Sumina's whimpering replies. With my limited command of Fante, I couldn't follow verbatim, but no precise words were needed. During my brief time at the house, I never saw Priscilla lose her cool, even with Prosper's misbehaving and tantrums. Then came something I understood clearly.

"*Sika wɔ hen!*" Priscilla exploded.

Where is the money?

I bolted upright in bed, instantly thinking of that duffel bag bulging with cedis and sensing she was referring to it. Mr. Sumina's response never came. A door slammed, followed by Priscilla's sobs. Another door banged, and all was quiet. My heart was racing, but I told myself to worry more about my fever and go to sleep.

Now Priscilla fidgets with the shiny lock of permed hair emerging from her headscarf.

"Yaa," she says in a raspy voice, "I have not prepared your breakfast yet."

"That's okay," I say, pointing upstairs. "I just wanted to tell you—"

An all-too-familiar gagging comes from behind the closed door. My mouth fills with a bitter taste.

"I hope he hasn't caught what I have."

Priscilla gives me a funny look. The door flies open, making us all jump. Mr. Sumina stands there shirtless. His eyes are bloodshot. He walks past us and into the bathroom as though we're not there.

"Yaa. Please." Priscilla avoids my eyes. "Wait for me in the dining room, eh?"

I turn to go but nearly trip over Esi. She stares vacantly at the floor of the bedroom, where there are several empty bottles of beer.

· · ·

Ato Ashun has a crush on me. Either that, or he likes to smile as much as I do. I can see that smile from twenty feet away as I approach Elmina Castle, where he works as a tour guide. Although it's a welcome sight, it's not one I hoped for my first month working with Mr. Sumina. He did manage to find a family for me during Edina Bronya's first day, just by parking in front of a large house and hailing the family members milling outside. They agreed to Mr. Sumina and me photographing them as they opened the ceremony, pouring libations for their ancestors. Without asking for anything in return, they also invited us to eat and drink gin, and receive New Year's blessings with them in the form of clay painted on our forearms. I was glad that my appearance went largely ignored—ideal for my intended role as participant-observer—but the family revealed no heirlooms or secrets about slavery.

Since then, Mr. Sumina has found hardly any interviewees for me, so

I've spent time observing tours at the castle, which I'd also proposed for my Fulbright. My novel alternates between the eighteenth century and the present day, where it explores the controversy over the castle's restoration, framed as preservation versus the whitewashing of history. My tour observations so far align with what I've read in academic studies about the issue: diaspora tourists who descend from slaves, like me, tend to react the most emotionally to the castle's history and prefer guides like Ato, who don't shy away from divulging the callous treatment of enslaved Africans in the castle's dungeons.

With Ato, I ignore the trusted advice of Naa, an American doctoral student I met in Accra. On one of our many seemingly chance encounters, she told me: "You should not smile so much here, Kim. People will take advantage of you." Her father is Ghanaian and she speaks his language fluently. Her mother is white, though, giving her the same cinnamon complexion as me and marking her as obviously *oburonyi*—a stranger, like me. Perhaps that commonality prompted her to play big sister whenever we met. "The guys will especially use you," she continued. "They think that all foreign women are loose. We are the ones they play with. Ghanaian women are the ones they marry."

I recalled the new hiplife song circulating on the radio stations: "Adwoa *yɛ me yere*; Yaa *yɛ me mpena*." *Adwoa is my wife; Yaa is my girlfriend.* For the moment, I didn't want to be Yaa. Naa was surprised to learn I didn't have a boyfriend already. I'd had many offers, in fact, but my prospects didn't seem appealing or sincere, such as the dreadlocked "wee"-smoking Rastas who called me "queen" and "sister," and the men who tried to dress and talk like American rappers. I ventured to date a man in Accra but dropped him after he asked for money to get to his friend's uncle's cousin's funeral.

"I think I'll trust my gut," I told Naa.

"But it is more than just your gut, Kim. People can seem so genuine."

She put a hand on my arm. "I do not mean to make you paranoid. But many people are desperate here. Make sure you realize what they want and what you can realistically give."

Ato seems to want nothing except my company, though. Mr. Sumina arranged an interview with him and advised treating him to a drink instead of the usual nominal payment. I've tried, to no avail. If I invite Ato to lunch or to a beer or taxi ride, he pays. When he refused to let me buy a sachet of water for him one day, I explained what I was trying to do. He pushed my money aside and handed the vendor two 100-cedi coins, purchasing waters for us both.

When he escorts me from the castle grounds to the taxis headed back to Cape Coast, he walks on the outside of me, shielding me from the traffic. When he talks to me, his eyes never stray to my chest. On our recent walks through Elmina, he's slipped his hand into mine. In Ghana, platonic friends of any gender hold hands in public, though I've sensed some men trying it with me to get a free feel. I don't get that vibe with Ato, even as many Elminans direct their eyes to our joined hands. With Ato at my side, I feel taller, safer.

One morning, I find him in the castle lobby, discussing politics with the receptionist. They debate whether some Ghanaians favored former president Jerry Rawlings because he was biracial with pale skin. Spotting me, Ato beams. I wave at him and go to flip through the visitor log, where the comments run from "An example of man's inhumanity against man . . . never forget!" to "What beautiful architecture!" Ato ends his conversation and joins me, reading over my shoulder.

"How do you do it, Ato, coming in here all the time and telling these sad stories?"

He flexes his biceps. "You must be strong-o. What happened here is done, the past. Nothing can change it. You cannot go around being angry or sad all the time."

Easy for you to say, I think. *It wasn't your ancestors who were sold.*

I immediately feel bad about my thought, knowing he isn't being insensitive. He also isn't like the many Ghanaian tourists who've horrified me by laughing when the castle guides detail the plights of the enslaved, including rape—Ato speculates that they laugh because the talk of sex embarrasses them. During my interview with him, I was excited to meet a Ghanaian who didn't suggest I "move on and forget" slavery since it happened "so long ago." He declared that if money weren't an issue, he'd bring his tour into town, since many Elminans grow up alongside the castle, as he did, unaware of the horrors that happened inside.

Staring at my hair, which I've styled in twists, he tells me I've just missed a group of diaspora tourists. Perhaps I might want to join them, he says, since they seem to be conducting a spiritual ceremony. I shrug and sit on the lobby bench, content to relax for a moment with him. I notice the receptionist, who always flirts with me, eying us with envy.

"I am curious," Ato says. "Is it that all African Americans wear Rasta?"

"What're you talking about? I don't have dreadlocks."

"I meant that you guys don't like to perm your hair."

I tell him that the tourists he's met are a microcosm of Americans, whether Black or white, and that most Black women back home straighten their hair, as in Ghana. I did myself before learning to appreciate my African ancestry.

Ato tsks. "Then maybe I don't want to visit your country, if the castle here is the main place where I can see hair like this." He tugs on my twists. "So, how is your research coming?"

"Slow, as usual." I sigh. "You're from Elmina. Don't you know some elders I can interview?"

He backs away. "Well, Mr. Sumina is working with you already. I don't want to interfere with his plans."

What plans? Mr. Sumina and I accomplished more in the two days in early December than we have since I hired him.

"He's not my boss, Ato. This is *my* research."

"Give me some time to think on it." He touches my hand. "So, my dear, I must be off to do some paperwork. Mr. Mensah's tour starts soon. Will you join him?"

I tell him I will, and he springs to his feet to give an impersonation of his colleague, capturing Mr. Mensah's dramatic, drawn-out syllables to perfection. I giggle till my stomach muscles burn. As I'm wiping my tears, I notice the small group of natural-haired diaspora tourists in the courtyard. They wear white and carry candles and glare as if I've lost my mind.

• • •

If laughing in a slave castle—which some equate to a graveyard—isn't inappropriate enough, a few weeks later, I'm partying there. Mr. Sumina has invited me to a celebration for his friend at Elmina Castle, and an impromptu drum circle has sprung up in the back courtyard, where tourists are never taken. After seeing me tapping my feet, one of the dancers dragged me before the drums, probably expecting to teach *oburonyi* some moves.

The female slave dungeons, the part of the castle I most detest, are just beyond a high, solid wall. After crying there so many times, I never thought I could find joy in this place. But now, I smile and sweat and shake my body. Dancing has been my release for a long time, and now, I truly need it. Lately I've regretted having paid Mr. Sumina in advance. During our down time, which comes much too often, he's treated me to many beers while bragging about his abilities. One of the Fulbrighters who referred me, he said, fired her other assistants after learning they'd faked data, and hired him. She was so pleased with his work that she donated him the used car she'd bought—the green sedan.

It's not that he's done nothing for me; he's located some interviewees, but they are well educated, despite my urging for otherwise. I'm in search of local and family histories, so I don't need informants with perfect English or PhDs. These people have recounted elaborate stories, but they often come from the same history books I've consulted. Foreign scholars who've conducted interviews in the area have referred to this phenomenon as "feedback." These mostly white men have also concluded that the history of slavery has been forgotten, since locals claimed to know nothing about it. They apparently hadn't met my research contacts, who claimed to have personal knowledge of familial slavery artifacts and the like, and who insisted that the history I sought was there, even if I was yet to find it.

Something else has bothered me about Mr. Sumina. When scheduling interviews with chiefs, he volunteered to make introductions for me. "They prefer it if a man does these things, you see," he said with a grin. Traditional protocol dictates bringing Schnapps for libations along with a monetary presentation. Before each visit, Mr. Sumina has shown me the bottle in its gray package, seemingly as proof that he spent my 70,000 cedis on it. Already sensing traces of dishonesty, I found myself wondering if he had a stash he'd bought wholesale, for much less. I also wondered if Mr. Sumina gave the chiefs my additional money and wished I could ask them, but it didn't seem appropriate.

When I notice Mr. Sumina sipping beer at the edge of the drum circle and smirking at me, I stop moving my butt so much. The man who got me to dance breaks into a sweat and stumbles away, unable to keep up. The crowd cheers me on in Fante, some of them pointing two fingers, the sign that someone's dancing well. They are wide-eyed as usual to discover that a "white person" like me has rhythm. I wonder if any of them will press cedis to my forehead, as I've seen done, but my skin is dry. By the time I do start sweating, my chest is burning and my throat feels parched, but I'm less tense about the progress of my research. I feel extra eyes on me and look up to see Ato leading tourists on the walkway high above. He smiles at me and waves before disappearing down the corridor.

I collapse onto the nearby covered cistern next to a drowsy-eyed Mr. Sumina. He gulps down the rest of his beer and places a hand on my shoulder. Squeezes.

"Yaa. I like the way you dance. The thing you do with your waist. It looks even more beautiful on a pretty girl like you."

I can feel his fermented breath on my temple. I stand abruptly and avoid looking at him.

"I think I hear Ato calling me," I say, and leave the yard.

• • •

The sky is clear and blue with a light cool breeze. Not too hot, not too dry, not too humid. A perfect day, made even better by the fact that I've finished mailing applications to five creative writing MFA programs, which was an ordeal. Internet cafés are as prevalent in Cape Coast as beauty salons, practically on every corner, but computer and dial-up speeds vary. I've had to sample several cafés to get all my documents printed properly, followed by visits over multiple days to two clerical shops to trim the A4 paper to the American size.

The clerk who made my day wore his pants in the Kumasi style Ghanaians joke about, the waistline coming up nearly to his chest. I held my snickers, seeing that he cut my papers meticulously. He was stunned when I tipped him, and I was shocked to have to explain that it was for excellent service. So many other Ghanaians, it seemed, were trying to squeeze every last pesewa from me, including the clerk the day before, who turned my paper into confetti and grew incensed when I refused to pay the full price. Then there are the taxi drivers and street vendors who give me the inflated *oborunyi* price.

Then there is Mr. Sumina. I've tried to ignore his increased flirting, but I can't disregard his business practices, and incidents have been piling up. The drum instructor he arranged for me, a tall, lanky Hausa man named Hassan, was late and moody showing up to the house one day. Never before had he been late. "On African Time today, huh?" I teased, and he cut me a look. He watched me stumble through the rhythms he'd taught over the past few weeks, drilling me until my fingers ached. When he noticed me wincing, he took hold of my hand. I flinched, thinking he might whip out a cane to crack across my palm, as Ghanaian children reported happening at school, but he lightly rested his hand faceup in mine. I made a face at his calluses and blisters, which finally got him to laugh. He suggested ending early so I could recover.

Before leaving, he asked for a donation for his dance troupe. I saw from his donation sheet that most sponsors had pledged 10,000 to 20,000 cedis—up to $3.00. When I offered 40,000, the amount I gave Mr. Sumina for a half hour of lesson time, Hassan shook my hand, thanked me profusely. I was further startled when he grabbed both my hands and pumped them again. On his way out, he waved the money over his head and blew kisses. Not long after, I saw him at an internet café and learned Mr. Sumina hadn't paid him until then. When I asked the rate Mr. Sumina had promised to him, I wasn't surprised to learn it was much less than the 40,000 I donated to Hassan's cause. In other words, Mr. Sumina had to be taking a cut of around 80 percent. I proposed to Hassan that I would take dance lessons with his troupe, and that I'd pay him the amount Mr. Sumina quoted me, directly.

Around the same time, a new tenant moved into the third bedroom down the hall, a Dutch high school student named Kaatje. She'd saved money over two years to come to Ghana for a monthlong volunteer program. She invited herself into my room not long after meeting me and shut the door.

"I can ask you something, Kim?" she said, sitting on my bed and fidgeting with her platinum blond dreadlocks. "How much is cedi to dollar?"

"About seven thousand five hundred."

"Everywhere?"

"Well, the forex bureaus or the black market exchange give you a better rate than the banks, but it's not much different."

"Mr. Sumina exchanged money for me yesterday. He told me rate is six thousand."

I stared at the drum I used for lessons, a medium-size djembe with crudely carved Adinkra symbols around the base. Mr. Sumina, of course, offered to procure it for me. I'd recently seen a larger, nicer one owned by an American exchange student at the nearby University of Cape Coast. Hers came with a padded batik cover, and she bargained for it on her own at the Accra crafts market, where the prices are notoriously inflated for foreigners. My stomach felt queasy when she told me she'd paid 100,000 cedis less than what Mr. Sumina charged me.

"Kim?" Kaatje was touching my arm. "Next time I think I exchange money myself."

I nodded. "I think that's a good idea, Kaatje."

The rhythmic thump of fufu being pounded in someone's yard echoes as I approach Mr. Sumina's house. I push open the front door and hear Kaatje and Mr. Sumina chatting in the living room, along with the faint sound of the TV. I halt when Mr. Sumina mentions my name.

"She say not to go to that one," Kaatje says.

"It is owned by a friend of my family," Mr. Sumina responds, chuckling. "Do you not think they will treat you well there?"

"But Kim saying computers too slow."

"These Black Americans." He sucks his teeth long and hard. "They gossip *paaaa*. I wish she would just get out of my house."

I go cold. "Gossipers"—just one of the many negative labels I'm learning Ghanaians have for African Americans, in addition to "stingy" and "unfriendly." Stingy, because we bargain hard, whereas white people—who know they're being cheated—don't want to cause a fuss. Unfriendly, because we get sick and tired of Ghanaians approaching us with bad acting, asking for a handout. Gossipy, because we don't keep silent about who's doing it to us.

Mr. Sumina swings into the hallway and stops short upon seeing me. He stares at the floor and strides past me. My eyes follow his shadow. The front door opens, flooding the hallway with bright light.

"I am going out," he says coolly behind me. "And Yaa, from now on, whenever my guests ask you about services here, you should refer them to me, understand? You do not know Ghana as well as you think.

"And Hassan told me you asked him about lessons. I don't appreciate you going behind my back and meddling with my relationships. You do not understand how we do business here."

The door slams shut.

Only after I'm in a taxi headed to Elmina Castle do I realize there was something odd about his reaction. I expected him to be irate that I realized he's been playing middleman—incidentally, the role Fantes played during the slave trade—without my knowledge or consent. But there was fear, not anger, behind his words.

• • •

The castle receptionist gives me a curious look as I trudge into the lobby. He doesn't flirt. He shuffles his papers noisily, saying, "Ato will come, eh? He is just completing a tour."

I continue to the central staircase inside the main courtyard and sit, slumping over. A few of the castle staff come into the yard, and I hear them whispering, "Is Yaa okay?" I consider the irony: the place I thought I'd hate most in Ghana, the place where my ancestors possibly passed through and suffered, has become my sanctuary. Kweku, a recent graduate of the University of Ghana who's doing his National Service as a tour guide, approaches me.

"Ei, Kim! What is it? Are you not feeling well?"

"Things aren't going well with Mr. Sumina. I'm ready to go back home."

"Oh, but Kim! Think about your research. It is not completed. You have only a few more months. You can make it."

I shake my head.

"It is that bad?"

My lips tremble, but I refuse to cry. I'm tired of crying in Ghana.

"Let me get Ato."

"No!" If I see him, I won't be able to hold my tears.

Kweku squeezes my hand. "I am coming."

He dashes away before I can stop him. He returns with the gift shop attendant, Patience, who is temperamental. Now, learning of my predicament, she hugs me and says, "My place is small-small, but Yaa, you can come stay with me. You let me know by this evening, and I will copy the key for you. Do not leave Ghana now. Okay?"

But I've moved so many times already and am sick of it. In the courtyard, Ato keeps turning to stare at us as he wraps up his tour. He makes a beeline for us as soon as he's done, and Kweku and Patience step aside. Ato kneels and grabs my hands and stares at me, and it's too late to turn my head. He passes me a handkerchief as the tears roll.

"Hey, hey, girl! What is it?"

"I can't stay there anymore, but I have no place to go."

He stands abruptly. "I am tired of this-o. Your stay here should not be so difficult. I will go today and ask my family if you can lodge with us. We have an extra room that no one is using."

"But Ato—"

"No buts. I will let you know soon what they decide." He touches my chin. "Be strong, Princess. All will be well."

• • •

I'm at a crossroad, literally and figuratively. I stand at an intersection on the University of Cape Coast campus in search of an internet café, feeling like the wretched ghost from Ama Ata Aidoo's seminal play—the one who stands at Elmina junction singing, "Shall I go to Cape Coast? Or to Elmina? I don't know, I can't tell." My gut tells me that if I part ways with Mr. Sumina now, he won't refund my remaining two months of money. And what if he spreads rumors about me to sabotage my research?

I finally decide to take the road to my right, having heard about a new café that way. Short trees line the winding street, their naked branches forming a canopy. I quicken my pace when I see the large satellite dish at the roadside, but sigh to find the café door locked. As I'm turning to leave, the door creaks open. The man standing there is tall, with the triangular eyes of a Nigerian Nok sculpture. He has that expectant look I've come to anticipate from Ghanaian men.

"My sister, are you coming to use the internet?"

I nod.

"Oh, but our connection is down."

"Yeah, I see." I start to walk away.

"Sister, exercise patience! It should be running again soon."

Maybe it's the way he's saying "sister." I fix him with a cautious stare and note the gold band on his left ring finger, not that it means anything. But his smile seems to overflow with innocence.

"My sister, come inside where it is cool. Rest yourself awhile."

I follow him into a small air-conditioned room, which contains five new computers with flat-screen monitors. We sit on stools facing each other. He extends a hand and tells me his name is Valentino, given to him because he was born on Valentine's Day. He cheeses, revealing a gap between his front teeth. My face breaks into a smile and I introduce myself in return, telling him my purpose in Ghana.

I remove my floppy disk from my bag. "How much do you charge for printing?"

"How many pages do you need to print?"

"Just one."

"Don't worry about it, Kim. Let me connect the printer."

I open my document as Valentino fiddles with cords beneath the desk. He avoids looking at the screen as he loads the printer. I click Print and hurriedly close the window. Valentino watches me scroll my printout. It's something I meant to prepare a long time ago: documentation of the transaction between Mr. Sumina and me at the Standard Chartered bank, with lines for our signatures.

Valentino stares as if waiting for me to continue some conversation we've been having half our lives. I roll the paper tighter.

"Valentino, I've been getting . . . would you say that Ghanaians look at African Americans unfavorably?"

"You know, Kim, we Ghanaians have something very unfortunate going on here." He eyes my paper again, as if he knows what it is. "There is a lot of deception and greediness in this country. Ghana is full of people who would not hesitate to sell their own flesh. There are some whites who come, and we treat them better than we do you."

He mentions the local saying I've heard during my interviews: "On your way to church Sunday morning, if you see a white man, turn around, because you've just met God."

I nod, recalling things I've observed since my semester abroad, such as Ghanaian waiters rushing to serve white people standing on line behind African Americans—we're "white" until the real white folks show up. I've sensed that it's because some white people treat Ghanaians well—better than they would ever treat African Americans back home. A white American Fulbrighter in neighboring Burkina Faso became vulnerable enough to confirm it for me. She admitted that she finds it easier interacting with Africans. African Americans, she said, have a defensiveness that intimidates white people, and she always fears she'll slip and say something racially inappropriate. In Ghana, I've recognized the same defensiveness of African Americans in Ewe people. I could only assume that as with us, it comes from having to prove yourself because some dominant group has relegated you to second place.

I ask Valentino where he thinks the negative attitude toward African Americans originated.

"Chiefs sold other Africans," he explains, "and we Ghanaians have carried that same mentality into the present day."

"But they weren't selling their own people. It was usually their enemies and war prisoners. And they didn't know what the white people did to us on the other side."

He shrugs. "Perhaps if they had known, they might have continued, out of plain greed. Regardless, their actions have affected Ghanaians today. I am an Anlo Ewe. I am sure you must have heard that there are tensions between the Asantes and us."

I nod, awed to have found an unanticipated informant for my research.

"It is not only tribalism. Some of it stems from the relationship we had during the slave trade." He taps on the Bible sitting on the counter near him. "There is a story here about what happens to the land when so many foul things happen on it. Eventually, the land will reject its own people. Take the Fantes, who bought slaves to sell to the whites. The Fantes were wealthy then, but now many of their descendants live in poverty. They may leave home, and they will thrive. But if they remain in places like Cape Coast or Elmina, they cannot advance."

He calls it a generational curse, just like he feels has happened with the Kennedys. The American political family earned their riches boot-legging, he points out, and look how tragically most of the men died. Valentino then tells me something I've been reminded of by Ghanaian friends, on the local radio stations, in the archival records: slavery still exists in Ghana in the form of house servants. They are usually poorer relations who do household chores in exchange for room, board, and school fees. While they are no longer bought at the market, they can still be exploited. The curse, Valentino avows, cannot be cleansed until local people stop practices like this and atone for the sins of their ancestors.

"There are too many greedy Ghanaians," he says. "But do not call them that! Oh no! They would rather be called a fornicator, because it is easier to prove one is a fornicator, yes?" He chuckles, and I manage a laugh.

"So why are there so many greedy people if they go to church so much here?"

His eyes widen. "Christian clones! What does church have to do with anything, Kim? True Christianity means striving to live the biblical principles daily. Many of us have nothing going. We are jobless, hungry, and poor. When you go to church, you are promised this place called heaven. So why not sit in church or prayer meetings most of the week? Basically give up your life and wait for some beautiful, painless promised land."

Mr. Sumina, unlike many Ghanaians in the south, is not a Christian, but my friends in Accra came to Valentino's conclusion when I shared my suspicions about his swindling: "It is because we Ghanaians are so poor." But he is most definitely not. His house is two stories and sprawling, and he inherited it from his family. His car was gifted. He has a full-time job and earns supplemental income from his occasional research assistance and from consistently renting to foreigners, at least two at any given time. That all seems more than enough to support his family—unless he has another one somewhere, as my friends suspect, in addition to his love of beer.

"This Mr. Sumina," said one of my friends, a Ga professor who opened her home to me for no cost in Accra when I struggled to find housing, "what is his tribe?"

"He's a Fante."

"Ah! You should have mentioned that first-o. Those Fantes are big cheats. It comes from when they collaborated with the whites long ago during slavery."

It's the most common condemnation I've heard against Fantes. But of course, as with most stereotypes, it isn't universal.

● ● ●

My latest residence at Ato's family house in Elmina has nothing of the luxury of Cape Coast. It has two stories as well but is made of hundred-year-old mud bricks. There is no running water, and the latrine is sometimes stocked with newspaper for wiping. My bedroom is much smaller. But Ato's multigenerational family of seven has embraced me like royalty. They won't let me iron my own clothes or sweep my floor. Like Priscilla, Ato's mother prepares me a daily breakfast of oatmeal and fresh pineapple, and she gives me the biggest portions of dinner.

A few weeks into my stay, Ato's nine-year-old niece announces at my room that I have a visitor. I push open my screen door and freeze. My breath comes jagged as Mr. Sumina rises from an armchair in the living room. A chair I don't want to sit in again. He's wringing a handkerchief and wearing a smirk like the one President George W. Bush can't quite hide as he labels everyone's actions evil except his own.

"I was in the neighborhood, Yaa, so I came to see how you've been faring."

"How dare you come here?"

Big Uncle, who is ironing a shirt in front of the TV, pauses to look at us.

Mr. Sumina laughs softly. "But, Yaa, why do you talk to me so rudely, when I have taken time from my schedule to come and ask of your well-being? What have I done to you?"

"You know what."

Shortly after moving out, I called to ask him for a refund for my remaining two months. As I anticipated, he refused, saying, "But you left on your own. We did not ask you to leave." Kaatje, whom I later saw at the market in Cape Coast, told me he filled my room with two foreign students less than a week after I left and charged them each what I paid. She also said she would have followed my example if she had another place to stay, and besides, she had only two more weeks to go.

Since leaving his home, I've encountered more people who've commiserated with me: Ghanaians Mr. Sumina introduced me to, either informally or through interviews. When I declined to detail why I moved out, they said, "That man you were running with is no good. He was cheating you, wasn't he?" One of them added: "And that other woman, the one who left him the car? He was cheating her, too!" I wish they could have hinted it earlier, but that would have been considered gossiping. I'm relieved at least to know there's no way Mr. Sumina could have bad-mouthed me to anyone.

Now he stands before me, looking like the child who denied dipping into the cookie jar, even though crumbs are on his mouth.

"So, Yaa, does this mean that you do not wish for me to call on you?"

"Exactly."

I feel myself snarling as he walks past me and down the front stair-case. I want to run to the porch and cry "Thief!" like Ghanaians do when someone's stolen something. It would incite the idle Elminans below in Trafalgar Square to chase him for all he's worth.

A hand touches my arm, and I jump. It's Big Uncle.

"Yaa, he has upset you. What is the matter?"

"He took something from me and won't return it."

"Then go and take it."

I shake my head and tell him it isn't so simple. I'll have to leave it up to Mr. Sumina's karma, something he should know well, since he studies East Asian spirituality. Maybe he'll spend all that *oburonyi* money drinking himself into jaundice. Maybe foreigners' "gossip" will spread until he's unable to get anyone to rent from him. Already, I met one of his new tenants on a castle tour, an African American college student. She isn't as rosy-eyed as I was during my semester abroad, perhaps because she's met Mr. Sumina during her first visit to Ghana. She mentioned that he installed a shower without asking if she wanted it, then charged her for it. When she complained, he acted indignant, arguing that he did it for her comfort. "Everyone's so damn dishonest here," she said, frowning. "I'm so bitter at this point and ready to go back home. It's not the price but the principle."

My thoughts exactly. I wouldn't have minded if Mr. Sumina told me up front that he was taking a cut, considering his prices were still affordable with my Fulbright stipend. I might have also been eager to tip him and extend my time with him—at least, had he not faltered with interviews and had not started flirting. Now the only thing he's earned from me is more gossip: a warning to anyone to stay away. On the flipside, Ato's family, who are supposedly dishonest Fantes, have not asked a pesewa of me, and I want to give and give, but as with the

Ga professor in Accra, Ato has told me they would take offense if I offered money.

Even so, my experiences in Ghana have taught me to be watchful with them, and I feel awful about it. *When will it come?* I wonder. *When will they ask for money to redo the flooring or install plumbing?* Because even if they aren't planning to scheme me, if they truly consider me an honorary family member, they might expect me to contribute something due to my financial situation. During one interview with an elder in a rural village, for example, I got wistful and told him he looked like my uncle. He responded without pause, without any trace of sentiment, "Well, then you are my family, and my roof has fallen, so fix it."

Many travel guides declare that friendliness—such as Ato's family's invitation to live with them—is one of Ghana's most distinguishing assets, but now I see that friendliness in a different light. For one, Ghanaians tell me they don't consider themselves more cordial just because they greet people more than the average Westerner; it's merely part of the culture. Further, there's the friendliness that comes with strings attached. When I returned home after my study-abroad semester, I told my Ghanaian classmates at college about people saying, "Welcome home, my sister." I was especially moved by the little boys at Elmina Castle, who pressed notes of homecoming into our hands. One friend of mine snickered, saying, "They were just trying to get money from you." That wasn't true of everyone, but I now know that those Elmina boys have made a racket out of pulling at diaspora tourists' heartstrings. A few years ago, Ato told me, an African American tourist was so moved as to shower them with hundreds of dollars, which encouraged them to hang out at the castle for more.

When preparing to return to Ghana for my Fulbright, Ghanaian friends urged me to always tell locals that I have connections or family in the country, even if I don't. It didn't make much sense then. I now understand if folks believe someone local will hold them accountable, they'll think twice about mistreating you. I forgot that advice in my dealings with Mr. Sumina.

I'm saddened for all those diaspora tourists who step foot in Ghana and remark that they've returned home. Who arrive to the castle dungeons with their anger and tears. I think of the Ghanaians who rain them with kindness—real or otherwise—and who designate them honorary chiefs and queen mothers and give them African names. These Ghanaians could very well descend from people who sold their ancestors. Today, we come to Africa without the facial markings or other physical markers of belonging, with little or no knowledge of the cultures and languages, and with our desired American dollars. And our fate is to get sold, again.

Joe Robert Cole

The Killmonger Doctrine
of Color and Humanity

ESSAY

[This essay is not part of Marvel canon or the Marvel Cinematic Universe, but the musings of a brown-skinned writer during quarantine.]

One evening in the winter of 2020, I was spiraling down a Google wormhole for a project that I was working on when a few YouTube clips of people talking about the complicated relationship between Africans and African Americans sparked my curiosity. At moments, the individuals in the clips were inspiring and insightful, while other moments were frustrating. The dynamic between African Americans and Africans is one that Ryan Coogler and I explored narratively in the screenplay for the movie *Black Panther*, so I had spent some time thinking about the subject in the process of writing the film. In *Black Panther*, the fictional African nation of Wakanda celebrates liberty among its own people while turning a blind eye to the generations of oppression of people of African ancestry outside its borders. It serves as a cautionary tale of the potential consequences that can arise when basic human and civil rights are not vigorously advocated for on behalf of all people. Inflamed by these injustices, the character of Killmonger envisions a world where the African Diaspora and the African continent come together and take a stand against the mistreatment of Black people everywhere.

In one of the YouTube clips, a woman from Africa, who does not specify her country of origin, charges that African Americans do not do enough to learn about Africa. As I listened, two questions crossed my mind: First, which country of the more than fifty African nations did she mean? All of them? Just hers? Second, when and where, in a practical sense, would the average African or African American meaningfully learn about one another? The connection is certainly not fostered in the elementary and high school systems in the United States, and from what I have been able to ascertain, the study of African Americans is not a part of many, if any, primary and secondary school African curriculums.

In the public schools that I attended in the United States, Africa received little or no attention. My early perception of the continent was formed by images of starving children on commercials, colloquial platitudes of past African kings and queens, and news stories of end-less wars. One would imagine that institutions of higher learning offer the most opportunities, outside of finding books on your own or social advocacy groups, to learn about the ties between the two groups—but how many academic programs exist with a focus on the through lines connecting Black Americans to Africa beyond the slave trade? I am sure there are some, but I am guessing not many.

When I was hired to write *Black Panther*, my knowledge of Africa weighed on my mind. I had written many scripts without walking in the door with a full grasp of the place at the center of a story, but this felt different, more personal. Throughout college and my adult life, I eagerly delved into books on African American history, African history, and the unpacking of white supremacy, but the prospect of representing a place and a people that all too often had been painted with a broad brush and woefully misrepresented was sobering. It was also, in many ways, similar to the challenges of representing African Americans onscreen. Everyone involved with the film felt a deep importance in depicting all our characters with respect. We consulted historians and collaborated with individuals from the continent, and members of the production visited Africa in preparation for the film. One reverberation after the film's release has been a heightened interest in African cultures, politics, and histories. Similar to the commercials and news stories from my childhood, popular culture has always played a role in shaping how we view each other, but our goal was never to educate, only to speak from a personal place through our lens on the world. The answer to learning about one another goes beyond entertainment.

There is a broad awareness of the concrete anthropological connections between Africans and African Americans, but for many reasons there is a limited sense of shared common ground. It is well documented that the familial and cultural ties Africans brought with them across the Atlantic starting in the seventeenth century were intentionally severed. Over time, that vacuum has been filled largely with misrepresentations and caricatures of Africans on the continent and members of the African Diaspora, which have been force-fed to people globally for centuries.

Let's look at the narratives Africans and African Americans likely have received about each other at some point in our lives: "Most Africans are impoverished and starving"/"Most African Americans are poor and needy." "Most Africans squander their resources"/"Most African Americans squander their opportunities." "Most Africans are primitive and hypersexual"/"Most African Americans are uncultured and hypersexual." "Most Africans are criminal and thirsty for war"/"Most African Americans are criminal and hyperviolent." The insidious similarities in these depictions are no coincidence. You will find analogous portrayals of members of the African Diaspora wherever they reside.

Anyone who doesn't fit into one of these pejorative boxes is framed an "exception," no matter how many exceptions there are—even if there are more exceptions than there are people who fit the stereotype.

For centuries, colonialism and the transatlantic slave trade provided the incentives of avarice and self-interest to spread the lie that whiteness was inherently superior to Blackness across the globe. These iniquitous motivations have impelled this fallacy to permeate most institutions in most cultures, and these institutionalized structures (like our aforementioned educational systems) have enduringly perpetuated this falsehood in a maddening loop. In tandem, to protect their gains, white-dominated nations have historically worked to keep Blacks on and off the continent from forming any substantive bonds, actively promoting the divisions and falsehoods that have some of us distanced from one another today.

Imagine if every indigenous African and Black person who lives outside Africa began to take our cues on recognizing our connection and shared interests in economic development, education, health care, representation, immigration, human and civil rights from a world whose treatment of us has, in application, rarely, if ever, been about merit or flag or culture as much as it has been about skin color—all in the pursuit of individual and national gain and the maintaining of power, resources, and profit. Pan-Africanism is certainly not a new concept. Leaders from Kwame Nkrumah to Malcolm X have argued for this shared sense of identity. You might question if it is reasonable to ask Black people from a diverse range of nations to feel connected simply because of our skin color. I would ask in response: Is it reasonable for the vast majority of white people to buy into a global system that benefits them because of their skin color? Has that not been our reality for the past several hundred years? Our world largely provides privilege to those with white skin and obstacles to those the darker your complexion gets. This is a fact that cannot be ignored in any honest discussion. Globally, whites have long rallied around their privilege despite their many nationalities, ethnicities, differences, and wars. That privilege has and continues to unite them, consciously and subconsciously.

Correspondingly, all too often, a single Black person represents all in the eyes of those who are not of African descent, and we are monolithically discriminated against despite our distinctions. This is sadly the case, at times, even by each other. We did not create this tent, but it is vital that we recognize that we are all in it together: Whether you are an African immigrant in the United States who perceives that you are treated better than African Americans, or an African American in Europe who perceives that you are treated better than Africans. Whether you are a Black conservative tired of "woke" culture, or you live in a wealthy enclave buffered from racial or socioeconomic strife, or you are an athlete, a celebrity, or a politician, or you live in a majority-Black or -Latino nation with limited interaction with non-Blacks, outside your window or your border, white supremacy is still at work. The umbrella of systemic racism hovers over all people of color in one form or another—regardless of our real or imagined safeguards. Make no mistake, even if you disregard all other factors, white supremacy is a powerful, unifying force connecting us.

I'm under no illusion that every African on the continent or member of the African Diaspora will buy into such an endeavor to unite around our collective oppression on the basis of our dark skin. Kwame Nkrumah was unsuccessful in convincing the bulk of his fellow African leaders to join forces, just as El Hajj Malik Shabazz's push for Pan-African unity was met with even more resistance than his calls for Black power as Malcolm X.

Some African Americans, Afro-Latinx, Afro-Caribbean, and indigenous Africans identify strongly with their African heritage, while others do not. Some see clearly the need to combat the relentless racialized color-based assaults against us, while others are not interested. The Killmonger Doctrine is simply a thought experiment into the conditions a vibrant Pan-African coalition might emerge from, and beyond that, the type of inclusive, big-picture collective mindset that would be necessary for it to flourish. It is easy for me to envision what an alliance like this could achieve in terms of social and economic equality, racial justice and human rights. But instead of delving into data and details that others are more qualified to speak about, I want to draw attention to a few human pitfalls that came to mind while watching those YouTube clips.

Members of the diaspora and Africans on the continent can't be beholden to knowing the ins and outs of everyone else's history and struggle as a prerequisite for unity. From media at every level to racist scholarship and curriculums, scientific and social research to legislation and laws, misinformation by omission and outright falsehoods has long been white supremacy's tool to obscure our knowledge of ourselves and each other. Pan-Africans have an opportunity to use these malign efforts as a call to unity, but to achieve that we must avoid casting the blame on each other.

Members of the diaspora and Africans on the continent can't be expected to dismiss our individual aspirations, cultures, or national pride. Calling for someone to brush aside a fundamental part of who they are in favor of their skin color misses the point. The ask here is not that Pan-Africans embrace each other in some utopia or put material demands on one another to prove our fidelity, but by acknowledging there is strength in numbers, we collectively and deliberately act in the best interest of the entire coalition when opportunities arise to lift all boats, in spite of our differences.

Members of the diaspora and Africans on the continent should not belittle or dismiss the ties that exist between us no matter how small or vestigial: hairstyles, recipes, and cultural practices that have survived slavery, and that many Black people who live outside Africa may not know have their origins in Africa; African spirituals and polyrhythms, which are central to so many musical styles in the Americas; religions like Santeria and Vodou; and the culture of oral tradition, from West African griot practices to African American folktales.

Building a collective fabric capable of uniting the diverse members of the entire African Diaspora and continental Africa will take empathy and acceptance. It will take the searching for and fostering of bridges among a breadth of tribes, nationalities, religions, customs, shades, and hues. A central question in *Black Panther* was "What does it mean to be my brother's keeper?" The isolationism of Wakanda fed Killmonger's pain in the film. In the real world, isolation from one another limits what each of us can accomplish standing on our own. Meaningful ties throughout the diaspora and continental Africa could open doors to deepened investment, opportunity, and advocacy across the globe. We have the chance to cultivate a stronger sense of unity if we choose.

Members of the diaspora and Africans on the continent should resist being pulled into the trap of litigating who has suffered the most under white supremacy and who has better responded to it. Our focus should be on the reality that white supremacy has been at work for centuries, targeting the African continent and the African Diaspora as a whole. Pitting one group's struggles against another's, and second-guessing how others have dealt with these daunting hurdles, does the work of disunity and division for those responsible. Examining all the successes and struggles within the diaspora and on the continent as a means to learn and have compassion for one another is a way to reframe the past to shape our future.

Lastly, members of the diaspora and Africans on the continent can't allow skin color to blind them. It has been true throughout history that the enemies of this cause can be any color, including Black. It should be a person's actions on behalf of combating systemic racism that dictate how they are seen—no matter their appearance. The fictional Killmonger rooted his solution to white supremacy in violence with an end goal of flipping Black for white in the current paradigm. That is not something that I am advocating in any way. The salient point is that Killmonger's failure was not in his point of view of the problem, but in the means by which he went about trying to solve it.

A unified front of all people of goodwill could wage the sustained fight necessary to expose, hold to account, and dismantle the white supremacist structures, messages, and messengers that have elevated skin color over merit. The greatest beneficiaries of white supremacy have shown they will fight every attempt at creating a more just world. Bigotry and bias will always exist, but leveling the playing field by rooting out global institutional racism will force those with those views to earn their sense of superiority, not simply rely on rigged systems to reinforce a manufactured lie. In that climate, fresh ideas and collaborations could spark new advancements and innovations to tackle the world's challenges. Bonds could be fostered where they were previously hindered, nurturing an expanded collective experience. The bet this coalition would be making is that the power to create a fairer world will come from the ability to unify people around the truth of our commonality.

The truth of our shared humanity.

Fatima Camara

Churai

Bring out the churai!
    The scented wood, that wet seed. Herbs plants and oils burned to
mask my mother's cooking.

    All the kids used to laugh. Cover their nose at the scent, but
their parents buy incense at the tobacco shop in the name of
aromatherapy. Fake oils, fake bamboo, set a blaze, trying to match
what has grounded my people for hundreds of years.
Bring out the churai!
    Back then, I knew nothing about ritual.

    When you are young, confused, and see no connection to what
has brought you, you cannot understand the dedication to the
burning of bark, dried flowers, and resin.
    How after cooking we spark. On Fridays, we spark.
    When visitors come, how we attempt to mirror Gambia &
conversations on the foyer of the compound. When all we have is
silence, when the entire house is cleaned, when we grieve

RELATIONS

Bring out the churai!

    In honor of the time my mother was missing warmth and sand the

most, so she sparked, the smoke filling the home and once cleared,

gifted my mother a memory.

    And in turn, she gifted me a story of land and dry heat. My

head

    on her pregnant belly, hoping the saying true, that the one who

rubs the belly most, is who the baby becomes.

    How mistaken I was, to see dirt instead of a beginning, to not see

them as one and the same.

Bring out the churai.

Sing me the melody I grew up on and in turn

sang to my sister when she was teething.

Ayo nay nay tuu ti

While the smoke traveled and became

part of

Tu tu baby Mariam

she sucked and nibbled on my knuckles

Ayo nay nay tuu ti

we cradled each other and found

Tuu tu baby Mariam

comfort

Ayo

and all we could smell

Nay nay

Was home.

Nay nay
Tu ti

Ayo nay nay
Tuu ti
Tuu tu baby
Mariam
Ayo nay nay
Tuu ti
Tuu tu baby
Mariam
Ayo
Nay nay
Nay nay
Tuu ti

Khal Torabully

[Coolitude: ce balisier-mirador]
[Coolitude: this balisier-mirador]

POEM

Coolitude: this balisier-mirador, my breath pushed into the abyss.

In the bays where swells subside, subdued,

history brought back to the time of mooring chains.

Here a reprieved land, a shout turned into a rallying cry

     in defiance of sentry-eyes . . .

My future will be tamed through audacious mosquitoes' confessions of

     thirst.

Coolitude: to put down my roots. I bend my resistance,

     refusing to make of myself an offering,

like flares elongated on the worried face of the sea's insurrection.

I know who bears high noon in the pulse of their quieted flesh.

Coolitude: to the climate recognized in the light of the rain,

my sword passes through the flash of the burnt mirror.

I lift the cover of coffers blackened by my elbows.

Khal Torabully

Who recovers my spices
from the fangs of overripe storms?
Polished by the patina of sea spray,
the ship's saffron unseals the bite of anoles.

Coolitude: tillers of Columbus, never tongue
without throat: Martinique, Guadeloupe, Trinidad, French Guiana . . .
Out of season, these beauties blighting the malanga harvest!

Coolitude: I know when the soft hands of a woman blaze
in the season of tales.
With calcareous defiance, she penetrates your glance,
her mouth smiling from the antics of her epic heroes.

Coolitude: how distant that land
where the tiger deepens the mystery of the secret country.
Let its mythical territory extend beyond our eyes!

Coolitude: oh, it's worse than all the fears from here,
the cobra dreaming in the middle of the cradle,
the mongoose leaping into the fire of its fangs!

Coolitude: your hands overcome monsoons,
accustomed to cutting the petals on rippled water.
You rock the shadows of children with eyelids of silences.
From your voice I only knew the scent of your veil, your hand
        where a verruca relates the melting-away of life.

Coolitude: I knew your full voice, this face encircled by my dreams, o
        maharaja on a white horse,

beheading the cutthroat thief of Cuttack.

Chameleons are only pale monsters

in the décor of His voice!

Coolitude: to submit to the word—

without forgetting memory

that still remembers nothing . . .

Translated from the French by Nancy Naomi Carlson

Translator's note: "Balisier-mirador" is a neologism combining "balisier" (a showy, tropical flower with petals arranged in spikes) and "mirador" (watchtower), with the intent of incorporating elements of verticality and transcendence.

Yejide Kilanko

This Tangible Thing

STORY

Bíbíire Kúkù's gnarled hands shook as she pushed open the heavy wooden shutters. A rush of cool air fanned her face leaving behind a tingling sensation.

In the far distance was the faint outline of Igbó Irúnmọlẹ̀. The enchanted forest gave their small village its name. Typical December morning, a Harmattan haze hovered above Lángbòdó, the lush green mountain at its core.

Bíbíire exhaled. Today, after eleven long years, she would get to hold her only grandchild, Àjọkẹ́. On the heel of the exhilarating thought came an acute wave of sadness. If only Bàbá Ẹniafẹ́ had waited to meet the precious child.

As she mentally pushed against the heavy feeling, Bíbíire reminded herself that her husband was resting. She had to let the man rest.

Latching on to a thread of fresh joy, Bíbíire adjusted her head wrap before hurrying out of the bedroom as fast as her slim octogenarian legs could manage. As she took careful steps down the flight of steep stairs, her housekeeper's melodic singing drifted toward her. Ìmọ́dòye arrived earlier than usual to help her get the house ready.

Ìmọ̀dòye stood in front of the gleaming double-burner kerosene stove. Her oval face, adorned with six short tribal marks on each cheek, lit up as soon as she saw Bíbíire. A fist went up in the air. "Màmá Seamstress for village president. This your cloth is fine o."

Bíbíire laughed. Her position as the first seamstress in Igbó Irúnmọlẹ̀ had earned her the title. The cotton fabric Ìmọ̀dòye complimented had a pattern of vibrant green leaves topped with bright gold flowers. At the market, Bíbíire could not resist the fabric's alluring call. "I see all your hard work," she said.

Ìmọ̀dòye inclined her head toward the stove. "When the fish stew is ready, I will fetch more water for the bathroom drums. Then everything will be ready."

Bíbíire nodded her appreciation. "Well done. I hope you are not in a hurry to leave? Ẹniafẹ́ wants to meet the person taking great care of his mother."

Ìmọ̀dòye looked pleased. "I will come back to greet him and Àjọkẹ́. I am sure you have many things to talk about."

Although Ẹniafẹ́ made regular telephone calls from Canada, it was not the same. Without their eyes meeting, it could not be the same. "I promise not to eat all the good things Ẹniafẹ́ brings."

"Since you are thinking about it," Ìmọ̀dòye said with a laugh. "I am not going home again."

Bíbíire snorted. "Who said you had an option?"

• • •

After Ìmọ̀dòye left, Bíbíire sat in the sitting room. Ẹniafẹ́ had called from the airport to tell her that their plane had landed safely and he was driving home in a rented car.

Three short horn blasts made Bíbíire jump to her feet. Finally! She gathered the folds of her ìró, tied the cloth securely around her waist, and hurried toward the front door.

Ẹniafẹ́ stepped out of the car and prostrated before her. "Ẹ káàsàn, Ma," he greeted.

"Káàsán, ọkọ mi." Bíbíire gestured at him to stand so she could wrap her arms around his expanding girth.

As she let go, Àjọkẹ́ came out of the vehicle. Bíbíire exhaled. The child looked like her! Tall and slim, one could easily say Àjọkẹ́ was thirteen instead of eleven. Bíbíire noticed how Àjọkẹ́'s dark brown eyes darted around the compound as if she anticipated danger.

Ẹniafẹ́ turned to his daughter and spoke to her in Yorùbá. "Aren't you going to greet your grandmother?"

Bíbíire's understanding was that while Àjọkẹ́ understood Yorùbá, she only spoke a few phrases.

Àjọkẹ́ mumbled something indecipherable under her breath as she held on to the sides of her long T-shirt, and curtsied like an English woman.

Bíbíire snorted her amusement. Ẹniafẹ́ should have taught his daughter how Yorùbá girls greet. She took the first step toward her granddaughter. Arms held to her sides, Àjọkẹ́'s rigid posture said, Don't touch me. Bíbíire's heart sank. To mask her disappointment, she turned her face away. "Let us go inside," she said. "You have come a long way."

Ẹniafẹ́ cleared his throat. "Màámi, I must head back to Lagos today."

Bíbíire frowned. Ẹniafẹ́ had told her they were coming home for a twelve-day visit. "Why?"

He sighed. "The airline placed our luggage on the wrong connecting flight. I need to be at the airport when they arrive. Ọdún sent some items to her family, and I must deliver them before we return. I came home because I knew you would be worried if you didn't see us today."

"You should eat something before you leave," Bíbíire said after swallowing the suddenly bitter taste in her mouth.

"Yes, Ma."

They walked into the house. "Where is the young woman helping you?" Ẹniafẹ́ asked as he looked around the sitting room.

"Ìmọ́dòye does not live here. She will visit later."

Ẹniafẹ́ frowned. "I thought we agreed that Ìmọ́dòye would move here?"

She and Ẹniafẹ́ had lengthy conversations before she'd agreed to hire a housekeeper. While she enjoyed the young woman's company, Bíbíire was determined to hold on to her dwindling independence for as long as she could.

Bíbíire shrugged. "The agreement must have slipped my mind."

Ẹniafẹ́ shook his head. "*Màámi.*"

"Yes, the son of his mother. I may be old, but I still have the right to live the way I want." She turned to Àjọkẹ́. "Come, my child. We need to set the table."

After sending her father a pleading look, Àjọkẹ́ reluctantly followed Bíbíire into the kitchen. Ẹniafẹ́ came along and helped. Head cocked, Àjọkẹ́ listened as she and Ẹniafẹ́ ate and discussed light family matters.

Àjọkẹ́ had barely touched her food. Bíbíire wondered if the pepper in the jollof rice was too much for her. She had asked Ìmọ́dòye to tone down the spice. As she opened her mouth to clarify, Ẹniafẹ́ groaned. "I think I overate."

Bíbíire clucked her tongue. "Your eyes were always bigger than your stomach."

"Màámi, Àjọkẹ́ is here."

"All the more reason why you should set a good example," she said.

Ẹniafẹ́ scowled. "You said I had to eat before leaving."

She sucked her teeth before turning to Àjọkẹ́. The child squirmed on her seat. "You want something?"

Àjọkẹ́ stayed silent.

"Your grandmother asked you a question," Ẹniafẹ́ said in a soft tone.

"The washroom," Àjọkẹ́ whispered.

She didn't understand the child's sudden need for cleanliness. "You can wash clothes after you finish your food."

Ẹniafẹ́ smiled. "Màámi, she needs to use the toilet." He pushed back his chair and turned to his daughter. "Come, I'll take you."

Several minutes later, he came back without Àjọkẹ́.

"Is she okay?" Bíbíire asked.

Ẹniafẹ́ sat next to her. "Yes. The toilet is Àjọkẹ́'s hiding place. I'll give her space while we talk."

A lump formed in her throat as she stared at Ẹniafẹ́'s sweaty face. "Son, you're too young to be this grey."

He ran a hand over his head. "I worry about Àjọkẹ́."

During their telephone conversations, Ẹniafẹ́ had hinted at some concerns. "What exactly is wrong with the child?"

Ẹniafẹ́ sighed. "The doctor diagnosed Àjọkẹ́ with an anxiety disorder called selective mutism."

Bíbíire frowned. "What is that?"

"Outside of our home and her best friend's house, Àjọkẹ́ barely speaks or responds to questions."

Bíbíire had never agreed with the saying that children should be seen and not heard. "Why?"

"We don't know. It is worse at school. Ọdún and I think something is going on there. We have tried, but Àjọkẹ́ refuses to speak to the professionals who can help or to us." Ẹniafẹ́ reached out and placed a hand on her arm. "You told me that as a child, there was a time when you stopped talking?"

Bíbíire went mute after her mother disappeared on a busy market day. But what she experienced afterward was not selective. Grief reached into her throat and took her voice. "I did."

"Màámi, I brought Àjọkẹ́ home so you could teach her what helped you."

An ancient Yorùbá proverb came to Bíbíire's mind. When a child kills a rat, he eats it alone; when he kills a bird, he eats it alone; but when he is in serious trouble, he drags it home to his father. She had to fill Bàbá Ẹniafẹ́'s large shoes.

Ẹniafẹ́ gave her a shaky smile. "Màámi, I missed you, too."

She missed him more. Ẹniafẹ́ was supposed to come back home after getting his graduate degree. His plans changed when he met his wife, Ọdún, at the same university. Home for him became a different country. Bíbíire placed her hand on top of her son's. It was not Ẹniafẹ́'s fault that he alone carried the total weight of their love and expectations because no other children came.

"Apart from this problem, you are happy over there?" she asked.

Ẹniafẹ́ pondered her question. "On most days," he finally said.

The response gave her some comfort. Being happy on most days was more than many people could say.

Ẹniafẹ́ moved away from her and pushed back his chair. "I need to tell Àjọkẹ́ I'm leaving her behind."

Bíbíire had assumed Àjọkẹ́ was going back with her father. "She would agree to stay?"

Ẹniafẹ́ looked uncertain. "I'm sure the process of retrieving our luggage won't be straightforward. She needs to spend our time here with you."

Àjọkẹ́ disagreed. She kept shaking her head and whispering no when her father informed her of his decision. From where she stood, Bíbíire could feel the intense distress bubbling underneath Àjọkẹ́'s skin.

"I know this is hard for you," Ẹniafẹ́ said in a soothing voice. "But sometimes we have to do hard things. Please speak to your grandmother. Remember, she can't read your mind, and she doesn't speak shrug. Will you do that for me?"

Tears ran down Àjọkẹ́'s cheeks. "Yes."

Ẹniafẹ́ pulled her close for a hug. "Thank you. I promise. I'll be back as soon as I can."

Long after her father left, Àjọkẹ́ sat on the verandah and stared in the direction of the road.

Seated on a nearby chair, an annoyed Bíbíire fanned her legs. It was dark, but Àjọkẹ́ had refused to go inside. When a loud screech pierced the air, a startled Àjọkẹ́ fell off her stool. She hurried to Bíbíire's side.

Happy that the child came to her, Bíbíire comforted Àjọkẹ́ with a touch. "It is okay, my child. There is nothing to fear. At night, an owl family perches on the walnut tree outside my bedroom window. They are just talking to each other."

She rose from her seat. "Come, let us go inside. It is long past this old woman's bedtime."

In the kitchen, Àjọkẹ́ watched as Bíbíire filled a large lantern with kerosene. While they were outside, the almighty Power Holding Company of Nigeria struck again. For as long as Bíbíire could remember, power outages were as sure as the rising sun.

Àjọkẹ́ held the lantern as they made their way upstairs.

Bíbíire led them to her bedroom. Judging by how Àjọkẹ́ had reacted to her father's departure, she did not think leaving her alone was the right decision.

After brushing her teeth and changing into a borrowed nightgown, Àjọkẹ́ took timid steps around the large room. In a corner was Bíbíire's sewing machine. The antique Singer sat on a wooden table mounted on a cast-iron treadle stand. Àjọkẹ́ bent and touched the wheel.

"I used to be a seamstress," Bíbíire said when Àjọkẹ́ stood and turned in her direction. "The proud proprietress of Àjọkẹ́ Sewing Institute."

Bíbíire chuckled when Àjọkẹ́'s right eyebrow shot up. The child probably thought she named the business after her. "The institute was established long before your parents met. Àjọkẹ́ is my name, too. It was what my father called me. But my mother loved the name Bíbíire. and that is what everyone knows. Your father named you Àjọkẹ́ to honor your great-grandfather and me." Bíbíire cocked her head. "Hmm. I wonder why he didn't tell you."

Àjọkẹ́'s gaze dropped.

There is a story there, Bíbíire thought. She covered a loud yawn before patting the bed. "This is my side."

Àjọkẹ́ sat on the mattress's edge. Then she lay down and curled into a ball, putting as much distance as she could between their bodies. Àjọkẹ́ soon nodded off. A restless sleeper, Àjọkẹ́'s arms and legs were everywhere. Bíbíire sighed with happiness when Àjọkẹ́ rolled over to her side. She had missed sleeping with someone next to her.

• • •

The days were passing too quickly. Ẹniafẹ́ was still in Lagos. Offering only short responses, Àjọkẹ́ followed Bíbíire around like a shadow, but she could tell Àjọkẹ́ was listening and digesting her lengthy monologues. Àjọkẹ́'s stoic expression slipped when Bíbíire told her about the party they threw after Ẹniafẹ́ called to announce Àjọkẹ́'s arrival.

Since Àjọkẹ́ arrived with only her hand luggage, Bíbíire decided to make her some simple outfits. She was pleased when Àjọkẹ́ sat at the dining table and drew pencil sketches of what she wanted. Bíbíire knew she was biased, but the child had evident talent.

Ẹniafẹ́ called every day. Bíbíire often stood near the toilet door to catch muffled snippets of the animated conversations. Speaking as if she had burning hot food in her mouth, the child couldn't get her words out fast enough.

Bedtime became Bíbíire's favorite time with her granddaughter. By the fourth night, Àjọkẹ́ no longer jerked away when their bodies touched.

On the morning of day five, Bíbíire woke up and found herself alone. Panicked, she hurried downstairs. The door to Bàbá Ẹniafẹ́'s study was wide open.

"Àjọkẹ́, are you in there?"

"Yes, Grandma."

The response calmed Bíbíire's racing pulse. In her nightgown, Àjọkẹ́ sat on the floor with her grandfather's old maps strewn around her. A guilty expression made her look like a child caught stealing a piece of meat from the pot. "Sorry."

"I am sure the maps are happy that someone is looking at them."

Àjọkẹ́ gave an audible sigh of relief.

"I have something for you," Bíbíire said as she brought the ancient bronze magnifying glass Bàbá Ẹniafẹ́ had kept in the top drawer of his large bureau-style desk. She handed it to Àjọkẹ́.

"You will be able to see more of the map symbols with this. I'm sure your grandfather would have wanted you to have it."

A big smile transformed Àjọkẹ́'s face. "Thank you, Grandma."

Bíbíire gave a dismissive wave. "It is nothing. We should go and get ready. I want us to take a walk around the village before it gets too hot for you."

Àjọkẹ́ began picking at her nails. It was not a good sign. "Child, what is the matter?" Bíbíire asked.

"If we're going to see stuff, I need my cell phone."

Àjọkẹ́ had left the phone behind in the hired car. Ẹniafẹ́ had found it. "Remember, your father will bring it for you."

"But I need my phone to take pictures."

"Pictures?"

Àjọkẹ́'s earnest words tumbled out. "Yes. For my best friend Panchita. When she and her family went to Chile, Panchita took pictures for me."

Bíbíire's cell phone was a basic one. Staring at Àjọkẹ́'s face, she

257

suddenly remembered the stash of disposable cameras her husband kept. It had been a couple of years, but they may still work, she thought.

As Bíbíire searched inside the large filing cabinet, Àjọkẹ́ stared at the framed family pictures lined up high on the wall. "What was Grandpa like?"

Bíbíire turned to look at her husband's picture. For his eightieth birthday, Bàbá Ẹniafẹ́ had reluctantly agreed to professional photographs. Dressed in an elaborate light brown *sányán* outfit decorated with the best gold embroidery she could afford, his tall, stiff cap sat at a rascally angle. A smile curved her lips. It was what he wanted.

"We Yorùbá people use the term *Ọmọlúàbí* to describe a person of good character, a courageous human with integrity. That was your grandfather. He was a small man with a larger-than-life personality. When he entered a room, people paid attention."

Àjọkẹ́ cocked her head. "How did you meet Grandpa?"

The vibrant memories warmed her. "The authorities brought your grandfather here to teach at the primary school. One day, he came to the shop where I was learning how to sew." She chuckled. "The headmaster said your grandfather needed trousers befitting a teacher and husband."

"So, you fell in love, married, and had Dad?"

"In those days, there was no falling, just choosing, and committing."

Bíbíire's heart leapt when she came across a stash of metal-cased disposable cameras. They were unused.

Àjọkẹ́ turned one over in her hand. "How do I check to make sure I like the picture after I take it?" she said.

"You can't see it. You will have to wait until you develop the pictures."

Àjọkẹ́ gave a heavy sigh. "*No filter*? That sucks. I never get perfect pictures the first or second time."

"It is this or nothing," she said.

"I'll take it."

She patted Àjọkẹ́'s shoulder. "It may not be a bad thing to take imperfect pictures."

The midafternoon sun was high in the sky when they ventured out of the house. As they walked down the stony path that curved along the river Ìyè, Àjọkẹ́ took several pictures. The water was so clear that one could see the bottom.

A woman wearing a wide-brimmed raffia hat and two small children drifted by in a bright blue canoe. Àjọkẹ́ returned their waves. She stared until the canoe came to a bend in the river and disappeared.

"Where does the river come from?" Àjọkẹ́ asked.

"The headwater is inside Mount Lángbòdó, which is at the center of the Igbó Irúnmọlẹ̀ forest."

Àjọkẹ́ sighed. "It's beautiful."

"There is something you can tell your friend when you show her the pictures," Bíbíire said. "Children with ancestral ties to this village cannot drown in the river."

"For real?"

Bíbíire took a moment to consider what Àjọkẹ́ was asking. "Are you asking if I'm telling the truth?"

Àjọkẹ́ nodded.

"In that case, yes."

Àjọkẹ́ narrowed her eyes. "Even if they can't swim?"

"The river carries them back to shore. I have seen it with my eyes."

"Hmm. How does the river know who belongs here?"

"It just does."

Àjọkẹ́ had a thoughtful expression. "Maybe the river keeps a database."

"What is that?" Bíbíire asked.

"Em, it's a collection of information, like names, addresses, or phone numbers."

The thought of river spirits keeping a database was laughable. "Perhaps we should visit the kábíyèsí to ask him about this database?"

"Who is the kábíyèsí?" Àjọkẹ́ asked.

"Ọba Aládégbayì, the king of our village."

"Does the king have a computer?"

Bíbíire shrugged. "I don't know what the king has."

Àjọkẹ́ glanced at the river. "If I were wearing my swimsuit, I would jump into the river to see what happens."

Bíbíire clucked her tongue. "You can do so after your father arrives."

"Maybe during our next visit to Nigeria, Dad will take me to the forest for a visit."

She doubted Ẹniafẹ́ would take his daughter into a forest teeming with ghommids, gnoms, and spirits. "We shall see."

Àjọkẹ́ looked disappointed. "That means no."

"That is not what I said."

Àjọkẹ́ pursed her lips. "Well, when Dad says those words, we never see."

Bíbíire let out a loud laugh.

During the walk back home, Àjọkẹ́ continued to talk without any prompting. Something had shifted for the child. Bíbíire thanked the ancestors for the gift.

• • •

That evening Àjọkẹ́ insisted on helping Bíbíire refill the lantern. She poured the kerosene and carefully adjusted the wick before striking the match.

"You have done a good job," Bíbíire said.

"Thank you, Grandma."

Àjọkẹ́ held the lantern as she led the way to the sitting room. "We will sit for some time before we go upstairs," Bíbíire said.

The lantern's flickering flame left huge shadows on the wall. Àjọkẹ́ stared at them. "It's almost like we're camping in the woods."

She liked the luxury of house walls. "Your parents take you?"

Àjọkẹ́ snorted. "No. I go with Panchita and her family."

"Panchita is a good best friend?"

"Oh, yes." Àjọkẹ́ smiled. "Panchita snorts when she laughs. And she laughs a lot."

"Laughter is good."

"That's what Panchita's mom says."

"She sounds like a wise woman."

"I like her a lot." Àjọkẹ́ glanced at the lantern. "The greenhouse at school uses solar panels. You should ask Dad to get you some for your roof."

"What do these things do?" Bíbíire asked.

"They use sunlight to make electricity. During wintertime, Dad always talks about missing the constant sunshine here."

She would ask Ẹ̀niafẹ̀ about these panels. "You are an intelligent child."

Àjọkẹ́ shrugged. "Everybody knows."

"I did not."

"Now you do. And when you come and visit us in Mapleville, you'll see what I mean."

The fear of being suspended in the air kept her at home. "If I come, will you take me to meet your teacher?"

Àjọkẹ́'s expression soured. "You don't want to come to my school. We have mean kids there."

"Mean?"

"They're not nice."

"What do they do?"

Àjọkẹ́ sang the words in a bitter tone. " 'Fie, fih, foh, fum, we smell the stench of the crazy mute.' " She threw up her hands. "Grandma, I

261

take a shower every single day. You can ask Dad. He says I use up all the hot water."

"That is what these children call you?"

Àjọkẹ́ nodded. "They also said I'm a joke. A crazy joke."

"Did you do something to them?" she asked.

"No! It's because of my horrible names."

Bíbíire frowned. "Horrible names?"

"Yeah. Think about it. Àjọkẹ́ *is* a joke."

She shook her head. "No, my child. Àjọkẹ́ is the name one gives to a daughter cherished by the entire family. I am a much-cherished child. You, too."

Àjọkẹ́ did not look convinced. "And my last name, Kúkù, sounds like 'cuckoo.'"

"The bird?"

"Yeah. That's what people at school call crazy people." Àjọkẹ́'s mouth tightened into a little ball. "I thought that if I stopped talking and stayed really quiet, I would blend into the background."

"God did not create you to blend into any background, my child."

"I wish he did."

A question nagged at her. "Why didn't you tell your parents about these children?"

Àjọkẹ́ shook her head. "Because they're both extra."

Bíbíire frowned. "What does that mean?"

"Their love is too much. I know they will come to school to cause a lot of trouble. It will only make things worse."

"My child, you are all that they have."

Àjọkẹ́ sighed. "Grandma, I just want to know why those kids at school won't leave me alone."

Bíbíire had always thought certain people, including children, feel important only when they're able to grind another in the dust.

"We only have one public high school in Mapleville. I'll never be able to escape them."

It was clear that Àjọkẹ́ needed to know who she was. "Listen. I am going to tell you the story of your ancestor. The first Kúkù."

Àjọkẹ́ sat up with an expectant look.

"Many, many moons ago, a child was born to an Ìjẹ̀bú family. The boy was his mother's seventh child. The six before him never drew a breath. Something terrible happened shortly after his birth. His mother died."

"That is sad," Àjọkẹ́ said.

Bíbíire nodded her agreement. "Stricken with grief, the maternal grandmother ordered that the newborn child be taken to the forest and left there."

Àjọkẹ́'s mouth opened. "How could they have left a baby in a forest?"

"Pain can make people do terrible things. Days later, a group of hunters found the baby. Astonished that he survived, they brought him back to the village. His contrite grandmother gave him the name, Ọmọwékúkù—'the child who did not die, lives.' As time went by, they shortened the name to Kúkù. He was a survivor."

Àjọkẹ́ cocked her head. "So, you're saying I'm a cherished survivor."

Bíbíire was pleased by Àjọkẹ́'s quick understanding. "Yes, my child."

"I guess it's better than being a crazy joke."

"Promise me that you will stop calling yourself those words. We must use our mouths to speak kind things to ourselves."

Àjọkẹ́ stayed silent for a while. "Grandma."

"Yes."

"How do you say 'I love you' in Yorùbá?" Àjọkẹ́ asked.

"Mo ní fẹ́ ẹ."

Àjọkẹ́'s brow furrowed. "'I have your love'?"

It was the literal translation. "Yes. We believe that love is tangible.

That no matter where we go, no matter how long we are apart, the love we carry stays with us."

A soft smile tugged at Àjọké's lips. "I like that."

. . .

Two days later, Ẹniafẹ́ called to let them know the suitcases were finally in Lagos. No one could explain their detour to Mozambique. He was coming to Igbó Irúnmọlẹ̀ the next day.

Tired out by another village excursion, Àjọké and Bíbíire both decided on an early night. Her chin propped in her hand, Àjọké laid next to Bíbíire and stared at her face.

"Grandma, the lines on your face, they look like the creases in Grandpa's maps."

Bíbíire smiled. "These lines tell plenty of stories."

"What kind of stories?"

It was hard to sum up a lifetime in a few words. "Stories about love, courage, deep secrets, sorrow, wisdom, joy, much joy."

"Which line is your favorite?" Àjọké asked.

She reached out for Àjọké's hand, brought it close, and traced Àjọké's index finger along the deep laugh line at the left corner of her mouth. "This one. When your father called to tell me you were born, I could not stop laughing."

Àjọké's expression sobered. "Grandma."

"Yes, my child."

Àjọké gave her a cautious look. "Dad said you also stopped talking to people."

"I did."

"Why?"

A familiar choking feeling welled up in her chest. "When I was seven, my mother went missing."

Àjọkẹ́'s eyes grew big. "Oh."

Bíbíire exhaled. "Màmá used to say I talked too much. Now I know she meant no harm. I told myself that was why she left us and that if I stopped talking, someone would tell Màmá so she would come home."

"Did your mom come back home?"

"No."

Àjọkẹ́ looked as if she was about to cry. "I'm sorry."

Grateful, Bíbíire reached out and stroked Àjọkẹ́'s face. Inside her eighty-five-year-old body was a seven-year-old who still wanted her mother.

"How did you start talking again?" Àjọkẹ́ asked.

It had been a journey of many months. "My father helped. He told me this folktale I am about to tell you and said my voice is a good gift. My child, when something is good for us, we must find a way to tolerate any discomfort. Now it is time for our folktale."

To Bíbíire's relief, Àjọkẹ́ sat up with a brighter face. The child loved hearing folktales just as much as her father did.

Bíbíire began the story the way their people have always done it. "*Àlọ́ o!*"

"*Àlọ̀!*" Àjọkẹ́ shouted back.

"One day, many, many, years ago, when most animals still walked upright, Alángbá Adánrípọ́n, the agama lizard, looked out of his window, saw that it was a sunny day, and decided to go on a leisure walk."

Àjọkẹ́ gave her a skeptical look. "That really happened?"

Bíbíire kept a straight face. "Child, one also does not say an elder is lying."

Àjọkẹ́ drawled the word. "Right."

Bíbíire pursed her lips. "Should I continue the story or not?"

"Yes, Grandma."

"The agama's stroll took him by his friend, Àkàlàmàgbò's home.

Alángbá Adánrípọ̀n remembered the hunting whistle he lent the friendly hornbill. He decided to collect it.

"Àkàlàmàgbò opened his door and invited him in. The hornbill was about to eat his evening meal. The aroma of the spicy pottage set on the raffia mat made Alángbá Adánrípọ̀n's mouth water.

"While his friend went to get the hunting whistle, Alángbá Adánrípọ̀n quickly dipped his fingers into the bowl of pottage and took a generous amount. His attempt to swallow the scalding-hot food without being caught sent the pottage down the wrong way."

Àjọkẹ́'s eyes widened. "Oho."

"Alángbá Adánrípọ̀n was in serious trouble. Àkàlàmàgbò returned and found the agama hopping from one foot to the other. Mystified by his friend's strange behavior, Àkàlàmàgbò asked for an explanation. Unwilling to say what he did, Alángbá Adánrípọ̀n stayed silent.

"As Alángbá Adánrípọ̀n's head glowed in a flaming-red color, a concerned Àkàlàmàgbò threw him inside a bucket of cold water. It was too late. The intense heat had destroyed Alángbá Adánrípọ̀n's vocal cords. That is why until this very day, all the agama lizard can do in response to any question is to nod its head sadly."

"Grandma, I didn't steal anyone's food," Àjọkẹ́ said.

"No, you did not, my child. Our folktales carry different lessons for different people in different seasons."

"What is the lesson for me?"

"I want you, Àjọkẹ́ Kúkù, always to remember that when we stay silent when we should not, we may lose our voices forever. Do you understand what I mean?"

Àjọkẹ́ nodded. "Like the agama lizard did."

"Yes. Like the lizard did."

"Grandma, talking when you're scared can be difficult."

"It can. And we also have to learn the wisdom of knowing when not to speak."

Àjọkẹ́ gave her a thoughtful look. "How do I know that?"

"It is something you will continue to learn for the rest of your life." She gave Àjọkẹ́ a soft smile. "You will speak to your parents and accept their help?"

Àjọkẹ́ took her time to think about the request. "I will."

Bíbíire pulled her close for a hug. "Thank you."

• • •

Àjọkẹ́ heard the honking sound before Bíbíire did. Eyes wide with excitement, Àjọkẹ́ ran out of the house.

A tired-looking Ẹniafẹ́ stepped out of the car. Bíbíire watched with gratitude as a laughing Àjọkẹ́ knelt on the sand to greet him before throwing herself at him. Mouth wide open, Ẹniafẹ́ held on to his daughter and swung her around.

After he and Àjọkẹ́ unpacked their suitcases, Ẹniafẹ́ brought a handful of gifts to her bedroom. He placed them down and sat beside her. "I'm sorry I didn't get to spend much time with you," he said.

The undivided time with Àjọkẹ́ had been priceless. "Then you have to come back soon."

"I will. How were your days with your granddaughter?"

"The best. Thank you for leaving Àjọkẹ́ with me."

Ẹniafẹ́ exhaled. "Her mother and I were worried that she would wear you out with her fretting."

"Àjọkẹ́ just needed time to know that she was safe with me."

"I'm still stunned by the change. I returned to meet a different child."

"Son, Àjọkẹ́ and I talked. There is trouble at her school. Some children there call her horrible names."

"But why didn't she tell us?"

"Àjọkẹ́ said she didn't because you and her mother are both extra."

Ẹniafẹ́ gaped at her. "For real?"

Bíbíire nodded. "For real."

Ẹniafẹ́ laughed. "I see Àjọkẹ́ has taught you her lingo."

"Please, do not be angry with the child over her silence. Àjọkẹ́ said it as she sees it. Yes, we love our children, but we must give them room to breathe."

"But Màámi, you did not give me the room to breathe."

Ẹniafẹ́ spoke the truth. "My son, one is never too old to learn."

"I have heard. We will make the necessary changes."

"Thank you. You and Ọdún are raising Àjọkẹ́ well. You should be proud."

Ẹniafẹ́ bent his head. "Thank you, Ma. *Ẹ̀ẹ́ pẹ́ fún wa.*"

The length of her days was in Olódùmarè's hands. "As the owner of life wishes."

Ẹniafẹ́ stood. "Àjọkẹ́ and I need to talk."

She nodded her agreement. "After you do, please send my child to me."

"I will."

A while later, Àjọkẹ́ entered the room. "Dad said you wanted me?"

"Yes, my child. Sit. I have a gift for you."

Àjọkẹ́ watched as Bíbíire dragged out the trunk under her bed. Opening it, she took out a piece of folded fabric and placed it in Àjọkẹ́'s lap. "This piece of *sányán* belonged to my mother. It is one of the few things they kept for me. I want you to have it."

Àjọkẹ́ held the fabric to her chest as she knelt on the linoleum tiles. "Thank you, Grandma."

Bíbíire smiled. "There is no need to thank one's self."

Àjọkẹ́ ran her fingers along the length of the wrap. "It's so smooth."

"Sányán is made with beige silk threads spun from the cocoons of the Anaphe moth."

Àjọkẹ́ whispered the words. "Grandma, I have your love."

She stared at her granddaughter's face, determined to stamp its features on her mind for the long nights ahead. "My child, I have your love, too."

. . .

As much as Bíbíire wished she could stop time, the day of their return arrived. Before Ẹniafẹ́ left for Lagos, he gave her Ọdún's list of items to buy. Bíbíire bought them all and more. Concerned the extra food items would lead to overweight luggage fees, Ẹniafẹ́ weighed their suitcases for the umpteenth time.

Bíbíire watched as Ẹniafẹ́ placed the suitcases in the car boot. "If you have to leave anything at the airport, make sure it is not your wife's requested items."

Ẹniafẹ́ dusted his hands. "Mrs. Bíbíire Kúkù, champion of women."

"A proud one."

"I won't leave Ọdún's things behind."

Bíbíire exhaled. *It is satisfying when a child you raise to adulthood continues to raise themselves to a higher standard.* "I know you're a good husband."

Ẹniafẹ́ prostrated before her. "Màámi, thank you for everything."

She held out her arms. Ẹniafẹ́ stood for her tight hug. "Son, I know our eyes will meet again." The words were a heartfelt plea to Olódùmarè.

Ẹniafẹ́ turned to Àjọkẹ́. "Before we leave, I should take a picture of you and your Grandma."

Àjọkẹ́'s face brightened. "Yes, please."

Ẹniafẹ́ looked surprised when Àjọkẹ́ pulled out a disposable camera from her backpack and held it out to him.

Bíbíire smiled. Àjọkẹ́ was leaving with the rest of her grandfather's cameras.

"You're sure you don't want me to use your cell phone?" Ẹniafẹ́ asked with a raised eyebrow.

Àjọkẹ́ moved close and wrapped her arm around Bíbíire's body. "Yes. Grandma said these cameras are the best."

To hide her tears, Bíbíire closed her eyes just as Ẹniafẹ́ took the picture.

Lillian Akampurira Aujo

In a Yellow Dress with Red Flowers

STORY

Daneri's heart pitched like a stone slung out of a catapult. The door to his two-room muzigo was shaking out of its frame from all the banging. Mariza, their dramatic neighbor, could be heard wailing like she had lost a child. He rolled off the bed and grabbed Dora's lesu from the nail in the doorframe. A whiff of her rosy scent stirred the air like she had just lathered on lotion after her bath. He wanted to believe that this was a usual morning and he had just woken up after Dora had left for the landing site. But whom was he lying to? The truth was that he was hobbling through the empty start of a day unlike many he had experienced. He draped the wide lesu around his thin torso twice before managing a rough knot at the side to secure it. Dora's hips filled it out easily, and even when it slipped it was held there until she fastened it again. Would she return to him after what he had said to her?

He unlatched the bolt and swung the door open in one go. Mariza almost fell through.

"What is it? What has happened, Mariza?"

Now she whimpered, striking her chest like a Catholic in penitence.

"Yesu! Yesu! What shall we do? Bikira Maria Omutukuvu!"

Daneri breathed deep: he was especially low on patience for his neighbor's theatrics today.

"Please tell me what is going on."

Now Mariza crossed herself, mouthing what Daneri took to be a silent prayer.

"They have killed her. It's another woman. They have killed her."

"What?" An alarm went off in his head like an ambulance siren. He had never thought he would find himself in a position where he had to contend with the possibility that the next murdered woman might be his wife.

For the last three months, the news had been reporting unidentified women found murdered. The killings were obviously related; a woman went to work and simply didn't come home. The bodies were dumped at random points on a road grid that connected Kampala and Entebbe. They were systematically defaced: missing breasts and lips, eviscerated stomachs, and sticks sticking out of their privates. Everyone was disturbed that the deceased's numbers had risen past the twenties and yet no culprit had been caught by the police to date.

"What are you telling me, Mariza?"

"I don't know, Daneri! All I know is that Toofa returned from his school dropping round saying they found another body."

"Oh God help us! Where did they find it?" Daneri shouted. He told himself to calm down. There was nothing to show that the latest victim was Dora. After all, they had quarreled and she was annoyed; rightly so. He didn't know why he had felt the need to poke at her ever open wound—hurt her where she was most vulnerable—like everyone else around them. It's not like there was anything wrong with being from a different part of the country than the central; he knew that, and yet at that moment he had reminded her that she was somehow less of a human being for being from the North. Before that he had always said that tribalism was wrong and backward. So what did that make him now? When had he become one of those bigots he despised? Something bitter rose in his throat but he swallowed it back. "And where is Toofa?"

"He's off to the stage to see what he can find out from the other boda guys. They said she was dumped in the big cassava garden before the Adventist schools on the Kajjansi exit."

"Let me rush and see what I can find out." Daneri whipped around into the house to throw some clothes on.

Mariza grabbed his hand. "Daneri, Dora . . ."

"She called you, right?" Hope fluttered in his chest. They had agreed last night that Mariza would let him know the minute she heard from Dora.

"No! I was going to say that she was wearing her yellow dress. The one with big red flowers."

Daneri swallowed hard, his Adam's apple bobbing up and down more quickly. He knew the dress; he had bought it for her to celebrate her breaking even in the fish-selling business after six months. But what did it have to do with anything? Dora had told him that Mariza considered women who "repeated" the same dress many times commoners, and that their men who allowed them to go around dressed like villagers were even more common.

"Don't start your dressing-standards nonsense with me, Mariza. You want to lecture me about my own woman?"

"No, Daneri! She dresses well, everyone knows it—"

"I don't have time for women talk. Especially today of all days."

"Look, Daneri, Toofa said the woman was in a yellow dress with red flowers."

He stopped breathing for a second. "What?"

"The dead woman. That's what she was wearing."

• • •

Daneri slumped into the only chair in his living room. The wood creaked loudly. A far-off part of him registered pain in his backside. His head thrummed like a generator. He told himself to calm down: it was a common dress, after all; one of those Chinese numbers with the same design in different colors. The hawker had had three identical ones the day he picked one out for Dora.

He reached over the armrest to the right and yanked the phone from its charger. He scrolled to the last dialed numbers. Dora. She was still not available. He checked their boda WhatsApp group, still nothing on Dora's whereabouts.

Last night, Toofa, Mariza's husband, had suggested he make use of the WhatsApp group to find her.

"You've checked the landing site, nothing. You asked around, nothing. You called the sister, nothing. You've been combing the whole town and the beaches and she's nowhere to be seen. Let's put a voice message on WhatsApp."

Daneri started shaking his head, not wanting the whole village to know he was having problems with his woman.

"I get it, Daneri, it's not easy for us men to expose our business," Toofa said, scratching his wrinkled chin and sneaking Daneri a sideways glance. "But these are hard times for our women, as you know."

"You're right. Of course you're right. The sooner we find her the better," Daneri said, wondering if he had glimpsed a wave of blame and pity on Toofa's face before sympathy smoothed it away.

"If anyone knows where she is, it will be a boda guy. Aren't we the ones who pick them and drop them off?" Toofa winked, but the joke flew right over Daneri: he was already thinking that their neighbors had overheard their fight the night before Dora went missing. He should have remembered that the walls were thin and not exploded, but only his anger had mattered that night.

• • •

He had come home to a meal of dried fish stew, millet bread, and nakati on the side. He noticed Dora was picking at her fish before pushing her bone-white melamine dish aside.

"Why aren't you eating? The fish is tasty."

"My stomach is turning. I'll just eat the nakati."

"You cooked it, and now you don't want it?"

"Maybe I am getting sick or something."

Daneri shook his head. "Sick, or tired of your good cooking?" He smiled as he threw in the compliment.

Dora smiled back. "I just lost my appetite, that's all."

"You're sure it's nothing else? Perhaps a pregnancy?"

Dora's smile shook before it disappeared altogether. "No, it's not that. I wish things were that simple. Let me go put the water for the tea on," she said. She picked up her dish and strode to the small kitchen outside.

Daneri spooned some soup into his mouth. Every time they talked about children his wife's dark skin lost its glow, as if the light beneath her face had been turned off. After almost a year of trying, they hadn't been lucky yet.

Meantime, Mariza had found ways to wedge the topic into the small talk he could not avoid having with her since she was their immediate neighbor and, more so, Toofa's wife. Only yesterday she had waved and shouted to Daneri as he wheeled his motorcycle out of their cramped multishared compound:

"I hope you don't ride like a muyaye now that you are about to be someone's father."

"Yes, Maama Mariza, I will be careful," Daneri replied, infusing his voice with faux humility because he knew she loved to think that everyone respected her opinions.

"I tell my Toofa every day not to rush to death on his boda and leave us behind. What about you and your new bride?"

Such occurrences were Daneri's feelers to know that people were already wagging their tongues about his childless marriage; besides, Mariza was called "the matchbox" for a good reason. He could take the talk, but he knew it was different with Dora. She was the woman, and childlessness, as everyone knew, was always the woman's fault. Then there was also the fact of her "strangeness," cemented by the fact that she was not from the greater Buganda region. Being from the north of the country, from somewhere beyond Jinja and even farther beyond the Nile, relegated Dora to the status of a stranger. It didn't matter that she had learned enough Luganda to get by: they said she butchered it so badly that it was smeared in shame each time she opened her mouth to speak. It didn't matter that she had her own fish-selling business, or that she could haggle down the wiliest of the fish brokers who traversed the shores of Lake Victoria. She was still a stranger to them, and now a barren stranger. Daneri arranged the empty plates on the low, small stool, starting with the widest at the bottom.

Dora returned with the small aluminum kettle of tea on a circular wooden tray. She set it on another small stool.

"I used lemongrass. Mama Mayi at the stage had some fresh bundles, I couldn't resist," Dora said as she poured the tea.

"No wonder it smells so good," Daneri said.

"It does, doesn't it?" She walked over to the cupboard for two ceramic mugs and started pouring out the tea. "There's something I need to tell you, Dan." She moved over to the other end of the three-seater chair.

"What is it, my oiled black night?"

"I had a coil put. Today."

"You what?"

"I went to the clinic, you know the one opposite Shell at the main road and I—"

"I heard you the first time! When were you going to tell me?"

"I am telling you now, Dan. Please don't be upset."

"We are supposed to be having children and you are telling me you went and put a coil?"

"I think we should not start with the child business right now."

"What? I thought we had agreed. What are you telling me?"

"We've been living in this muzigo for two years. I can't imagine having kids in this small space. We work hard, but money is not coming together quickly enough."

"So you decided all this on your own?"

Dora fell quiet for a while. She touched his hand and he flinched. "I know I grew up in the village. We were not rich, but my father owned land and there was enough room for all of us—"

"What kind of woman are you that doesn't want to have children for her man?"

"I didn't say I don't want to. I said not now. Look at this place."

"'Not now!' 'Not now,' she says. I should have listened, everyone warned me about you women from the North: you never listen to your men."

"Daneri, look—"

"Are you just wasting my time?" Daneri paced the small length of the living room. "I should not have married a mudokoro," he thundered.

"What did you just call me? Say that word again and I swear you'll see."

"Isn't that what you are with your dark skin?"

"My dark skin! Weren't you seeing my dark skin before?"

"Clearly I was blinded by your witchcraft!"

"So now I'm no longer an 'oiled black night'? And I practice witch-craft?" Dora jeered and faced the door. "Maybe you should get one of those pawpaw-colored women with black knuckles, the ones you said your eyes would never fall on."

"At least they listen to their men and bear children for them."

"I'll leave then, so you can marry one of those."

"Did you even just have it put today? Or have you had it all along?"

Dora threw him a cold stare and fished into her skirt pocket for a folded paper, which she tossed at him.

"There! Today's receipt from the clinic. Or will you say I forged that as well?" She stormed off to the bedroom and banged the door.

As the tea sat untouched and cooling on the stool, Daneri lay seething in the chair, where he dozed off. The next thing he heard was the front door shutting as Dora left for work at six in the morning. He hadn't seen her since.

. . .

Daneri called Dora's sister Joy in Mukono.

"Nothing yet. I have called everyone I can think of. No one has seen her," Joy said.

Daneri's heart slumped. Joy's was the only place he had expected her to go, because she had no other relatives in the city center. She had friends, yes, but none close enough for her to spend the night with unless there was a funeral.

"Okay. Let me link up with my fellow boda guys to widen the search. Someone is bound to know something."

"Shouldn't we go to the police? These are bad days for women, espe-cially in your area."

"They'll just tell me to sit and wait for her. And when they find out we quarreled before she stormed off to work they will just send me to the family division desk for counseling."

"What did you two quarrel about anyway? What was so bad that she had to run off?"

"I can't talk about that now. I'm sure she'll tell you when you see her. Okay?"

"Okay. When she comes back. We'll talk about it when she comes back." Joy drew each word out in a sort of incantation, as if it needed to be believed for it to manifest into truth. At his end of the line, Daneri mouthed "Amen," although he had never been a praying man.

• • •

Daneri's motorcycle shuddered as he maneuvered over the stones jutting through the dirt road. He was climbing uphill and revved it harder, in a hurry to leave the incline behind and get onto the leveled wind before finally reaching the stage. There he hoped someone would have seen Dora, since she was known to most of them: last night he hadn't been able to ask after her there, since they had closed their stalls by the time he rode by, toward ten o'clock.

On both sides of the narrow road, small matooke plantations waved their dark green fronds in the slight but sharp breeze, and mounds of sweet potatoes with shimmery vines spilled over the black soil. The high concrete fences ending in razor wire and their equally high metallic gates emitted nearly no sound, the children having left for school and their parents for work. Daneri was jarred by how normal it all looked, yet Dora remained missing—and a woman who might be her had been found dead. If things turned out that way he would have no one to blame but himself, and he doubted he could live with that sort of guilt sitting on his heart. Maybe he would become one of those men who wandered the roads unkempt, with no thoughts in their heads except where the butterflies were going. He brought the motorcycle to a screeching halt in the middle of the road. The black Prado that had been at his flank for the last minute nearly bumped into him but the driver stopped just in time.

"I almost knocked you, man! Get your spoilt boda off the road before someone kills you," the man shouted.

Daneri wheeled the motorcycle to the side of the road and stood staring ahead, suddenly too afraid to face whatever he would learn when he got to the stage. He slumped to the ground, waiting for courage to infuse his bones.

• • •

Ten minutes later, he was parked in front of Mama Mayi's fruit and vegetable stand. He limped over to the side where she was seated on a low three-legged stool washing passion fruits in a small blue basin.

"How did you sleep, madam?"

"Very well, sir, how about you?" Mama Mayi said, averting her eyes a little to the side.

"I would have slept well if Dora had come home."

"I beg your pardon?"

"I came to ask if you have seen her."

"Jesus! Dora was here the evening before last. She took some lemongrass, tomatoes, onions, and green peppers. You mean you don't know where she is?"

"She went to work yesterday morning but didn't return last evening. I went to the landing site, but they said she left at about four o'clock, after selling her fish. Yesterday I drove around looking for her, until ten o'clock in the night. Her phone is off."

"Eeh! But where could she have gone?"

"That's what I'm trying to find out. Could you spread the word, see if anyone knows anything?"

"Yes, I will do that. Let me record a WhatsApp and put it on our women trader's association group."

"Is it okay if I leave my boda here as I ask around?"

"Yes, just move it over to this side where I can keep a close eye on it."

"Thank you, Mama Mayi."

"No problem."

"Stay well," Daneri said.

"And you too," said Mama Mayi.

Daneri moved a few paces over to Micaiah's rolex shack. Micaiah was Dora's go-to guy when she was late or too tired from work to cook supper. She said he had the best chapatis and Daneri could not argue. He looked up as Daneri approached. He set his rolling pin aside and they bumped fists.

"How are you, man? Have your heard that they killed another woman?" Micaiah shook his head.

"Yes. I heard from Mariza, Toofa's woman. But I'm here to ask if you've seen Dora. She didn't come home yesterday. We had a small disagreement, but you know women."

"Aah, my friend, if you find a man who always agrees with his woman, let me know, because they are as rare as white goats. Me, I know these things happen. She'll get back to her senses and before you know it, she will be back. She passed here after six the other morning. I had just put the first chapati on the frying pan," Micaiah added.

"I see. Have you seen Toofa anyway?"

"He was here earlier, but it seems he took a passenger. As for these murders, I don't understand why police can't do something."

"What else do you know about the woman they found?"

"Nothing much, except that they killed her so badly that she is un-recognizable. Just like the others: no ID, no phone, nothing to show who she is."

"Such a shame. One wonders where humanity has gone to."

"Have you called the police?"

"I am going to, I just want to make sure she is not nearby before I involve them."

"That's wise. Because you have to cough something small before they even take your statement."

"Yes. But what can we do? We need them and they know it," Daneri said. "So will you help me ask around for Dora?"

"Of course, man. I'll let you know if I hear anything. If I don't see you at least I'll tell Toofa."

"Thanks, man."

Daneri made as many stops, as there were stalls and shops lining the road. Some women appeared from their dim vantage points with the hope that he had not found what he was looking to buy from the previous stall. They retreated with downcast eyes when they realized he was looking for his missing wife and not fruit or vegetables. The profusion of color from all the fresh produce on display made him dizzy. His nose thickened with the smell of mold from the open sacks of flour and grain in the window-less retail shops. Farther along the road, the air was thick with the smell of frying cassava, pancakes, samosas, mandazi, and chapati, and Daneri felt that he would never stomach another fried snack. He crossed the main road to the Kampala minibus stage and asked the touts, who sat play-ing ludo when they were not harassing women, to enter their particular commissioned taxi. He moved back and forth across the stage, asking the other boda guys as they picked up and dropped people off if they had seen Dora. He kept checking his phone, but there was no news.

An hour later, he went back to Mama Mayi's and picked up the mo-torcycle. He headed toward Entebbe and turned left off the main road after twenty minutes. As he rode farther inland, the breeze cooled and sharpened more. Soon he could see the blue waves of Lake Victoria bobbing with the light of the sun, and the wooden canoes roped to the pillars sticking out of the dark water along the shore. He milled through the small crowd; no one had seen her since one evening ago. He checked his phone again; nothing. He called Toofa, who said he was home for an early lunch and they could talk there before he left for work again. He turned his motorcycle around and began the ride home, making the same inquiries he had made only a few hours ago, and getting the same response: no one had seen Dora.

• • •

A wave of fatigue assailed Daneri as he approached his compound. He stumbled as he wheeled the motorcycle toward the entrance. He braced it by the hedge and wiped his brow with the back of a dusty hand. Usually, home meant Dora's warm voice and smile seeping through everything in the house. Today, however, it would mean staring up at the iron roof and watching dewdrops gather as the cold and night thickened. He would have his phone by the pillow, vibration and volume at maximum levels. He sighed and pushed the motorcycle farther on, entering the compound. A policeman and another man in a dark blue shirt and black trousers were chatting on Toofa's veranda. The policeman pointed at Daneri and shouted, "Are you Daneri?"

"Yes, I am? How may I help you?" Daneri replied.

"We hear you have been looking for your wife."

Daneri stopped and wiped cold sweat off his forehead. "Yes, I've been looking for her since last evening. She didn't come back from work."

"Is that so? Why haven't you reported her missing?"

"Because I thought she would turn up soon. We had a small disagreement."

"A small disagreement. That's not what we hear from your neighbors."

Daneri crept over to the two men. Toofa, drawing the curtain aside, stepped out of his house, and Mariza rushed out after him.

"They just arrived, asking all sorts of questions about you and Dora and what she was wearing," Mariza said.

Toofa gestured with his hand for her to keep quiet.

"I told them you're a good man. That one tried to corner me into saying you probably killed your wife," Toofa said, pointing at the man in plain clothes.

"I am a whole police detective. Don't point at me like I'm your child." The man shook a finger in Toofa's direction.

"I am sorry, Detective," Toofa said.

"You people have no respect for officers of the law. How can you talk to us like that? Don't you know we can arrest all of you just for that?" the detective said. "Anyway, let's not waste time. We have come for you to help us with a murder investigation." The two policemen flanked Daneri, and the detective clamped cold handcuffs on his wrists.

His stomach fell and he turned widened eyes to Toofa.

"I haven't done anything! I'm just searching for my wife."

"Officers, why are you arresting him? I told you he is not a murderer," said Toofa.

"Are you an investigator? Let us do our job. If we need you, we shall send someone to pick you up as well."

"Why would you also arrest my husband? He has already helped in the investigation by answering your questions."

"Don't tell us how to do our job, woman!" said the uniformed policeman.

They led Daneri away, and into the back of the dark blue double-cabin police pickup that had just pulled up as if on cue.

. . .

At the police station, the two policemen pushed Daneri down a labyrinth of corridors and into a dark cell. They shoved him to the floor and ordered him to take his shoes off.

"Where were you last night?" the investigator asked.

"I was searching for my wife. I told you she didn't come home yesterday."

The two policemen exchanged flat glances. "And you expect us to believe that when a woman was murdered last night! Who was searching with you? Where did you spend the night?"

"I slept in my house. I went looking for her alone."

"Isn't that convenient?" the uniformed one said. "And what do you know about the dead woman?"

"Nothing, *Afande*. Just what my neighbor's wife said. That she was wearing a dress like my wife's."

"And you expect us to believe you are innocent?" the detective shouted with so much strength Daneri began shaking.

"Please let me go. I haven't done anything. I'm innocent," Daneri cried out.

"You murderers always cry your innocence. But we shall see if you will not be calling your mother by the time we are done with you."

"Please, I need to find my wife."

"But aren't you the one who murdered her? You think police are miracle workers, and we are going to resurrect someone you already killed?"

They started kicking Daneri and he hit the damp floor hard. The kicks were joined by blows and Daneri tried to shield his face. He groaned as he waited for death to put him out of his misery. He choked on his own blood.

285

"Please, I am innocent. You need to help me find my wife. Please, I beg you."

"We are only here for your confession," the detective said with a dry laugh. "So please don't waste our time."

"If you tell us the truth we can even be merciful. How did you kill her?" the other one asked.

"Please! I didn't kill anyone. At least let me see the body. Let me see if she is my wife."

The policemen exchanged looks and smiled cold smiles.

The thin one produced a thick black cloth, which he tied roughly over Daneri's eyes.

"Looks like you're going where many don't like to go, since you won't tell us what we want."

Daneri tried to resist but he was no match for the two men. They forced him out of the cell and dragged him up three flight of steep sharp steps at the end of the corridor. They opened a door that creaked on rough hinges. The room was musky with rot and strong chemicals. They took the blindfold off, but Daneri could not open his eyes. They punched and kicked him like a gym bag until he keeled over.

"Get up, you murderer! Get up! Isn't this your wife?"

"Look at her," the detective said. "Isn't this the dress she was wearing? Isn't this the red dress with yellow flowers you said she was wearing?"

They shoved his groin into a metallic table. Over his own moaning, Daneri heard the brief sound of wheels coming to a slow stop, like a toy car that had ran out of batteries. He opened his eyes and stared at the dress with the yellow flowers. It was caked in dried blood. And what he could see of the woman's body was yellow pawpaw skin, complete with dark veins showing through. His heart bled relief; Dora was out there somewhere—but whether he would be alive to see her was another matter altogether.

Nana Nyarko Boateng

A Honey-Headed Child

STORY

Maa laughed out through her dreams and woke up Papa and me. I was dazed. Knocked quietly on my parents' bedroom door; was addled, when it was Papa's voice that said,

"Come."

Maa was turned to the wall, subsumed by her soft, rickety snore. A large illuminable crucifix cast a green Jesus on the wall, head bowed and shackled up by Maa's favorite rosary.

"Brema, what is it? Are you okay?"

I nodded to my papa, inching closer to my parents' bed. Papa stretched out his neck to look at me. Lifting the rest of his body onto his feet, he picked me up, placed me on his side of the bed, and went to the floor to sleep.

We did not fall asleep immediately. We couldn't, Papa and me.

Maa had roared from her soul and out came birdsongs and a bright sunset that rose the temperature in our home. It was the same as watching an egg uncrack. A true miracle. Even more spectacular than walking on seas, unblinding the blind, or turning barrels of water into the finest wine. I am not exaggerating. Maa never laughed, not this loud, not so abundantly. Papa shifted on the floor, struggling to find a comfortable spot for rest. I wanted to sleep next to my papa, coiling into his chest to hear his heavy breathing, to smell the brandy from his pores.

I waited for him to call me, but Papa didn't say, "Come sleep by me if you're scared." When the lights went off, I pretended to be afraid because Papa would pull me into his chest, his arms tightening around me as I fake shivered. Papa did not know that I feared only three things, and the dark wasn't one of them. In his godlike voice he would say, "If you close your eyes, you can see the biggest and the brightest light. You are that light. You are a star." Then Papa would tickle my stomach until I melted into giggles. The scariest things in the world were three: Maa's yells, a room emptied of people, and a dirty woman, because Maa said women are not to be dirty; but if I told Papa that the dark did not scare me, maybe he wouldn't tickle my stomach anymore, maybe he wouldn't call me a star.

"Brema, stop drumming the mattress with your feet!" Papa whispered; his breath riven in three rushes as he exhaled.

"Papa," I, too, whispered.

But either he did not hear me or was pretending he hadn't.

"Papa . . . Papa . . ." I called a little while later.

He snored, thundering, muddling the melody from Maa's muffled snore.

• • •

In the morning, Maa woke me up with the back of her palm touching my forehead. She put a hand on my cheek.

"Are you sick?" Maa asked.

"She's not," Papa said.

"Why didn't you send her back to her bed then? We are not raising a honey-headed child."

Without fail, at daybreak, Papa's voice filled our home. Papa loved to talk, and he loved talking to Maa the most, his thought patterns moving freely in any direction. His monologues were more than words, his hands danced, shoulders shrugged gently, head tilted to the left, eyes lit with zeal whether he was talking about a tree or increased fuel price. Maa listened, humming, cleaning, ordering the day, the way only she could.

Sunken in a simmering anger that encircled her each day, Maa got up and tied the curtains to let in the rays of the early morning sun. There was no pretense, we all knew that no day could turn out joyful through Maa's eye. Maa only had one eye. The dead right eye was sealed; darkened where the eyelids met. Maa told me the day I touched it that there was nothing inside that eye. It had been removed.

"But how? Can't you put it back?" I had asked.

"Stop asking useless questions. Have you finished your homework?"

I knew Maa once had both eyes, because in her wedding photo, her eyes were open wide, glittering with love as Papa looked into them. Maa wasn't going to tell me how she lost it, ever. It didn't matter, anyway, that Maa lost an eye. The remaining eye detected everything with an intense, penetrating stare. It could see through walls. There was nothing I could ever hide from my mother. She knew things I didn't tell her about, like when I put five cubes of sugar in my breakfast instead of two. When I walked back from school because I lost my tro tro money or used the money to buy FanIce instead. She scolded me then. Maa wasn't like Papa, she didn't like to play, she pushed my head away when I tried to lay it on her lap.

"You are not a baby anymore; your head is way too heavy now."

And my laughter, to her, was earsplitting, uncouth, inconsiderate of our neighbors. I was terrified of her yells, but I wanted nothing more than to make her laugh, the way she laughed in her sleep. When Papa was away, I wanted her to play with me, to tickle my stomach, to call me a star; but she was Maa, had no time to spare. If all of reality was under my mother's control, she would never have allowed it to shift and turn. Change was a threat to her. Maa shunned newness, redoing what she knew how to do, living the life that hadn't killed her yet, living in a way that fended off fresh cracks. When life threw her into the deep waters, she stayed there, breathing underwater. I kept the memory of my mother's midnight laugh astir in my heart for many years. Often dusted it and let it fill the air whenever Maa looked sad.

"Go and take your shower now or you'll be late for school," Maa said.

I rolled out of my parents' bed and went to lean against their bedroom door, causing Papa's big blue towel hanging on the door to fall to the ground.

Papa was forcing another shirt into his small traveling bag. At first glance, Papa knew I was going to cry. He came and squeezed my shoulders.

"Go on, I'll be back before you know it, okay?"

"Okay, Papa," I said, my voice cracking.

"Don't. I already put extra money in your school bag for ice cream."

I nodded, fastening myself around my father's leg.

"Brema, stop that! You'll wrinkle his trousers," Maa yelled, pulling me off Papa. She smoothed his gray trousers with her palms.

"Just count up to ten days and I'll be here already," Papa said.

"Brema, you can't waste everybody's time with your tears whenever your father has to travel. Don't you want him to work? Go and bathe!"

Papa was a merchant; he went to Togo to buy fashion items: clothes, bags, shoes, fabric, and perfumes. He supplied these to the small boutiques in Accra.

As Maa's voice rose higher, I felt glued to their door.

"In one-two-three-four-five-six-seven-eight-nine-ten days." Papa counted his fingers breathless, lifting them up at ten to show me. "You'll have brand-new toys and a big bowl of strawberry ice cream," he said.

"And chocolate," I said.

"And chocolate, of course."

Maa kissed her teeth. Papa winked at me.

I left to gather my sponge, soap, and bucket. Wrapped my towel around my body just like Maa taught me and trudged to fetch my bathwater.

We lived in a big compound house shared by other families. Our neighbors were friendly except for the few times fights broke out over whose turn it was to scrub our shared toilets and bathrooms. We had three toilets and three bathrooms on the compound: one allotted to every four families. In the mornings, the compound had its own rush hour. Queues formed for the toilet, and another stretched for bathing. Maa always made sure that I bathed before the other families woke up. I was never late for school. Maa wouldn't ever allow that to happen. Of all the things I had to share with my neighbors, I wished I didn't have to share the tap that stood right at the center of the compound like a shrine, a splattering shrine. It thrilled me to turn it open and watch the water gush out, drumming itself into my bucket and onto the ground. But always, someone would rush me away from the tap and push their buckets under it as if I couldn't see that my bucket was already full and overflowing.

From the tap, I could see every corner of our large compound, open to the sky, cluttered porches with water barrels and makeshift kitchens. Small square rooms we made homes—partitioned with plywood. And at night on our porches—couples eating from the same bowl, children doing their homework, highlife songs playing from portable radios, sleeping babies on mats covered by mosquito nets. Flanked by each other's noises, we lived gaily, competitively, with no privacy.

Papa stepped down our stairs, waved goodbye at me, and headed for our giant gray wooden gate. The gate was big enough to hold three or four children at a time. We would step on the bottom rail while one of us swung the gate open and closed. We weren't supposed to do this; the hinges were weak. "The gate will collapse on us to our deaths," the adults in the house were always cautioning. Sometimes, a mother would shout from a window for us to stop. On other days, we were rounded up and punished.

Punishments ranged from doing *m'aso-yɛ-den* to distilling the gutters in front of our house. We preferred jumping into our garbage-choked gutters with shovels and hoes. The first few squats of *m'aso-yɛ-den*, we would usually giggle, but by the time we got to twenty, our cries reverberated around the compound, pitches rising, hoping to find mercy, but none of the rota of adults who punished us ever relented to relieve our aching thighs. Those who stopped to clean their tears had to start counting again from one to a hundred, hands pulling on ears, up and down in fiery lunges. On those days, I was sure that Satan himself invented *m'aso-yɛ-den*. But on most days, the adults just left us alone to swing and swing on our giant gray gate, hanging on its rusty hinges, until our own selfishness halted the fun. There was always one person who did not want to get off the bottom rail to push the rest of us, and this resulted in a wild assortment of cries, name-calling, and empty threats.

My bucket was already full. I wanted to run after Papa, but I knew better. If someone else went to the bathroom before I did, Maa was going to yell the entire morning. So I just washed my face to hide the tears.

The compound was mostly quiet in the mornings, except for the endless exchange of greetings between neighbors.

"Good morning o."

"Good morning."

"Na mo ho yɛ deɛ?"

"Nyame adom o."

"Yeda Yesu ase."

"Mo nsoɛ? Mmofra no ho yɛ?"

"Nyame adom, obiara ho yɛ."

"Yoo . . ."

Whenever Papa traveled, I got sick, had headaches that made me scream for Maa, vomited after eating. Maa would give me cold baths and two spoons of Living Bitters Tonic, but it never worked. My temperature would rise in the middle of the night and Maa would blame the devil, speaking to the holy, listening, wise God. In the space that should have been filled with Papa's voice, his stories, his tickling my stomach, there was a void so dark that nothing could reach me. Maa was often down on her knees, rosary in hand, holy water by my bedside, sprinkling holiness on me every few hours. And God was there, watching his children suffer.

• • •

The night after Papa left, Maa put a rosary around my neck and another under my pillow. I hadn't vomited my dinner yet. I was busy doing math. *Ten minus one equals nine.* I prayed for a new day. *Minus two equals eight.* On the third day, I couldn't fall asleep. I was suspended between wakefulness and sleep, floating on top of my bed, shifting right to left. On the morning of the fourth day, I was drowsy, stared at my breakfast, had chills. Maa said it was malaria. Two spoons of Living Bitters Tonic and off to school I went. Maa monitored my temperature when I got back home, threatened me with more spoons of Living Bitters if I didn't eat my food. Even after the sixth day, when my forehead wasn't hot at all, Maa felt my forehead with the back of her hand and cleansed my spirit with blessed water at night.

The tenth day felt so stretched. I waited for Papa by the door. Anytime I heard footfalls, I rushed outside to check if they were his.

"Brema, if you open that door one more time eh!"

Maa shouted from the living room. She was doing three things at the same time, sifting through beans in a pan to remove the bad ones, watching the evening news, and running her own side commentary along the headlines.

"Kai, this country eh. People die, people die over things that shouldn't kill a person.

"Which policy? Which policy? *Apuutɔɔ*! The health care system itself is the ultimate death trap.

"Brema! Didn't I say close the door!"

I was still inside but my head was popped out through the door. While Maa feared mosquitoes entering our room, I feared Papa had had enough of Maa's yelling. He was never going to come back home, was he?

Two shadow heads appeared on our neighbor's wall, the closest wall to the main gate; the heads waved into one and then separated, showing the rest of the shadow bodies. The shadows became man and boy holding hands. As they walked toward the light of our porch, the boy rubbed his eyes, Papa's eyes dropped when he saw me, his pace slackened.

"Papa?!"

I ran down the stairs to hug him. He didn't lift me up into the air as he usually did. The boy held on to Papa's hand.

"Papa, carry me, carry me!" I cried.

"Not now, Brema. Where is your mother?"

"Inside," I said.

My heart both sank and rose. I looked at the little boy in Papa's hand. He was sleepy-eyed and thin. Maybe five years old or six, but I was eight years old. I smiled at him, and he returned a groggy grin.

"Okay, Brema, take your brother's bag to your room. Kwame, go with your sister."

A warm liquid ran down the back of my neck into my spine. And in my heart, there was hammering, increasing loudly in my ears. Papa had promised brand-new toys and ice cream, but he brought me a brother. A real brother.

Taking his hand into mine, looking into his heavy eyes, I pursed my lips and held my breath. My brother. Was he really mine? Papa rushed ahead of Kwame and me into the room.

The beans Maa was sifting through were scattered on the floor when we entered the living room, the pan well turned to the ground. The news was still on, but Maa wasn't there running her commentary. Her voice and Papa's were loud from their bedroom. I knew well to start collecting the beans before being asked. Kwame came to kneel by my side and helped me collect my mother's beans.

"What do you mean 'I had no choice'?"

"Baaba, please calm down."

"Don't ask me to calm down. What do you want me to do with somebody's son?"

"He isn't somebody's son, Baaba, he is mine."

"How could you, Kofi? How could you?"

"Baaba, Baaba, please listen to me. I didn't know."

Papa started to cry. "His mother . . . she just dumped him on me two days ago. She recently remarried, and her husband doesn't want him."

"Remarried? Did you have another wife in Togo, Kofi?"

"No, Baaba, she was never my wife."

"Your mistress then? My God! Kofi, you?"

"Baaba, it was a one-time thing, I swear. I was drunk. I made a mistake, Baaba. *Mepa wo kyɛw.*"

"A mistake. How old is he?"

"Seven."

"You made a mistake for seven years?"

"I did not know, Baaba. You have to believe me."

"You did not know when you were taking off your pants? You did not know you were sleeping with another woman?"

"Baaba, I am sorry, it was that time. I was in so much pain."

"What time?"

"The time you wanted to leave. You know how pain distorts a person. I wasn't myself. Please."

"Oh, so it's my fault?"

"No, that's not what I'm saying, *mepa wo kyɛw . . .*"

Words I never thought Maa would even think flew out of her mouth. Papa was the carcass of a dead animal, his nostrils were large like a hotel, his head like a knife sharpener, his legs crooked like cassava from a barren land, his face like a witch who had fallen into blood, his mouth red like fire. A beetle bug—was the last thing Maa called Papa.

"He cannot stay here!" Maa yelled and went silent for the rest of the night.

I heard sobs through the walls. I was certain it was Papa crying, because Maa never did. Kwame was scared, but I told him he would get used to the nightly quarrels. He fell asleep by my side. I couldn't sleep.

• • •

Things weren't supposed to turn out the way they did after Papa returned with Kwame. The first few days after his arrival into our home, Kwame was "the boy" to Maa.

"Brema, tell the boy to come for his food."

"Give this cover cloth to the boy."

"Where is the boy?"

Maa began to sound like she had something caught in her throat when she spoke. Her voice didn't seem to fit her anymore. Her voice was distant, at odds with her tailing presence, even when she was talking to me. The strain at home, on her, on everyone, lasted for weeks. Maa no longer sat by Papa when he had his dinner. Each day, the strain moved nearer to the point where everything would rip apart; it was a quiet strong wind, drifting with no clear direction. Nothing was safe—not our brown curtains, the doormat, half-eaten by time, or Papa's fragile heart. Papa begged. He said "sorry" and "please" like children are told to say to adults.

Papa bathed Kwame and helped him dress up. Maa didn't get involved. Papa reminded Kwame to call Maa "Maa" not "Madame."

Kwame was funny. He spoke little English and would race through an entire conversation in French as if I understood. I taught him Twi, which he picked up fast. Sometimes I corrected his English too. I liked to teach him Twi the most because his accent in Twi was the funniest. Even Maa and Papa sometimes tittered when Kwame tried to speak Twi. Kwame didn't fear Maa the way I did. He liked to tell Maa things.

"Madame, *mepa wo kyɛw, me pɛ agyinamoa, le chat*, a pussy cat!" He blurted out.

He made paper animals to show Maa even after Maa told him not to rip any more pages from my exercise book. Maa never yelled at him.

Nothing would ever be the same again at home, but Papa tried to make things better. He started to buy Maa clothes and shoes and bags, but he didn't know Maa's favorite colors, red and gray. Papa bought yellow and orange and green shoes. Maa said thank you, yet she never wore a single pair. The shoes were lined up under their bed.

Kwame talked nonstop like Papa.

"When Papa come to Togo, he and *ma mère* take me to *le cinéma*," Kwame said.

Night after night, Kwame retold the movies they had watched, laughing at his own jokes, jokes I didn't get. But I had a brother. Papa had brought me a brother, a real brother.

Kwame and I held each other's hands and promised to never ever fight. One day we would go and visit Kwame's mother, we swore to each other. Every morning, we went into Maa and Papa's room to greet them. Papa would lift us up onto his lap, Kwame first, and say we grew bigger in our sleep. Maa never got involved but she had stopped calling Kwame "the boy." Kwame liked to hide behind the couch, jumping out to scare whoever entered the living room. The first time Maa called him by name, he had tried to scare her.

Over time, Maa's anger thawed, and she began to treat Kwame like a guest. She was kind, warm, and patient toward him. She combed his hair every morning. She washed our clothes on weekends; never complained that Kwame's was too dirty. Papa ironed our church clothes and school uniforms. Maa explained to Kwame, gently, how he must wash his plate after eating. But Maa seemed angry with me for loving Kwame so dearly. She always found something for me to do when Kwame and I were playing.

"Go and sweep under your bed."

"Go and find me a thread."

"Go, read your books; you must become a doctor."

• • •

It was a Sunday morning. We were running late for Mass, and it was Papa's fault. Maa didn't like to be late for anything, but Papa had gone and ironed a shirt too big for Kwame. Papa didn't go to the same church as Maa. He rarely went to church at all, but he was Presbyterian. Maa was Catholic. Papa was a member of the Presbyterian Men's Fellowship, but he went to service only when there was something to celebrate. Christmas, New Year, death.

Kwame was standing between Papa's thighs, getting his big blue shirt buttoned up.

"Is he going to follow me in that sack? It's three times bigger than him, can't you see?" Maa's voice was saturated with disdain.

"Baaba, I think the shirt is okay o," Papa said.

"So, I don't know how to raise a child anymore?"

"I'm sorry, Baaba. I'll help him find another one that doesn't need ironing."

"Brema, go and clean your shoes," Maa said.

I left with Kwame as Maa boiled in the living room. Papa went with us to help Kwame find a smaller shirt.

Kwame ran back to Maa with a brown T-shirt.

"Have you cleaned your shoes well?" Papa asked me.

I nodded. He looked down at my feet and took an old rag from my hand.

"Take them off," Papa said.

Papa cleaned my shoes. As he was helping me buckle them, Maa was helping Kwame get dressed again. No one knew what Kwame said to Maa.

Musical peals of laughter rushed out Maa's mouth, like when she had laughed so loud in her sleep that it woke me and Papa up. It was the second time I heard Maa laugh that way. Spurting. Wild. Like the ocean waves. I ran out of my room, leaving Papa kneeling with a jelly sandal in his hand. I wanted to check if maybe Maa had fallen asleep.

"Where is your other shoe?"

Maa's laughter crashed to a halt when she saw me.

"Papa was helping me buckle them," I said.

"Go and wear your shoe. We are running late."

· · ·

When we got to church, Kwame and I went to Sunday school. Maa didn't have to tell us where to find her when Sunday school closed. It was easy to find Maa at church. Morning and evening Mass, she always sat on the front pew facing the catechist.

At Sunday school, Kwame and I sat right next to a picture of Jonah being swallowed by the whale.

"What did you tell Maa?" I whispered.

Kwame brought mirth wherever he went, and yet it was bizarre how he had made Maa laugh so hard that Sunday morning. I could never make Maa laugh that way, but I wanted to.

"Kwame, what did you tell Maa?" I whispered again.

"*Rien du tout*," Kwame said.

"English, please."

"I tell Maa nothing."

I had never felt like Maa belonged to me. When people said I had my mother's beautiful head, the shape of a pear, I nodded eagerly, but Maa never agreed. She said I had my father's head, full of faraway dreams and mushy nonsense. I wanted Maa to be mine. I wanted to make her laugh her ocean laugh, but my jokes crashed in her thick silence.

"Nothing? So why did she laugh?" I pushed Kwame for an answer.

"Brema, quiet!" Auntie Nancy, the Sunday school teacher, said.

"Who can tell me how many days God took to create the entire world?" Auntie Nancy asked.

"Me, me, me, me, me, me, me!"

Shrieking voices pleaded to be heard.

"Settle down! Settle down! You shoot your hand up if you think you know the answer. You don't open your mouth, until I call your name, okay?"

"Yes, Auntie Nancy," the class chorused.

"What did you tell Maa?"

"Tell Maa what?" Kwame said.

"No, what did you tell her? Why was she laughing?"

"Brema, move over here," Auntie Nancy pointed to a seat in the front row.

Kwame got up to follow me.

"No, you remain seated over there," Auntie Nancy told Kwame. His eyes welled up with tears.

"Don't cry, I'm just going to sit over there," I said.

. . .

I knew Papa was at the door when the gingerly sweet smell of kelewele seeped into our room. Kwame's eyes were alight with pleasure, the kind only chopped and deep-fried ripe plantain, drenched in ground spices, could bring. We raced to Papa. I got to him first and took the black polythene bag from his hand. Kwame chased me for it. Papa asked us both to stop fooling around and hand over the kelewele to Maa.

"Your mother will share it for you," he said.

"Yes, Papa," we chorused.

Maa removed the kelewele from the bag, greasing the paper that wrapped it, and asked me to go get two plates. Kwame's grin widened as he went to sit back on the couch. I ran out to get the plates.

"Brema," Maa called me back.

"Have you taken your evening shower?"

"No, Maa," I said.

"No kelewele for you then. Go and bathe. I am not raising a dirty daughter."

My eyes drifted, as usual, to Papa. I wanted him to say something. That he bought the kelewele for me and Maa couldn't just take what was mine. But Papa never contradicted Maa, even when he needed to. Like the day Maa said it wasn't a holiday; but it was, and I went all the way to an empty school and came to an empty home.

"Papa," I called.

"Do as your mother says, Brema," he snapped.

I slammed the door and went to bathe. Every thought in my mind was imbued by a crippling rage. It was hard for me to tell which one of us Maa lived to torment the most, Papa or me.

"I leave two for you," Kwame said when I came back from the bathroom.

"Two what?"

He put his hand in his pocket. Two tiny pieces of kelewele came out, specked with lint.

"Just two?"

"*Oui*. I think Maa will give you your own one when you have *bathe* finished."

"No, she won't give it to me today, maybe tomorrow, I don't know. I don't even want it anymore."

"Just take. Tomorrow when Maa give you, you give me back."

"Okay, thank you."

I picked out the lint from the kelewele and ate it.

"What did you tell Maa?"

"Brema, I tell Maa many things, many, many, many."

"I know, but you told her something that made her laugh big, remember?"

"No, I asked her question."

"What question?"

"Her eye. She can't open it, like my Mama eye."

"Your mother is also one-eyed?"

"Yes, you can ask Papa."

Conceição Lima

Napoleão

It was Dad who decided to name him Napoleão. He was white, with a face that was feline but not frightening, and he had light brown spots on his neck, hips, and feet. We never observed the slightest air of meek humility. A good boy nonetheless, he carried his neck high and his muzzle turned up in the air. When he went out with us, he behaved like a faithful companion, never a lackey.

Dad brought him home one day, at nightfall, on his powerful BMW motorcycle and we, at hearing the meows, gathered around him in a cluster. Mom, who, like us, still gravely missed the light, prissy Minerva, came down the stairs with her hurried but cautious steps. When she saw him, with us already fighting over him, she smiled sweetly and petted his neck.

We loved him at first sight and that love was reciprocal. As soon as morning came, we squatted around him and saw the sweet, attentive hazel light in his eyes. The boys made him a house, but he preferred to lounge on the veranda, climbing up all those steps. From there, from the heights of the veranda that circled the entire house, he maintained order over the enormous yard, reacting to the slightest sign of the unusual.

One day, two neighboring dogs dared to cross the property line, advancing into the yard. We saw him in the air, in near vertical flight like an eagle, and then falling, landing on all four of his feet just in front of the two intruders who immediately understood that they weren't welcome. They recoiled apologetically. The feat astonished us and the boys recounted the story with huge gestures and impassioned words to their playmates from around the neighborhood, who listened, awestruck with incredulity. The veranda was very high, designed to provide a view of the surrounding landscape. From that day onward, Napoleão was a hero to the young men of São João and the surrounding area.

While we were at school, he was almost inseparable from my mom. After she sat down on her low stool to scale or clean the fish, he kept a slight distance, his back feet tucked beneath him, his front feet extended, neck cocked to one side, ears gently fallen, eyes, at moments, closed.

It was enough for Mom to get up to do any little thing for a total metamorphosis: all his muscles entered high alert, his ears pricked, his eyes aflame.

He loved fish heads, which Mom cooked with corn flour, in a yellow Nido milk tin. During the season when squids, sardines, or nzanvés washed ashore to be collected in baskets, it was a real feast. He liked sardines. He especially liked a type of paste that mother made him, mixing sardines, braised squid, and grilled or stewed breadfruit.

When needed, especially during the festive seasons, his talent for hunting shone brightly. All you had to do was say, "Sic, Napoleão!" or point with your finger. The selected hen was seized by the neck without a nip and brought over between the teeth, like a trophy. If the target was a pig or small goat the technique was to chase them until wearing them out, then corral them into a corner. He liked soccer, and often ran with the boys after the ball. We said that it was the effects of Lifebuoy soap, publicized by Eusébio, who used it to shower. One doubt vaguely concerned us: whether that made him a Benfica fan. An unrepentant Sporting fan like the rest of the family, Dad laughed and reminded us that in Mozambique, his birthplace, Eusébio played for Sporting.

I don't remember seeing him, even once, in a group of dogs, no matter how small. He steadfastly guarded his territory and the inhabitants of his territory, but was a loner within his own tribe.

One day, he didn't come down from the veranda and we had to take him his food, which he barely touched, clearly lacking any appetite. His once gleaming white fur was now dull and patchy, as if small tufts of it had been pulled out. The injections Dad administered no longer seemed to have any effect. He sluggishly circled the house on the veranda, although he rarely went down to the yard. For weeks, months, we would visit him over the course of the day, to take him his food, which he only sniffed and licked from a slight distance. He listened for us without raising his head, eyes distant, his formerly lively, dancing tail still. Of the effusive meows that had greeted us over the course of all those years, all that remained was a drawn-out, drained imitation, more like a restrained lament.

One Saturday, first thing in the morning, we found him completely still, eyes closed, lying on his side. He wasn't stiff yet. The boys picked him up by the feet and carried him toward the yard.

At the foot of the strongest kimi tree on the hillside leading up to Cóbo Gita, they dug a deep grave that we coated with leaves from the breadfruit tree, over which we placed bits of *upa*, the cottony fluff of the palm tree, old rags, and anything that seemed soft and fluffy.

Leading the procession, slowly, so that the body wouldn't swing much, Minho and Buggy. Behind them, in a single-file line of children and teenagers, girls and boys, eyes brimming with water and silence.

Mom said that many humans didn't get such a farewell.

The night that he became a member of our family, Dad told us that he was a pointer, a *perdigueiro*.

Translated from the Portuguese by David Shook

Arao Ameny

Atat

When I heard the sharp, rhythmic *snip-snip* of stainless-steel scissors, each blade taking turns cutting the thick, warm air and Ayaa's black curls, I knew someone had died back home. After a phone call from Uganda, my mother had gone from the closed door of her bedroom to shut herself in the bathroom and shear her hair.

I've learned to loathe long-distance phone calls, avoiding buying phone cards for my mother from the store around the corner, pretending to have forgotten so that she would have to buy them herself. I'd put the two folded five-dollar bills on her mahogany nightstand, unspent, and walk away quietly. I couldn't bear how so-and-so was making Ayaa worry.

Usually, so-and-so needed school fees or medicine. Sometimes, so-and-so needed to renovate their house, even though Ayaa sold her house and some of the family land to pay for documents and buy plane tickets for all four of us to join Papa in America. We lived in a small apartment that my parents did not own. They had to pay the landlord on the first and fifteenth of the month, or get evicted.

I didn't want to know who was sick or worse. I didn't want to know who Ayaa needed to send money to for two burials—the traditional one and the Christian one, one after the other, in no particular order. I wondered if the dead cared—if the sayings of elders or the Twenty-Third Psalm actually warmed their cool bodies. Ayaa said all of it matters, but I don't know. I didn't like seeing my mother worry herself into another headache.

It's only year two in America, and this was the second phone card conversation that ended with Ayaa locking herself in the bathroom to cut her hair after her hands steadied from the shock. She took a razor to shave the rest.

Back home, Atat and my aunties greeted death with scissors to their hair, too. Whether it was Uncle or Grandfather, or a neighbor who had a stillborn child, a line of round shaved heads lined up one by one to meet at dawn with plates of cooked food, cakes, and condolences. They would come again at night with more saucepans of food and jugs of mango juice, each woman taking turns to visit, never leaving the main mourner alone. The length of a woman's hair would tell you what was happening in her life. But we were in America now, where a girl with a shaved head would get made fun of for looking like a boy.

"Who is it this time?" I asked Ayaa, waiting for an answer I knew I wasn't going to get right away. Whenever anyone passed on, my mother took her time telling me whom we'd lost. She said I was a kid—her way of saying "When the time is right."

Ayaa turned her head slowly, as if it was heavy on her neck. "We've only been in this country for two years and already you've forgotten how to greet?"

"Sorry, Ayaa. Good morning."

"Good morning."

"Who is it now?" I tried again, defiance bubbling up inside me. "My mother and you share the same stubborn spirit," Ayaa often told me.

307

"Atat lives here in my house. Little fire woman," she would sing over me. "Tough pumpkin seed, my firstborn girl!"

"Make sure you walk Atim and Okello to the bus stop," Ayaa said now, like I didn't walk my brother and sister to the bus stop every day.

"Does Papa know?"

"Then straight to school," she continued. "Make sure you sit at the front in all your classes. Don't open your mouth too much—"

"But, Ayaa, at school here, you have to talk a lot, or they think your head is empty."

"*Wun woto wuno.* And when you finish school, come straight home. If I see you walk-walking around with those foolish girls, my daughter, you will see me."

"Okay." I swallowed saliva in my mouth that wasn't there.

It was getting wearisome juggling two sets of rules. At home, I might as well have never left Uganda. It was: Don't speak unless spoken to, don't look an elder in the eye, don't don't don't—it's disrespectful. Outside our house, where "America" started, it was disrespectful not to look elders in the eye.

I stood at the doorway, waiting for Atim. I could see my sister's straight, lean ten-year-old body scurrying around looking for the pair that matched the white shoe on her left foot. I rolled my eyes. Atim was always making me late.

"You're going to miss the bus—why don't you just wear the black shoes?"

"They don't match my outfit," she said, dashing from one room to the next, looking under the sofa and then her bed and then inside the laundry basket.

Okello, still sleepy, stumbled toward me, struggling to keep his eyes open. He groaned as he walked toward the front door, waddling from side to side.

"Ayaa said we have to leave now," he whispered in his usual morning raspy voice. Sometimes I wondered if Okello was an old man trapped in a little boy's body. He was just twelve, but he moved and spoke like the seventy-two-year-old neighbor across the street whom he regularly played chess with. "Ayaa said we need to leave on time," he repeated, brushing the lint off his old-man sweater.

"I know, O. We're just waiting on Atim, okay?"

He tucked his shirt in the front first and then the back. He closed his eyes as he leaned against the wall, sleeping while standing. My body loosened with relief when I saw both of Atim's white shoes running toward the door. She pounded her feet for effect, strutted, and spun in a circle, showing off her white dress. It looked like those fluffy milk-white confections little girls wore at Easter time. As always, Atim was overdressed for school. Ayaa would never let me wear such clothes to classes. "You are the firstborn," she would say, "as long as you lead, your sister will come to follow your example." Back home, being the firstborn was a burden—it felt like a big curse—and here in America, it just continued. Ayaa called Atim and Okello "my little Americans" since they had come here so young and started "picking things so fast," but me—she expected me to be an example to her "little Americans." It was tiring. "At least one of my children will be Ugandan in this country, I beg," she would say, hands raised up to Obanga.

Okello rolled his eyes into his head. "Mr. Turetsky said that school isn't a fashion show, Atim. Every morning, 'My shoes, my this, my that . . .'"

"You and that old man are just jealous because all you do is boring chess," she said.

"Let's go, please." I wrapped my arms around them and pushed them toward the door. "The only person Ayaa will yell at is me."

Before we left, I stood outside Ayaa's bedroom. "Mummy, see you later," I said to the closed door.

I heard her on the phone again. *"Kop ango? Kop ango?"*

The connection didn't sound good. She must have bought the two-dollar phone cards instead of the five-dollar ones.

"Hold on, hold on," Ayaa said. She came out and surveyed me. Up, down, and then up again. *"Ibutu aber?"*

"Yes, Mummy, I slept well. *Abutu aber.*" Then she looked down the long hallway to see Atim and Okello waving at her by the door.

"My children, I'll see you." She folded me into her arms before conceding one answer to my earlier questions. "Papa will be here later today."

I tensed. My father was due back from the Netherlands tomorrow. "But—"

"You go."

It was getting late. I ran with Atim and Okello to the bus stop, the blinking headlights already visible in the fog.

I fell back in my seat on the crowded bus and watched my mates shout over each other in the presence of an adult who wouldn't tell them not to talk "too much." The bus driver remained mute the whole ride, his eyes firmly fixed on the road. In America, parents talk to their kids like they are old people. They even argue back and forth in the supermarket about what to buy. I tried it once and caught a swift slap across the face.

If my grandmother could hear the kids around me, she would let out a quick "Ehhh!" and hold her right hand to her chest in disbelief before telling them to keep quiet. Atat preferred her rebellion unspoken, smiling slyly at me when Ayaa would ask how much jackfruit, pineapples, and passion fruit I had eaten to get a stomachache. I could see Atat's sticky-sweet hands now, the scent of fruit enveloping my bus seat. I didn't think everything had to be said, or shouted. Sometimes silence was the smart choice, but sometimes it was a prison where it wasn't quite clear if you or your feelings were the jailer. I envied my mates' vocal abandon.

When I reached school, the concrete slab in front of the building was wet from last night's rain, the moisture darkening the letters for the name of the school ominously. I shuffled through the sea of bodies, holding my backpack in front of me to soften the blow from the bumps. My book bag felt like a ton of bricks hanging from my right shoulder.

"Hello, Anna," the history teacher said as I walked through the large metal doors.

"It's Auma. *Aaah-Whou-Maaa*," I reminded him for the third time this week, looking straight at him and forcing a smile. Ayaa called this "smiling with only your mouth" because the eyes refused to participate—no creases or lines of genuine pleasure. I was becoming an expert at this kind of smile in America.

"Come on, Anna, I can pronounce that one at least," Mr. Dobbin said, half laughing. A week ago, he had taught our fifth-period class about the Russian composer Tchaikovsky, and before that, we learned about Polish American diplomat Zbigniew Brzezinski, yet it was hard for him to pronounce my four-letter name.

In English Lit, I sat down in the second row. Noticing a vacant seat in the front, I raised my hand to ask the teacher if I could move. I didn't want to just crawl into a seat that didn't belong to me like I watched Victor and Cindy do without asking Mrs. Mitchell.

"Come on," Cindy called to me after scurrying to the front row. "Rhonda won't mind."

"I'll ask Mrs. Mitchell first," I whispered before raising my hand again.

"You can call me Rhonda." The teacher smiled.

I didn't even want to imagine what would happen if Atat heard me calling an adult by her first name. "Thank you, Mrs. Mitchell."

The day had barely begun, and I was already tired from trying to be respectful in two cultures. I thought back to my mother's shaved head, and Papa's early return. Who had died?

I scanned my memory to see if I could, by a process of elimination, figure out who it was. It wasn't Aunty Dorcas. That woman refused to die. One time, she was knocked down by a car, but walked away with only a bruise that needed stitches. She beat breast cancer. She beat the man across the street who cheated on his wife, throwing her slippers at him while he ran away with his trousers unbuttoned. It couldn't be her.

It wasn't Papa's brother either. Uncle's sickness would come and go and come and go, and then he would go back to drinking his waragi into a Tuesday. He had a long throat, the kind that could drink alcohol for days and days before drunkenness kicked in. I couldn't remember him ever being sober. Even when Atim was born, Ayaa had to stop him from carrying her. But drunk or not, his sicknesses always passed. I doubted it was him.

It wasn't Ayaa's stepmother. She worried so much about everything that she called the doctor early in the morning if the pitch and volume of her sneeze wasn't just right.

The last school bell of the day temporarily interrupted the litany of family members I had crossed off in my mind. I looked for the school bus and remembered that it was Friday, when Ayaa usually picks up Atim and Okello. My seat on the bus felt bigger than usual as I resumed ticking relatives off the list of possible dead.

Everyone else was healthy, so it had to be some third or fourth cousin we weren't close to. The thought comforted me even though I knew the distance of the relation made no difference to Ayaa. The house would be different because of this death. I just wanted Ayaa to be normal again, without constantly worrying that there would be no one left by the time we went back to Uganda.

As I walked on the long stretch of sidewalk to the apartment, I saw Papa's black sedan in the driveway. It had been parked in the airport garage for a week while he was gone and there was dust built up on it from sitting still in an open parking lot. Six other cars I didn't recognize were also in the driveway, squeezed next to Papa's and Ayaa's cars. A big station wagon was double-parked in the street in front of our building, next to Mr. Turetsky's Volkswagen Beetle. Last year when Aunty died, there were only two cars outside.

A seed of fear started growing in my stomach.

Maybe there was a party nearby. The Acostas always had big parties when their family visited from Belize. Their guests' cars would fill up all the spots on the street and all the building parking spaces. Once, the landlord had to knock on their door repeatedly, and tell them to free up some parking for the tenants. Maybe the cars were there for the Acostas. But there was no music.

I broke into a slow jog to the house. At the entrance, I noticed the bird feeder that Papa had hung up for the hummingbirds had fallen over. The nectar was leaking into the grass and the bright red and yellow feeder was dotted with ants eating the sugar water. Ayaa's potted plants in the doorway drooped, withered. The purple flowers, my mother's favorite because of the color, had shriveled into flaky black and brown plant paper.

I opened the door to find Atim and Okello sitting at the table in the dining room with "Aunty" Agnes. There were so many aunties in the house, and half of them "didn't eat from the same plate as we did." I wanted to pull Ayaa aside and demand to know what was happening, but that would be disrespectful. "Respect," Ayaa would say, a never-ending rebuke to Okello, Atim, and me to be "good, proper people." Sometimes respect was a vise around my neck squeezing until I couldn't breathe.

Papa walked toward me, his eyes fixed on mine. He was holding a blue airmail envelope with my name on it. I knew it was more photographs from my grandmother. Atat regularly sent me photos of all my cousins and my best friend, Florence. Sometimes she sent Ayaa jars of Moo Yao in dark containers and bracelets for Ayaa to sell at church for extra money. But Papa had flown in from Amsterdam, not Lira—where had he gotten this letter from Atat?

I could hear Ayaa's muffled sobs from the living room. Papa put his hand on my shoulder. "This is the last letter your grandmother sent me, but it is addressed to you, my daughter." I nodded at him and quickly scanned the room to look for Ayaa. So many women were huddled around her, it looked like a ring of arms was smothering her. My father took my hand and we marched past aunty after aunty toward the kitchen. Some had buried their faces inside their handkerchiefs and shawls, their shoulders shaking. Others gave me no-teeth smiles behind burgundy, rouge, and burnt orange lipstick—the kind of smile strangers give when they know something about you that you haven't figured out yet. I didn't want their smiles, I wanted to know what was going on.

"Papa, who is it?" I gasped for air, the seed of fear in my stomach now a jackfruit.

Papa's tall, lean frame hovered over me, mountains of plates and closed saucepans filling the air with the scent of grief. His shoulders looked squarer than usual in his newly ironed white shirt. I knew he had ironed it himself because the creases weren't gentle like Ayaa's; my father liked to use extra starch.

He sat me down on a stool in the doorway of the kitchen.

"Papa—" I asked again.

He held my chin still. He looked straight into my eyes and said one word that I couldn't make out over all the talking and crying and humming and singing. I watched his lips mouth the words again. I repeated the word, only louder, almost shouting. For a few seconds, the house grew quiet until the word was all I could hear.

"Atat."

My chest clenched as I clasped the blue envelope he gave me now. I could feel the photos Grandmother had sent me inside. I looked at Papa, my stomach aching. My knees felt weak and wet, like I was stuck in cement. Papa put his hand behind my back to catch my fall.

Atat hadn't been sick. She drank moringa tea and walked half a mile every day. We were just supposed to be here for a few years until Papa finished his research at the university, and then we'd go back to Uganda. Back to Lira. Back to Atat and her mango tree, where we would sit in the shade, and she would tell me stories about when she was a little girl. Back home.

Papa's arms swallowed me as he whispered, *"Itye wunu kede kumu. Itye wunu kede kumu."*

I found myself on the sofa in the living room with a white knitted shawl over my legs, surrounded by Ayaa and the aunties. I sat there numb, thinking about Atat and her hands sticky with the sweetest fruits, until I could see her stretching to pluck a mango for me. Why couldn't it be another so-and-so?

I felt shame for all the times I asked my mother not to come to school with her head shaved—and all the times, since I'd come to America, that I vowed I'd never shave mine if someone died because I didn't want the girls at school to stare at me, or the boys at school to whisper. All of that seemed to fall away as I rose from the couch and walked to the bathroom. I closed the door, I picked up the scissors, and started to cut through the thick hair my mother struggled to plait, chopping off handfuls and clumps. I cut each section lower and lower and lower, until it was all gone.

Under the yellow light, some strands stood defiantly, like young grass on a field, determined to sprout. For the first time, I saw the familiar roundness of my grandmother's head in the mirror. Even her small ears, I recognized them. I smiled at my reflection as warm tears ran down my face. Ayaa was right: Atat lives in her house. She was staring back at me.

Recaredo Silebo Boturu

Sontem
Sometimes

Sontem,

A want flae lek pambot

Sontem,

A want jala lek frok,

Sontem,

A want gui bris lek stick

Bot, a de na dis yel: a no fit laf, a no fit krae,

   a no fit dans.

Sometimes,

I want to fly like a bird,

Sometimes,

I want to croak like a frog,

Sometimes,

I want to offer a cool breeze like a tree

But I'm penned in this prison: I can't laugh,

   can't cry, can't dance.

Translated from the Pichinglis by David Shook

Në na'a mpúrí haalo
I want to leave this place

Nta láai, wáè, në na'a mpúrí haalo.	I don't know why, but I want to leave this place.
Mpááte la sípatyípattyí,	To fly like a tiny grasshopper,
Ntyatyè lá kísókisö.	To glimmer like a firefly.
Nta láai, wáè, n tyi ná'a m púrí haalo.	I don't know why, but I don't want to leave this place.
Na tyuè báubaa tö purí,	If all of us leave,
Ká lë kásá'ó wètya wéría?	Who will tidy up our village's house?
Ká lë írèré béata yénòkonoko?	Who will write down our nòkonoko monster stories?
Ënökönökö ë hëtáárí,	There's too much racket,
Ë ityeketyeke ri hëtáárí,	There's too much clutter,
Ë rihúla ri'a perí sòbò së, wáè,	A plague of ants has arrived at the house, but,
A bola bë Bíòko ba tòrí haalo.	Bioko's children should be there.

Translated from the Bubi by David Shook

En la puerta primavera
At the gate of spring

At the gate of spring
I don't want my poems to be clad in oxen.
They will not wear Hermès ties.
I don't want them handsome and attractive to anyone.
I want them as they are: rebellious, racy.
Half-naked. Provocative.
Full of truths and warmth: exuberant.

Let my poems be like veins through which Black blood flows like gunpowder,
Raw adrenaline blast,
Relaxed lake, withheld waterfall,
Match lit at night in the distance,
Lit match in the depths of the sea.

Mask-wearing verses
That vociferate their complaints to botuku.
Verses scattered like hugs
Extended to all colors, without prejudice.
Without foolish divisions. Without pinches.
Verses that help us keep
The darkness out of us.
Verses of music and witchcraft
That sprinkle us with love for our neighbors,
All neighbors, here and there.
Verses held by the hand of a friend
Able to withstand a hard heatstroke,

RELATIONS

A snowfall, or a hurricane,

And become, in the end, a loud voice

Alerting our brothers who left

That here we are still

Adrift, searching for our voice.

Translated from the Spanish by Johnson Asunka

Vanessa Walters

Lagos Wives Club

STORY

"Why are you here?"

The question startled and confused Simone.

The older woman leaned over the two empty chairs between them, dabbing at her red face with a handkerchief. Simone had seen her at Nigerwives meetings before but didn't know her name.

"For the meeting," she replied. Wasn't it the reason they were all there?

"No, hot! Why so hot in here?"

Simone was unsure whether it was the woman's Scandinavian accent that had caused her to mishear the question or her own troubled spirit.

"It shouldn't be so hot like now," the woman continued. "This is Harmattan, when it is usually cool and dry. The weather used to run like a clock. December to January, Harmattan. May to September, rainy season."

Simone nodded politely, hoping this wasn't a segue into a conversation about the Nigeria of thirty years ago. Lagos so green, no trash anywhere, no traffic, never any crime, 55 kobos got you a whole US dollar, yadda, yadda, yadda. The aunties all told the same stories.

"The air, it's so thick, like pap. You know, pap!" The woman leaned back in her seat. "I weaned my babies on the pap," she muttered almost to herself now.

Everyone in the school hall seemed to complain about the heat, showing off the sweat patches on their ankara dresses, pointing to their skulls boiling under the wigs some of them wore. The very high ceiling and fully opened wall-to-wall sliding glass doors made little difference.

"There's no NEPA!" someone announced periodically, as if they were new to the national power grid, the acronym of which had come to be known as Never Expect Power Always. "The school hasn't put the generator on!" The school never put the generator on. That wasn't part of the agreement. They could use the hall for their monthly meetings, but good luck with Nigeria's electricity. "No power even to run a fan!" exclaimed another. Somebody optimistic had brought one, but it stood useless and forlorn in a corner, the cord still wrapped around its foot.

Simone hadn't thought of coming to the meeting initially. The Saturday catamaran crew were out, crisscrossing the lagoon. It was fun to watch them from the shade of her balcony, enjoying fresh pineapple, betting which of them would capsize next. She hadn't been coming to meetings for a while. Not since Genevieve, a former Nigerwife, had left. They used to arrange to come together, save each other a seat near the front and catch up on the funny things they had seen and done during the week.

She glanced around at the rows of about forty women in the room, wondering as she often did at the odd patchwork quilt of cultures and ethnicities they must seem. Brown skin, peach skin, blond hair, Afro, long, oiled braids, sleek, straight hair, dreadlocks, redheads. Their multiaccented chatter sounded like an orchestra warming up. She liked that international feeling about the group. It felt normal, like growing up in London's melting pot, but in London, you chose your friends, with the same interests or understandings as you.

Among this group, not all skin folk were kinfolk, and it was rare to find shared interests. Oh, they were mostly agreeable, kind, and helpful, but building genuine, deep friendships was hard. Simone found more affinity with the few Nigerian friends she had. They were gregarious and cosmopolitan. Often they had recently moved back from London, too. But their lives revolved around their large, extended families and childhood friends.

After being Black in the United Kingdom, she found it a pleasant change, to disappear into a crowd, to navigate stores without being trailed by security, to not have the host or hostess at an upscale restaurant look at you doubtfully when you walked in. But just because she wasn't othered in Lagos, it didn't mean that she belonged.

Her husband, Preye, belonged, and he reveled in it, casting aside his polo shirts for traditional tunics and swapping his British accent for the local cadence. He walked taller, took his time with simple actions like rising from his chair or washing his hands, and smiled more.

Their time in Nigeria was only supposed to be temporary. When Preye had asked Simone to move to Nigeria for a few years, she had agreed without thinking about it too much. She'd just had a baby. He made it sound fantastic. Their lifestyle would be better. More space and staff, too. He would be working for his father, getting the opportunity to start his own business, so he would be around more. Their son would get to grow up in Nigeria—an African man. But "a few years" had become seven in the blink of an eye. There were two boys now alongside the apartment that looked out onto the lagoon, and the nanny, the steward, and the driver. Preye wouldn't hear about moving back to the United Kingdom, so there they were. She sighed. He would never leave Nigeria again, not permanently. He was home.

She'd tried to make it her home, too. A poetic narrative about being a descendent of slavery circling back to the home of her ancestors sustained her at first. But seven years later, she still felt like a visitor. A foreign object. She would never be of this place.

The conversations about moving back to the United Kingdom became heated arguments. Preye poked at her relationship with her mother and sister. The family she was crying about was dysfunctional, he reminded her; wasn't she glad to be away from them? He couldn't understand why she would want to leave a life of servants and sunny days to go back to dreary London, where you cleaned up after yourself and had to jump on the Tube every day to face the endless grind of the nine-to-five, and racist white people. He didn't see any reason to live anywhere else. Certainly not the United Kingdom, where people were as miserable as the weather. It wasn't a country for Black people, he said.

He spoke more vehemently than Simone had ever known him to, and she wondered if he was shouting at her or himself. He seemed to be out to prove something, about all the times he'd been overlooked at work in London, or feared by white women opting not to share a lift with only him, all the landlords who wouldn't rent to him, and the taxis that didn't stop: that there wasn't something inadequate in him, after all.

Years of ignoring and dismissing her had made Preye unable to see or hear Simone. She was the problem, he said. It was all in her perspective. She asked if they could try couple's therapy, but, oh no, he was an "African man" who didn't need that "useless rubbish."

Preye hadn't always taken himself so seriously. He had laughed about bringing swim shorts to Idawari's water birth, and he stuck up for her constantly carping mother, trying to build a bridge between them. But now he was haughty, closed off, and hard to talk to. If she got upset about something, he was dismissive. "There are no victims in this house."

And things had taken a turn for the worse after she'd caught him in a lie about his whereabouts. He laughed when she said a friend saw him in the Sheraton Hotel in Ikeja when he'd claimed to be in Abuja. "You women are always seeing ghosts."

"They all change," complained Genevieve, before she left Nigeria for good last summer. For more than a year, Genevieve had been obviously depressed, griping about how awful everything was. The economy. The mold in her apartment. The theft of jewelry by her house girl. Her children's substandard tennis instructor. Finally, she admitted the problem was her husband having women on the side. Before she went back to the United States, they'd held a somber tea party for her, a kind of wake, because although she promised to visit every holiday, they knew they'd probably never see her again.

Officially, Genevieve's reason for leaving was to settle her children at college. But tongues wagged regardless. Nigerwives gossiped—gisted—relentlessly. What else was there to do when the sun's pink fingers found you by a pool with a cold vodka and Sprite, and the kids were away with the nannies?

Simone remembered clearly the talk about the Nigerwife who ran away from her husband's jealous fists. Another vanished when the money ran out. This one was hysterical about the pollution. Apparently, that one had confessed she "couldn't get used to all the Black people," the secret leaked during an infamously boozy playdate. Another had seemed nice until she dubbed them 1950s housewives on social media and returned to Lahore to resume her legal career, taking her husband with her. *But many of us are happy, aren't we?* That was always the refrain.

Sure, some seemed marooned, and others had fallen on hard times, but many had built enviable lives, started businesses, and cultivated social networks they were justly proud of and didn't want to leave. It was never said, but most of them were elevated by their husbands' status and a lifestyle they wouldn't enjoy in the countries they had come from. There was also their exotic foreignness, the privilege of lighter skin, a Western education, or the belief that they were culturally superior, one often encouraged and validated by people they met. But how long could such affirmation trump connection?

She wasn't going to get the answer from Preye's mother.

"Don't leave your husband in Nigeria to travel, not even for a weekend," was the opener to one of Mother-in-Law's many TED talks on how to be a good Nigerian wife, delivered in her dressing room while their lashes were glued, faces powdered, and wrappers tied for a wedding. As the gele was pleated and wound around her head in a viselike grip, making Simone's ears shriek, Mother-in-Law explained, scolded, and commiserated. "Without a wife's vigilance, the husband is a sitting duck for an unscrupulous woman." Divorce made little sense to her. "Your husband is your house. Your house is your children. Your children are your life, and what is life without all three?"

Simone had been happy their first years in Lagos. Why would she not? Preye was well connected, from a wealthy family. She moved in elite circles. She threw herself into making friends and spending time with her in-laws, re-creating herself into a person she thought they would like: glamorous, sociable. She spent hours at playdates sipping Prosecco and gisting. But none of the bonds she tried to forge from these surface connections ever took root. No one wanted to go deeper with her—they were fine with the facade. When Genevieve ghosted her, she realized how useless it all was. These were only superficial relationships for here and now. It was so painful, she stopped trying.

At least the playdates had worked for the boys. Idawari and Tubo were of this place. Even better, they were on a pedestal, already strutting about like roosters, their loud voices gobbling up space. If she followed through on her threats to take them and leave, how would they cope with life in London, without their privilege, without their sense of belonging, without their father?

The Nigerwives Lagos president, a stout Indonesian in her late fifties, welcomed the attendees and complained about the heat. They stood and sang the anthem as they did every month, led by a wrinkled wisp of a woman with the energy of a gospel choir conductor, her silky white hair floating above her.

> *Nigerwives from many lands, many lands*
> *Sharing lives and joining hands, joining hands*
> *We are one, we are one, we are one*
>
> *Nigerwives are truly blessed, truly blessed*
> *In all things we do our best, do our best*
> *Strong to serve, strong to serve, strong to serve*
>
> *Nigerwives across the nation, 'cross the nation*
> *Sing our song of celebration, celebration*
> *Sisters all, sisters all, sis . . . ters . . . all!*

Through the open windows that mercifully sucked their dreary warbling out of the room, Simone could see her driver Azeez sitting on an upturned cement bucket in the shade of a tree. He stared at nothing, his face sullen because she wouldn't let him enjoy AC in the car, burning through diesel while she sweated in the hall. Simone and Preye had hired him because of his excellent references, which had omitted his nonstop commentary. He had an opinion on everything from Manchester United's Premiership chances to whether cats were a medium to the underworld. She was just tired.

Sitting down, the president began with the day's agenda: actions needing to be taken for the Small World festival, membership ID cards, immigration, and welfare. The items were routine—things they usually discussed at meetings. Of course, there were constant interruptions.

"Is it definitely confirmed?" someone piped up. "About Small World? Because you can't support the same charity year after year in case of fraud. They don't like it. For two or three years now, we have chosen Braille."

The president said yes. She had confirmed they could donate to the Braille Centre this year, but after that, they needed to find another charity.

"This year or next, it's not right to ask us to choose a different charity," someone else interrupted. "Braille is our own charity, built with our sweat and blood. We still have salaries to pay and books to produce!"

"Those are the rules," interjected someone else. "They are allowed to have rules, you know!"

There was a lot of tutting and shaking of heads. Soon the aunties were quarreling like fruit bats. Sometimes Simone wondered if they enjoyed arguing, if it was the reason they came to meetings. She drifted back to the question she had misheard. Her son had asked the same thing this morning.

"Mummy, why are you here?"

Focused on the lagoon, she hadn't noticed Idawari watching her from the open doorway, his little head cocked to one side.

"Getting some air," she had said with a sigh.

"No, not here. Why are you here in Nigeria?" The effort of articulating himself had caused his forehead to pucker.

It didn't feel like something her son would say.

"Why do you ask that?" she said, and he shrank back and said nothing. It made her suspicious that he'd overheard a conversation about her on the compound. Maybe something an in-law said. They probably knew things with her and Preye were rocky. Heard the fights. The staff talked. But she smiled. "I'm here for the family. So we could all live here together."

His face brightened, and he drew closer again. They hugged, and he climbed onto her lap to enjoy the Day-Glo-colored catamarans that twirled like pinwheels in the Atlantic gusts. But his words had sat with her.

A bang on the table from the VP brought Simone back to the meeting. They had moved on to the welfare committee's forthcoming trip to the Regina Mundi Home for the Elderly being organized by Welfare Officer "Eboni with an 'i,'" as she always introduced herself. The dimple-cheeked American spoke with such idealistic zeal that Simone imagined Eboni dotted her precious "i" with a heart.

"The Nigerwives community is a wonderful family of friends," said Eboni, addressing the hall. "Some of you may not know the association started in the seventies."

"Nineteen seventy-nine!" someone yelled. Eboni smiled and nodded. She explained that the younger members owed a debt to the aunties who started the group and others who were getting older and needed assistance.

"Nigerwives are not just here for socializing. Every so often, we hear of elderly Nigerwives in distress and we try to help," she said. "We've heard there is a Nigerwife in the Regina Mundi Home for the Elderly who is destitute and has no family, so I've arranged a welfare visit for Monday to see what she needs and to support the home. Please attend if you can."

Simone listened sympathetically but with no desire to go. She didn't do Nigerwife stuff like that anymore, not really. Time-consuming, and too many arguments.

"What if they aren't paid-up members?" called out one aunty, which set the arguing off again, a cacophony of complaints quickly cascading into tangents.

The president clapped her hands—starting a new, fruitless discussion about how Nigerwives were supposed to be exempt from visa charges yet each new minister of immigration kept forgetting they existed—brought the meeting to an official close. The women bought raffle tickets for prizes laid out on the trestle table. This month, obvious Christmas regifts included a box of tumblers with green spots and a few bottles of wine. Also, a dozen eggs from someone's farm, and an unopened box of dates. The women got up to stretch their legs and snack. Simone gathered her things and headed for the door.

Eboni stepped into her path. "Hey, Simone, can I put you down for that Regina Mundi visit?"

"Well actually, I—"

"The Nigerwife I spoke about is actually Caribbean, and the Caribbean aunties are coming."

"It's just that—" Simone desperately tried to think of an excuse.

"We hardly see you at meetings anymore," pleaded Eboni. "It would be really great if you could make it."

"Fine," Simone said with a sigh.

Eboni seemed hysterical with happiness. "Don't you just love the Nigerwives? We're like a surrogate family, always there with advice and support. Honestly, I was happy in Atlanta, but after we got married, Lekan wanted to move back. I had my doubts."

Oh God, not another Nigerwife origin story, Simone thought. *They never tell you how much they want to move back when they meet you.*

"You know, all those stereotypes," said Eboni. "But, now I'm here, I love Lagos. So much to do!"

Eboni still gave off cringe tourist vibes even after two years in Lagos, posting photos on social media of herself posing by tricycle taxis and pretending to shop in the local market. One day she'd question what it really meant to live here for years, decades, a lifetime as an outsider, somebody who wouldn't be missed. After eighteen years in Lagos, now that she was gone, no one asked about Genevieve.

Simone and Eboni parted, promising to meet for coffee as usual. But they never did. Simone always made an excuse. Not that she didn't like Eboni. She was kind of endearing, like those fluffy dogs hawkers sold by the roadside. But what was the point of putting two years into someone only for them to leave? Each time felt like a bereavement. Genevieve never replied to the WhatsApp messages Simone had sent asking how she was doing, even though they had sat on committees and worked on fundraisers together. They had confided in each other over the éclairs at Cakes and Cream. And she could tell the messages had been read from the double blue tick beside them.

Simone slipped out to the car park, where a slightly happier Azeez now sat inside the SUV, chugging and chilled for her, ready to go.

• • •

Azeez was sulking again on the drive to Mushin two days later. It turned out he'd missed some sort of family memorial because she had made him work the Sunday. That's what Preye said, anyway. He self-righteously preached about overworking the staff, which was maddeningly hypocritical since he didn't think twice about calling a driver up out of his sleep at midnight to go to a strip club. "He's fine now. I've given him soothe money. Just forget it."

Mushin was deeper into the mainland than she usually went alone. Their first few years in Lagos, Preye asked her not to leave the "safe" environs of Victoria Island, Ikoyi, and Lekki Phase 1. Then Yaba, just over the bridge, became doable. The market there was an excellent place to find fabric for curtains. Ikeja Mall opened with a cinema, and that also became an acceptable destination. Gradually, she ventured farther. More recently, she had made trips to the Ikeja Saddle Club for Idawari and Tubo to feed the horses. But when Simone mentioned the welfare trip to Mushin, Preye thought it too close to Oshodi, a rough neighborhood known for its area-boy clashes. Nevertheless, he considered the idea for a while before deciding that, since it was daytime and the boys were not going, it wasn't such a risk. "Just plan to be back by four," Preye warned.

For all his concerns, the journey to Mushin was unremarkable. It was after the morning rush, so any traffic was heading into the center, and Mushin seemed quiet compared with the frenetic commercial activity on Victoria Island. Apart from the insistent street hawkers and beggars banging on the SUV for attention, it was fine.

The high-walled Regina Mundi compound was on the main road lined with street traders sitting under large umbrellas, their goods laid out in piles on the ground. Keke maruwas rattled past precariously on their three wheels. Inside was an orderly and peaceful courtyard surrounded on four sides by peach-colored buildings, what looked like a hospital, offices, and modest apartments. Nuns walked through the square in their pale blue habits, and Simone could see Eboni with a group of women clustered underneath a sign that read HOME FOR THE ELDERLY.

As Azeez parked the car, Eboni waved eagerly at her. Simone recognized most of the West Indian Nigerwives. They loved to tell Simone how they had met their Nigerian husbands in the 1950s and 1960s, when they were sent to the University of the West Indies to study civil administration to prepare for Nigeria's independence. They often spoke about the close-knit group they had formed to keep each other sane in a culture they didn't understand. Their closeness was evident in how they finished each other's sentences and referenced each other's children as if they were their own.

On the whole, Simone found them to be a quaint, old-fashioned type of Caribbean. They still grew their food in their gardens and obsessed over Queen Elizabeth, displaying a prissy Englishness that was fading away among the Caribbean community in the United Kingdom today. They were kind, always asking after her boys. But she didn't really feel like one of them. Their world was created out of a need that no longer existed. She was a visitor there, too.

Several elderly residents sat outside the home enjoying the comings and goings or snoozing, dressed in matching ankara clothes as if there was an event. A guide greeted the Nigerwife delegation in the parking lot and rattled off a quick history of the residence. She led them inside, through large communal rooms, male and female dormitories, and a sitting room with scattered sofas and armchairs, and a wooden dining table that could seat twenty. She showed them the kitchen where staff cooked. Donated foodstuffs were stacked up like a woodpile. Saucepan-size cans of powdered Peak milk. Boxes of Indomie noodles. Cooking oil. Poundo yam flour. Barrels of rice. It was well stocked. Clearly, the home was a popular cause of the community.

The guide made a big show of their chief attraction, the Nigerwife Eboni had organized the trip to see: an old woman called Theresa sitting dazed in an armchair, squinting as if the world hurt her eyes. She had scraps of frosted hair and the frailty of someone in her nineties, even a hundred. Her skin crinkled on her arms like a plastic bag, and her head drooped to one side as if it was too heavy. When the representative touched her shoulder and said, "Good Morning, Mummy!" Theresa frowned slightly, as if she'd heard a floorboard creak or a whistling draft, but nothing more.

"Theresa can't see or hear much now," the guide explained. "She's our precious mystery. About twenty years ago, locals found her destitute and brought her here. They said she was from Barbados. But she doesn't speak, so that's all we can say."

The Caribbean women consulted each other like they were internet search engines. "Did you know about a Theresa?" "Who is Bajan here?" "Yuh think she really Bajan? She look Saint Lucian from dat forehead?" "Inez might remember her." "Inez is ninety-plus!" "But her memory is sharp!" "Who has Inez phone number?" However, they eventually reached a blank, and stared at Theresa in silent concern until the representative moved them on.

On the drive back, Azeez warmed up enough to ask some questions. He turned down the radio.

"Madame, what happens in that place?"

"The old people's home? They live there until they die."

"Why are they there? Why not with their families?"

"They don't have any family."

He digested this poorly. "Ah no, madame, everyone has family. Where are their children?"

"Who knows? They're alone in the world."

"Does this happen in the white man's country? I can't understand who would abandon senior relatives to this place. This is not African at all!" Azeez seemed entirely worked up. Angry, even.

"These people have been alone a long time," she said. "Perhaps their relatives are dead."

"Ah-ah, this is an abomination, madame," he said.

It didn't take much to make Azeez's list of abominations, the things he couldn't fathom: so far, unmarried mothers, married women who still partied in nightclubs as she did, the country's corrupt leaders, and now, putting elders in homes. Never having left Nigeria and rarely exposed to non-Black people, the strangeness of the West mystified him—the weird and wonderful "Obodo Oyinbo." Some of his questions or comments made her laugh, but others were sad, like when he'd asked her once if white people never got sick, since "they invented medicine, madame."

For the most part, Africa, at least the countries she'd visited, Ghana and Benin, felt like an escape from racism, but she still frequently encountered Black people who viewed white people through white savior lenses.

This abomination, though, Simone agreed with.

The journey home was straightforward. The traffic was on the opposite side of the road. The evening rush from the islands had begun. Already, a never-ending train of cars shuddered along with a lot of honking and hollering. Eventually, the radio volume went back up and Azeez lapsed into silence. But still, Simone couldn't get Theresa out of her head. Especially the thought of her being so alone, thousands of miles from her home country, her people, anyone who cared.

She had heard of this happening to Nigerwives. After their husbands had passed away, and their children, if they had any, had gone. Eventually, the local community discovered them, rotting away in some old house, as useless and objectionable as the weeds that forced themselves up through the paving stones. Even if they were once familiar and well-liked, they might go back to being strange and foreign to their neighbors. If they were once generous madames, they might end up at the mercy of servants who kept them alive only to steal what they could. Sometimes, as the welfare team reported in meetings, it might only be the proliferation of rats that motivated neighbors to act on behalf of such women. Simone wondered when the point of no return was for them. For her. When do the slender blood ties to your place of origin expire, leaving you marooned in a country?

Although Theresa seemed well taken care of—and now that they knew she was there, the Caribbean women would check up on her—the circumstances of her abandonment bothered Simone. How had she ended up there? Why was there nowhere to send her and, worse, no one to remember her? She would have had a home once, maybe children, friends, in-laws, a husband. Why was she alone? Where were the records of her life? It was as Simone's grandmother used to say of long-gone family members. "Only God knew they lived."

But if she left, would it be much better? She thought of her mother, who rarely called, and her friends—there weren't many. Long-distance friendships were hard to maintain. Already not much to go home to. By the time the boys were grown up and off to college, there might be nothing left there for her. Or if her mother died. The younger relatives didn't know her. Would it still be home if you no longer had an identity there? People who knew you? Any place to go? Would she eventually become a fan in the corner, forlorn, useless, one day to be abandoned like Theresa? Had Idawari's innocent eyes noticed she was already out of place here, unnecessary? Someone who could also be forgotten?

They crossed the bridge into still-busy Victoria Island and were swallowed up by the afternoon crush.

Richard Ali A Mutu K

I Am Lost!

STORY

At least 19 civilians killed in another bloodbath suspected to have been carried out by the ADF in the eastern region of DRC, where a week of violent demonstrations has been criticizing the passivity of the UN and local authorities.

Six Years Since the Beni Slaughters: The Horrors of the Killings Are Still Visible at Ngadi

Since October 30, 2019, the LUCHA movement has counted 1,206 human casualties in Beni, and noted a growth in killings around Ruwenzori and a part of Ituri, the neighboring province—areas once safe.

On Tuesday, Daesh claimed, via their own media, a new raid against a military camp in Beni. 15 soldiers reported dead, government weapons and explosive devices seized.

DRC—Beni: Nearly 100 Dead in Less Than 5 Months, a Disaster That Moves (Almost) Nobody

In less than two years, over 1,100 people have been killed in Lubero and mostly in Beni, Northern Kivu, where the death toll is almost 100 since the beginning of the year. The murders continue, despite the presence of UN forces and the Congolese army.

Pregnant women are ripped out in Beni, babies are mutilated, human beings are tied before their throats are cut. —Dr. Denis Mukwege, Nobel Peace laureate

How do you write about something else when the country you live in is plagued by recurrent violence? When brothers and sisters are killed on a daily basis, I mean slaughtered, tied up, beheaded? When babies are cut out of their mothers' bodies and crushed alive in mortars or butchered and minced like meat? How can you think of anything else under such circumstances? How do you create, or imagine? How can anyone close their eyes in the face of such barbarity, such horror, such tragedy? How long will this go on, this human madness, this unheard-of violence and animosity, these unspeakable massacres?

For days I've been trying to write something to escape these images, these videos, the news on the killings in the eastern region of my country, this vast African country at the heart of the world's issues, the navel of world peace and world war. To live in Congo is, without a doubt, to live in the center of history and the future of the planet. My father used to say, "As long as Congo is Congo, it will always be in charge of the world and burdened by it." Then he would add that Fanon's vision of Congo was limited when he said that it was merely the trigger of Africa. "No," my father said, "Congo is the trigger of the world, figuratively and literally. We turn to Congo for everything: yesterday for the atomic bomb, today for technology, and tomorrow it shall certainly be for water, the forest, to save humanity."

I vowed to read more novels to get my mind on other things, let my soul stroll in someone else's head, as Aline advised, but I failed. I couldn't get the images in my phone out of my head. One in particular haunts me: a dead woman, shot down, lying on the floor, a frail, innocent kid by her side, not more than two years old, alive, his little mouth hanging at her left breast, sucking.

What goes on in the mind of a man who leaves his home, grabs a machete, enters someone else's house, lifts that machete, grips it tightly, and disembowels or beheads his victim in cold blood? Good God, what is going on in his mind at that very moment? I want to say that only mad lunacy can push a person to such a shameful act, but "shameful" is too weak an adjective or conclusion.

This macabre situation has been going on for an eternity, and the so-called international community keeps silent, as do its media. How many dead should we count before the world considers for a second this part of the globe? How long must we wait for a word to be said about the Congolese genocide? Every day, the eastern part of Congo counts its share of dead! Every day.

Some blame the curse of the subsoil. They say the land is suffering because of its mineral wealth. The coltan, cobalt, copper—all the raw materials we're aware of. It seems we just find ourselves on the wrong side of the globe: where everyone dreams of getting rich.

Who's behind all of this? For some time, rumors have been circulating that there could be some Congolese among the executioners and the string-pullers, compatriots complicit in the illegal exploitation of our mineral resources, working hand in hand with the foreign militias. I decided to investigate and unmask these people, find their names, their identities. Young people from Beni and other collaborators have been sending me tips, pictures, and videos about what is happening in their region. Most of the alleged live in Kinshasa, where they occupy senior positions in politics, the army, and the police. Sons of this country, accomplices in these atrocities.

Once upon a time, I used to blog about these things, anonymously, of course. I was still a student when my posts started causing a stir in the country and abroad. I even started contributing to one of the foreign wire services. Income from those posts didn't cover my university fees, but they helped. After graduation, though, I had to make a decision: live undercover, naming and shaming the powerful and corrupt, or find a stable job, and eventually settle down with Aline. I chose the latter, and I am mostly happy.

Aline and I have been seeing each other for almost two years—from our last year in university to now. She's a walking exclamation point. A neckbreaking beauty, extravagant in her tastes and gifts—not the type I usually go for, because that type usually doesn't go for me, but it's working, and I feel myself falling for her. Hard. On the job front, I work for a daily Kinshasa paper covering local news. It's steady, it keeps me on the pulse of the city I love, and I can write opinion pieces on the issues in the country as long as I keep my observations philosophical. Lately though, especially with the endless conflict in the eastern region, I haven't been satisfied writing these toothless editorials. Aline tells me I need to stop focusing on the evil I can't control and enjoy my life. "You can't help anyone until you help yourself." Spoken like a politician's daughter.

I've reached out to one of the outlets I used to write for when I was in school and sent them an article with my findings—the first in what I hope will be an investigative series about the politician enabling the conflict. I haven't yet uncovered all the personalities involved in the eastern region mafia, but I'm convinced that I will soon. In the meantime I'm gathering more info, more names, more leads. This story has consumed me. I want to expose each murderer of the republic, the crooks, the fake citizens, the politicians who plunder the country's resources.

I mentioned to Aline that I was doing an investigative piece on compatriots involved in that illegal trafficking of natural resources, blood minerals, but I didn't give her any details and she didn't want any, which I suppose is best, for her safety and mine. For my security, I write under a pseudonym. No one, except my editor, knows I'm the author of the exposés unearthing the corruption enabling the slaughters in Beni.

. . .

2:13 p.m. My iPhone is ringing. A birthday gift from Aline. At first I refused it, daring to tell her, "Sorry, darling, but I don't think I can use this device." She almost choked.

"I'm having a hard time, and I don't really know what's wrong with me, Aline. A few days ago, I came across *Blood in the Mobile*. Do you know that documentary?"

"No!" she said. "And? Are you saying I've given you a bloody phone?"

"No, that's not what I mean. What I—"

"Alain!"

"In fact, that documentary has upset me ever since I watched it. Darling, the situation is critical."

"Pfft!" she hissed.

"I know, I know, I'm raving again."

"Seriously, Alain! Seriously!"

Aline was furious, she didn't want to hear anything from me. She demanded that I return her gift, her phone. I couldn't. I didn't want to jeopardize our relationship. I still had plans for her, for us. I couldn't just let things end for a phone matter of which she understood nothing, nothing at all.

I tried to quickly tell her about the blood-soaked history of cellphones, about what was actually happening in the mining areas where coltan was exploited, about the women and children who've died because of continuous dangerous work, and the endless conflicts in the east, owing to our natural resources, and particularly coltan, which is vital to the mobile phone, computer, and other technology industries. I didn't get very far—Aline was incensed and, at that point, had tuned me out. She was not happy I had shunned her gift. Everything I was trying to explain was just smoke to her. Our relationship almost fizzled out that night.

Anyway, as I said earlier, the iPhone rang. I pulled it from the right pocket of my blue jeans, and checked the screen. It was "Al-love." Aline. I picked up.

"Where are you?" she asked without so much as a hello. Strange. I looked over my shoulder to make sure no one was tailing me. She wasn't around, nor was anyone she knows whom I know. I told her where I was: "Total Filling Station, Force-Assossa. What about you?"

"We need to meet right now! Come quickly to City Market, please!"

"Right now?"

"Alain, I told you it's urgent! I have important news."

"Uh . . ."

"I'll be there in less than five minutes. Hurry up, please!"

Aline lived at Gombe, an uptown district of Kinshasa, while I came from Matongé, the city, the lungs and heart of Kin, where the capital lives and vibrates! Kinshasa has always been special to me. It's quite a complex and strange town, always thrilling, teasing, exciting, surprising, shaky, hectic, a mysterious and mythical metropolis. I've been living there since my childhood, and she has been living in me, but still I don't fully know her: she is elusive and troubling, but that's another story.

Aline prefers quiet places, relaxed, chic restaurants located in her neighborhood. Makes sense. Her father is a senator she still hasn't introduced me to. They lead a "good life" and lack nothing. I know she only loves me because I'm a handsome and intelligent guy, and I'm not a liar. She once told me, "Alain, you know you're not only cute, you're very smart! I love you so much and I feel good with you!" When she said that, lightning shot up my spine. It's a special thing to be loved by someone, but when it's by someone whose beauty is nearly universal, trust me, that's another sensation altogether: you have the world at your feet!

I had no idea why Aline was insisting we meet right away, and no inkling what she wanted to talk about. We can chat about everything and nothing, we hardly plan a topic. But still, she gave no clue, only that it was important.

"Important news!" My sister got me worried when I told her Aline insisted we meet because she had something urgent to tell me. "She is probably pregnant."

"What!?"

"Yeah, I bet I'm right, bro! Get ready for that!"

"Oh no! No! Not that!" My skin went slick with sweat at the thought.

My sister could be right. Women can smell these things. But how could Aline do such a thing to me? She knows perfectly well we agreed to avoid having a baby before marriage. Every time we've gotten down, Aline has assured me she has everything under control, that she would never let herself get pregnant at her age. She has plans, so no kids for now. So why on earth is she telling me she is pregnant? Maybe Aline just wanted to fool me, or ask me if we should have an abortion. Abortion? I don't think so. Aline is a Christian. She's even a cantor in her church. She could never do such a thing, never ever. Yet, if she did opt for that, what should be my reaction? Do I have a choice? The truth is, I'm not ready to have a baby, but telling her to have an abortion doesn't seem the best option either. That would bother me a lot.

I became such a sweaty mess I forgot it was just an assumption. Nothing more. My sister didn't know what Aline had to tell me; she barely knew Aline. My Aline. My girlfriend. I know her better than anyone. She would never ever drop such news on me.

I pulled myself together as I parked at City Market. The restaurant was a bit empty, even though it was the afternoon, when it's usually full and busy. Strange. I found Aline sitting at a table. How beautiful my girlfriend is. Ebony skin. Hoop earrings shining at each lobe. Upturned eyes, slightly elongated nose, lips not too plump.

"You took forever, you know?"

Aline never welcomes me this way. I took the seat facing her. I kept my cool and played the guy as she stared at me. I escaped her penetrating gaze and directed my eyes to the waiter who had approached our table.

"Pineapple juice, please."

He jotted my order down in his small notebook. "Anything else?"

"That will be all. Thanks." Aline was already drinking a Coke.

"Everything okay?" I asked casually.

Her lips remained sealed around her straw. Her nod said everything was fine, but her face showed something was terribly wrong. I had never seen her like this.

"Darling, what is it?"

Aline put her big Coke can on the table. She pushed back a lock of hair and said, "Alain, you have to save my father!"

I frowned, then leaned back in the chair to hear her clearly.

"You're the only one that my family can count on right now! My father needs you. He was just named in a new article about the conflict in Beni. They're saying he's been siphoning funds from the mines, that some of the militia work for him. You have to help him!"

"Your father?" I didn't even know her father. I rifled through the few names I had been able to gather for the article I sent my editor. Aline hadn't introduced me to her dad precisely because she knew what I did, only referring to him by his title whenever I prodded. "His name is 'Honorable.' That's all you need to know."

"What's your father's name, Aline?!"

She bowed her head. "Honorable Mawouzi."

I sat there, speechless, breathless. "But . . ." I shook my head. That despicable man could not be my girlfriend's father. Among the senators I had listed, Mawouzi Tshela, the parliamentarian representing North Kivu in the upper chamber, was the most sickening. He had been born in Beni. A son of the soil turning a profit at the massacre of his own.

Aline covered her face with her sweaty hands. She couldn't look at me. I sat there lost, unsure how to reconcile that my Al-love was the daughter of a lying, thieving murderer. She started to tremble. Tears slipped from her chin and tore at my heart. Her slow build of gasping sobs destroyed me.

"Calm down, Aline! Calm down, honey." I left my chair and went to comfort her. "Calm down. Stop crying."

"Will you help my father, please, Alain?"

Aline has helped me a lot. She paid for a big part of my studies. When I was finishing up my bachelor's in journalism, she's the one who gave me the money to pay the last tuition installment and covered all the costs I incurred for the defense of my dissertation, "Investigative Journalism in a Country of Permanent Violence."

"Alain!"

"Yes, honey?"

"You're so quiet. Will you help us?"

I held her tight, but I could not answer. All I could see was that kid sucking his dead mother's breast as Aline cried into my shirt, my iPhone vibrating in my pocket.

Translated from the French by Ray Ndebi

Edwige-Renée Dro

Poor Men Have Too Much Ego

STORY

We all know how it ended for Queen Vashti.
She was replaced by Esther.

That was last Sunday's sermon. The Sunday I discovered the missed calls in Didier's phone history and the string of WhatsApp messages, each incoming text more desperately blasé than the next. Here we were again. Despite all the promises he made the first time. If that had indeed been his first time. Maybe the first time he got caught.

And his reply, sent just before church, before that sermon:

Je vais passer t'apporter des viennoiseries.

At what moment was he planning to leave the house, go to the bakery, get her the viennoiseries, and make it on time to church? And the certitude with which he wrote. I *will* come over. Not "might" or "could." *Je* vais *passer.* This man was sure about what he was writing—and what he was going to do.

I decided to stop looking at his phone, to stop torturing myself like that and get Cécile ready.

Still, I couldn't help wondering. What would he have done had she said yes?

What kinds of viennoiseries does she like? Chocolate croissants? Almond? Financiers?

Is she one of those girls who only likes eating in a man's pocket? Whose expensive tastes only appear when a man is paying? She must be, if after all those messages, he was now having to butter her up with an offer of popping over to hers with *des viennoiseries*!

The pastor sermonized, punctuating each sentence with an "amen." Every pause. Amen. Every trailing thought. Amen. The congregation, too. Amen. They said it. I didn't. Amen to what?

What kind of showing off did Vashti refuse to do for a man who had a harem—access to many other women—to banish her? *Hein*? Presumably, Vashti was used to being shown off. So if she refused on that day, why didn't anyone ask why? Perhaps Xerxes had said to one of the many women of his harem, *"Je vais passer t'apporter des viennoiseries."*

Maybe that was why, on that particular day, Queen Vashti said, "Fuck the dignitaries! Fuck his kingship. I will not be my husband's crown."

The head that wants to wear a crown must sit straight. You move your head here and there, and you want the crown to stay on? That thing is heavy! And it falls, if the head doesn't stay put wanting to see every delight passing by.

Some will say that it is up to the crown to position herself in such a way that however much the king moves his head, his crown covers him and stays put—in the same way that the Proverbs 31 Woman, through her rising before the dawn, never eating the bread of idleness but working vigorously, brought respect to her husband at the city gate and made him take his seat among the elders. But, did nameless Proverbs 31 Woman's nameless husband text anyone, *"Je vais passer t'apporter des viennoiseries?"*

Or was she the kind of woman who didn't place any stock in men's egos anyway?

I remember carefully watching the pastor's wife as her husband preached. She sat in the front row looking all "first lady"—a recent and full-force makeover she had given herself when she decided to rebrand from *Maman* Liliane to *Pasteure* Liliane.

For starters, she began preaching more, because God created all of us equal. She set up a Facebook page, where she hosted a Facebook Live series on how Christian women should behave. How we should be submissive to our husbands. How no person on God's earth could come to her and say that her husband, Pasteur Jean-Charles, has done this or that, because she wouldn't even open that door. Her husband is covered in the blood of Jesus. Sometimes there were talks addressed to single women. How they should pray for a God-fearing husband, and for a vision from God to show them how to be suitable helpmates once they got their husbands.

Then there was the makeup that became more caked, done by a professional. Or professionals. Because there were enough makeup artists who saw doing *Pasteure* Liliane's makeup as sowing into the kingdom, and enough hairdressers who kept her up on the human hair-weave front.

There was a time when I used to admire this woman, or perhaps her marriage. Her simplicity. Her prayer life. The fact that she was always available when you wanted to speak to her after church. I think everything changed the day she gave that sermon and advised us ladies to look good for our husbands. She told us she was now going to the gym four times a week, and it was Pasteur Jean-Charles, "my darling" (she always feels the need to add that after she mentions his name), who purchased the gym membership for her.

Today, as her husband preached about Queen Vashti's refusal to submit to her husband, *Pasteure* Liliane's right hand was raised, her palm open, her expression an impassive state of composed rapture. Not a "why" on her carefully made-up face. She was drinking in the Word. No, sir! Whys were not her portion. She wasn't worrying her well-coiffed head about why Xerxes was throwing away Queen Vashti without a second thought, and when I had gone to her the first time Didier cheated on me, she had advised me not to question Didier's motives either.

"A wise woman builds her house!" she told me. She, of course, was the quintessential wise woman who wouldn't throw away her marriage to Pasteur Jean-Charles (her darling), their three boys, and the ministry by behaving in a way that wasn't submissive. Vashti she wasn't.

Pasteur Jean-Charles spoke with Didier over multiple sessions, once with me. We spoke of submission, of not paying heed to all the gossips out there, and of the Jezebels trying to create discord.

If you don't open the door, the devil can't enter.

You are a young, beautiful, engaged couple. Filled with the Holy Spirit.

Of course that doesn't please the devil.

I gave Didier another chance.

• • •

Something gnawed at me over the course of the days and weeks that followed our counseling sessions. Even though Didier seemed to be behaving after I ordered him to delete the whore's number and never contact her again. Even though he got busy winning me over.

Candlelight dinners. Flowers. Day trips. Viennoiseries.

Instead of leaving me to visit my parents alone, Didier made time and we went together. He didn't hesitate in showing his love to me. Kisses here. Caresses there.

My parents indulgently looked on like a bad wind had blown by, especially Maman. "When happiness is on its way," Maman echoed the pastor's wife, "the devil is busy working hard—he doesn't like it when people progress."

Tantie Georgette disagreed with Maman's assertion when I told her what had happened. "You people do know that you insult this devil, if he even exists, when you say things like that, *non*? You think that he cares for your frolicking?"

My immediate family kept their distance from my mother's sister, but I needed another opinion about what to do about Didier. I had accepted Didier's apology and submitted to the counsel from Pasteur, First Lady, and Maman, but still I felt unsettled in my spirit.

"What would you have done, Tantie, had it been you?"

She took a slow sip from the glass of wine she had just poured. "Do you see a man here?"

"But if Tonton Richard cheated on you? Or at least, had an *écart*."

"Is that what they call it these days? Darling girl, I've always been interested in being rich. When you are rich, there are some things that don't even enter your mind."

"But you are a woman!" I burst into tears, as if it wasn't bad enough that our conversation was happening within earshot of her housemaids.

"My child! Men are what they are. The question is what do you want to do?"

My body shook in answer. And I cried. Because I didn't know what I wanted to do. I never imagined that Didier, my Didier, could or would betray me. Not again.

How was he to be my head if he was behaving like those other men who didn't know better and let themselves be seduced by the honeyed voices of the sirens outside? Did he not know that he was giving his strength to another household just when we were about to build our own?

I was ready to answer "madame" the next time someone asked me "*C'est madame ou mademoiselle?*" I was ready to stop ticking the *célibataire* box. I wanted a next of kin who wasn't my mother or my father. I wanted to build a life with a man! With Didier.

I didn't see the tears coming. I thought that I had gotten over it, but obviously not. It—Didier's *écart*—had not stopped gnawing.

"Baby girl, I'm going to talk to you as I would Amanda or Lara," she said of her daughters. "You may not like what I'm going to say, but that's the job of a mother. This man you are going to marry, what does he do?"

"He works in communications."

"Where?"

"Tantie . . ."

"Just answer the question." She took another sip of her wine.

"He is freelance. He works for himself."

"And how much money does he make in this working for himself that he does?"

"It varies."

"But you earn more than him. A lot more!"

"Well, I have a good job."

"So why are you choosing to shack up with a man who is counting pennies? What's the rush?"

"I'm not expecting him to support me."

"And he isn't! You are supporting him."

"We are both supporting each other. He is a good man."

"He is 'good' and he is dipping his wick in other women before you have even tied the knot? I wouldn't want to see his 'bad.'"

That's when I asked myself, *Why did I come to Tantie about this?*

I was seeking advice from someone who did not share the same belief about marriage as me.

"You know, this church thing, I have done it," she said. "I have a Bible that I read. God is God and He is One. But even the man after God's own heart was rich. This your one, how is he going to be your head when he can't even provide for himself? *Hein*? Or is he going to lift you from your mother and father's house and make you make do in some rental?"

I couldn't hear her above the gnawing. If *I* was feeling horny, what must be going on with Didier? Saving ourselves was hard, even if we were doing it for the Lord—and for the devil not to have any hold over us, for a stronghold not to be built in our lives. Biology is biology.

I decided to move the wedding date up.

• • •

"She came to Abidjan and instead of keeping her eyes on her job, she got knocked up."

I've heard Maman say this about Tantie Georgette many times, and I have often wondered—even if I have asked forgiveness and prayed not to dishonor my mother or admire the things of this world—if Maman wasn't maybe a little jealous of Tantie Georgette. I know I wished I had Tantie Georgette's independent spirit. Even though she wasn't a Christian, I admired her.

Maman was a woman of her generation. She and her friends were content standing behind their men, going to endless church services, busying themselves with looking after their grandchildren. No point putting Cécile at nursery, she said. No point getting a nanny. She came over every day to look after Cécile.

My generation is busy building businesses, being ambitious without shame or compromise, dumping men who show any hint of flexing muscles on them. Well, not many of my friends, but some.

Charlotte is living on her own in an apartment in Bonoumin. Fatou is in her very own villa in 2-Plateaux. Not married. And even if they speak about marriage at times, they make it sound more like a fantasy.

"He needs to have his own house, too. Because at this my age, he is bound to have children, and I don't fancy playing maman to someone else's child!"

"But he will come as a package, Fatou!" I tell them, cringing at the thought of someone making such a judgment about me because of Cécile. Not that I even considered anything like my package being damaged when Didier and I were engaged in those conversations.

"Nobody is saying he wouldn't come as a package. Even me, I come as a package, *non*? But I don't want someone playing daddy of the year with my Khady when it's convenient. You know those men: ever smiling despite the child's demands, but not getting involved in the day-to-day stress of raising them! The kind of man who is full of great child-friendly adventures, but when you tell him 'I'm stuck at work, could you please go and pick my child up from this and that place,' will have headless and tailless excuses?" Fatou shook her head. "Oh, and while we are choosing qualities, brother needs to be rich o! Poor men have too much ego."

"Fatou!"

"I lie? From whose mouth are you always hearing, 'I'm a man, I'm a man'? Poor men!"

Those conversations don't happen so often. Fear stops me from being too close to those girls. I imagine them to be like the purple cloth seller in the Bible, even after she heard Paul and was converted.

Something of the purple was bound to remain inside her, *non*? Of all the multitude of colors, why choose to sell purple clothes in the first place? Purple, the color of royalty. This may have been a woman who marked a pause when Paul told women to dress modestly. This was a woman with some purple in her. Dignity. Regalia. Power. A woman about her business, like Fatou and Charlotte, who are never around much.

Fatou is busy making back-and-forth trips to Dubai and Abidjan for her cosmetics and clothing stores, and Charlotte is as careerist as they come. We might have started together as accountants at SODECI, but soon after Charlotte left and launched her own event-management company.

A big part of me wants to ask the girls what I should do about Didier's indiscretions. Maybe I will. I need Fatou's honesty. Charlotte will ask me, like Tantie Georgette did then, "What do you want to do?" I still don't have an answer. Or maybe I do?

Every so often, the word "divorce" pops into my head, but I get so scared that I stuff it down. God hates divorce. And there is no proof that Didier has slept with this latest woman. Still, I hurt. I don't want anyone to tell me that this is how men are. That's why I have not spoken to anyone about the viennoiseries messages yet. Not even Didier, even if he's noticed that I seem to be down.

"It's just work."

"It will be fine. Cécile doesn't need to see her maman like this, and I don't want to see the love of my life looking unhappy."

He hugs me. I smile, and tell him to look after himself as he goes out to some meetings at church or a *vié père*, where he goes to network with politicians and businessmen. That's how he might win a contract, and bring money home.

Back then, I didn't mind the "freelance" nature of his work.

"He is an influencer," Charlotte told Fatou when she asked what my husband did.

We were at a party and Fatou had been talking about and pointing at some man, telling me that he seemed to be looking in my direction. "I could introduce you. He is loaded, but he likes to be free!"

I didn't ask her why she didn't go there herself. "I'm married."

"And she is a Christian," Charlotte added for good measure. A good measure that I didn't mind. It is good witness when people know that, because of your belief, there are some conversations that will not be pursued. Had, but not pursued. I am no prude.

"Have you brought him to the party then?"

"We are not attached at the hip, you know."

"Ooohhh! Influencer. Anyone we know?" Fatou asked, ready to rank Didier against the other social media personalities she followed.

"Didier Ogou," Charlotte said. She didn't have to add anything else because the name was sufficient. It still is, in some circles, but maybe the scales have fallen off my eyes. Having name recognition on Facebook to people in Cocody—a few people out of Cocody's 200,000 populace—is not what I call influence.

Fatou nodded, and said, "I have heard that name." The change of temperature in her voice made me shiver, but I didn't know what to think then. I still don't. Did she know him?

. . .

The next time I found messages in Didier's phone, I went to visit Tantie Georgette. She had been right about my misplaced focus the last time I had come to her for advice. Instead of worrying about Didier's cheating, I should have been thinking about his ability to contribute to our household.

I decided to take it as an answer to prayer when I called and she was not in Europe, or in the village buying aubergines, okra, shea butter, or plantains to sell in Abidjan. She was at home, in her kitchen with her two housemaids, grinding spices, making up sauces. There were quite a few pots going on the huge six-fire cooker.

"Bring water for my daughter, kèh! Look at these girls!" She shook her head at the housemaids and hugged me, asked me to wait for her in the living room.

"No, I'll sit here with you." I plonked myself at the kitchen table and drank the water one of the girls poured for me.

"Well then, taste this!" She passed me a piece of chicken. "I'm opening a shop in Beverly Hills here soon!"

I might have marked a pause when she gave me the chicken, a pause during which I told myself that it was just a piece of chicken. A piece among many pieces. Tantie wouldn't have had the time to make a ritual sacrifice in the hour that it took for me to leave Koumassi to her place. Besides, the housemaids were in the kitchen. Weren't sacrifices made when nobody was around? So I ate the chicken, because the blood of Jesus is stronger.

It would have just been easier if Tantie were a Christian. Even a Muslim would have worked for me. But Tantie Georgette was an out-and-out animist, and she was in a polygamous marriage. Or rather, a union. The law doesn't know her, only her children, although Amanda and Lara are not Tonton Richard's.

As I ate the chicken, I dissolved into sobs.

"Let's go to my bedroom."

She grabbed a bottle of wine out of the fridge and my bottle of water, and led the way up the stairs.

"So all these tears are over Didier," she said as she plopped herself down on her chaise longue and opened the bottle of wine. "Have a glass. Sangaré will drop you back home."

"Why would he do something like this? Again."

She took a sip of her wine and again, she asked me, "What do you want to do?"

Apart from the hum of the air conditioner and the birds singing outside in the garden, there was no other sound. She didn't say anything more, just sipping slowly and sitting with me as I leaned back in my seat and allowed myself to think about the answer.

I looked around the bedroom Tantie had decorated simply but elegantly. White sheets on the bed, plumped-up pillows. A white chaise longue and two armchairs. The wooden floor was painted a powder blue, and uncovered. The delicious smell of jasmine wafting through. This was her sanctuary. Hers alone. Tonton Richard had his own bed-room but, of course, that was out of bounds to me.

Of those men whose names were said in whispers in Abidjan, Tonton Richard was one. One whom not many people had access to. One of the real *riches*, as opposed to the *nouveaux riches* who needed everyone to acknowledge when they broke wind. Not even Fatou and Charlotte knew that he was my tonton. Partly because I didn't care and partly because I didn't want to deal with any raised eyebrows or questions trying to understand how exactly he was my uncle.

"But he is married. *Han han*, so, you mean, that's your auntie?"

That unclickable name on his Wikipedia page wasn't my aunt. Tantie has her own Wikipedia page, created when she was awarded Prix d'excellence for being the top businesswoman in Côte d'Ivoire last year. Fatou and Charlotte know Tantie Georgette as my aunt; not that other woman officially known as Tonton Richard's wife. In the family, everyone knows Richard as Tantie's husband, his children know her as the other wife of their father, and his first wife knows it, too. But that knowledge is family knowledge. Not national knowledge.

Tonton Richard might have bought Tantie Georgette that place in Beverly Hills, but she had a fat villa of her own in 2-Plateaux. With her own money, she sent Amanda and Lara to Canada and the States for their education. The villa is now providing her with rental income.

When Tantie had first asked me to consider Didier's finances, I was focused on light not yoking with darkness. That part about Jesus dying for my abundant life, I had put aside. And that was why I was in some rental in the back end of Koumassi, when I could afford a flat in Bonoumin. Maybe, not just when I got married, but three years into the marriage when I was promoted to *expert-comptable*, I could have moved. But men are men, and their ego must be dealt with softly. And gently. And carefully. Although that was no guarantee. They could still go ahead and make offers like *Je vais passer t'apporter des viennoiseries.*

• • •

Why does dignity need to be translated into never meeting and confronting the husband's mistress? I met her one lunchtime at Fondation Donwahi. It wasn't difficult to arrange at all. What is the use of Facebook, if not for such things? To know what they look like. What they do. What their movements are.

She was at the terrace, having a glass of wine and smoking a cigarette. Her dark sunglasses firmly in place over her eyes. No doubt taking a well-deserved break. This woman was accomplished, really accomplished, a photographer you could Google who was exhibiting her work all over the world: Dakar, Berlin, Addis Ababa, Abidjan. Her pictures on Facebook showed her chilling with her fellow artist friends in the coolest spots in these cities. There was not one photograph with her and Didier—I examined every single photo in her albums, and there were a lot! I checked for posts that might allude to their relationship, nothing. Or maybe one cryptic one. It just said, "Ah, my brothers from Abidjan!" with a sunglassed smiley face. So what was she doing with my husband? What did she see in Didier? His beauty? He is beautiful, my husband. Tall, muscular, gregarious, always smiling. But let's be honest: the man is broke!

I had started asking myself what I saw in him when, three years into the marriage, he was still describing his employment status as "freelance" instead of "jobless," but I would stuff down the thought. It was the devil whispering such things into my mind about my husband. These days, I have begun to think that it is no devil but life staring me right in the face and asking real questions. Questions like: What is an influencer? Why am I with a man who cannot even pay for my birthday trip? One with whom I must go half on my own birthday trip! Surely God didn't mean that when he made man head over the wife!

I pulled a chair and sat at her table. She lowered the glasses and frowned, probably assuming I was a fan.

"I'm Abigael. Didier's wife."

She smiled brightly now. "The wife he hides. Well, nice to meet you, sister."

"I'm not your sister. You are sleeping with my husband."

That's when she took off her sunglasses and looked deeply into my eyes. If she thought that I was going to be the one to break the gaze, she was sorely mistaken. She put her glasses back on and took another drag of her cigarette.

"I call every woman a sister. Call it a tic." The corners of her mouth inched upward into another condescending grin. "As for your husband, I'm no longer sleeping with him. We did it maybe twice, but you know, it was shit."

"Why did you even go there?"

"*Ahi*? Shouldn't you be asking him? He is the one who made promises to you, *hein*!" She clicked her finger and a waiter appeared. "*L'addition*."

"Don't you care that you are destroying a marriage? We have a child."

I was aware I sounded pathetic, and I'm now glad that she didn't answer that question. Instead, she paid her bill, grabbed her bag, and threw me a glance that I do not know how to qualify today. I knew, however, that it wasn't pitying. She left without another word.

I stopped stalking her on Facebook. I deleted her number, which I had pinched from Didier's phone, and tried my best to forget it. Because she was right. Didier is the one who made promises to me. My beef is with him. Not with her, or any pastor, or pastor's wife.

. . .

"I want a divorce."

I dropped the bomb as he was preparing to go out to "influence" at an event. No ifs, no buts.

He has been busy delegating people to talk to me ever since, to convince me otherwise. I have been busy going to the tribunal.

How does one go about getting a divorce in this country?

Jacquelynn Kerubo

Sundays in Nairobi

STORY

The water splashed Nancy's feet as she rinsed the laundry. Her boyfriend, Martin, sat on the grass, watching with a bemused look. And then a chuckle as she wrung the water from his white Calvin Klein briefs.

"What's funny, Mato?" she asked.

On their first date, Martin described himself as a village boy, a son of farmers who would soon return to his roots. As they spent more time together, Nancy had doubted that he'd move to a place without reliable water, electricity, and a dry cleaner. He wore Burberry dress shirts and perfumes, tastes acquired during his student years in the United Kingdom. He watched reruns of *Ally McBeal* and JLo music videos on MTV. Still, having met two of his ex-girlfriends, Nancy sensed that his tastes were more like those of their grandparents' generation, when men chose women who'd take on more traditional roles. He was probably laughing because back when she was still resisting him, he had told her that he would one day tame her. Now there she was, with her American graduate degree and an accent acquired from her years in New York, submitting to the humility of hand-washing his undergarments.

"I feel really bad, really guilty, for letting you do this," he said, heaving slightly, although the glee in his eyes betrayed him.

Looking helpless, he had gathered the handful of clothes and put them in the basin in the washing area in the backyard. His houseboy, Joseph, came around on Tuesdays, and though Martin had sufficient dry cleaning and laundry to last him a couple of weeks, Nancy had felt this new pressure to be more of a girlfriend. A woman. A possible wife. She was afraid to lose him.

Dating in Nairobi was different from dating in New York, where a relationship could progress to a meaningful plane without apparent domestication. Kenyan men were different. A friend in New York, a man who enjoyed theater and Saturday dinners and Sunday brunches at the starriest Yelp recommendations, became annoyed with the wife he had brought back home to Nairobi. "She didn't even bother to *personally* make me a cup of tea, asking the maid to do so. I spent tens of thousands of dollars courting her around the world." Martin was conservative, too, and Nancy wanted this thing with him to advance. She was down with hand-washing laundry.

Nancy welcomed the ice-cold comfort of the water. It was rarely this warm in Nairobi. Earlier that morning, it was Mato's heated body and lovemaking that had offered warmth against the usual Nairobi chill. They had slept in as they did on Sundays, after a night of nyama choma and beer with friends at Chomazone on Mombasa Road. As usual, they had followed the feasting with a drive to the marshy land by the airport, where they took turns driving his Subaru sports car through the mud, competing to see who was better skilled at navigating the wheels. Their very own safari rally.

Nancy was once a church girl, keen to keep the commandments. One evening after service at New York's Times Square Church, she had found herself in the arms of a fellow member. She was too embarrassed to return to God, punishing herself with enduring guilt. When she returned to Kenya, she tried church again, hopping from one to another in the hope of finding one where she'd feel comfortable. Hanging Martin's undies up to dry, the sound of worshippers wailing to God for mercy and prosperity in churches across the city, desperate for divine intervention, rang in her memories. They were lonely, tired from their often-unrewarded hustle. At home on these Sundays, husbands, after a workweek filled with evenings at the bar with friends, were forced to finally spend time with their families. They sat at the dining table and marveled at their wives' pancakes and their children's banter. Then they'd hatch a plot to escape for a drink with male friends, which sometimes meant seeing a side chick. Their wives had come to accept this Nairobi male proclivity.

For nonreligious singles like Nancy and Martin, Sundays were a complicated dance. It was the day the women woke up in the arms of lovers or prospective lovers, the day that signaled a new week with new questions regarding which way the winds were blowing toward the ultimate goal of joining the mostly miserable married. But Nancy was desperate to join the happily obliging women. Martin was a smart businessman. He once made her laugh until she peed when he told her someone walked like a bean planter. His lovemaking wasn't theatrical, but rather generous and satisfying, like a buffalo in the wild. He called or texted every night to make sure she was home safe. He was amused by her American ways, like when she wanted to talk to the manager at a restaurant after subpar service. Yet he was also empathetic when she told him she was seeing a therapist to recover from the internalized racism she'd learned in the United States. Still emerging from all of the tangled weeds of a Black life attempted abroad, she felt safety in Martin's steady ways and confidence made her feel safe. She always thought that he, too, had endured some indignities as a Black African male in the United Kingdom. He was just better at disguising his wounds behind the village man identity. Yes, she wouldn't mind joining the married, and looked forward to twenty years down the marital road, when she might be irritated by his hovering presence.

From the kitchen window, Nancy could see the washed clothes swaying in the breeze. One pair of the Calvin Klein underwear dangled where the wooden peg had come loose. So what if it fell and dried on the grass? It would survive.

For now, lunch was more urgent. Martin's new stove was unfamiliar to both, and Joseph wouldn't be back to clean and organize and explain until Tuesday. They lay flat on the kitchen's polished red floor, spending an hour trying to figure it out, lighting matches to test if the gas was leaking.

"I once read a joke about a girl whose gravestone read 'Here lies so-and-so, who went looking for a gas leak with a match,'" said Nancy. They laughed, glowing in their new depth of intimacy, okay with the idea of dying together in a blaze of love.

"Well, if we survive this, you'll have a slower learning curve when you get your stove," Martin said. Her electric stove had short-circuited the past week. She was looking to replace it with a gas cooker, since Nairobi's power company wasn't reliable.

At last, they found the manual Joseph had saved in a drawer in the kitchen. Nancy went about scraping together a meal with the limited groceries in the fridge. Some beef chunks. Potatoes. Peas. Carrots. Rice. Not so fancy, but a wholesome Kenyan meal.

Martin paced around the house, sorting his mail, rummaging through closets, taking a smoke outside, trying to adjust to this newness. By now, he would have dropped off Nancy at her apartment twenty-five minutes away, and he'd be back home, a JLo video in the background, newspaper in hand, marinating in his postcopulation smells. Now he had to pretend to have a semblance of domesticity, a somewhat impressive routine, and to sit through a first meal at home together.

"Don't worry, Mato. I'm going to leave as soon as I'm done with the dishes," Nancy said, desperate to reassure Martin that she wasn't trying to trap him. As they ate on the couch in the living room, she tried to swallow her food with speed as if it would hasten time, love, a deepening of the relationship.

Martin laughed. He was never one to say much, but underneath his stoicism and easy laughter lay plenty of softness and some insecurity. Sometimes she was terrified of this unknown part of him. When they gossiped about a local handsome news anchor whose romance travails were splashed in tabloids, Nancy had said that it was a good thing Martin wasn't so handsome. It hurt her to see tears spring to his eyes.

The knock at the gate came just as Nancy was packing her weekend bag, or fornication bag as she called it. Even though they'd been going out for a year now, she had some lingering doubts, a nagging feeling she couldn't quite place, and she preferred not to leave any personal effects behind. Maybe she should stay this day? A bra or a thong? The banging at the gate got louder.

"Mato! Mato! There's someone at the gate. Do you want me to get it?" Nancy shouted through the bedroom window to alert Martin, who was smoking another cigarette in the backyard.

"Please. If you don't mind. Probably the watchman with my news-paper delivery."

It was a petite woman drenched in the Elizabeth Arden Red Door perfume that saturated Nairobi's Central Business District. Her bur-gundy lipstick defined her shapely, full lips. Her carefully crafted outfit—the floral mididress, the faux leather purse, the polished pumps with the slight terpenic smell of Kiwi shoe polish—were an effort at sophistication. Nancy remained calm as she confirmed that the woman was indeed here to see Martin. She invited her in.

"Would you like some water?" Nancy asked the woman, who'd

introduced herself as Liz. The sweat on Liz's face and the thin layer of dust on her shoes suggested she'd taken public transport.

"Yes, please, thank you," Liz said with authority.

She's been here before, Nancy thought. The way she moved swiftly to the living room and chose the armchair with the vantage lighting that made her look ethereal. To travel by public transport to Martin's place took great effort—there weren't many matatus on this proper middle-class estate's route, particularly on the weekend. She had to take a matatu and alight on Mombasa Road, then trek the dusty mile or more to the main gate, and after a security check, trek another half a mile or more to the smaller security gate that led to the section of homes where Martin's was. That was a lot of commitment. Liz had to be an aspiring girlfriend.

"Nancy Obare. That's what you said your name is, right? Are you a Luo?" asked Liz. She emphasized the Luo part in the way that people who despised the tribe did.

"No, I'm not." Nancy didn't want to engage in the hierarchy of tribes.

"Oh, really. Obare sounds like a Luo name," Liz said, again lacing the tribe's name with spite. "You even look like one."

"I'll take that as a compliment. Luo women are beautiful," said Nancy. Because she and Martin were from different tribes, she'd gotten used to people hinting that men from his tribe rarely married outside their own. But no one had ever been this persistent and almost hateful. Nancy didn't bother to ask the woman what her last name was, instead hurrying out to tell Martin to come greet his guest.

Martin came through the bedroom door and joined Nancy so that they walked side by side into the sitting room. He froze when he saw his guest, his pupils darkening, a look of disgust crossing his face. "What are you doing here?"

"I'm visiting you," said Liz.

Martin shouted some words in Kikuyu, which Nancy didn't understand. Liz responded harshly in Kikuyu. Without warning, Martin descended on her, slapping her several times across the face. Her earrings flew across the room.

"Stop it. Stop it. Mato, please. Stop it," said Nancy, scrambling to pick up the scattered earrings.

"You came here to disrespect my girlfriend?" Martin shouted in English, now raining blows all over Liz's face and body.

Liz fled barefoot. Nancy gathered Liz's stuff and ran after her. She quietly handed over the belongings and watched as Liz walked away, shoes in hands, her confidence, her whole person, diminished.

Nancy didn't know how to face Martin now. She'd never seen this side of him, never noticed any flashes of anger. He was always agreeable, always laughing, always admitting to guilt when he felt he'd been unkind or inconsiderate or a prick. Was he really that angry about the woman's surprise visit? Would he have been as angry if the woman had shown up after Nancy had left? What had the woman said to provoke him so? How did they know each other? So many questions she was now afraid to ask.

"I have to leave soon. Are you still able to drop me off?" an eerily calm Nancy asked Martin, who still had tremors of anger.

"You shouldn't have seen that. She shouldn't have come here to disrespect you."

"Who is she?" Nancy finally asked, her eyes fixated outside the window, where the underwear that had fallen off the peg now lay on the grass.

"She showed up at the bar with some guys from my village."

"How did it progress from a bar to here?" Nancy asked, even though she already knew the answer. He was likely introduced to Liz by the village mate who didn't like Nancy. Martin probably brought Liz home on the nights they didn't spend together. How did she fool herself into thinking that Martin, an eligible bachelor, couldn't possibly have other women in the periphery?

"I'm a fairly known guy around here. It wouldn't be hard to find me if you talked nicely to the guards."

Sunday evenings in Nairobi are filled with emptiness and bitter disappointment. The churchgoer finds that the glow from the sermon that promised healing is gone with the tithe they offered, but their infirmity is even more present. In these hours, the week ahead threatening a burst of capitalistic pursuits, husbands once again stressed about establishing status in society, acutely aware of their wives' shortcomings, and vice versa. They both welcomed the misery, if only to return to a familiar pain rather than languish in forced familial intimacy. They snapped at each other, at the children, at the house help whose only mistake was to announce dinner.

As Martin's Subaru sped through Mombasa Road, Nancy took in this shutting-down of hope. On other Sunday afternoons, she had allowed herself to fantasize about the mythical Nairobi, whose inhabitants were the polite, laid-back sort, given to cooking indoors or laundering underwear outdoors. That she could one day be a member of the well-heeled rarefied few, who escaped the city center for the safari parks or private clubs with swimming pools, where their children ate cheeseburgers and chicken wings. But this was it. The city in the sun had no sunshine, in fact.

They drove past the airport, what once was a playground of theirs, now turned gray. Chomazone, their preferred hangout joint, was dimly lit, tables occupied by the few incurable optimists. The roar of the Subaru's engine filled the vacuum left by a lack of conversation. What was there to say? Nancy marveled at the happenstance that the day she made up her mind that she wanted to be *wifed* by Martin was the day their relationship took a turn for the worse.

In the back seat, parts of Martin's old stovetop, which Joseph hadn't disposed of, rattled as the car caught the end of a pothole, then one of those pesky tiny speed bumps meant to curb the rush of deadly matatus and people late to catch their flights.

"Why don't you take this, hmm? It'll serve you well while you wait to replace your broken stove," Martin had said before they left his house, wrapping the stove with newspaper, his low voice hinting that he'd already figured she wouldn't be back.

Makanaka Mavengere

Mbuya Baines

STORY

They started calling her "Mbuya Baines" for the simple fact that she erected her shelter, a surprisingly well thought out design, on the corner of Fife and Baines Avenues. Her home, made of cardboard boxes deconstructed to resemble the houses that surrounded it, was carefully encased with plastic bags emblazoned with TM Pick n Pay, OK, and Spar logos, a waterproof shield from the rain. The meticulousness of the structure had the attendants who manned the local shops and cafés, the area hair salon workers, and their regular customers all guessing at her origin story. Those who dared to ask never got an answer.

Mbuya Baines spoke not when spoken to, but when she felt the need.

"Work hard," she often told the friendly waiter from the café who gave her leftover sandwiches. "Be content with what you have," she would continue as she scratched her wig, a fractious mess of tangles vaguely resembling a bird's nest, which she wore back to front. Her delivery was so articulate you almost wanted to strip her of her faltering looks to find the woman she might have been before she became who she was.

She was always looking over her shoulder, sniffing audibly, as if whatever was hovering around her had a smell that overpowered the stench of the rot, filth, and waste from the nearby trash cans and open gutters streaming with sewerage. One cold June morning, she went into an olfactory panic, her nostrils flaring alarm after a black SUV drove past her shelter.

"Stop! Please, stop that car!" she screamed as she ran frantically after the vehicle, almost hurtling herself into a taxi that slammed to a halt.

"Get out of the road you crazy woman!" the taxi driver shouted.

"I want to help her," Mbuya Baines said, her head sharply jerking over one shoulder, then the other as she sniffed violently. "Do you smell that?"

. . .

Memory is a funny thing, isn't it, Daisy? As much as you want to believe you are who you choose to remember, the things you wish would stay in the past refuse to remain there. As you drive to your favorite spot along Baines Avenue, you pray that what you are about to do will not take you back to being who you wish you could forget.

You are Daisy Beta, wife to a well-known businessman. Your face is a picture of perfection, and that pitch-black curly weave you have on accentuates your oval face well. Yet, as you drive your brand-new car, the one he got you for your birthday, there is something you are hiding in your small, round nose. Even still, you smile to yourself, relieved that you no longer have to live the life your mind won't stop replaying. "Lord, please help me," you say out loud as you turn onto Fife Avenue toward the shopping center on Baines.

Your smile disappears as you step out of the car, your red-bottom heels the first thing people see. It's the smell, isn't it? The funk of abject poverty. The stink of the boiled egg seller's hopeful hopelessness. The pong of the cost, effort, and time spent in the heat that won't amount to the pittance he will make at the end of the day. The egg seller begs for your support. The quiet desperation in his eyes takes you back to Mbare, where you grew up.

You lived with your family in the famously overcrowded Matapi flats. The filth and dilapidation made you promise yourself that you would do whatever you had to do to get out. The broken water taps, lack of electricity, and communal bathrooms are things you can hardly believe you lived through now that your current home could easily house all the occupants of two blocks of Matapi.

You remember how it felt living in that tiny room with your father, mother, and two siblings Tendai and Kuda, as well as your mum's sisters Aunt Shorai and Aunt Shatai. It was a room smaller than your current shoe closet where every movement, or sniff, could be heard. You cringe as you think of the many nights you, your siblings, and your aunts had to endure the noises your parents made. "*Chemerera, Mai Daisy, chemerera kani*," your father would say to your mother, asking her to moan and groan as a sign that she, too, was enjoying their perfunctory union. Years later, as you lay underneath different men, your parents' sounds replayed in your head. The sight of your father on top of Aunt Shorai when you walked in early from school one day, his eyes closed, so into his adulterous act that he did not even notice you standing there, shocked, also haunted you.

You despised your father for his selfishness and how his insatiable desires had made it impossible for you and your siblings to have normal conversations. "What was Baba doing on top of Aunty Shorai?" your six-year-old sister, Tendai, asked as you were queuing for water at the borehole. You hated how ridiculous you sounded telling her they were just playing a game. You snapped at Tendai when she probed further, inquiring why he did not play that game with you or her. You winced when your young brother, Kuda, chuckled as you told her to stop asking silly questions.

For a long time you did not understand why your mother turned a blind eye to the whole charade. You felt so let down by how easily she had given up, leaving you in the hands of fate and your promiscuous father and Aunt Shorai, who kicked out Aunt Shatai after the funeral. Thinking about it now, remembering how the cancer ravaged your mother's body so there was hardly anything left of her, you realize she had no more strength to fight. As you take a sip of your latte in your favorite café, you wonder why she insisted on not taking the prescribed medication. Why had she instead opted for the holy water Madzibaba Jezman had given her?

You did not blame Aunt Shorai for spewing frustrated insults at you after your father left for Johannesburg. She had been left pregnant with twins and had you and your siblings to take care of with the 1,500 rands your dad sent every month, rent included. This was nowhere near the life you heard him promising her in bed. *"Ndichakutengera mota,"* he would tell her and go on to describe the car in detail, the color and make changing every time he made that vow.

The croissant melts in your mouth as you check your phone. There are no messages from your younger brother or sister, who sometimes text you asking for money, so you sip your latte again as your mind takes you back.

At fourteen, you decided that you were going to become an architect so you could design and live in the house of your dreams. You used to close your eyes and imagine yourself living in the beautiful suburban houses in the magazines. You are living this dream now, Daisy, but the memories of how you got here refuse to stay in the past where they belong.

Your father never returned and he stopped sending money. Your aunt took off with the twins and went to live with the man she had been rumored to be having an affair with. It was then that the landlord, Jaravaza, started threatening to kick you and your siblings out.

You tried selling scones and boiled eggs during and after school to raise the rent money, but the food you got from the welfare feeding scheme at school was not enough. You and your siblings always ended up having the remaining stock for supper.

"How can you allow yourself to starve and get to the brink of home-lessness when you have the well of all wisdom between your legs," Jaravaza said one day as you stood by his car begging him to give you more time to look for the three months' rent that was due.

You completely disregarded his comment and ran off, telling him you were going to call your father in South Africa. You sat emotionless on the floor as you tried to comfort your siblings when you heard of your father's passing two weeks later. It was on that same day you gave in to Jaravaza.

Two years later you graduated from sleeping with Jaravaza to a cote-rie of regulars who enabled you to ensure your siblings never lacked to a point of them becoming like you. You told yourself that if sex could get you where you needed to go, you were going to use it, at least until you got there.

You completed your diploma in technical drawing and design at nine-teen, but the in-the-gutter economy refused to allow you to turn your back on the life of poverty and lack you knew. All you could find was a job at Greta's Hair Salon sweeping hair. The skills you obtained from months of careful observation, helping finish off customers' long braid styles and occasionally being asked to do washes, amounted to nothing for your advancement as long as you did not have one hundred US dollars to rent your own chair. For this reason you continued to engage in your night work.

You worked in Greta's salon for nine months and knew most of the regular customers by name. You laughed at their stories of abuse, situations, and entanglements. You inquired about their lives and well-being as you removed nail polish or endured the cheese-like smell emanating from in between their well-manicured toes, but none of them knew anything about you, nor did they show interest. You scrambled for their leftover chips and drinks as well as their hairpieces, which you used for your own braids, to "keep up appearances" or risk losing your job. You hated that they did not really see you, and wondered what it was about your face that made people forget you even while they were looking straight at you.

Aunty Theresa had surprised you. She entered the salon in all black, holding a snakeskin bag with red handles. Her fresh rose scent captured the customers, hairdressers, and Greta herself. She stood by the door for a few beats, taking in the vibe of the salon before taking off her black sunglasses. You remember her dark brown eyes darting across the room as she walked straight to where you were crouching behind the sink refilling the Dark and Lovely shampoo bottles with a no-name shampoo.

"I need my hair deep-conditioned," she said.

"You can take a seat, I will be with you shortly," Greta said from across the room, avoiding the questioning look on the customer whose hair she had just started braiding.

"You are busy and she is not," Theresa said as a matter of fact. "Unless you are telling me she is incapable?"

"Ermm," Greta stammered.

"Well?" Theresa said.

"Yes, she can do it," Greta said putting on her best fake smile.

Your heart skipped with the excitement of having a real client for the first time. You straightened yourself up, ready to take on the opportunity, hoping this would be the beginning of a new phase for you. As she sat down and rested her snakeskin bag on her lap, you picked up a strange smell underneath the heavy rose that had initially preceded her into the salon, but you focused on the task at hand, just as you did when you were washing calloused feet, determined to do a good-enough job to keep this woman as a client.

Despite being old enough to be your mother, Theresa insisted you call her by her first name. Her interest in your life was invasive but refreshing, and you politely engaged her without giving out too much information.

"No, I do not have children. My parents are both late. I have to take care of my siblings. No, I am very single," you responded to her many questions.

"You are a beautiful girl," Theresa said, putting her bag under the chair as you lathered shampoo onto her scalp and hair. "I wouldn't mind you being my daughter-in-law."

You chuckled uncomfortably, but just as you were wrapping a towel around her head a violent thud sounded from outside, yanking your attention.

Every head in the salon turned to the windows as the pedestrians who, just moments before were casually strolling, were now panic-running as distant chants came closer and grew louder. Just like that, a crowd filled the streets, roaring and stomping their feet to an accompaniment of hooting car horns.

Inside the salon, screeching customers and hairdressers grabbed their bags and fled. You had not been able to grab your small bag, which was in a drawer, because a barrage of people trooped in. You ran for your life as the invaders grabbed towels, bottles of shampoo, hairpieces, a group of them shoving and fighting each other for whatever was in the cash register.

When the streets eventually emptied, you and a few other terrified souls emerged from behind the rubbish bins lined up in an alley. You walked back to the salon hoping to find your bag. It had five US dollars in it—your payment for the all-nighter you endured.

The cash register had been violently opened, there was broken glass everywhere. Smashed containers leaked shampoo and oozed hair gel. Cracked nail polish bottles trickled streaks of hot pink, lime green, and white down the plastic shelves that now dangled from the wall. You were shocked to find that, on the floor next to the sink, there it was, Theresa's snakeskin handbag, untouched, even though the invaders had found and taken yours.

You took the bag, sure a woman like Theresa carried more than five US, but you were disappointed to find just a few thousand ZWDs inside. You guessed Theresa had been smart enough to pocket her bigger bills before she fled. At home, you shoved the bag under your bed before your first customer for the night walked in. As he grunted and sweated on top of you, you wondered again how such an expensive-looking bag could have been left behind by the desperate eyes who had looted even old, used, dirty towels. You stood silently under the shower as droplets of cold water trickled down your body one at a time after your second customer paid and left. You regarded the bag again before going through the vacancies section of the newspaper, an exercise you did every night before resigning to bed.

A movement woke you up in the dead of night—the silent type you heard with your eyes even in pitch darkness. You squinted, trying to make out what it could have been, as a strange, cold, foul smell arrested you. You felt a presence in the room, slowly crawling closer as your body shook in terror.

The next morning, you wrote off the incident as a bad dream. Your drenched sheets and the lingering stink, however, pointed to a truth you refused to acknowledge until you pulled the bag from underneath the bed. You almost fell over, shocked by the handbag's weight and the bundles of US dollars stuffed inside—and the smell.

Without a word, when you reported for work at the ransacked salon, you handed the bag to Theresa, who was waiting outside. In her eyes you saw an inexplicable darkness, and she wore a knowing and loud smile, daring you to ask about the bag. You wanted no part of the evil she carried, so you walked off as soon as she took her bag and you watched from inside the shop minutes later as she drove away in her red Range Rover.

You look down at your car keys now. Your black Range Rover is parked outside and you chuckle to yourself, shaking your head slightly, as you watch three young men taking selfies next to your car.

"Anything else I can help you with," the waiter says as he smiles politely. You acknowledge him with a grin and shake your head. He walks off.

You rummage inside your red handbag and come up with some lip gloss, which you apply. You smile at a small picture of your husband, Craig. He is the man you dreamed would share your suburban magazine house. Sometimes you lie awake staring at him, afraid you will wake up to find he really is a dream.

"I want to introduce you to my son," Theresa said when she accosted you outside Greta's on your way home. You'll never forget that day—a Tuesday, a day to the month after your first encounter with her—or your rush to escape her presence. You doubled your pace, not interested in making any bargains with the evil this woman represented, desperate to escape the odor that fought with her perfume.

"What do you want with me?" you asked as she matched your hurried strides.

"There is something about you that reminds me of myself," she said. "You don't have to work here getting paid next to nothing. How do you even survive on that? My son is single and he will be able to take care of you and the siblings you mentioned."

You slow your steps, but the smell keeps you moving.

"Call me when you change your mind," she had said, handing you a piece of paper.

"*Wakapusa stereki.*" Wadzanai, one of the new hairdressers who occasionally spoke to you, chastised you for not taking some of the money when you told her about Theresa.

"I couldn't!" you replied. "It was so strange how the dollar bills appeared. Bundles! I have heard of these stories before, but it's another thing when you see it with your own eyes."

"People do a lot of things for money. I am sure she conjured up some spirit or has made great sacrifices for that bag. If I had been you, I would have taken a few hundreds and dealt with consequences later," she said nonchalantly.

Theresa started crossing your mind more and more. You asked yourself what could be worse than having your body ravaged by different men every night, trying to dissociate your mind from your body.

The morning you woke up on the floor, barely remembering how you got there until the piercing pain all over your body reminded you your client had beaten and raped you when you confronted him for trying to pay with a fake twenty-dollar note, you searched for the little piece of paper Theresa had given you. He left without paying.

It was on that day you decided to not ask any questions and heed Theresa's proposal. You did not care what it entailed, you felt your sacrifices over the years to provide for your siblings had not been enough. Your younger sister had been rumored to be sleeping with the landlord, and your brother was now always both drunk and high, empty bottles of codeine cough syrup his intoxicant of choice. He was violent at times. Sometimes he was wide-awake, unresponsive at other times, and the few pieces of furniture—the only things in the flat that could be sold for more than a few dollars—had started disappearing. This was your final attempt to help them.

Craig was not like all the other guys you had been with. He was gentle, kind, nonjudgmental, and there was something about his warm smile that made you feel safe. Theresa had set up the meeting in the same café you were sitting in now by the corner table, which has become your favorite spot. You had expected there to be many awkward silences seeing the very different lifestyles and backgrounds, but you had hit it off quite well and he seemed genuinely interested in you as you were in him.

Four months after Theresa introduced you to Craig, he proposed, and you accepted without hesitation. The two of you were joined in matrimony in Theresa's well-manicured garden in the posh Borrowdale Brooke estate.

You remember how happy you were to finally be free from want. You did not mind that you had to move into Theresa's house as the building of your own house was underway. Theresa allowed you to invite your siblings, Tendai and Kuda, to move into the house. None of them lasted long. They could not get used to the lingering stench in the house, which you had somehow coaxed your nose to accept. The same scent that had emanated from Theresa's handbag the night you had it tucked under your bed.

Your sister, Tendai, ran off to South Africa with her boyfriend barely a month after she moved in. She calls you once in a while, but only when she needs help. Your brother, Kuda, was never able to free himself from the clutches of his addiction. You had, after many attempts to help him, left him to his own devices. You call him every week and take parcels of food to him every month to ensure he never goes hungry. You feel you have done all you could for your siblings, it is now left to them to decide their own fates as you had chosen yours.

The smell, and the feeling that someone or something was watching you, alerted you to the fact that there was something not quite right about your house when you finally moved in. You discovered that the source of the smell was the corner room at the end of the passage on the third floor. The room you had been forbidden from entering.

"It's a good thing you brought that up," Theresa said to you when she paid you a visit in your new house and you were complaining about the smell. "My son and I have, over the years, had to do certain things and make sacrifices to be able to amass all the wealth you see here. Now that you are part of us, you too will have to play your part."

You shifted nervously when Theresa said this. You had known that the time was going to come when she would demand something for the comfort she had afforded you, you just did not expect that it would be so soon.

"From now on, every Thursday I need you to cook two big pots of porridge and place them by the door of that room on the third floor. Do not go in. Place them by the door, knock three times, and walk away," Theresa said.

"What's in the room?" you asked.

"Ask no questions, hear no lies," she replied as she took a sip of the Tanganda Tea you had made for her with some Baker's Inn soft buns.

Something changed about Craig when you moved into your house. He no longer desired you like before, lovemaking becoming a strange ritual you performed in the dead of night at random intervals and days. You remember your first encounter; you had been woken up by the smell overpowering your senses, causing your eyes to water. There was an icy soft slithering sound that seemed to get more intense as the stench became stronger. You had tried to move but couldn't, and all you remember is seeing a dark silhouette towering over you. You felt a strange cold sensation crawling up your body from your feet up; as though someone were rubbing a very wet towel on your skin.

You woke up the next morning with no recollection of what had happened after the strange coldness, but the wetness in between your legs and a strange emptiness told you something had indeed happened. Craig avoided your gaze that day as he would in the days that followed.

Thinking back, the anxiety and fear you felt especially when you were home alone did not stop you from wanting to know the origin of the smell that seemed to permeate everything you had now.

Your need to know grew stronger with each pot of porridge you prepared every Thursday. You watched as Craig and Theresa entered the room, emerging hours later looking drained, each holding bags of cash you could spend at will.

"There are some things you cannot unsee," Theresa said when you started insisting.

"What do you mean?"

"Don't look for things that you don't want to find," was all she added.

"I give you everything that you want," Craig said. "Why can't you just let this one go?"

"Where is the money coming from?" you would say.

"Please, Daisy, just trust me," Craig would say.

You turn around when, as the door of the restaurant closes, the gentle breeze that whiffs in carries with it a waft of that smell. You feel a coldness within and your heart starts beating a little faster, maybe it's a warning not to enter the forbidden room. You ignore all these thoughts. You have made up your mind and today is the day you will know the truth. You breathe in deeply to calm your beating heart as you lift your hand to summon the waiter. You hand him a crisp twenty-dollar bill. "You can keep the change," you say to him as you pick up your bag, phone, and car keys, and walk out.

Your body shakes as you approach the room, almost causing you to spill the pot of porridge you were carrying. You knock three times. You wait, your whole being fighting within, but you ignore it. You open the door.

· · ·

Her heart still beating at the Range Rover sighting, Mbuya Baines walked back to her cardboard mansion. The fear in her wide eyes as palpable as the day she had seen it: the inexplicable thing, hanging from the ceiling, crawling ever so slowly toward Craig and Theresa. Her nostrils flared at the memory, the stench so loud she could hear it.

"Do you smell that?"

Chuma Nwokolo

The Swagger Stick Man
of June Fifteen

STORY

June fifteen was the day an interstate taxi brought the bearded man to Waterside's Wednesday Market. He was an elderly sort, although he wore black, ripped jeans that suggested he did not consider himself elderly, as such. A fading prison tattoo peered from under a black collar, and he carried an ominous crocodile swagger stick, the sort reputed to have made Major General Aguiyi-Ironsi bulletproof, at least until he died in a hail of bullets. He hauled a large box down from the trunk and paused awhile where the taxi had dropped him, staring intently at the townsfolk, who were staring intently at him. Finally, turning toward the seafood section of the market at the waterline, he raised his voice and cried, "*UwaBabe'm! UwaBabe'm!*" The marketplace fell silent. It was the most interesting thing anyone had seen in many a month. Someone asked him if all was well, to which he replied that he was looking for Cynthia Uwalaka, who sold periwinkles at the waterline. "Oho, Cynti?" said Maria Utoms, who did not know how to mind her own business, "Cynti has die na! More than five years ago, even." This information seemed to sear the stranger like the flame of a blowtorch and his black swagger stick recoiled and struck Maria on the head (which is why Watersiders say that the sensible bearer of bad news delivers it from a distance). If you don't believe me, go to Bene's Hospice near the cemetery, where Maria Utoms has been lying ever since that blow, unable to move her head, or to discuss anything other than the Swagger Stick Man of June Fifteen.

Before Maria hit the ground, he had turned away, that Swagger Stick Man. His face was now as savage as a Calabar masquerade's and the crowd parted before him as he crossed the road to the bank of commercial motorbikes. There he mounted a smoking okada and scooted off, leaving his luggage behind. People have abused Waterside traders for their lack of balls, in not apprehending a stranger who had assaulted their fellow trader so unwarrantedly. Yet the thieves of Waterside were even more pathetic, and here's the evidence: that expensive box stood there two days and two nights, despite the Ethiopian stickers that suggested untold treasures from abroad. Yet the rumors of the diabolism of the owners of crocodile swagger sticks had been proved in the sight of all Waterside, and children were fleeing the Wednesday Market before Maria hit the ground.

Cynthia Uwalaka's headstrong daughter, Emi, returned from her trip to Sapele a little after noon on the third day after the incident. Her best friend, Leticia, brought her directly to the market square from the Sapele taxi park, and the lanky Emi, with a protective palm on her four-month-old baby bump, circled the box suspiciously. By the time she finished her third circuit of the box, a decent crowd had gathered and watched her from a distance. "And this is the box?" asked Cynthia Uwalaka's headstrong daughter, Emi.

"That's the very box he brought," swore the hauler from the tray of his wheelbarrow, where he spent his downtime waiting for customers.

It was Saturday afternoon, not quite as busy as Waterside's famous Wednesday Market, but all Emi's friends were there. The butcher described the prodigious height of the Swagger Stick Man, which seemed to lose an inch or so after he was charred by the news of Cynthia's death. And the orange seller described his contorted face, as though he had not just heard of her death but had seen the ghost of Cynthia Uwalaka as well. And the shoemaker described the timbre of his foreign-accented voice and demonstrated how he staggered across the road to the okada, as though he had received a fatal wound. Emi wiped her brow, and her tears, and swallowed. Her friend, Leticia, had been emphatic about this, but she had to be sure: "And this tall man, was he . . . dark skinned, or light complexioned?" The suya man laughed. "That man na charcoal, o, he black pass you, sef!" The seamstress agreed, "*Black* in complexion and *black* in dress!" She pointed at the abandoned luggage, which—to be fair—was the color of pitch. "Can't you see? That's the very box he brought!"

The twenty-three-year-old Emi then did what no Watersider had had the courage to do: she took the box and rolled it all the way down Agina Street. To be fair, that box was more than just a box to Emi Uwalaka, who had stood out, all her life, for her coal-black complexion. She had never known the identity of her father, and when her mother died five years earlier in a road accident on a journey to Yenagoa, all hopes of someday winkling that information out of her had died as well. When Emi pumped her mother's relatives and old friends for information, all she ever got were hints of a mysterious, malevolent lover who had left Cynthia in the lurch and gone abroad, never to be heard from again. So, when she heard of the swagger stick stranger so publicly devastated by news of Cynthia's death, the prospect that he was an ex-convict versed in the diabolical arts did not dampen the excitement that she might finally be on the trail of her father. Confirmation should come from the box.

Yet it was only sensible to take precautions, so she dragged it across the zebra crossing near the bank, all the way down to the Catholic church. She was followed, from a safe distance, by Leticia and a queue of curious Watersiders shouting warnings to the twenty-three-year-old Emi.

The parish priest was away all week on a retreat, unfortunately. The catechist—who had just wrapped up a catechism class—was startled by the request to stand in for the priest and exorcise a box. "That's a job for a witch doctor," he said, laughing. "God forbid," replied Emi, "I was born and bred in the Catholic church." But the catechist had heard how Maria Utoms had been laid low by a crocodilian blow from the box's owner and he dug in his heels. "There's a papal bull that forbids the exorcism of boxes," he lied. "Which particular papal bull is that?" asked Emi. "I can't lay my mind on the particular bull now, now," hedged the cate-chist. This wrangling continued for a while until the disappointed crowd dissipated, returning to their businesses in the market. Emi then left the box at the gatehouse of the church and retired with the catechist and her friend Leticia to Bintu's Buka, for an indulgent lunch, which gave her time to elevate her swollen feet. After that amenable bribe, the catechist dallied over his beers while Emi held forth on the agonies of a childhood without a father figure, and the cruelties of a patrilineal playground where she answered to her mother's surname and not a father's. Then her baby kicked, and she held her womb and smiled, remembering her boyfriend's pledge to stay in her daughter's life in all the ways her father had not stayed in hers. By the end of his third beer, the catechist rose and led them, unsteadily, back to church. There, newly fortified in his spiritual faith by an alcoholic spirit, he filled a retired soap dispenser with holy water from the marble font. By the time he returned, impressive in borrowed vestments, the ladies had dragged the box into the grotto of the Marian shrine. He walked down a grove of pitanga bushes gleaming red with ripened fruit and took his position in front of the statue of Mary, under her outstretched arms of plaster. He spooned incense on the burning coals of a censer as they pulled out their rosaries. Under Mother Mary's puzzled gaze, an Exorcism of Luggage began in the Catholic church, even though the parish priest was away all week on a retreat.

The congregation of two crossed themselves fluidly as the catechist's prayers petered out. He put away the censer and spray bottle. The box was wet with holy water and the grotto misty with holy incense. Emi's baby kicked in her womb again as she unzipped the box, liberating the smell of camphor. Trembling, she took out and shook out an overwhelming succession of clothes. Gowns and old-fashioned frocks of a style that might once have been fashionable in the 1970s, in a convent, lay in mute embarrassment on the manicured hedge. They were all size eight, which was poignant, in a tragicomic way, for Cynthia Uwalaka had ballooned to a size eighteen by the time she died. It was as though the Swagger Stick Man's trip to see his lover had been interrupted by a long sentence in a prison—or asylum. As though, once free, he had waited only to grab the box he had packed decades earlier before flying home to an interrupted rendezvous with his belle. Then Emi found an ominous slew of black necklaces and, instinctively, the congregation of two crossed themselves fluidly.

Emi sat down abruptly and blinked back her tears. With no clue in the box, it was another dead end in her lifelong search for a father. "This was a bullet that you dodged," whispered Leticia, who was both fishwife and philosopher. She pulled her friend up and hugged her tight. "Don't be sad. This was a *wizard* that you lost, not a father!" But Emi had decided that June fifteen was her new birthday, for a child could not be born without two parents, and June fifteen was the day a man who shared her coal-black complexion materialized in an elemental, devastating demonstration of love for her mother, in the sight of a town that had forever questioned his existence. Emi had grown up stained with the conviction that her father was a "hit-and-run artist" whose lust for her mum had expired in the moment of her conception. June fifteen was her intimation of a father who still called her mum "My Babe Uwa," whose thunderous love still resounded down the decades since her birth. The catechist took his glasses off and wiped them clear of holy water. Then he replaced them and took a closer look at the Ethiopian baggage tag on the box, which had been scrunched up and taped upside down. "Al-phon-sus Nkuzi . . ." he read, haltingly. Emi's eyes grew round. "Emi Nkuzi . . ." she said slowly, testing the three new syllables in her name. Tears welled spontaneously in her eyes. Leticia darted to the box to confirm the new surname of her best friend, as Emi sat down abruptly.

The name of her father provoked a healing at Bene's Hospice later that evening, for when Maria Utoms heard about Emi's name change she left her bed abruptly. Taking an urgent trike from Cemetery Junction, she taxied all the way up to the compound where Leticia and her best friend smoked fish for a living. The two friends were dressed in their blackened aprons as they stacked their smoker with gutted and seasoned catfish. "See as you're drawing Devil with your own hand!" panted Maria, glaring over her shoulder at Emi. "Your head correct so?" Emi looked askance at her visitor. The question seemed more relevant to Maria herself, whose face was now permanently set at three o'clock. Maria continued, "You're answering the name of Devil that slaps people with crocodile? Is that the name of the person you want to give your baby? Is that?" Emi paused. For a moment, the diabolism of a man in black who brought gifts for a dead lover preyed on her mind. Then, slowly, as she tugged at the frills of the new frock under her old apron, her womb was warmed by the recklessness of the love that sired her. The serendipity of his romanticism swamped all, for the visit of the man in black was no mere outreach to his dead lover. It was an overture to his living daughter. "Nkuzi is *my* name"—she smiled—"my baby will take the name of *her* father."

Enuma Okoro

The Heart of the Father

STORY

"Who has the heart of your husband?" Pastor asks Mama. "It's important to know before we reach the burial site and start our prayers."

I look up from my coloring book, the family I have been shading with my brown color pencils since takeoff. All of them are the same color. Me too, I want to know who took my daddy's heart.

Pastor keeps talking. "This thing that happened, Mummy, no be small matter."

I think Pastor has started to fear me small since I saw Papa. Saturday before last, I told Mama that I saw him. And Mama told Pastor. And Pastor came to the house. Since then he cannot look me in my eye. This trip, it is his own idea. He asked the church to raise money for us to go to my daddy's village to "settle this matter." Me, I listen to Pastor now, and cover my mouth with one hand before a giggle slips out. I still think it is funny that Pastor calls Mama "Mummy," as if he is a simple driver or house help. A whole man like Pastor, who speaks to God and holds our heads under water until our spirits are born again.

"Brother Obinna's spirit wants something," Pastor says. "He will come to her again."

I thought Papa came because of me, that God was going to answer my prayer and Papa came to tell me what would be done. Like I was Mary, found with favor, and Papa was my angel Gabriel. A messenger I would not fear. Full of good news. But Papa did not speak that time. So, me, I have been waiting for his second coming. But now I hear Pastor saying that Papa wants something, it makes more sense. I cannot imagine anybody coming from heaven for me.

I steal a glance now at Pastor from the corner of my eye. I catch the glimmer of his freshly ironed shine-shine suit. The whole one-hour flight from Abuja, he has been sitting straight up in his aisle seat, so his suit does not wrinkle. Pastor dresses like he himself has come from heaven, his clothes like Moses's face in that story when he comes down from the mountain. I know I would have to look different if God called me to something, because there is no one like me in the Bible. People like me, we are not Chosen Ones. Me, I know nobody will remember my name. But today, I will try not to let those things fill my head. Today, me, I am so happy to miss school and to not see Aisha them, and to be on an aeroplane. And it is still only morning. I have not felt like this before, as if the whole day can just open up from here and treat me like, me too, I belong inside it.

Before Mama can answer Pastor, the plane rolls down the runway, shaking like one of those old taxis Mama waves away from us on the road sometimes, like all the parts are held together by cellophane. I grab Mama's arm tight until the plane jolts to a stop. We have landed in Enugu. People begin to clap their hands as if the pilot has performed a miracle. As far as I am concerned, he has. I know there is science, but me, ehn, I think it is either a miracle or juju to keep this machine in the air. Pastor makes the sign of the cross. I mouth the words with him out of habit. "Father, Son, Holy Ghost." Sometimes when I am praying by myself, asking God for the things that have not yet come, I change the word. I say "Father, Daughter, Holy Ghost." Because in the beginning was the Word and the Word was with God, and I want a Word with me that makes God see me. If he will not fix me, I want him to look at me and tell me why he made me like this. As if he himself, a whole God, ran out of color.

I use my middle finger to push my pink glasses back up my nose and peer out the oval window at the layers of tinted color, rust, brown, wheat, and shades of green. They build up from the gray tarmac steadily up to the empty blue sky, bleeding into one another like dye running backward from one of Mama's adire dresses. Everything blurs like a watercolor picture.

I need Mama to clean my glasses. I told her once that somebody should invent eyeglasses with a tiny nozzle on one side that sprays water, and little windshield wipers on the lenses, like on our car. The one we had before we had to sell it. When it was only me and Mama inside it, and nobody would shift their body away from me, or open the door and leave, like on the bus or in drop. Anyhow, I remember how Mama laughed a lot that time I told her about the glasses. The sound caught me by surprise, entering my body and filling me up like a balloon about to lift up into the air so that I had to look down and check that my own feet were still on the ground. I feel weightless like a spirit, those times when Mama's eyes crinkle in the corners, and her mouth stretches open like one of those sacred chambers of the Lord that Pastor is always talking about, and all these jewels of laughter fall out clinking and tinkling and shining together and somehow falling into me. So that for one minute I imagine I have changed and maybe, me too, I can be called to something. Nothing as important as "Pastor." But still something good anyhow.

"Ozioma! You this child," Mama says turning to me as if she knows I am thinking of her just now. "Put that coloring book away." I like to hear my mother say my name. It sounds like the end of a long prayer, all the syllables curved like grateful sticky fingers clutching the answered prayer even before it has arrived. Even when Mama is scolding me, my name comes out of her mouth like praise.

I know how to listen for how my name falls from people's lips. There are many ways to hear it, to close my eyes and dip down to soak in the calling of it, until the sound rises like water above my head. Sometimes it feels like when Pastor baptized me in the house last year, like when I pulled my head back up and out from the bathtub, coughing and spitting out water, thinking everything was about to change. "Father, Daughter, Holy Ghost." Like how I waited, soaked in new life, with hope dripping off me in small crystal-clear droplets. How I waited for a word from the Lord. Sometimes, I hear my name, and it feels like I have fallen into the deep end of a swimming pool. Like with Aisha them. My name rises over my head and I cannot breathe. Drowning.

Mama puts her hand in my lap to take the book but I drop my color pencil to clasp her hand in both of my own first. A chocolate-filled vanilla biscuit. The only time I can see my own skin and smile.

"Oya, now, pack your things. The queue is forming. We still have a long drive ahead of us." Mama sounds annoyed small. But I lean my head on her shoulder instead. She smells like a morning bath, the flowery scent of her pink Lux soap still clinging to her skin. I shift my face slightly and stick my nose on her dark brown neck. I sniff and inhale. "Are you okay? Did you not hear me?" She shakes her arm free, and gathers my coloring book and pencils, before I can even finish coloring the small daughter in the picture brown.

"In fact, Mummy," Pastor says, "I should have asked you who has your husband's heart before we left Abuja. It will help if that person is gathered with us. I was assuming it is Mama Obinna. Every mother has her son's heart, is it not so?"

I shift in my seat, trying to ignore how my heart pounds at my grandmother's name. My grandmother who thinks I am juju. I do not think there is a good kind of juju. So Mama Obinna means I'm the one that is not good, even if she has not seen me in my whole life. Aisha them says only a witch can kill her own father on the same day she is born.

I try to remember how Mama tells me that I am like a white star shining in the sky. So bright that it made my skin explode with light and drained all the other color from me. That is why I am like this. That is why too much sun makes my skin break out into all these dots that pain me like matches are being lit inside my body. I imagine their glowing tips striking against the under of my arms, starting a sacrifice. As if I am an offering to no god in particular because, me, I do not know a god yet that needs me. But Mama says God is already inside me. Sometimes when she comes into my room to turn off the light after I have crawled into my bed, she sits by me on the bed first. She presses her fingers into my arms softly and then watches the light pink imprint it leaves for a few seconds afterward.

"And because you have so much light inside you, you do not need any more. You do not even need the sun. Can you imagine how lucky you are? Of all of us, you are the luckiest, *inugo*?"

Then she stares at my face until she thinks I believe it. Me, I want to believe that I, too, am a house for God. Like Pastor is always telling us, "You are a temple of the Holy Ghost." I want to make Aisha them believe that God lounges in me like rest at the end of all holy days. Like these arms and legs and head and heart and skin are God's way of saying, "It is finished." Anyhow, I am hoping Pastor is right, that Papa will come to me again, for this his heart that Pastor is talking about, or whatever the reason. And today I will see the place that Papa comes from.

Mama brings Pastor to our house once a month to pray over us, over me most of the time. When Pastor prays, he casts out our enemies by

Holy Ghost fire. He claps loudly and shakes his fists in the air. I imagine that there are small demons with wings flying around us. They have huge gaping eyes that bulge out of their tiny heads, and their mouths stay wide open with pointed fangs just like bats, except I think the demons are bright red instead of black. Pastor is always asking Father God to put a hedge of protection around me and Mama. I wonder why nobody put a hedge around Papa. Or if they did and somebody tore it down. I wonder if they can tear down our own too.

He clears his throat like garri is stuck to the back, like he did that time he came to the house for Thanksgiving prayer (because we should thank God for what we know God will yet do) and I asked him again to please ask God what is taking so long for him to answer my prayer. He answered as if I do not know how to pray.

"My dear, how long have you been praying? We do not serve an overnight God." He opened his mouth to laugh as if it was only yesterday that I laid my burdens down before the Lord. Anyhow, I stuck up my hands to his face and counted on my fingers for him. "I have been praying from my sixth birthday when I started school and, so, Pastor Chike, that is four years already."

Pastor closed his mouth into a frown, and shifted his eyes into his head so he could look for something there.

"A day is like a thousand years to the Lord, and a thousand years is like one day. Second Peter chapter three, verse eight." Pastor smiled. He was happy with what he had found. "It is good to know the Word of the Lord. Remember it and trust in the Lord's timing."

I remember how Pastor patted my head and walked away, leaving me with my pink palms still open in the air. I did not tell him what I have been praying for, how I want to wake up one day and look like Mama and him and Aisha them, with my body like Milo. When I was small Mama said I poured the chocolate drink on my hand because I wanted to see if the color would stay. "We thank God that the drink had cooled." And Pastor said, "Our Father is a miracle-working God." I tell myself maybe my prayer is not impossible. It took three days to raise the temple and the temple was the body of God (made flesh) and Pastor says we are one body in the Lord, and me, I think that means that part of me is God's body (whether God likes it or not) and if God can raise a dead God (made flesh) then God can change a living me and my own flesh. So see ehn, me, I cannot stop praying.

Finally, Mama says something. She makes it clear to Pastor that it is not my grandmother who has Papa's heart.

"*Mcheew.* That wicked woman. Obinna loved her but, please, she is not the one. God forbid. Is she not the reason we are even making special prayers? How are we even sure her hand is not inside this thing? She cannot be amongst us o!" Mama's voice has increased. She sucks her teeth and snaps her fingers in the air.

"*Ndo*, Mummy. It's okay. It's okay." Pastor pats Mama's arm gently, forgetting his suit and looking at the line behind him as we walk off the plane. If anybody stares it is only at me.

"Pastor, it's not okay, *inugo*? We have to settle this matter. God has to settle this matter for us, ehn? If Obinna wants to tell us something, let him come and communicate to me. I am not afraid. Let his soul rest, *biko*. But as for that woman, I do not want her near my child."

We do not talk about Mama Obinna in our house. Like we do not talk about Papa. Until he came back. Now, ever since I told Mama I saw him, I hear her trying to talk to him when she thinks I am asleep. But Papa does not answer or come to her. Papa did not come when Pastor was at the house and held me down and spoke in tongues and told Mama to bring olive oil which we did not have and so Mama brought Mamador instead and Pastor prayed over it and called it anointed and poured the vegetable oil all over my body and I kept my eyes closed tight and my hands frozen by my side and pretended I was a holy offering acceptable to the Lord.

Mama makes me put on my sun hat just to walk from the plane to the small building of the airport and then again to wait for the driver. I have four hats. Purple, blue, pink, and black. I brought the purple one. But now, I am wishing I had my pink one so it would match my dress and glasses. It is a two-and-a-half-hour drive from Enugu to Papa's village. We only have one small suitcase we carried on the plane because Mama said we were not staying around those people long, and that we were "definitely not sleeping in Mama Obinna's place." She told me not to drink or eat anything they offer me. "But what if I'm hungry?" I asked her. "You will not be hungry, *inugo*?" And anyhow, she looked at me so that I, too, knew that I would not be hungry.

Outside, a man looks straight at me and smiles. He walks toward us. I slip my hand in Mama's, use the other to push my glasses back up my nose, and then stare right back at him. As he comes closer, I watch his face to see his reaction. There is always a reaction. He stops in front of me.

"Welcome, Pastor, Mummy."

Pastor steps in front of Mama and smooths his hand over the front of his satin suit. It is shimmering in the early-afternoon sun and switches color from blue to gray every few seconds. He nods at the man. "Eh hen. Oliver. *Kedu?* On time. You have done well. We want to reach the village, conduct our business, and start coming back by nightfall. *Inugo?*"

It is the driver. "No problem, sah. *Anyi ga-eme oso oso.*" He takes the suitcase Mama packed for her and me and the suitcase Pastor brought. I wonder how he knows we are the ones he is to carry. He glances at me again. Then, of course, I know. "*Nna, kedu? Y na su Igbo?*" he asks me.

I understand, but I have to answer in English. "Fine, thank you. I only speak a little." He smiles again at me and pats me on the head. I am not used to this, to someone besides my family and Pastor not afraid to touch my skin. I hope Mama and Pastor do not talk about me seeing a spirit while we are with Mr. Oliver. He has parked the car somewhere and we follow him. I see a large billboard ahead of us toward the car park. A giant yellow woman is rubbing her arms like it is a dog, and smiling like somebody just gave her a whole packet of chocolate biscuits. Next to her arm is a jar of cream. As we get closer to the car the advertisement gets larger, until she is hanging above our heads and I can read what it says. I crank my neck up, and underneath the jar, I read the words CAROWHITE 100% LIGHTENING SKIN CREAM. YOUR DREAMS COME TRUE. I want to ask Mama a question, but just as I open my mouth, I hear her say my name. Her voice is thick. You can use it to scoop up soup.

I turn my face to answer her, but she is not calling me. She is talking to Pastor. She is walking much slower than him and Mr. Oliver, who has already reached the car, and I can see Pastor is trying to be respectful and wait for her. He has not learned that Mama does everything on her own time.

"Your question that you asked me before on the plane, about Obinna's heart. Ozioma has it. I told you she came after we had given up. After how many years of trying." Mama drops my hand and I feel her fingers rest lightly on my hat. "Obinna saw her that day in hospital." Mama's voice is like a wave of water, up and down before it breaks heavy on the shoreline of her next thought. "I didn't know how he would react. You know how our people can be. And she was a girl on top of it. But he said she was beautiful." Mama sighs heavy. Her hand falls from my head. "It is a strange thing to say. But sometimes I thank God the accident happened on his way from the hospital, instead of while he was going there. It was like he and his Chi agreed he must see his child before leaving this world."

There is a tiny breath that escapes me before I can catch it. Surprise slips between my lips and floats about like a feather, light and white and circling the air. I watch it fall softly and land on my pink dress by my stomach. I stare down at it, my mouth still slightly open. *I am the one with Papa's heart.*

We have reached the car and Pastor opens the passenger door for Mama, one hand grabbing the top of the doorframe, and the other on the handle.

"*O bu eziokwu,*" Pastor sighs in agreement. "It is true. God's mercies are beyond our understanding."

Mama says I can sit in front, as she adjusts the blouse of her wrapper and gathers her skirt, bending herself into the car.

"Have any of his people met her?" Pastor asks.

She looks up at Pastor like he is a seller at the market who has offered her a foolish price. "*Mba.*" She says it like a full stop. She slams the door and Pastor jumps, pulling his hand back just in time.

When we are all inside the car, I take off my hat and pull my seat belt across my chest. I face my front, with Mama and Pastor's voices in the back like a cinema I cannot see. I strain my ears to hear.

"After the accident, Mama Obinna did not want to see her," Mama says.

"I understand. Mummy, *ndo*, ehn. Our people sometimes, it takes time," Pastor says. "But, Mummy, they know we are coming today, to the compound?"

There is no answer.

"Mummy? Does anyone know we are coming?"

I hear Mama suck her teeth. Me, ehn, I know Pastor is about to get a blast.

"Can you imagine that foolish old woman said it was Ozioma's fault! A newborn baby still in the hospital causing a motor accident! Can you imagine? And she calls herself a Christian. I should take Ozioma to look her straight in that her eye, while the she-goat is still alive! She should see the granddaughter she has been denying, and support her from all that Ozioma's father left her. He was not a small man, Pastor. But all this village thinking and backward superstition. Is this not the reason we are suffering like this now? Ehn? They refuse to open their hand for Obinna's daughter. Do they think it is only me that made her like this?"

"Mummy, *biko*. Calm down," Pastor says.

Mr. Oliver turns to glance at me, as if to ask me about the she-goat, and why my Mama is talking like this about her elders. I shrug my shoulders at his silent question and turn to stare out the window. The roads are dusty and orange, and the tall trees green pass by in a blur. I watch them and try to capture my own thoughts. They come in from nowhere and buzz around me like mosquitoes. In my mind I see my own hand open and grasp after them. *Me, I have Papa's heart?*

We pass through small towns and villages and I look at everything, straining my eyes. Hawkers selling sticks of cooked snails or tiny plastic triangles of groundnuts pass by our windows and look in at me, hesitating before offering their food to us. I stare past them at the leaning houses falling off the sides of the roads into wide ditch gutters; the tin roofs are gray and brown and red, all meshing into a color I do not have a name for. There are stacks of yellow and blue and orange plastic jerry cans piled high, like the ones by the generator in our compound back home. The streets are swollen with old dingy cars, and rickety three-wheeled kekes. There is one blue bloated lorry tipping dangerously to the side. GOD'S OWN is painted in big pink letters across the back of it. Mr. Oliver slows down for the potholes and presses feverishly on his horn as he jerks the car suddenly to avoid the okadas that zip out of nowhere carrying passengers without helmets.

We come to a town where traffic lights seem to pop up randomly on the road. When the car stops, I see a rusty iron sign in front of a fading blue building the color of the sky. It says MIRACLE WORD CHRISTIAN SEMINARY. The windows are broken, and the hanging pieces of glass are caked with the orange dust that is everywhere here. It is an empty building.

The light changes and we enter go-slow, the cars piling up behind one another. I see children walking back from school, holding hands and dragging their feet. Their skinny brown bodies swimming in their school uniforms. As the car slows down along the narrow roads, they nudge each other in their ribs and stop walking to stare into the car. Maybe it is because of everything that is happening, Papa's heart, going to his place, Mr. Oliver patting my head. I feel like maybe anything is possible. So I wave at them. I am surprised sha, when some of them wave back. Butterflies flap their light wings inside my stomach, and I want to laugh out loud with happiness. The traffic light turns green and when Mr. Oliver picks up speed, I wind down the window and stick my head out small. I look back at them as the car moves forward, squinting my eyes against the sun until the hands of the children shrink into a memory.

"Ozioma! What is wrong with you? Come on, sit properly and close that window!" Mama's voice cuts against the wind on my face.

I lean back in my seat still smiling. For the first time all day I wonder if there will be other children where we are going. I bend my fingers and stare as the little yellow creases in my knuckles become short straight cracked lines. I pinch my thin flesh together at my wrist. Not as hard as Aisha them do at school. Not enough to make me cry. I leave it and reach up for the little gold crucifix at my neck, holding it for a few seconds. It is from Papa. Not from God. Everybody said he used to wear it for protection. Mama said it fell from his neck during the accident. Pastor said we are lucky nobody stole it. When I told Mama about seeing Papa, she said I should wear it. There is no magic in it, but sometimes I rub it between my fingers hoping it will make me forget some of the things Aisha them say at school.

"They will use you for medicine."

"Mind yourself before we sell you for five thousand naira."

My mind cannot stop it. The smile slips down with my hand. I start to see again, how during class break they circle me, their mouths full and heavy like a bucket full of sloshing water. The words spill out from between their slick lips, and I slip and slide and fall in them. Inside my chest, I think there is bruising. Inside, my heart pains more than everywhere else, more than the pulling and shoving, all the falls to the ground.

That day, when they say they will sell me, I reach home, I go to the bathroom and lock the door. I am using Dettol to clean the wound on my elbow and the small scratches on my arm. The sting makes me squeeze my face. I look at myself in the mirror and I am crying, my cream skin botched in patches, itchy and irritated. There is sand on my scalp. I see the brown dust in between my white braids.

"White demon." I have carried their voices back with me. But it is my own lips moving in the mirror. It is my own voice I hear. My tears begin to fall faster, and I close my mouth into a thick line watching it tremble up and down, listening to the muffling, whimpering sound of everything trapped inside that wants to come out. That is when I see him. In the mirror behind my reflection, an outline, like in my coloring books. A shape filled in roughly but lightly with color pencil, like the person was in a hurry and could not stay inside the lines. Papa is a filled-in figure, orange brown like the skin of Udara fruit. And me, almost the color of the inside of a kola nut. Papa does not touch me. He does not speak. But I know it is him. I hear my heart racing inside my chest. But me, I do not scream. I am not afraid. I step backward, slowly

keeping my eyes on the mirror, until I am standing inside the outline, inside him. Until I am not alone. And it is good.

I lean my head against the car window as a new thought sneaks into my mind. I place my hand on my chest. If I have Papa's heart, am I feeling what he feels or is Papa feeling what I feel? Aisha them, are they paining me or are they paining Papa? I think of words from the Holy Gospel of John. Am I in my father like he is in me? My heart starts to beat fast. I say in my head, "Father, Daughter, Holy Ghost."

"Mummy, if nobody knows we are coming, what if we reach and Mama Obinna does not allow us to enter?" Pastor is still asking his questions. Me, I am starting to feel hungry. I am tired of sitting. I want to reach Papa's place even if I am still scared small. I kick my legs up and down and my canvas hits the dark place under the small compartment by mistake. I glance quickly at Mr. Oliver and cover my mouth with both my hands.

"It's okay." He turns and looks at me. I let my hands drop, and a breath escapes my mouth. I relax.

"Long journey. You must be tired."

"Yes, sah. And hungry." It comes out before I can catch it. I cannot remember if I am supposed to not be hungry yet or just when we reach the village. I cover my mouth again quickly and look through the side of my eye to see if Mama heard me. Also, because of the things Mama has told me in the past, I am not used to talking to strangers. Someone like me cannot trust them. But Mr. Oliver has been nice. Anyhow, Mama and Pastor are still talking.

"She cannot keep me from visiting my husband's grave. Before, Pastor, do you want me to announce our arrival over FM radio, so their people have time to prepare trouble for us?"

"Mummy, that is not what I am saying, ehn. Just that we cannot travel this far and not do the prayers."

"Pastor, is it me that should be telling you that if God is for us who can be against us? No weapon fashioned against us shall prevail. Are you not the one that has been quoting that scripture up and down since I told you what happened?"

"Yes, because it is true, Mummy. It is the Word of God. But we ourselves must still do what we know we have been called to do once a situation presents itself."

"Is it not possible that Obinna came so we ourselves are forced to come and settle this matter once and for all? You know, somehow, I always believed he was still fighting for us, this his small family he just left like this." Mama sighs, and I listen to her string her grief to hope, tied with a thinning thread to the thing that happened to me, and not to her. "It took ten years, but maybe this is his sign. Mama Obinna will not see Ozioma, but it's time she provide something for her only son's child. I am believing it is God who led us here. He will not close the way, *inugo*? You sef, Pastor. Was it not your mouth that God used to say we should come? Have faith small. One way or another, me, I am not leaving here the same as I am coming."

Pastor does not say anything. But his words poke me in the open places where I hold all my questions like pockets in my skin. Outside, the people and the market shacks thin out until the weary roads stop abruptly and the car humps over onto a stretch of paved highway. We are going faster now. Past a thick forest of palm trees and wide fanned out banana leaves. I lean back in the seat and close my eyes, and the sounds of voices in the back become a faint lull as I fall asleep.

• • •

"Ozioma, wake up. We have reached." Mama's hand is gently shaking my shoulder. Mr. Oliver is pulling up on an unpaved and bumpy orange-red road. I sit up and sigh deeply, wiping my mouth with the back of my hand. I can smell fresh bread. My stomach is grumbling now. I glance behind to the back and see that Mama has a soiled paper bag by her side. We must have passed a Mama-Put on the roadside while I was sleeping. Now I just want to eat. I stretch my arms, my back and look outside. On one side there is a large, empty space with half a house on it, just the cement structure, as if a giant child was building a giant sandcastle and his giant mama yelled at him halfway that it was time to go.

"See the place," Mama says to Pastor. "He was still building when he died. He only finished the small guesthouse in the back so we would have our own space when we came for Christmas. But that is where he is buried, on the land his father gave him. It is too far to be visiting, but you know our culture, in the end we all have to bring each other home."

"*O bu eziokwu*, Mummy. It is true," Pastor repeats. "It is even good he is buried here. When we pray, we will be covering his paternal lineage. We will have to walk around the whole property. Let holy water seal the perimeter." Pastor points to the old house on the other side of the car. "And what of that place?"

"That one is her house. See how she has closed all the windows and curtains. How does air even enter that place, sef? Just shutting herself up in a tomb of wickedness. In fact, are you sure you don't want to just go and pour all the holy water there, sef?" Mama kisses her teeth. "Nonsense and ingredient. See, it's already two o'clock. Let's unload, please. If we pray by four p.m., we can get back on the road by five p.m. I will not spend up to twenty-four hours here."

I slip my hands under my knees. The seat is warm and damp with sweat. I lean forward to get a better look from Mr. Oliver's window at Mama Obinna's house. The house is two floors high and the color of a banana, but the walls are dirty and brown in some places. Like the fruit is going bad. I wonder where she is inside and what she is doing. I try to imagine Papa as a little boy running in and out of rooms in that house. Mama Obinna yelling at him to go outside and play, and him coming back with orange clay dust rising up from his feet to his legs, like he is slowly changing color.

Mr. Oliver parks the car and we all come down. I put my hat back on my head and Mama stands by the boot holding the food and waiting for our suitcase. Me, I walk around her just to see the rotten banana house proper from the ground. There is an old man sitting on a piece of plywood stacked on big cement blocks right by the gate. His legs are crossed, and he is working hard on his chewing stick like there is a prophecy from God stuck between his teeth that he needs to spit out. He sees me. He drops his chewing stick and scrambles to his feet screaming.

"*Chineke! Chineke!* He has come back. Brother Obinna has come back o! Wonders shall never end!" His hands are on his head and he is hopping from one foot to the other. I step back and bump into Mr. Oliver, who puts one hand on my shoulder. I let him. Mama starts to yell at the gateman.

"*Biko, emechi onu!* Be quiet!" She goes toward him, waving her hand down for him to stop yelling. I hear her say, "Village people," under her breath. They talk for a few minutes. At first, he is the one talking fast, pointing back toward Mama Obinna's house, staring at me over Mama's shoulder. Then Mama is the one talking, pointing her finger in his face. He puts his arms behind his back, holding one with the other at the elbow, his head hanging down, nodding. Soon she is walking back to us, her slippers kicking circles of orange-red dust behind her.

"Mummy, what? What is it?" Pastor asks.

"Don't mind that bush man." She kisses her teeth. Then she looks down at me and puts one hand on my chin with a small smile on her face. "I told you that you and your father are carbon copy." Her voice is soft. But the sadness in her eyes removes some of the sweetness.

She turns back toward Pastor, all the fire flaring up in her throat again. "But can you imagine? The man says Mama Obinna is very sick. That she has not left her bed for two weeks." Mama snaps her fingers in the air. "*Tufeakwa!* Says she has been crying for Obinna. What does she want her dead son to come and do for her now? Instead of her to be crying for God's mercy."

"Ah-ahn, Mummy. It's okay. It's enough. But two weeks?" Pastor rubs his own chin as if there is a beard there. "Isn't that when you said Brother Obinna appeared to Ozioma?" He raises his palms into the air and shakes them. "Mummy, I told you this thing was serious."

"*Biko*, Pastor, what are you saying? Ozioma and this woman have nothing to do with each other." Mama is annoyed. She looks at her watch and waves her hand for Mr. Oliver to follow us with the suitcase. "Please, Pastor, let us take our things to the guesthouse. Ozioma needs to eat. All of us in fact. Thank God, we bought meat pie in town."

Pastor is shaking his head. "Mummy, you have to go and see Mama Obinna. *Odighi nma,*" he repeats. "It is not good."

"Pastor?" Mama wipes her hands together like she is cleaning them. "Please don't be offended, you hear? But I have told you. Practically ten years, and I did not hear from that woman." She takes my arm and pulls me toward the unfinished house. I see a lizard scurry past us as if leading the way. Its gray body and orange head shaking as it goes, as if it agrees with Mama.

"Did you not say, you will not leave here the way you came?" Pastor is still standing by the car, calling out to us.

Mama stops walking. The lizard continues. She turns to face Pastor, nodding her head slowly and still holding me by my arm. Me, even in my sunhat, I am already ready to get out of the heat.

"It is true. This one that she is sick and crying for Obinna. Maybe sense will enter her head, and she will do the right thing by this child before something worse happens to her. Okay. I will go and see her. By myself. Just before we leave. I don't want her interfering with us this afternoon."

. . .

After lunch, Mama and Pastor are resting in the guesthouse's two bedrooms. Me, I have the couch in the parlor because I can't sleep when Mama snores. But the couch smells of camphor. I am trying to rest but nothing is happening. Mama's words to Pastor twist around inside my stomach, paining me. What if Mama Obinna is dying? I am afraid of her. But, I am more afraid that she will die and I will never see my father's mother. I get up and peek into the hallway. Both the doors are closed where Mama and Pastor are sleeping. My heart is beating so loud that I have to hurry before the sound wakes them up. I take my hat from the table, and decide to also take my last box of mango juice remaining from lunch. Maybe a present will help somehow. I hold my slippers in my hand and tiptoe through the parlor and outside the front door of the guesthouse. The sky is clear, and the heat has reduced. I put on my slippers and follow the path back toward where the car brought us, then run across the compound to Mama Obinna's gate.

The old man is dozing on the bench. He jolts awake when I tap him, and jumps up, his eyes wide like a full moon. I find my voice while he is struggling with himself.

"I want to see Mama Obinna. I am her granddaughter," I whisper.

He is afraid. He looks at me like I can change him into a cat. He nods his head slowly and opens the gate, pointing inside toward the house. I leave him.

I try the front door handle. It is unlocked. When I open it, sunlight floods into the dark entrance. I pretend I am one of the women finding the stone rolled away. It is not Jesus I am looking for but, as I enter

Mama Obinna's house, I pray in my head that he too is here. It feels cold inside, like Harmattan season, and I shiver small. There is a staircase directly in front of me. There is nobody downstairs, not even a house girl. But even from here I can hear somebody crying upstairs. I climb the stairs slowly, holding on to the railing and following the sound. Along the wall there are old black-and-white photographs of people I do not know. The frames are dusty and thick cobwebs cover some of the corners. There is a large painting of Jesus in the middle of all the pictures. His long yellow hair flowing at his shoulders and his blue eyes staring at me. I stop and look at it. His heart glowing with red paint in the center of his chest. I lean into the painting and whisper, "Oya, remember me o." I make the sign of the cross. "Father, Daughter, Holy Ghost." At the top of the stairs there is a stream of light coming out from under one of the doors. I put my ear to the door, listening to the old woman.

"Obi, Obi. Obinna, my son. *Biko*, forgive me, *inugo*? Do not let me die without you hearing me, ehn? My son." Her words break between wails. I put my hand on the doorknob and turn it.

When I enter the room, she has her back toward me, but I can see she is holding her head in her hands, facing the wall. She is crying so much that her large body is shaking, and she doesn't hear me come in. I stand there. Suddenly unafraid. Like I am not alone with her.

"Mama Obinna."

The black headscarf she is wearing falls to the floor as she lifts her head from her hands and slowly turns to me. It is as if somebody poured flour on her head. It is all white, almost like my own. Her wrinkly face is Milo brown like Mama. Her eyes are swollen and puffy. She does not scream like the gateman. She stares at me, her mouth open without words. Like she is seeing a ghost.

"Jesus is Lord. You are my son. My Obinna."

"No, Mama Obinna. I am Ozioma. His daughter."

"Jesus is Lord. You are Obinna." She says it again, sitting up in bed. "You are his spitting image. And that pendant on your neck, the one I gave him. If not for." She stops speaking for a few seconds, and stares at me up and down again, her mouth slightly open. When she finds her voice again she says quietly, "Your skin."

I know I don't have much time before Mama discovers I am gone. I watch her look at me. I see how she is afraid, even if she is not yelling. I do not know how a grown woman can fear me. The mother of my papa. I am sad and I am sorry, for her and for me. I wonder if Papa can feel that. And that is why I say the next thing. Because I do not want Papa to feel sad or sorry for anything. I do not want to risk anything that might make him not come back to me. So I say it quickly. I spit it out. "Mama Obinna. I forgive you."

"Ehn?" She sits up straighter in bed and puts her hands over her mouth.

"I heard you, just now. Crying to Papa. And I forgive you."

"But how can you . . . can you forgive me?" She pulls herself back, and I see her red eyes widen.

"Mama Obinna, it's okay." I walk to her bed and stick out my hand to give her my mango juice box. My bare arms almost match her light pink sheets. She takes it hesitantly, her eyes never leaving my face. I place one hand on my heart and the other on her leg. "It's okay, Mama Obinna. I have Papa's heart. So that must mean I, too, can forgive you."

"Jesus is Lord." She starts to cry again. "Obinna, *nwa m nwoke*. Is this how you come? Through the one I denied? Ehn, Obinna?" She is sobbing so hard now that my fear comes back. I step back from the bed and turn to leave the room. That's when I see Mama standing in the doorway. Her hand is on the doorknob, but her body is frozen, like a statue. My heart starts beating faster even though she hasn't started screaming at me yet. I glance over her face quickly trying to see how angry she is. But her mouth is in a line and her eyes are bright and glaring past me straight at Mama Obinna. The only thing moving is her left eyebrow. Twitching. I have not seen that happen before.

"Ozioma. Leave this room." Mama speaks in a voice I do not know. I stay silent and just inch toward her without even looking back at Mama Obinna. I cannot pass because Mama is in the doorway. So I stand there keeping my head bent and staring at the floor.

"You." Mama speaks to Mama Obinna and steps inside the room. I slip out behind her. But I do not close the door. Once in the hallway, I just take one step to the side and stand with my back against the wall next to the open door. My heart still racing in my chest. I see Pastor at the bottom of the staircase, pacing up and down in the shadowy dark.

"How did you use your wickedness to bring my daughter to this godforsaken house?" Mama's voice is sharp but quiet. It sounds worse than if she was yelling.

"Amara, *biko, gee m nti.*" Mama Obinna is still sobbing as she begs Mama to listen to her. "I do not know what is happening, ehn. What are you people doing here even? It is as if my Obinna is inside this your daughter. I am sorry, *inugo.* I am sorry."

My back softens against the wall and I let myself slide down to sit on the floor. Is this the tired old woman Mama has spent ten years hating?

"Ehn-ehn? It is now you know to be sorry because you are afraid of dying and facing God. Do you even know what the last ten years have been like for us? You think my daughter is—" I hear Mama stop and snap her fingers. "God forbid. I won't even repeat your nonsense."

I want Mama to stop being angry. I want to run back inside and tell Mama Obinna that I am not juju, that my skin is just showing the light inside me. I look at the Jesus painting and move my lips in silence, asking for a miracle.

"Amara, please, I take God beg you. Anything you want. I just want your daughter to pray for me, ehn. She has lived up to the name you people gave her, *inugo*? Please. Obinna, *mee ya ka o gee m nti*," Mama Obinna pleads, crying loudly again.

I take a deep breath and stand up. I know Mama is so angry she might even slap me, but I walk slowly back to the doorway and stand there. "Mama. Please." I swallow hard. "I am not afraid of her again." Mama turns and stares at me. She looks me up and down slowly and tilts her head, as if she has not seen me in a long time. She sighs deeply and I can hear a tremble in the breath. Water coming into her eyes.

"Go and call Pastor," she says.

As I turn back toward the staircase for Pastor, Mama Obinna blesses Mama again and again. "*Chukwu gozie gi.* Ehn, Amara. *Chukwu gozie gi.*"

When Pastor comes, he tells Mama and me to stand on either side of Mama Obinna's bed. He will stand at the foot. Mama Obinna is sitting up with her head in her hands, shaking softly and trying to hold her tears. I look at Mama and she gives me a sad smile. She is not happy, but she is not angry. That is enough for me. Pastor removes a small bottle of water from his pocket. He holds it up with both hands.

"Father God, it is you that knows our comings and goings, what we keep inside our hearts, where we have fallen short and sinned before you. Father God it is you that protects and redeems us. I call on you, Father God, by the power of the Holy Ghost, to cleanse this woman, to redeem her heart and her transgressions."

I sneak one eye open and see Pastor move his hand between Mama and Mama Obinna, so that I am not sure who the prayer is for. He opens the water, cups his hand, and pours some into his palm. I close my eyes just as he throws his hand and I feel some of the drops sprinkle on my face. Then I hear his footsteps and sneak my eyes open again. Pastor is at the bedroom door. He starts walking along the wall around the whole room, letting the water drip from his fingers, his mouth moving quietly. When everything is finished and we open our eyes, nobody speaks. Mama Obinna's crying is a whimper now. Pastor goes to the head of her bed and puts his hand on her arm. "It's okay, Mummy. It's okay. *O ga-adi mma.*" Mama Obinna's shoulders shake even more as he comforts her.

Mama sighs again. "Pastor, it's already five p.m. Let us come and be going."

Mama Obinna cannot look at us. But still, I go, and I put my hand over her own hand that is just lying in her lap. Her skin is dry, and the wrinkles make it feel rough. I feel a drop fall on mine, the tear slides down over the brown sunspots on my hand. Mama Obinna uses her other hand and wipes it away. Then she leaves her hand on top of mine.

"Ozioma. *Ka a puo,*" Mama calls to me.

I pull my hand away and follow Mama and Pastor out the door, down the stairs, and out of the banana house.

The sun has gone down, and the daylight is slipping into a dark blue. The three of us walk back across the road to Papa's plot of land and toward the guesthouse.

As we pass the unfinished house I ask, "Pastor, what of our prayers at the burial site?"

He pats my white braids. "It is finished. It is enough."

I see him steal a glance at Mama. Her head is down and she is walking like her legs are heavy. Like her whole body is tired.

"Mummy, it is well. Something has touched her. She will do the right thing." He tries but his words do not make her body less heavy.

"It is between her and her God." She sighs, and I hear her say Papa's name very quietly under her breath, like an amen. I slip my hand into Mama's and remember something Mama Obinna said before.

"Mama?"

"Yes, Ozioma?"

"Mama, please tell me again how I got my name."

"Ehn?"

"Mama Obinna, in the room she said, I have lived up to my name. I want to hear that story again please, Mama."

Mama stops walking. She steps back and bends down. Her hands find my arms and she caresses them for a minute then holds me still. "Ozioma, you know it is your father that named you." She looks into my eyes. I do not even know that I am crying until she wipes my tears away. "I have told you this story many times. The day you were born, he held you in his arms and said you were his little miracle. He said a child like you can only be a message from God. So he named you Ozioma, Good News."

I release my arm from Mama, and raise my hand to cover the smile I feel spreading suddenly across my mouth. It feels like our secret.

Nana Ekua Brew-Hammond

Trophy

POEM

How could you have known

when you were running home in your high waters
tears clinging to your tangled lashes
your boyhood stomped on
by other boys born under a boot

when you were sitting in that chair
combing paraffin through your hair
waiting for alcohol and parabens
to activate your naps into submission

when you were working so hard in class
to make them laugh
and make them love you
all the things you did so your kids wouldn't look like
you

RELATIONS

that you

black as the limo you pulled up in
African as the name you abbreviate
so beautiful they had to convince you
you were a beast

(yes, you)

back when you were
named for the day and the
order of your birth, clay
on your arms
sugar, salt, and gin
on your gums
everyone rejoicing

you are the trophy

just as you were
when you were running.

In two generations, your heirs will show your picture
as proof they can't be racist.
Look where I come from, they'll say
Look who.

clinging by a strand
to that Black
you were running so hard from.

Salma Khalil

Célebrons la culture
Let's Celebrate Culture

POEM

Fresh and running, they water me,
Clear and elusive, they brighten me.
Those little drops escaped from a cluster of clouds,
Suddenly send us a particular message.

A message with a familiar fragrance that promises a season
With scents reminiscent of the fertile and wet soil,
Cradling the cone-roofed huts crammed together,
Illuminating both candid and sunken faces.

It is the rainy season, the season of happiness,
The season of hoe, seed, and labor,
We hurry to dust off the drums,
Virtuous messengers to answer her with poetry;

The hoots matching richly embroidered robes,
Harmoniously compose the rhythms of the culture.

RELATIONS

And as the braids spice up some beauties,

Children are already running to the village square.

That is where frenzy and gathering meet,

The arena celebrating rain, the source of life.

Like excited bees flying to their hive,

We run, absorbed by the vibrant drums.

The choirs of men refresh the lively atmosphere,

As they stomp their feet, the wet soil is backfilled.

The songs of women spring from their chords,

Encouraging the laughing and handsome dancers.

With spiritual tears hanging on his fingertips,

Whispering heavenly incantations to the ancestors,

The father, features sunken, purifies the mother earth,

Nursery of our breath, source of our richness.

Tea springs from humility and empathy,

Bodies move to the rhythm of friendliness;

The whole village melts in a positive energy,

Where the waves of inspired silhouettes are drawn.

Soon, at dawn, when the roosters crow,

The concert of hoes will enliven our days;

We will then start the noble labor inherited

By our hands, carrying seeds of each generation.

Translated from the French by Ray Ndebi

Ayi Renaud Dossavi-Alipoeh

Word maker.

My mother's words

Life is the words we share.

We live in words as we sleep in bed. For us, they are a link not only with others, but also with our inner selves. We clothe every moment of our existence with them, every form of our thoughts, every fold of our brains.

> *Let my words, forks, and scythes,*
> *cut in the dawn of the dream merchant moon*
> *A hint of salt for a unique lantern*
> *I palaver with mountains and skyscrapers*
> *The word is vast like the ocean when it falls*
> *the shadow of things to come and the distant reflection of the past*
> *Tomorrow, or someday, I will die, but my plural heart will bloom in my people's words*
> *Speak to me in Mother's language, friend, It is my shroud and my eternal altar*

The experience of a French speaker in a world increasingly immersed in the English-speaking matrix, for example, is particular. It is difficult at first to understand that one lives on an island called "Francophonie," which floats on an even-larger ocean of meaning, so immense is the island itself!

There is everything, or almost everything, in the French-speaking world: history, technology, philosophy, an ethos, and a being-in-the-world of its own, millions and millions of pages of knowledge already written and compiled. It is a wide world whose limits seem infinite. One only realizes its limits when, precisely, the time comes to explore more "modern" data, especially in the scientific and technical field. There the world dresses itself in "The," "Yes," and "preterite."

The experience of the Francophone, in a world technically and conceptually subjugated by Anglophone thought, gets even more complicated for the Francophone African. The experience starts from the shores of the Atlantic Ocean, somewhere in the Gulf of Guinea. It is a double colonization—one leaves one's mother tongue to live in French, and then one has to move, at least with one's feet, to put down one's bags in English—which calls for a double decolonization.

Imagine the scene: taking one's suitcases to leave one's mountains or native valley, and groping one's way to the banks of the Thames (or rather the Washingtonian Potomac), passing with great noise through the French Seine.

> *One does not chase with stones*
> *the shadow of our forgotten dreams*
> *My words in the pockets of the void*
> *sing the hymn to rebellion*
> *Rebellion to Life and Death*
> *To oblivion and to Nothingness*
> *I was here, on this piece of lagoon*
> *when eternity eternalized its whims*
> *I will be here, on this end of the lagoon*

when the water says its last word
Mother's tongue is an ocean of love
that falls, again and again, against the rocks of History

A particular experience, first of solitude then of rediscovery. Like a cutting, one must quickly regain one's footing, and let the new plant flourish, which carries within it the traces of the old soil. For each new word learned, better, for each facility to express oneself in the "language of others," it is like a new self which is born, which thinks a little in its own way, which draws, a little differently and as it pleases, the sketches and the outlines of the world. We quickly regain our footing. And without realizing it, we take with us all the languages that live in us, or that we live in. It depends.

Words are the heat of our thoughts
the fertile ebullition of our hands weaving laughter
at the crossroads of a thousand skins and a thousand faces
Words to make circle and unity, trapeze and diversity
Words have the flesh of wrestling arms, transforming into greeting hands

We can see it as a double uprooting, but also, could we (and should we) see it as a double rerooting? We carry our languages like so many bouquets of roses and ilang-ilang and sunflowers, a motley, multicolored bunch. The languages are worlds and dusty trails in the sparkling night.

Words are larger than the world

Words have the same flesh as the world and the same taste as the raindrops that water our
dreams and our breaths and our lives as simple men and women,
walking on the surface of the earth.

Words have a softer skin than all the women in the world,

RELATIONS

Words are the brick of the building, and the plank of the ship.

Words and languages are universes in themselves, which possess and inhabit us. From Lomé, Abidjan, or Lagos, the world is an ocean of colors and spices that is constantly reinvented, to the rhythm of breaths, today of the internet and its passions. We are connected to the thousand and one lives of the world by the infinite pulsations of the zeros and ones that go around the world. And we make society, from the margin, the periphery of the world and our screens, with all the distant citizens of the world. If most idiosyncrasies remain in the linguistic and creative universe that gave birth to them, many artifacts break the barrier and escape from their cradle of creation, to impact and amaze other peoples, to make other hearts laugh and throb. Whether through the magic of translation, subtitling, or even multilingualism.

Words are swords in the hand of the king and revolt in the mouth of the weak.
Words are breasts in the bra, the kiss on the cheek of the traitor, and cake under the cherry
The Word is heat in the thermometer, boat in the storm, drop in the rain, and kiss in the
night embrace.
Words are a world to conquer, a kingdom to draw, and blood to spill on the battlefield,
of the white sheet.

Humans live in the world, and take root in memories. Every day, we connect with our fellow human beings through words, we build words and intimate universes. Fragments of eternity. There are so many words in so many different languages. Forty in the country-*mien*, Togo, a tiny rectangle nestled in the back of the Gulf of Guinea. Forty! So many unique stories, marked by sacrifices and wars and bloodshed and cries and tears and joys and wanderings. So many ancestors and women moaning in the thickets to give birth to the next generation and make the crossing possible.

Give my words
Fruit baskets and Swiss chocolate
Indian tea and Chinese silk

Ayi Renaud Dossavi-Alipoeh

Give my words
Singapore velvet and Papua drums
Invisible threads attached to the Great Puppeteer
My crying-smiling words contemplate the world and the world's laughter
God, coughing after his clop break, sips a glass of whiskey
Singing my words

Faced with birth, all women moan in the stubborn language of existence. The whole earth witnesses the spectacle: life that is born from life.

At birth, all children speak a universal language, the words, borders and scars on thought, come later.

Speak to me the language of my mother, friend
She is my cradle and my ultimate down word
She is my moon that muddies with impatience the infinity of the night
the child, rebellious to the years that flow, rolls his hump beside the adult
and it is in the language of my mother that the eternal child reminds the man who grows old
the original cry
the founding cry
the first cry that gives birth to the adventure
When the hours are dark and my heart too stony
Speak to me the language of my mother, friend
It is my refuge, my eternal

We have always feared Death. Like all species before us, we have always feared to die. The disappearance, the oblivion, the fateful "RIP."

So what do we do to mark our passage? We scribble our names on the walls of houses. We write our names in the sand of the beach, giving them to the timeless ocean to drink.

RELATIONS

We shout our names in buses and cabs. We engrave our names on books and medals. Our names on our identity cards, our names in the evening with strangers, our names and our nicknames on profiles and walls and statuses. We want to live, a thousand and one times, by proxy if need be. And names—words—are emissaries.

> *My mother's words taste like dried chili pepper*
> *that I pour on the hot rice dish*
> *when I come home hungry from having run too much after life*
> *my memory as the only sentinel, I smile*
> *when I chew on life, with the words of my mother*

We pray to God to live after death, we write to live after death, we paint to live after death, freeze life on canvas, and we sing. Why do we sing? To celebrate life or death, or both?

Today, otherness is just a click away, eternity, too. One day, someone somewhere will be able to find our tracks, our photos, and our name, whether we were in New York or London, Addis Ababa or Jakarta. Our words will tell someone that we were there.

> *We, the loneliness engraved in the words without flesh and bones*
> *We, the sum of laughter at the edge of the lagoons of Bè and Ebrié*
> *We, the fertile storm after the rain*
> *We, the dance of those who know how to say "Life" and "Death" with a smile*
> *To live is a solemn act, a beautiful gesture to deceive the nothingness*
> *. . . only death is eternal*

This is why our goal is to make words, words of all the colors of the rainbow, to color the universe and our memories. It is in memories that men live, it is in words that they are implanted.

Ayi Renaud Dossavi-Alipoeh

Through our respective adventures, we want to be one with all the movements of the world, to be one with all the palpitations and trepidations of the world. With clicks and taps, hashtags and symbols, we make the world with the word.

> *Dances the light on my windowsill*
> *Dies the moon stranded on the banks of our dreams*
> *Flows the fire, heavy with our sparse star existences and heavy dreams*
> *sings the rain that draws eternity*
> *dances the rebellious light to the tears of the night*
> *My existence, timeless flower, dances like a woman in the words of my mother*
> *My existence, bloody dagger of splitting the nothingness like the words of my mother*
> *And when the shadow of dark days survives the rope of the hanged man*
> *It is in my mother's language that I will give my accounts*
> *There, on the other side of the mirror and doubts, an eternity awaits*

I appeal to our capacity to create, again and again. Flood the universe and the web with our thousands of words with our own eyes. It's about telling the world, about giving it an A from our unique and particular perspectives, about setting the tone for the sacred music of the earth. Wherever you are, type a word on a keyboard, engrave a name on a stone, in the flesh of a tom-tom under the palaver tree, under the walls of the law courts, in the hand of the mother who has just passed away, on the gates of your houses, in the trunk of the thousand-year-old trees. Engrave words everywhere, in all the languages you know!

We need words, words that taste like mango and watermelon and wild apple and broken rice and hot chili and black pudding and yellow laughter and cats and dogs and run after me if you can!

> *Give us words in suits and agbadas*
> *Words that know how to dance the agbadja and do the whirling dervish*
> *Words in broccoli and words in sauce-gombo-paste-akoumè*

RELATIONS

"Exotic" words and "diversity" words
Give us words of all the flavors of the rainbow
To make the world smile, and men cry
To ignore the Night that comes for us,
And plant the flag, in the eternal flesh of the world

Put words in every throat, sing words in every sound and tone. Make acrostics with "Africa" or "Kama" or "Kameta" or "Ifriqiya" or "Europe."

Behind each breath, an eternity awaits.

I am here, at the edge of my lagoon. I hear these words in the language of my mother. And I write them in the language of Molière. In what language will they end up, at the end of the journey?

CONTRIBUTORS

Arao Ameny is a Uganda-born, Maryland-based poet and writer from Lira, Lango region, Northern Uganda. She spent her early childhood in Uganda and grew up in the United States, earning her MFA in fiction at the University of Baltimore. A former journalist and communications professional, she has an MA in journalism from Indiana University and a BA in political science from the University of Indianapolis. Her first published poem, "Home Is a Woman," appeared in *The Southern Review* in 2020 and won the James Olney Award. She was a winner of the 2020 Brooklyn Poets Fellowship, a finalist for the 2021 Brunel International African Poetry Prize, and a nominee for the *Best New Poets 2021* anthology. She is an alumna of the 2021 Tin House Workshop (fiction writing) and the 2021 Kenyon Review Writers Workshop (poetry). Currently, she has a one-year contract role as a biography writer and editor at the Poetry Foundation.

Ayesha Harruna Attah is a Ghana-born writer living in Senegal. She was educated at Mount Holyoke College, Columbia University, and New York University. She is the author of the Commonwealth Writers Prize–nominated *Harmattan Rain*; *Saturday's Shadows*; *The Hundred Wells of Salaga*, currently translated into four languages; *The Deep Blue Between*, a book for teen readers; and *Zainab Takes New York*, a rom-com recently optioned for TV/film adaptation. Her writing has appeared in the *New York Times*, the *New York Times Magazine*, *Elle Italia*, *Asymptote*, and the 2010 Caine Prize Writers' Anthology.

Ayi Renaud Dossavi-Alipoeh is a writer, business journalist, and blogger from Togo. The author of poetry, short stories, and essays, he is the winner of the France Togo prize in 2018 for his collection of poems *Chants de sable*; that year, he also won first prize in the "Africa of My Dreams" writing competition sponsored by the African Development Bank. In 2020, he was awarded the rank of officier de l'ordre national du mérite (officer of the national order of merit) for his accomplishments in literature nationwide and abroad. He is currently the secretary-general of the association of writers and people of letters PEN Togo, where he promotes writing and freedom of expression, especially among the younger generation.

Bahia Mahmud H. Awah holds a master's and doctorate degree in social anthropology and public orientation from the Autonomous University of Madrid. He has a diploma in translation studies, and serves as an honorary professor of the Autonomous University of Madrid. A humanist, writer, poet, and anthropologist, he is a member of Antroplogía en Accíon, Centro de Estudios AfroHispánicos of the National University Distance Education, and a member of the Asociación Española de Africanistas.

A lecturer at various universities in the United States, Canada, Spain, Italy, Great Britain, the Caribbean, and South America, he is the author of several articles in academic and cultural journals in the United States, Brazil, France, Nigeria, Mexico, Japan, and Spain.

He has several published books of anthropology, history, poetry, and literary and historical-anthropological essays on the culture of Western Sahara and Mauritania, as well as being the coauthor of more than fourteen prose and verse anthologies. In addition, he is the codirector of the film *Legna, habla el verso Saharaui*, the winner of the first prize of the Sahara International Film Festival in 2014. Some of his most notable works include *La Entidad Política Pantribal Precolonial Saharaui* (2017), *Tiris, rutas literárias* (2016), *Cuentos saharauis de mi abuelo* (2015), *El sueño de volver* (2012), *La maestra que me enseñó una table de madera* (2011), and *Versos Refugiados* (2007). His work may be viewed on the web at https://www.bahiaawah.net/ and the blog *Sahrawi Writers in Exile*, http://generaciondelaamistad.blogspot.com/.

Bidi Salec is an Arabic-English-Spanish translator/interpreter providing accuracy along with a deep understanding of both source and target languages, and taking into consideration the culture of the reader receiving the final text. He holds a master's degree in translation and interpretation, and has eleven years of experience in the field of interpretation and translation in different jargons, especially international development, mine action, arts and literary works, IT, media, and journalism. He has provided both translation and interpretation services for two mine action projects implemented by UNOPS/UNMAS in the Sahrawi refugee camps near Tindouf, South-West Algeria, and worked as a volunteer English-language teacher, a translator journalist, a translator/interpreter, and an information management and translation officer.

Boakyewaa Glover is a Ghanaian writer and organizational psychologist. She is the author of *Circles* (2009, romantic drama), *Tendai* (2013, science fiction), and *The Justice* (2013, political thriller), as well as a plethora of articles, short stories, poems, and other works.

Boakyewaa was a 2014 finalist for Africa's Most Influential Women (organized by CEO Communications, South Africa), the 2018 winner for Ghana's 40 under 40 Awards in the authorship and creative writing category, and a 2020 nominee in the category of English/Literature/ Poetry for the prestigious Ghana Millennium Excellence Awards.

Boakyewaa's current book project is *Commitment*, which tells the story of the thousands who sacrifice personal lives and careers and choose to prioritize family. *Commitment* also tells the story of the particular way that some women in Ghana get by—through the benevolence of older, predatory men, and the physical and psychological abuse these women tolerate in order to protect their lifestyles. *Commitment* is a passion project that Boakyewaa hopes to publish someday soon.

Boakyewaa considers herself an avid connoisseur of life, and when she is not taking care of her mother, foster son, and dogs, is watching movies and TV, listening to music, swimming, reading, blogging, and writing short stories, including her COVID-19 romantic drama, "Connected, Yet Separated." She hopes to resume her lifelong interest in travel soon. Boakyewaa currently works as a freelance consultant and writer.

Chiké Frankie Edozien is the author of the Lambda Literary Award– winner *Lives of Great Men*. He lives in Accra, Ghana.

Chuma Nwokolo was called to the bar in 1984 and appointed a notary public in 1995. He is the convener of the good-governance advocacy project Bribecode (www.bribecode.org). He cofounded *African Writing* magazine (www.african-writing.com) and was writer in residence at the Ashmolean Museum. His short stories and essays have been widely published, and his work has been translated into Italian, Slovene, Arabic, Yoruba, and Slovak.

His first novel, *The Extortionist*, was published in 1983. His latest, *The Extinction of Menai*, centers issues of language and cultural extinction. He has published two other novels, *Dangerous Inheritance* (1988) and *Diaries of a Dead African* (2003); the novel in stories *African Tales at Jailpoint* (1999) and *One More Tale for the Road* (2003); the poetry collections *Memories of Stone* (2006) and *The Final Testament of a Minor God* (2014); the short story collections *The Ghost of Sani Abacha* (2012), and *How to Spell Naija in 100 Short Stories* (vol. 1, 2013 and vol. 2, 2016); as well as essays, including "Law & Justice in the Service of Humanity" (2014).

Conceição Lima was born on December 8, 1961, in Santana, on the island of São Tomé, São Tomé and Príncipe, in the Gulf of Guinea. A journalist, poet, and chronicler, she was among the founders of the National Union of Writers and Artists São Tomé, UNEAS, inspired by Alda Espírito Santo, a poet and a fundamental nationalist and literary reference. Lima attended primary and secondary school in São Tomé, where she currently lives and works as a journalist of TVS, the state television network. For many years she worked as a journalist and a producer for the Portuguese Service of the BBC World Service, based in London. She is the national coordinator of the World Poetry Movement for São Tomé and Príncipe. She is a graduate of King's College London, with a BA in African, Portuguese, and Brazilian studies (first class honors), and the School of Oriental and African Studies, London, with a specialization in governments and politics in sub-Saharan Africa. Her published books of poetry include *O Útero da Casa* (2004), *A Dolorosa Raiz do Micondó* (2006/2008), *O País de Akendengué* (2011), *Quando Florirem Salambás no Tecto do Pico* (2015). Her poems have been translated into German, Arabic, English, Spanish, French, Italian, Galician, Turkish, Czech, and Serbian-Croatian. In 2010, the books *O Útero da Casa* and *A Dolorosa Raiz do Micondó* were both translated into German by DELTA Publishing, in a bilingual edition. In 2014, *A Dolorosa Raiz do Micondó* was translated into Italian by Edizioni

Kolibris. The same book was translated into Spanish by Baile del Sol, of Tenerife, and El perro y la rana, of Caracas. Published in Brazil by Geração Editorial, in 2014, it was selected among more than four hundred titles by the Programa Nacional de Bibliotecas Escolares, with an edition of 35,500. Her poems have been published in several periodicals, magazines, and anthologies, including: *Revista Metamorfoses*, *Revista Prometeo*, *Revista Arquitrave*, *Revista Caransari*, *Antologia da Poesia Feminina dos PALOP*, *The World Record*, *Anthology of Poems on Capital Cities*, *Jornal Cultura*, *Jornal en el Camino*, *World Literature Today*, *Words without Borders*, and *The Literary Review*.

Dami Ajayi studied medicine and surgery at Obafemi Awolowo University, Ile-Ife, Nigeria, where he cofounded the literary magazine *Saraba*. Since then, he has cofounded *The Lagos Review* and most recently *Yaba Left Review*.

His first volume of poems, *Clinical Blues*, was longlisted for the Melita Hume Prize and the Wole Soyinka Prize for Literature in Africa. His second volume of poems, *A Woman's Body Is a Country*, was a finalist for the Luschei Prize for African Poetry. He coedited the anthology *Limbe to Lagos: Nonfiction from Cameroon and Nigeria*.

His essays on literature, music, film, and popular culture have appeared in the *Chimurenga Chronic*, the *Guardian*, *The Africa Report*, *Lost in Lagos*, *The Elephant*, *Bakwa*, *Afropolitan Vibes*, and also in translation in *Das Goethe* (a *Die Ziet* supplement).

He works as a psychiatrist in London.

David Shook is a Californian poet, editor, and translator whose work has focused on underrepresented languages and literatures. Their translations and cotranslations from the African continent include work from Burundi, Cabo Verde, the Democratic Republic of the Congo, Ethiopia,

Equatorial Guinea, Guinea-Bissau, Rwanda, and São Tomé and Príncipe, rendered into English from the Bubi, French, Kinyarwanda, Kirundi, Lingala, Pichinglis, Portuguese, Spanish, Swahili, and Tigrinya languages. *No Gods Live Here*, Shook's book-length translation of São Toméan poet Conceição Lima's selected poems, is forthcoming from Deep Vellum in 2023, and their translation of the Cabo Verdean poet Jorge Carlos Fonseca's *Pigs in Delirium* is forthcoming from Insert Blanc Press. They are a 2021 Global Africa Translation Fellow at The Africa Institute.

Edwige-Renée Dro is a writer, literary translator, and literary activist from Côte d'Ivoire whose writings have been published by HarperCollins, Myriad Editions, and Bloomsbury, among others. She is the cofounder of Abidjan Lit, a collective that seeks to put books at the center of lives and at the heart of cities. Other literary ventures with which she has been involved include Jalada, Writivism, and the AfroYoungAdult project, of which she was a facilitator and the French translator of the stories selected for the anthology.

She was awarded a Morland writing scholarship in 2018 and was a resident at the Iowa International Writing Program in 2021.

In March 2020, she set up 1949, a library of women's writing from Africa and the Black world, in Yopougon (Abidjan).

Enuma Okoro is a Nigerian American writer, speaker, and cultural curator. She is a columnist for *FT Weekend*. Her work explores arts and culture, story and identity, women's interiority, and contemplative spirituality. Her bylines include the *New York Times*, *Vogue*, *Artsy*, *Cultured*, *The Cut*, *The Atlantic*, *Harper's Bazaar*, *Aeon Magazine*, *Catapult*, *Washington Square Review*, *The Guardian*, the *Washington Post*, *Essence*, NPR, ABC's *Good Morning America*, and more. As a speaker, she is represented by the Harry Walker Agency. For more information, please visit www.enumaokoro.com.

Fatima Camara is a writer and spoken word artist from Minneapolis. Not only a TruArtSpeaks (TAS) program alumna, Fatima has worked as the Re-Verb Open Mic host, the program's associate, and Be Heard liaison for TAS. She currently serves as the program's administrative associate.

Camara is a recent graduate of Metropolitan State University with a degree in professional/organizational communications, with a minor in community development and organizing.

Her chapbook, *Yellowline*, was published through Akashic Books and the African Poetry Book Fund. Fatima's passion for writing comes from her desire to highlight the stories and experiences of first-generation people in the United States. Through her creative work, she hopes for future first generations to have narratives they can reference and relate to. Follow her on Instagram @fatima.cl, and on Twitter @fatimac_1.

Jacquelynn Kerubo is a New York–based writer. Her nonfiction has been published in the *New York Times*, the *Wall Street Journal*, *Business Insider*, *Quartz*, the *Independent* (UK), and more. Her fiction has been published in the *Golden Handcuffs Review*. She's currently working on a memoir and a novel.

Joe Robert Cole co-wrote the Academy Award–nominated *Black Panther*, for which he received a National Association for the Advancement of Colored People Image Award. His critically acclaimed Netflix directorial debut, *All Day and a Night*, starring Ashton Sanders (*Moonlight*) and Jeffrey Wright was released in May 2020. He produced the Emmy-winning FX series *The People vs. O. J. Simpson*, for which he received an Emmy nomination for writing the episode "The Race Card" and earned a Writers Guild of America Award for Outstanding Writing. Joe is attached to create and executive produce a new series adaptation of *In the Heat of the Night* for MGM and recently completed co-writing *Black Panther 2*.

Johnson Asunka is a lecturer of Spanish and translation at the University of Ghana. He had his secondary education at Kanton Secondary School, Tumu, in the Upper East Region, from 1972 to 1977, and his postsecondary education at Mount Mary College, Somanya, where he trained as a teacher of French between 1978 and 1981. Thereafter, he taught French and English in secondary schools in Ghana and Nigeria over a ten-year period before enrolling at the University of Ghana, from where he graduated with a BA (first class honors) degree in French/Spanish (with a minor in linguistics) in 1996. He took up a temporary teaching appointment with the Ghana Institute of Languages (GIL) and then proceeded to Kent State University, Ohio, where he pursued postgraduate studies in Spanish/French/English translation and undergraduate studies in the Italian and German languages. He returned to Ghana in 2001 and taught at the GIL for four years before joining the academic staff at the University of Ghana in 2006. His research interest is in contrastive language studies and editing/proofreading in translation. He has over thirty years of experience as a translator, translating between English, Spanish, Italian, and French for various units in the University of Ghana, embassies (particularly the Spanish and Italian embassies), banks and other financial institutions, and state organizations such as the Ghana Accreditation Board. He also translates from Portuguese and German into English.

Khal Torabully is a prizewinning poet, essayist, film director, and semiologist from Mauritius who has authored more than twenty-five books.

Born in 1956, Torabully gives voice to the unimaginable suffering of the millions of indentured men and women brought to Port Louis between 1849 and 1923 as a source of cheap labor. Some remained in Mauritius, while others were forced to endure terrible voyages overseas to other European colonies. Torabully coined the term "coolitude" in a way that echoes Aimé Césaire's concept of "Negritude," transforming a pejorative term into one reflecting a vibrant and resilient cultural identity and language.

Kim Coleman Foote, born and raised in New Jersey, is the author of the forthcoming novels, *Coleman Hill*, which fictionalizes her family's experience of the Great Migration, and *Salt Water Sister*, a woman-centered account of the trans-Atlantic slave trade in 1700s and 1990s Ghana. Her writing has appeared or is forthcoming in *The Best American Short Stories 2022*, *The Rumpus*, *Ecotone*, *Iron Horse Literary Review*, and elsewhere. She is the recipient of several writing fellowships, including from the National Endowment for the Arts, New York Foundation for the Arts, Center for Fiction, Yaddo, MacDowell, Hedgebrook, and Phillips Exeter Academy. Kim was a Fulbright Fellow in 2002-03 in Ghana, where she conducted research for her novel and also wrote a memoir about her experiences. She received an MFA in creative writing from Chicago State University.

Lillian Akampurira Aujo is a poet and fiction writer from Uganda. She is the recipient of the 2015 Jalada Prize for Literature and the 2009 Babishai-Niwe Poetry Award. She was shortlisted for the 2019 Gerald Kraak Award and the 2018 Brittle Paper Anniversary Award, and longlisted for the 2018 Nommo Award.

She has performed poetry at the Gender Is My Agenda Campaign in Ethiopia.

Her writing has been published by *New Internationalist*, *Prairie Schooner*, *Transition*, *Jalada Africa*, the Jacana Literary Foundation, and *Omenana* magazine, among others, with her most recent poems appearing in *Lolwe* literary magazine. She is preoccupied with women's place in the spaces of time, history, and genealogy.

She works as a creative writing mentor, facilitator, and editor.

Makanaka Mavengere was born and raised in Harare, Zimbabwe. She is the author of the novel *Perfect Imperfections*, which was published in South Africa in August 2019. Makanaka currently resides in Johannesburg, South Africa, where she continues her storytelling journey as a screenwriter, playwright, and content creator.

Miral al-Tahawy is an award-winning Egyptian novelist and short story writer, and an affiliated member of the Virginia G. Piper Center for Creative Writing at Arizona State University in Tempe, where she is associate professor of modern Arabic literature and head of classics and Middle Eastern studies at the School of International Letters and Cultures. She has written four award-winning novels, each of which has garnered national and international recognition. Most are now taught around the world as part of standard curricula in Arabic literature in translation. Her literary work has now been translated into more than fifteen world languages.

Her creative works include *Al-Khibaa'* (*The Tent*), which came out in 1996. It focuses on women and Bedouin life in Egypt, and was selected as the best literary work in English translation by the American University of Cairo. It became a bestseller. The novel was published in Arabic in more than six editions. *The Tent* was translated into English, French, Italian, German, Spanish, Swedish, Norwegian, Hindi, Urdu, Dutch, and fourteen other languages.

Al-Bazingana Al-Zarka'a (*Blue Aubergine*), about the 1980s Islamic uprising in Egypt, followed in 2000. For this book, Miral won the Egyptian National Prize. She is the first woman novelist to do so. Like *The Tent*, *Blue Aubergine* was translated into several foreign languages, including English, French, German, Danish, and Italian.

Miral's third book, *Nakarat El-Zeba'a* (*Gazelle Tracks*), is a historical novel about Bedouin families in Egypt at the beginning of the nineteenth century; it traces the changes in women's lives through this time. *Gazelle Tracks* won Best Novel of the Year at the Cairo Book Fair and was translated into many languages.

Miral's fourth novel, *Brooklyn Heights*, released in Arabic in 2010, is an intimate look at a woman's sudden immersion into American culture. It was awarded the 2010 Naguib Mahfouz Medal for Literature at the American University in Cairo. The English translation of *Brooklyn Heights*, published in 2011 by Faber and Faber in the United Kingdom, was chosen as the best translated Arabic book and was shortlisted for the International Prize for Arabic Fiction.

Mogolodi Bond is a writer, poet, and rapper. He was born in Botswana, lives in Harlem, and is the author of two chapbooks: *placidity.* and *no turning back.*

Nana Ekua Brew-Hammond is the author of the children's picture book *BLUE: A History of the Color as Deep as the Sea and as Wide as the Sky*, illustrated by Caldecott Honor Artist Daniel Minter, and the young adult novel *Powder Necklace*, which *Publishers Weekly* called "a winning debut." Her short fiction for adult readers is included in the anthologies *Accra Noir*, edited by Nana-Ama Danquah; *Africa39: New Writing from Africa South of the Sahara*, edited by Ellah Wakatama Allfrey; *New Daughters of Africa*, edited by Margaret Busby, CBE,

Hon. FIRSL; *Everyday People: The Color of Life*, edited by Jennifer Baker; and *Woman's Work*, edited by Michelle Sewell, among others. Forthcoming from Brew-Hammond are a novel and children's picture book.

Brew-Hammond was a 2019 Edward F. Albee Foundation fellow, a 2018 Aké Arts and Book Festival guest author, a 2017 Aspen Ideas Festival Scholar, a 2016 Hedgebrook writer in residence, and a 2015 Rhode Island Writers Colony writer in residence. Every month, Brew-Hammond coleads a writing fellowship whose mission is to write light into darkness.

Nana Nyarko Boateng is a writer and an editor. She works at Gird Center, a writing, editing, and training services company in Accra. Her work has appeared in several publications, including *Lusaka Punk and Other Stories* (the Caine Prize for African Writing 2015 anthology), *Reflections: An Anthology of New Work by African Women Poets*, *Summoning the Rains* (an anthology of the Third FEMRITE Regional Residency for African Women Writers), and *Look Where You Have Gone to Sit: New Ghanaian Poets*.

Nancy Naomi Carlson is a translator, poet, essayist, and author of twelve titles (eight translated), including Khal Torabully's *Cargo Hold of Stars: Coolitude* (Seagull Books, 2021). *An Infusion of Violets* (Seagull, 2019), her second full-length poetry collection, was named "New & Noteworthy" by the *New York Times*. A recipient of two translation grants from the National Endowment for the Arts, she was a finalist for the Best Translated Book Award and the CLMP Firecracker Poetry Award. Decorated with the rank of chevalier in the Order of the Academic Palms, she is the translation editor for *On the Seawall*.

Phillippa Yaa de Villiers writes, performs, and lectures in creative writing at Wits University, Johannesburg. Her poetry collections include *Taller Than Buildings* (2006), *The Everyday Wife* (2010, winner of the South African Literary Award in 2011), and *ice-cream headache in my bone* (2017). She coedited *Keorapetse Kgositsile: Collected Poems, 1969–2018* for the University of Nebraska Press (forthcoming), and her poems appear in *New Daughters of Africa* (2019) and various journals, including *New Coin, Stanzas,* and *Wasafiri.* She edited a special edition of the *Atlanta Review* on South African women poets (2018) and coedited *No Serenity Here,* an anthology of African poetry translated into Mandarin (2010). She wrote an essay and contributed to another in *Our Words, Our Worlds: Writing on Black South African Women Poets, 2000–2018* (2019). Since 2016 she has been a member of the editorial board of the African Poetry Book Fund. She was the 2014 Commonwealth Poet.

Ray Ndebi is a Cameroonian writer, literary translator, and analyst based in Yaoundé. He is the author of *The Last Ghost: Son of Struggle,* published in 2013 by AuthorHouse, which appears in many international anthologies such as *Between the Generations: An Anthology for Ama Ata Aidoo at 80,* and a translation of a short story in the anthology *Your Feet Will Lead You Where Your Heart Is* (Bakwa Books, 2020). He has translated many children's books for local publishers, and is currently completing the translation of a poetry collection by Danielle Eyango (Cameroon), and short stories by Boube Hama. He also works in collaboration with the author Nana Ekua Brew-Hammond for poetry and short story translation projects. He is the cofounder of Ônoan Literary Agency and Academy of Creative Writing and Literary Translation, which seeks to promote quality output in literature, especially in the African context. Every day he works to produce modules that can help authors, readers, and translators best achieve their writings. He has been leading workshops and mentoring authors and readers for almost twenty years in Cameroon, across Africa (physically and virtually, private and public). He has notably led workshops in poetry (Lomé International Book Fair, November 2018), creative writing and reading (University of Lomé, April 2019), translation and bilingual fusion in creative writing (Pa Gya! festival, Accra, 2019), translation (University of Bristol, Yaoundé, 2019), and literary critique and creative writing (Lomé, November 2019). He has also led several online workshops due to the COVID-19 pandemic, and an art of reading workshop at the University of Lomé in August 2021. He aims at making African literature stronger for young authors, and for future generations to benefit from the best possible support and direction.

Recaredo Silebo Boturu is a poet, actor, playwright, director, and cofounder of the Bocamandja theater company in Equatorial Guinea. An "artivist" defender of the arts, Boturu is a passionate advocate of the dramatic art of Equatorial Guinea. He is the author of *Luz en la noche* (Editorial Verbum, 2010), *Crónicas de Lágrimas annuladas* (Editorial Verbum, 2014), and *From the Mediterranean* (Editorial AUGE, 2019). He has given talks, conferences, and workshops on the culture of Equatorial Guinea in Colombia, the United States, Spain, France, Austria, Nigeria, and Italy. Likewise, his works have appeared in anthologies and magazines such as *Afro-Hispanic Review, La Palabra y La Memoria: Guinea Ecuatorial 25 Años Después, Caminos y Veredas: Narrativas de Guinea Ecuatorial, Revista Iberoamericana, Chronic Chimurenga, GuinGuinBali, Molossus* magazine, *Best "New" African Poets 2018 Anthology, Nuevas Voces de la Litertura de Guinea Ecuatorial, Antología de la Literatura Hisapanoafricana y Afrodescendiente,* and *The name of the sun,* among others. In 2014, he was chosen for inclusion in the "Africa 39"—thirty-nine African writers under forty years old published in the corresponding anthology *Africa39: New Writing from Africa South of the Sahara* to celebrate the selection of Port Harcourt, Nigeria, as that year's UNESCO World Book Capital.

Reem Gaafar is a public health physician, writer, researcher and mother of three boys, with more than fifteen years of experience in the Middle East, Africa, and North America. A graduate of Juba University in Sudan, she obtained her masters in Public Health from the University of Liverpool and is currently working toward a PhD at the University of Ontario, Institute of Technology in Canada. She writes for several platforms and has accumulated nearly two hundred publications including blog posts, peer-reviewed and magazine articles, short stories, and book contributions. Her work has garnered honorable mentions, and she was recently shortlisted for the prestigious Miles Morland Foundation Scholarship awarded to published African writers.

Rémy Ngamije is a Rwandan-born Namibian writer and photographer. He is the founder, chairperson, and artministrator of Doek, an independent arts organization in Namibia supporting the literary arts. He is also the cofounder and editor in chief of *Doek!*, Namibia's first and only literary magazine. His debut novel, *The Eternal Audience of One*, is available from Scout Press. His work has appeared in the *Johannesburg Review of Books*, *American Chordata*, *Lolwe*, *Granta*, and many other places.

He won the Africa Regional Prize of the 2021 Commonwealth Short Story Prize. He was shortlisted for the AKO Caine Prize for African Writing in 2020 and 2021. He was also longlisted and shortlisted for the 2020 and 2021 Afritondo Short Story Prizes, respectively. In 2019 he was shortlisted for the Best Original Fiction award by Stack Magazines. More of his writing can be read on his website, remythequill.com.

Born July 11 in Mbandaka (Democratic Republic of the Congo), **Richard Ali A Mutu K**, known as "Richard Ali," was selected in 2014 among the thirty-nine young authors of sub-Saharan Africa under forty considered the most promising in Africa for the anthology *Africa39*. Founder of the Association des Jeunes Écrivains du Congo in 2011, and currently secretary-general of the association Écrivains du Congo, he has been working since 2016 as head of the Wallonia-Brussels Library at Kinshasa, where he organizes literary activities that thrill the Congolese literary scene. In 2009, he was one of the winners of the Mark Twain Literary Prize (from the US embassy in Kinshasa) with his short story "Le cauchemardesque de Tabu." He is also the author of a bestselling novel written entirely in Lingala, *Ebamba: Kinshasa-Makambo*, and translated into French and English under the title *Mr. Fix-It*, published by Phoneme Media. The English version was officially presented in Los Angeles by the great Kenyan author Ngũgĩ wa Thiong'o. Richard Ali is also the founder and CEO of Alibooks.cd, a digital platform dedicated to the sale of books in the DRC. Among his publications are the following:

Le Cauchemardesque de Tabu. Kinshasa/Wavre: Mabiki, 2011. Short stories.

Ebamba: Kinshasa-Makambo. Wavre: Mabiki, 2014. Novel.

Mr. Fix-It. Los Angeles: Phoneme Media, 2017. English translation of *Ebamba: Kinshasa-Makambo*.

Okozonga Maboko pamba, masolo ya mikuse. Kinshasa/Wavre: Mabiki, 2017. Short stories.

"Ebola ++," in *Jalada Africa*, 2015.

Génève: Kin 2020 la correspondance. Geneva: BSN Press, 2020. Collective novel.

Et les portes sont des bouches. Kinshasa-Wavre: Mabiki, 2021. Novel.

Salma Khalil is a multidisciplinary artist of committed visual expression who has inherited much from her parents. (Her father, Professor Khalil Alio, is the author of the books *Pour Qui File la Comète* and *Sússúnà: Contes Bidiya*, and the son of a veteran of the French army of the Second World War. Her mother, Khadidja Hamit, is a storyteller and embroiderer, and the daughter of a veteran of the French army of the Indochina War.) She is part of a movement of visual artists who use local materials to create paintings made from recycled products and natural pigments inspired by the know-how of the Kotoko, an ancient civilization of Chad.

Also a graphic designer and photoreporter, with a master's degree in urban geography from the University of N'Djamena, she develops many social subjects with an artist's eye, navigating between human rights and cultural heritages. With the support of the Service de Coopération et d'Action Culturelle of the French embassy in Chad, and in collaboration with the sociologist Aché Ahmat Moustapha, she codirected the book *Portrait de femmes tchadiennes*. She created her company Zarlinga in 2014, through which she sells her photographic work and her talent as a graphic designer.

Khalil is also a published writer. She authored the poetry collection *Passion de la Pensée*, published in 2004 by Éditions le Manuscrit, and in 2020, her storybook *Afaf et l'oeuf dorè* was borne of her experience with the organization JRS, working with refugee girls from Sudan (Darfur) and the Central African Republic to highlight the violence experienced and to offer perspectives. Additionally, she has contributed to numerous French-language short story collections in Chad.

Named one of *New African* magazine's 100 Africans of the year in 2017, Khalil seeks to promote women's empowerment, the arts and culture of Chad, and help improve the living conditions of future generations. To learn more about her work, visit artistetchadienne.org.

Sarah Uheida is a twenty-four-year-old Libyan poet and experimental memoirist who received her bachelor of arts in English studies and psychology from Stellenbosch University in South Africa. At the age of thirteen, Sarah and her family escaped the Libyan Civil War and emigrated to South Africa, where she learned English and is currently residing. As the recipient of the international 2021 Miles Morland scholarship, she is currently penning her fictionalized memoir of the Libyan Civil War and the female refugee experience. She was also the winner of the 2020 Dan Veach Prize for Younger Poets. Her work features in or is forthcoming in literary journals such as *New Contrast*, *Eunoia Review*, *The Shore*, *fresh.ink*, *Plume*, the *South African*, *Sonder Midwest*, *Stone Thursday*, *Every Day Fiction*, *Wend*, *Flock*, *SliP*, *Atlanta Review*, and in the anthology *We Call to the Eye and the Night: Love Poems by Writers of Arab Descent*, which Persea Books will publish in 2023.

Vanessa Walters is an author and playwright originally from the UK, now based in the US. She is a fellow and former resident of Tin House and The Millay Colony. Her forthcoming novel, *The Nigerwife*, will be published in June 2023 by Atria Books.

Vivian Solana is an assistant professor at Carleton University's Department of Sociology and Anthropology in Ottawa, Canada. Her long-term ethnographic research in Sahrawi refugee camps and in the diaspora focuses on the forms of labor that socially reproduce a Sahrawi revolutionary nationalism in exile. Her most recent publications can be found in *PoLAR: Political and Legal Anthropology Review*; *Comparative Studies of South Asia, Africa and the Middle East*; *History and Anthropology*; and *MERIP*.

Yejide Kilanko's debut novel, *Daughters Who Walk This Path*, a Canadian national bestseller, was longlisted for the 2016 Nigeria Prize for Literature. Her work includes a novella, *Chasing Butterflies* (2015), and two children's picture books, *There Is an Elephant in My Wardrobe* (2019) and *Juba and the Fireball* (2020). Her latest novel, *A Good Name*, was published in 2021. Born in Ibadan, Nigeria, Kilanko lives in Canada, where she also practices as a therapist in children's mental health.

THANK YOU

Jesus.

Judith Curr, for your friendship and confidence in me.

Rosie Black, for your ready support.

Rakesh Satyal, for being an incredible editor and literary partner.

Ryan Amato, for shepherding this through all the necessary stages from edit to publication.

The copyeditors and proofreaders, for your eagle-eyed expertise.

Every single contributor who crafted these original works.

Ray Ndebi, for the multi–time zone WhatsApp meetings with various writers to translate edits, and for your introduction to Ayi Dossavi.

David Shook, for all the care you took to ensure we didn't miss any nuances in the works you translated, and for introducing me to Conceiçao's work, among others.

Johnson Asunka, for all your translation support.

Martin Egblewogbe, for connecting me with Ray and Johnson Asunka, and for —along with Nana Awere Damoah, Nana Yaw Sarpong, Kofi Akpabli, Mamle Wolo, Lizz Johnson, and Elikem M. Aflakpui— welcoming me so warmly into Ghana's literary community.

Zukiswa Wanner, for making introductions and connecting me with writers for this anthology, and for your support and sisterhood through the years.

Fanta and Ako Mutota, for your encouragement. You will never know what that 2012 phone call meant to me!

Kwam, Delphine, and Nii Allotey Brew-Hammond, I love you.

Malaika Adero, for making time for me.

Todd Hunter, for your day one support.

Binyavanga Wainaina, for all you did to welcome me into the world of words. I miss you!

Brook Stephenson, for believing in me and telling me so when I needed it most. Your legacy lives in many ways, including through the Rhode Island Writers Colony.

Rhode Island Writers Colony fam, for inspiring, challenging, and supporting me.

Jennifer Baker, for helping me believe I could be a writer again after many years of rejection.

Hedgebrook Writers sisterhood, for sharing your truths with vulnerability and extending compassion so I could share mine.

Hobart Writers Festival family, for creating the most welcoming space for writers.

Charlotte and Ally Sheedy, for not giving up on me!

Lola Shoneyin, for being a massive inspiration to me and so many.

Maya Nusbaum and the Girls Write Now team past and present, for being foundational to my growth as a writer and editor and literary citizen.

Kwame Alexander, for your generously extending advice and opportunity.

The Book-in-a-Day crew, for being you!

Delphine and Nii Allotey Brew-Hammond, I love you.

Essie Brew-Hammond McCabe, for listening to multiple drafts of this intro *and* the novel I've been writing in tandem.

Dustin Haffner, for making sure I took breaks to eat and get fresh air, and your "You got this" notes exactly when I needed them.

Nimma Bhusri, for your daily prayers.

Stephanie Nikolopoulos, Jane Park, Debra Ayis, Tricia Clarke, Cristina Spataro, and Elle Maldonado, for your support in more ways than one.

Redeemed Writers Group.

Readers, for receiving this anthology with love.

A NOTE ON THE COVER

Relations being a collection of work by writers throughout Africa and the diaspora, it was clear that the cover should feature artwork by an African artist as well. I had previously come across the work of Nigerian artist Damola Ayegbayo and filed it away in my mind with the hopes of using it on a cover when the right assignment came along. *Relations* proved to be the perfect opportunity. The painting, created especially for this cover, is as powerful as the writing within the book. Damola's Expressionist style of depicting Black faces by using countless colorful brushstrokes aptly speaks to the many voices, personalities, and lived experiences in *Relations*.

–Alicia Tatone

ABOUT THE EDITOR

Nana Ekua Brew-Hammond is the author of the children's picture book *BLUE: A History of the Color as Deep as the Sea and as Wide as the Sky,* illustrated by Caldecott Honor Artist Daniel Minter, and the young adult novel *Powder Necklace,* which *Publishers Weekly* called "a winning debut." Her short fiction for adult readers is included in the anthologies *Accra Noir,* edited by Nana-Ama Danquah; *Africa39: New Writing from Africa South of the Sahara,* edited by Ellah Wakatama Allfrey; *New Daughters of Africa,* edited by Margaret Busby, CBE, Hon. FIRSL; *Everyday People: The Color of Life,* edited by Jennifer Baker; and *Woman's Work,* edited by Michelle Sewell, among others. Forthcoming from Brew-Hammond are a novel and children's picture book.

Brew-Hammond was a 2019 Edward F. Albee Foundation fellow, a 2018 Aké Arts and Book Festival guest author, a 2017 Aspen Ideas Festival Scholar, a 2016 Hedgebrook writer in residence, and a 2015 Rhode Island Writers Colony writer in residence. Every month, Brew-Hammond coleads a writing fellowship whose mission is to write light into darkness.

Here ends Nana Ekua Brew-Hammond's
Relations.

The first edition of the book was printed and
bound at Lakeside Book Company
in Harrisonburg, Virginia, December 2022.

A NOTE ON THE TYPE

The text of this novel was set in Times New Roman, a serif type-
face designed by Stanley Morison and Victor Lardent in 1931
as a commission for British newspaper *The Times*. Inspired by
eighteenth-century printing traditions and early Baroque print-
ing, Times New Roman is a high-contrast, robust design that
moved away from the old-style model. It has become one of the
most popular typefaces of all time.

HARPERVIA

An imprint dedicated to publishing international voices,
offering readers a chance to encounter other lives and other
points of view via the language of the imagination.